THE KILLING CURSE

ALSO BY H.B. MOORE

The Omar Zagouri Thrillers:

Finding Sheba
Lost King
Slave Queen
The Killing Curse
Beneath: An Omar Zagouri Short Story
First Heist: An Omar Zagouri Short Story

Esther the Queen
Daughters of Jared
Eve: In the Beginning
Ruth
The Moses Chronicles series
The Out of Jerusalem series

Writing as Heather B. Moore

Heart of the Ocean
Power of the Matchmaker
Love is Come
Condemn Me Not: Accused of Witchcraft
The Tangerine Street Romance series
The Newport Ladies Book Club series
A Timeless Romance Anthology series
Timeless Regency Collection
The Aliso Creek series
The Falling series

THE KILLING CURSE

AN OMAR ZAGOURI THRILLER

H.B. MOORE

Interior design by Heather Justesen
Edited by Charlotte Herscher, Daniel Born, and Lisa Shepherd

Cover design by Rachael Anderson
Image Credit: Adobe Stock #101846055, Ihor Voloshyn

Published by Mirror Press, LLC

ISBN-10: 1-947152-00-9
ISBN-13: 978-1-947152-00-7

DEDICATION:

I've been surrounded by courageous and strong women all my life. My husband teases me about how many writer friends I have with the name Julie, yet each of them have been a strength to me personally. Their friendship and inspiration have kept *me* strong and courageous:

Julie Wright
Julie Daines
Julie Donaldson
Julie Bellon

HISTORICAL CHARACTERS

Raynald of Châtillon, AD 1125–1187
Stephanie of Milly
Humphrey IV, son of Stephanie
Isabella, daughter of Stephanie
Alix, daughter of Raynald and Stephanie
Azzo VI, married Alix

Saladin (Salah ad-Din Yusuf ibn Ayyub), AD 1137–1193

CHAPTER ONE

AL KARAK, CITY OF JORDAN

Taheer Sayid picked up his cell phone and selected his most trustworthy contact. The phone call would take only moments, but the result would teach the entire Sayid tribe what honor meant. He shut his third-floor office window, blocking out the rising heat of the Jordanian desert's summer morning. He and his only brother owned the bank in the Jordanian city of Al Karak, and having started it three decades before, now they were among the town's wealthy elite.

"Yes?" Yamil answered.

"We have proof," Taheer said into the phone.

"Four male witnesses?" Yamil asked.

Taheer sighed. Yamil was a stickler for rules. An execution couldn't be ordered unless there were four respected male witnesses to the crime. In this case, there were actually no witnesses, but Taheer knew his daughter was guilty. He had plenty of video footage of her leaving her university apartment more than once after midnight, and he also possessed other, less legally-binding evidence. There could be only one reason for his daughter's midnight forays. Worst-case scenario, Aamira was no longer a virgin. Or else she'd been tainted in some way by a relationship with a man other than her fiancé. Taheer was still trying to find out whom she was meeting. But now it was time to put the execution order into motion. She would be returning home for summer very soon.

Taheer would have no problem bribing four men to sign the official document. That way, if the killing were questioned by the authorities, the paperwork would already be in place. And once the paperwork was submitted to the judge, another bribe would be offered to bypass a trial.

"Yes, the witnesses are ready to sign," Taheer told Yamil. "When can you complete the task?"

"Two weeks," Yamil said.

Taheer's left hand curled into a fist. "One week."

"The process is complicated," Yamil said. "Especially if you want the paperwork legalized."

"My daughter . . ." Taheer dropped his voice to a whisper. "My daughter has dishonored her family and my extended family. My family will not be put through this shame for two more weeks."

A pause, then Yamil said, "Ten days at the earliest. That is, if you want the right signatures. And my fee for that short schedule will double."

Taheer considered for a moment. With Al Karak's stricter laws now against honor killings and the authorities' recent practice of imprisoning all involved family members, Taheer knew that waiting the full ten days for the paperwork was the best procedure. If he had his daughter executed, and was found out of compliance with the law, then his family, including his nephew, could pay the price.

Taheer was already taking a risk by obtaining witness signatures and bribing a judge. Most honor killings in the town were done completely privately with no criminal paperwork filed. When authorities questioned the family about their missing female relative, stories were invented about the girl running away, or traveling out of the city, or even suicide. But suicide didn't have to be used as an excuse unless the body was found.

Aamira would be buried, without traditional honors, but Taheer refused to hide the cause and reason for her death. Her crimes needed to serve as a lesson for everyone in their community, and everyone in their tribe. Only then could his family hold up their heads proudly and restore their tribe's honor.

"Ten days," Taheer said. Money was no issue. And two weeks seemed a lifetime.

"I want those signatures by tomorrow," Yamil said.

"You will have them." Taheer ended the call.

For a few moments after the phone call ended, Taheer remained at the window, overlooking the dust-spewing streets and crawling traffic below. He took pride in his city of Al Karak, the city of his ancestors. He wouldn't let a stranger—another man—come between all that he'd envisioned for his daughter and family. One part of Taheer grieved for the crumbled hopes he'd allowed himself to depend on. The other part of him knew that his honor as a man had been put to the test. He could not let any sentiment interfere with enforcing discipline.

If his daughter got away with her immoral actions, then it would set a precedent for others in the family. Taheer thought of his son Ehan. Years down the road, when Ehan took over as the family's patriarch, Taheer wanted his son to have a pure family blood line. Not one tainted with dishonor and infidelity.

Now, because of his daughter's betrayal, Taheer would need to select the bride for his son very carefully. One who wouldn't bring disgrace onto the family. One who would be a faithful wife and devoted mother. One who would stand by her husband no matter what.

Taheer's heart seemed to twist until he felt a twinge of physical pain. His own beloved wife would not be pleased when she learned of their daughter's actions. He dreaded telling her the news. And he would need her absolute allegiance.

Their marriage had felt off lately, and Taheer couldn't explain why. He supposed that most long-term marriages went through low points. But his wife had seemed more distant than her normally introverted self. He would have to speak to her about that. It wouldn't be good if others in the family noticed and began to talk about their relationship.

Two women walking below in the street caught his attention. They both wore dresses, and their heads were uncovered. The younger woman linked her arm through the older woman's, and for a moment, Taheer was reminded of his wife and daughter. He watched the women idly, until he realized it indeed was his wife, this time with his niece.

Taheer stiffened at the realization. The women crossed the street, turning so that he caught a glimpse of their faces. Both of them smiled as they talked; it seemed the women were close and shared many secrets. Doubt flashed through him. How many secrets did women share between them? Perhaps when he told his wife of their daughter's infidelity, it wouldn't be such a surprise after all. Icy cold settled in his stomach. Perhaps . . . his wife already knew.

And if that was the case, it meant that his wife was part of Aamira's deception.

CHAPTER TWO

LONDON

Omar Zagouri didn't know how he got himself into these situations. All right. He knew. But it didn't mean he was happy about it. Why did he think he could attend his cousin's graduation from the London School of Economics, and bring down a notorious art thief, all in the same weekend? Ehan Sayid had proved elusive.

Omar had largely ignored the email invitation from his aunt about his cousin Chad's upcoming academic honors, until Omar's father sent an instant message. When that was followed by a phone call from his mother, life rerouted itself.

So here he was in front of his hotel, wearing a recently dry-cleaned, gray suit, and hailing a cab on crowded Charles Street. A taxi mercifully slowed. Omar climbed in and spoke to the driver.

"Ah," the driver said. He was possibly Lebanese. "There's a blockade around the university. Extra security, you know, after the theft last week. Did you hear?" The driver's dark eyes studied Omar for a couple of seconds. The cab pulled into the crawling traffic. Omar knew the look. Everyone was a person of interest when the news media blared unverified information about the possible art thief. And Omar had to admit, he and Ehan Sayid were similar in appearance. At least to the untrained eye.

"Where did you say you're from?" the driver asked Omar.

"I didn't say," Omar replied. Maybe it would be faster if he walked, although he was in no real hurry, which was rare for him. He'd be about an hour early to the ceremony and planned to use the time to catch up with his aunt.

The driver's eyes were on him again, and Omar looked out the window. The gray London morning had seemed promising at first, but now raindrops started to splatter on the window. So much for hope. The last time Omar had been in London he'd spoken at an archaeology conference, as the assigned representative of the Israel Heritage Preservation Commission.

Omar had recently been promoted from undercover agent to director of the Israeli Preservation of Cultural Heritage and Ancient Artifacts Agency. And his current assignment was to train Joseph Bar, the newest agent, in the fine art of tracking an art thief. Pun intended.

The taxi jerked to a stop at a lengthy traffic light, and Omar pulled out his phone and scrolled through the texts he'd saved. Typically, he deleted everything upon reading, but he'd saved a few messages from his girlfriend Mia.

Good luck with the training. I'll see you when you return, she had texted.

Technically, he was Mia's superior, although she reported directly to the big boss, Simon Greif, just as Omar did. As undercover agents, they knew the very basics of each other's assignments, such as locations, but that was about it. Her current assignment was at the Petit Palais museum in Paris, to befriend the curator. The French government suspected him of running a cover operation for a black market dealer in ancient artifacts.

Joseph is a smart man, Omar had typed. *Don't think we'll have much trouble tracking down this guy. I have a few theories and if they're correct, we'll be bringing in more than just one. Be home before the week is out.* Of course, he'd sent that text before the whole university graduation event became number one priority. He hoped it would only set back his plans for a day. He'd assigned Joseph enough research that the new agent probably wouldn't even notice Omar had left the hotel.

Then I'll make myself available for dinner, read Mia's next message.

You think you'll beat me home? he'd answered.

Easy.

At that point, Omar had smiled and been tempted to call her, but she might not be able to answer anyway. And he knew it would just make him distracted.

It was a good thing that Omar had talked Mia into living with him at his Tel Aviv apartment a few months earlier. Otherwise, he'd have a hard time keeping protocol in order to see her more. As it was, he wanted to be careful that he didn't push her away. He'd asked her to marry him, and, well, that hadn't gone so well.

But at least they were still together. Omar decided to be grateful for the smaller things in life.

Just as he was about to put away his phone, it rang. He frowned when he saw the incoming caller was Joseph. Omar had told the man that he wasn't to be disturbed for the next couple of hours unless it was an emergency. Exhaling, he answered.

"Interpol just logged in an alarm breach at the National Portrait Gallery," Joseph said. "Do you think—"

It was too much of a coincidence. The National Portrait Gallery had been one of the museums under surveillance for the art thief, and the museum director, Mrs. Shira Moberg, had added extra guards at Omar's recommendation. On display at the museum were a couple of paintings that belonged to a series that Ehan Sayid had been systematically stealing from other museums.

"How close are you?" Omar asked Joseph.

"I'm heading there now, cutting through alleys."

"On foot?" Omar scanned the thick traffic. It was at least another ten minutes to the museum. This snarl would double or triple his travel time.

"Yes," Joseph said.

"When you get there, go to the back of the museum," Omar told Joseph. "And keep your eyes on the roof."

"The roof?" Joseph started to say, but Omar hung up and dragged out some bills from his wallet. He dropped the money onto the seat by the driver.

"Stop the car," Omar said, opening his door.

The driver's eyes widened, and before the taxi came to a full stop, Omar was out, running in the drizzle. Of course he didn't have an umbrella with him, which meant he couldn't claim to be a respected local. Multiple umbrellas were popping up among those headed to the university entrance. He dodged several honking cars, and wished he wasn't wearing a suit and dress shoes. The slick pavement and slicker shoes slowed him down. Regardless, he ran hard, ignoring the stares of the passersby.

Just as he left Strand and started down Bedford, looking for a shortcut, Joseph called again.

"He's on the roof," Joseph said. "At least I think it's him, unless another random man decided to go up there. Do I follow him?"

"It's not like he can jump buildings," Omar said. "Is he carrying anything?"

"No," Joseph said.

"All right," Omar continued. "He'll be up there until the commotion dies down and he can escape, probably until dark. I'll be there in a few minutes."

"Police are everywhere," Joseph said in a quieter voice. "No one's looking up, though. How did you know?"

"I've been chasing thieves for years," Omar said. "Guess I got lucky this time." He hung up and continued running, and by the time he reached the museum, the police had started to block off the street.

Omar found Joseph behind the museum, his face pale, his blue eyes wide. "Where's the maintenance ladder?" Omar asked, trying to catch his breath.

Joseph pointed to a half-rusted bit of metal. It would have to do. Omar shrugged off his suit jacket, although there was little to salvage of it from the rain. He handed it over to Joseph, and noted that the other agent had had some sense to don a mackintosh. "I need your gun."

Joseph handed over his Glock.

Without another word, Omar pocketed it and started to ascend the ladder. Moments later he stepped onto the wet roof. He drew his weapon and scanned the undulating roof, staying low. It took him only seconds to spot Ehan Sayid. The man was crouched on the far side, his face turned toward the street beyond, as he looked down at the police chaos he'd caused.

Ehan was not only a cocky bugger, but also stupid, Omar decided. He rose, staying hunched over, and started to creep toward the thief. Omar was surprised to see the man alone on the roof, but he knew Ehan had a getaway plan, and he fully intended to thwart it. He'd be home even earlier than he'd told Mia.

Gun raised, Omar hurried as fast as he could without making a sound or drawing premature attention to his approach. The closer Omar was when Ehan noticed him, the better. And then Omar heard the roar of a truck's engine. Ehan snapped his head to the left, and Omar knew he'd just lost the chase.

The truck was for Ehan, and even as Omar straightened and started his sprint across the rooftop, he knew he'd be too late.

Ehan turned, and his eyes locked with Omar's. For a moment, time seemed to shift, and Omar saw into a desperate man's soul—a man who would do anything to defend what he thought was his. Omar was the same kind of man. So he was not surprised when Ehan turned back toward the edge of the building and stepped off.

Omar ran to the spot where the thief had disappeared, just in time to see the truck that had served as a landing spot for Ehan roar down the street, cut through the police barricades with barely any deceleration, and continue on.

"Damn." It was an understatement. Not only had Ehan Sayid gotten away, but he'd seen Omar. And as much as Omar hated to admit it, he had screwed up. Now Ehan knew exactly who was following him.

Omar turned and hurried back across the roof, pocketed the Glock, and climbed down the metal ladder.

Before Joseph could question him, Omar said, "He's gone. For now. But he'll be back to get the paintings. Get Mrs. Moberg on the line and tell her this is far from over."

Joseph pulled out his phone.

"But first," Omar said, handing over Joseph's Glock, "I need your mackintosh. I'm soaked."

Joseph fumbled with the rain gear and handed it over. Omar tried it on. He hoped he wouldn't look too pathetic for the graduation.

"I'll meet you back at the hotel in a couple of hours. Text me any updates." Omar left Joseph standing there with his to-do's and made his way to the street, heading in the opposite direction of the police barricades.

There wasn't much use in catching another taxi. The traffic had slowed to a standstill, so he set off at a jog.

By the time he reached the front of the university, the cops were redirecting all traffic away from the main entrance. It seemed no one was being allowed to park close to campus. Omar hurried along, knowing he was later than his aunt had expected him. She wouldn't be happy.

"Omar!" It was unmistakably Aunt Jasmin's voice. Her deep, rich tones had always reminded Omar of a lounge singer, even though she claimed she couldn't carry a note.

He looked up the set of stairs he was climbing to see the thin figure of his father's sister. Long, dark hair intertwined with silver strands cascaded over one shoulder, and her bright red lipstick was a familiar sight.

"You're late," Aunt Jasmin said, but she was smiling.

As soon as Omar reached the top step, Jasmin enveloped him in a quick embrace, then drew back and squeezed his cheek.

"I'm not four years old anymore."

"Oh, but you're still adorable," she said, and checked the

delicate gold watch on her wrist. "The first speaker has already started."

People surged around them and through the auditorium doors. The blocked roads and police barricade had delayed everyone. The university should have offered a late start to the graduation event.

Omar linked his arm through his aunt's. "How's Chadi doing?"

"He hates it when you call him that, you know," Jasmin said. "He goes by Chad now."

"I know," Omar said. "But you still pinched my cheek."

His aunt laughed, and Omar smiled. It was good to be with family. Perhaps his mother had been right. Too bad it had to be right in the middle of one of his assignments.

"Chad *is* very happy. Not only is he graduating today, but he plans to propose to his girlfriend tonight."

"Propose? I didn't even know he had a girlfriend." Of course he didn't. Omar hadn't seen Chad since another cousin's wedding a couple of years before. At that stage, Chad still had a face full of pimples. Well, maybe it had been more than a couple of years.

"Oh, yes," Jasmin said, lowering her voice. "And get this. She's from Al Karak, in Jordan. A very small, but noteworthy town. Have you heard of it?"

"I have," Omar said, unable to explain the tightening in his stomach. It didn't have anything to do with the security check up ahead before the interior auditorium doors. He was familiar with Al Karak, famous for its castle that had been won and lost multiples times during the medieval Crusades. Not that he'd been there himself, but he made a mental note that it was Ehan Sayid's hometown.

Omar and his aunt stopped and waited in line. The security officers riffled through his aunt's purse, then ran a scanner over both of them. This was why Omar hadn't come armed. Soon they were inside the dim auditorium while a woman's British-accented voice regaled the crowd with testimony of her last four years at the university as “stupendous” and “exhilarating.”

Finding seats halfway up the left aisle, Omar settled next to his aunt.

“There he is,” she said, pointing to the rows of graduates on the stage facing him.

It appeared that Chad had finally lost the pimples.

“And there’s Chad’s girlfriend,” his aunt said. “Second from the right on the first row. She’s graduating with top honors. A very sweet girl.”

Omar glanced to where his aunt pointed. The girlfriend was pretty. Smooth, dark hair, high cheekbones, copper skin, dark eyes. “What’s her name?” he asked.

“Aamira Sayid.”

Omar froze. He knew the name well. Very well, in fact. She was art thief Ehan Sayid’s younger sister.

CHAPTER THREE

LONDON

Aamira glanced at Chad, knowing she couldn't allow her gaze to linger or a smile to escape. Her father Taheer and Uncle Kahul were in the audience, and would be taking her to dinner following the graduation ceremony. Her brother Ehan was traveling as part of his art collection business, so she didn't hold out much hope to see him. She wished her mother had been able to attend, but her father had said she wasn't feeling well enough to travel.

Aamira could hardly believe she was graduating already from the London School of Economics. The hours of study and loss of sleep seemed but a small sacrifice to pay for the experience and freedom she'd enjoyed living in England.

She moved her gaze from Chad before he could notice her looking at him. If their eyes connected, she wouldn't be able to hide a blush or tamp down a smile. She straightened her skirt and crossed her ankles. Aamira didn't need to see beyond the bright lights shining on the stage to know that her father and uncle were in the audience.

All week she'd felt the heaviness in her limbs. She wouldn't just be going home for the summer months. She'd be staying this time. And she also knew she was expected to start planning a wedding to her cousin Sadan, son of Uncle Kahul.

Sadan was five years older, and when they were children,

Aamira and Sadan's parents had talked about marriage between the two of them. The week before she left for England, the two sets of parents had organized an old-fashioned betrothal ceremony. Aamira, more than ready to leave her small town for a college experience, had agreed with almost anything they said. But now she regretted agreeing.

As the first speaker began her speech, Aamira wondered what might have happened if she'd refused to participate in the betrothal. It wasn't hard to guess. Other girls in her town who'd showed such defiance were subject to censure. Sometimes it was paying a fine to the young man's family, and other times it was serving in the community for a set amount of time. Almost like carrying out a probation sentence.

It was the way the family could save face.

Aamira released a breath. And to break an engagement after the fact . . . Her head started to pound at the thought of telling her father that she'd fallen in love with Chad. That she didn't want to marry her cousin, and that she wanted to start a different life, a new life with the man she loved.

Chad was originally from Morocco, but his family had moved to England when he was a boy. Chad wasn't a member of any specific religion, but when they'd talked of her Islamic beliefs, he'd been very interested and open to learning more. He was a good man, a good son, and took care of his widowed mother while working part-time and going to school on an academic scholarship. It was a wonder he'd even had time to court Aamira.

She flushed at the thought. That's what he'd called it, teasingly, of course: courting. Which, it didn't take much deduction, meant that he was just as serious about her as she was about him. The only trouble was that she'd kept one important fact from him all of these months. She hadn't found the courage to tell him she was engaged to her cousin Sadan back home.

Aamira knew she'd allowed herself to live in a dream world, where she could still be part of her family and entertain thoughts of marrying someone like Chad. But the truth was, she didn't know if her family and Chad could ever be harmonious. She'd either have to give up Chad, or give up her family.

The audience burst into applause, bringing Aamira out of her thoughts. The speaker had concluded her remarks, and Aamira began to clap. Although she wasn't exactly listening to the speakers, she didn't want the ceremony to end. When it ended, she'd be leaving the university with her father and uncle.

The next speakers' words were also a blur, no matter how Aamira tried to concentrate. And then she was suddenly walking across the stage and accepting her diploma and congratulations. When the ceremony ended and all the graduates filed off stage to join their families, she felt a familiar hand brush against hers.

Chad. She turned to see him right behind her. She wanted to throw her arms around him and hug him, to tell him congratulations.

His hazel eyes were more green tonight. It was what first drew her to him, and pretty much the first thing she'd seen after she slipped on the sidewalk one rainy morning, and Chad had helped her to her feet. She couldn't believe she hadn't seen him on campus until then. When he told her later that he'd noticed her months before, she was more than surprised. So maybe it wasn't entirely coincidence that he'd been nearby when she'd suffered her minor accident.

Chad was not a tall man, but lean and muscular—he ran to relieve the stress of school and work and having responsibility for his widowed mother. It endeared him more to Aamira. He was barely taller than Aamira, and she knew that if she stepped closer and embraced him, her body would fit perfectly against his.

Instead, she ignored every desire she had to be closer to him, and smiled and turned forward again. He knew that she hadn't told her father about their relationship yet. So Chad had agreed not to interact with her.

Still, he gave her a half wink, then let her move again in front of him. They planned to meet later that evening at a graduation party. Aamira couldn't wait.

"Father," Aamira said, when she stepped off the last step and nearly collided with a tall man in a black suit. Somehow he'd made it past all the other families to get to this spot. Had he seen the small interchange with Chad?

But he was smiling, and he didn't look upset or suspicious.

"Congratulations," he said, and grasped her hand. He kissed her on both cheeks. Then her uncle came into view.

Uncle Kahul kissed her cheek, and her eyes immediately started to well with tears. Kahul looked like an older version of Sadan. The same thick lashes framing deep brown eyes, the long chin, and the quick smile. All of her betrayals seemed to course through her at lightning speed, and it was like a punch in the stomach. She was surprised she could still stand and smile at her uncle.

If he only knew. A shudder ran through her, but she tried to cover it up by brushing a hand over her hair. "Thank you both for coming."

"We'll take a picture and then we'll leave," her father said.

Aamira had almost forgotten what it was like to be around her father—always commanding, never inviting her to do something. Never asking. She swallowed back the threatening emotions and said, "Let's take a picture over here." She led the two men to a place below the stage where there was a graduate banner.

She wondered where Chad had gone and if he was with his mother. She'd met his mother once and would have liked to see her again.

After finding someone to snap their picture with a disposable camera she'd brought, she released a sigh of resignation. She'd have to be content with seeing Chad later on tonight, and not worry about looking for him again in the crowd.

"We have a surprise for you," her father said in a pleased voice, as he steered her by the elbow out of the auditorium.

"What is it?"

"You have to wait until we're in the car," he said.

Outside it was raining and Uncle Kahul opened up an umbrella. The three of them walked to a rented sedan. Once inside, her father turned to face her in the back seat.

He held up a cell phone, and Aamira couldn't help but be surprised. He'd not allowed her to have a cell phone, since he didn't trust the security, and feared she'd somehow be exploited.

Chad had bought her one, though, and it had streamlined so many things for her at the university. She wasn't looking forward to giving it up when she returned home.

"Do you know what FaceTime is?" her father asked.

She shook her head, even though she knew exactly what it was.

"Watch," her father continued, then tapped on the contacts app and pulled up a contact named Sadan.

Aamira's stomach nearly turned over. She wasn't prepared for this—not now. Not today. She still had three more days before her flight back home. And she'd planned to spend those days reliving all of her university memories before she redirected her thoughts to what the reality of home would bring.

Before Aamira could mentally prepare herself, Sadan answered the call and his face appeared on the small phone screen. His hair was a little longer, and he'd grown a mustache. Otherwise, his eyes and his intense gaze were just as she remembered them.

"Hello, Aamira," Sadan said. "Congratulations on your accomplishments."

To some his greeting might have sounded innocuous, but Aamira knew it was really saying that she was now educated and sophisticated enough to be the wife of the son of the prominent Sayid family in Karak. It didn't matter that her father was the oldest Sayid brother. She clasped her hands together, wishing she wasn't sitting in the back of a car with her father and uncle, and now her fiancé onscreen, all watching her.

"Hello, Sadan," she said in a determined tone of voice that she hoped hid the trembling. "How have you been?"

There had been no communication between them during the university semesters, and when she'd returned home for the summers, she'd only seen him at family gatherings. Suffice it to say, there had been no romance between them, and no interest beyond politeness from Sadan.

It was to be expected, Aamira knew. She was entering into an arranged marriage, not one of fantasies and dream worlds described in the novels she'd read between homework projects at the university. She'd have to leave all of her novels behind, as well.

Sadan had asked her a question, and now she concentrated hard on what he was saying.

"My mother is already planning a celebration for your return. Which day do you arrive?" Sadan asked.

Surely he knew. He was just acting on formality. "I fly out on Monday," she said. "I'm willing to help your mother with whatever she needs." Already she was acting the part of a conciliatory and dutiful daughter-in-law.

Sadan smiled, a quick grin that made him seem friendly and approachable. But all too soon, his dark gaze returned to its usual intensity.

Aamira wondered if he could see through the phone into her heart. What would he find there? A long crack that was deepening by the moment, she was sure. They spoke about a few other things, most of which Aamira knew she'd forget.

When Sadan finally hung up, her father reached back and grasped her hand. "We're proud of you, daughter, and your accomplishments. Your education will help you raise and teach fine sons." He released her hand and turned back to the steering wheel and started the car.

Aamira remained silent as her father drove along the rainy streets to the hotel where he and her uncle were staying. She hardly paid attention to what the men were talking about, and wondered where Chad was right now, where he and his mother were eating. He'd told her that his cousin from Israel might come to his graduation. Aamira imagined Chad's family dinner as vastly different from the one Aamira would have with her relatives.

When her brother's name came up in the conversation, Aamira tuned back in. "Where's Ehan now?"

"He's actually in England," her father said. "He really wanted to come tonight and surprise you, but I'm afraid business detained him."

Aamira wasn't surprised. Her brother Ehan was always working, building his business. Their father had given him a one-time loan, and then told him if he failed to make a success of himself, he'd be relegated to working at the bank.

She and Ehan used to sneak up on their home's roof at night when they were teenagers and confide in each other about what they wanted to be when they grew up. Ehan had a lot more choices than Aamira, of course, but she liked to dream as well. And Ehan was nice enough not to laugh at her when she told him one night she wanted to be a helicopter pilot, and then changed her mind the next day and dreamed of becoming an archaeologist. Ehan had encouraged her to seek both, so that she could fly to her dig sites.

But that had all changed after Aamira was promised to Sadan and she'd left for England. Aamira didn't even have an email or a phone number for her brother. All communication had been through their family.

Her father stopped the rented car. She climbed out and followed her father and uncle into the hotel. While they waited to be seated at the hotel's restaurant, her attention was caught by another family celebrating a graduate as well. Aamira recognized the young woman as the one who'd spoken at commencement. The woman's pale blonde hair was pulled into a twist, and she wore a short, dark red dress.

Aamira wasn't surprised to see her father and uncle shake

their heads when they saw what the woman wore, and turned their heads away, as if even looking at her was a sin.

But she felt her face heat up, both in embarrassment for the graduate and in shame for her father and uncle. Just because the woman wasn't dressed to *their* ideals didn't mean she deserved their censure.

Once they were seated at a table, her father set into a familiar lecture, about how women should dress and act, especially in public. The truth was that Aamira agreed, but she also didn't believe she should treat someone else poorly because of the choices they made. She'd met many wonderful people at the university—students, professors, and employees—all with different beliefs. Although she hadn't allowed herself to become close to anyone other than Chad, she had learned to appreciate differences.

"We're grateful you've had this chance at a superior education," her father continued. "But it's also time for you to return to your roots and to follow your path of destiny."

Aamira nodded. She knew there was no use arguing with her father. And if she was to argue with him, it wouldn't be in a public restaurant.

Taheer looked over at the table where the other graduate sat with her family. His eyes narrowed, and he returned his gaze to Aamira. "If she were *my* daughter," he hissed, "she'd be punished."

A shiver ran through Aamira. She took a sip of her water, giving her heart a chance to stop racing. Compared to wearing an immodest dress, Aamira's actions were much worse. Even if she hadn't fallen in love with Chad, she'd been alone with him—and once would be enough for her father. If things had been completely innocent and platonic between them, her father would still see it as a betrayal. Unmarried women simply didn't keep company with unmarried men.

The irony of sitting in a restaurant in England, where her

father's traditional notions lined up with those of the Regency era, wasn't lost on her. Somehow, though, she didn't think her father would find it all that amusing if she pointed it out.

"Ah," her uncle said, looking down at the phone he carried. "The confirmation just came in. Aamira's flight has been changed for tomorrow morning."

"What?" she said. "My flight back home?"

Her uncle grinned, and her father smiled.

"It will be a surprise for your mother," her father said. "You'll come home early, and we'll surprise her."

"But . . ." Tears burned in her eyes. She had planned to spend her last couple of days finding a way to say goodbye to Chad. "I have to go through a clean check for my apartment and—"

"We'll coordinate over the phone," her father said, watching her carefully.

Aamira exhaled slowly. She couldn't cry in front of them. She couldn't allow them to become suspicious of the real reasons she didn't want to leave early.

"All right," she said. "I'll finish packing tonight."

It was enough, it seemed, because her father nodded. Just then the waiter approached, and they ordered dinner. Aamira didn't know if she could last over the next hour, keeping everything inside and pretending to enjoy her meal. But she had to.

CHAPTER FOUR

LONDON

Omar couldn't move as quickly as he wanted through the jam-packed aisles because he had to stay with his aunt. Aamira and her family had already left, so it was too late to get a better view of them, and possibly take a picture. Aamira had been with two men wearing expensive and immaculately tailored suits. During the graduation ceremony, Omar had sent a series of texts to Joseph, requesting updates on the museum breach and Ehan Sayid. He had also asked Joseph to send over file pictures of Taheer Sayid and Kahul Sayid. Joseph had still not replied to the first texts, and Omar was starting to perspire under his shirt collar.

Aunt Jasmin linked her arm through Omar's, and said, "Isn't it wonderful? Chad has worked so hard, and now he has a university degree."

"Yes," Omar said, as they maneuvered in Chad's direction through the press of bodies.

Omar wished he were free to follow Aamira. He would bet everything he owned that the two men with her were her father, Taheer, and her uncle, Kahul.

His phone buzzed, and he looked discreetly at it. Ehan Sayid had made a clean getaway, said Joseph's message, and the museum director, Mrs. Moberg, had been informed. The pictures that came across his phone told Omar that he hadn't been mistaken about the identities of Taheer and Kahul Sayid.

Just moments ago, Omar had been in shouting distance of three members of the Sayid family. And it wasn't a stretch to believe that the Sayid men were all connected and most likely working together. Ehan Sayid just happened to be the front man for the thievery.

From the beginning, Omar had suspected that the notorious London thief wasn't working alone. Now he wondered if he'd just found evidence that the Sayid family was in fact very close. The coincidence of all of them being in London at the same time as the graduation might indicate that Ehan wasn't the only guilty party.

"There you are, Chad," his aunt called out. She tugged Omar along and waved her free hand toward a dark-haired man a couple of dozen feet away.

Chad turned and grinned at his mother. For an instant, Omar was reminded of himself, about fifteen years ago when he'd been a fresh-faced college graduate. Now, at thirty-seven, he no longer considered the world his oyster. He was just lucky to make it alive from one week to the next. Sometimes by the hour.

As Chad walked toward them, Omar studied his cousin and wondered if the young man truly knew anything about the Sayid woman. The cousin he remembered was a hard worker, but not necessarily the type of man to engage in a complicated deception. Perhaps Chad had just fallen in love with the wrong woman.

"Omar!" Chad said, his eyes wide. "Mum said you were coming, but I didn't believe it." He kissed his mother's cheek, then took Omar's extended hand and shook it. "You're looking old and tired."

Omar smiled despite his distraction. "Thanks. And you must be thanking God every day that you finally sprouted some whiskers."

Chad scoffed. "Wait until you meet my girlfriend, then you'll be choking on your words."

"I'm looking forward to it," Omar deadpanned.

"Oh, you boys," Jasmin cut in, grasping both of their hands. "I thought you'd both be more mature by now."

Chad shrugged and gave his mother an impish smile.

"Is there somewhere we can talk privately?" Omar asked Chad. The crowd had started to thin, but with each passing moment, Aamira and her family were getting farther away. What if her brother Ehan was meeting them somewhere?

Jasmin furrowed her brow. "Aren't you going to join us for dinner?" she asked. "I've made reservations."

Omar hesitated. He needed to find out how much Chad actually knew about his girlfriend. Dinner with his aunt would only delay the opportunity to question his cousin. But he could also imagine the berating his mother would give him if she discovered he'd skipped a dinner invitation with Chad and Jasmin. "Of course, I'd be happy to come along."

"All right, then," Jasmin said. "Let's grab a taxi before they're all gone."

If there was one thing that London wasn't short on, it was taxis.

"Will the elusive and mysterious girlfriend be joining us?" Omar asked, looking from his aunt to Chad.

"I'll be seeing her later," Chad said.

"How well do you know her family?" Omar couldn't help but ask.

Chad's eyebrows lifted, and Omar realized that he was pushing too hard, too fast. He'd have to wait until they weren't around so many people. Not that anyone was trying to eavesdrop.

"I haven't met her family, if that's what you're asking," Chad said. "They all live in a small town in Jordan."

"I wasn't asking if you'd met them," Omar said.

Chad wasn't smiling anymore. Maybe the guy wasn't so dense after all. And maybe Omar would be able to get answers from him. Eventually. It would be best if his aunt knew nothing of Omar's agenda. The fewer people involved, the better. And when it came to family, he didn't want anyone close to him involved.

His cell phone buzzed again, but he didn't have a chance to

check it until they were outside, in the drizzling rain, walking toward a line of taxicabs. The screen lit up with a half dozen texts.

Taheer Sayid: male, 54, owns Bank of Al Karak, married to Deena Sayid, two children. Twenty-five-year old son: Ehan. Twenty-three-year old daughter: Aamira.

Kahul Sayid: male, 51, manages Bank of Al Karak. Three children, all sons. Twenty-eight-year old son: Sadan Sayid . . .

Omar skipped the rest of the information to study again the two pictures Joseph had sent over. Both of them were grainy, black-and-white photos and probably at least five years out of date. Omar sent along the picture he'd snapped of Aamira at the graduation.

A definite match, he typed. Joseph would see for himself. Then Omar continued the message: *They're both in the area, most likely staying at a hotel within a few kilometers of the university. Start a run on the hotel registrations. Message Simon Greif for a reliable contact.*

Omar could only hope the investigation of these two men would connect them to Ehan. And it might be as early as tonight. He'd have to come up with an excuse if he needed to suddenly leave his cousin.

Omar looked up from his phone just as Jasmin and Chad secured a taxi. The driver motioned them inside, and Omar sat in front while his aunt and cousin slid into the back seat. As Jasmin gave the name of the restaurant to the driver, Omar searched the milling people outside the taxi row for any sign of Aamira or her father or uncle. Nothing.

They had exited only a couple of minutes before Omar, if that. Omar typed another message to Joseph. *Check local rental car agencies*. He slipped his phone into his pocket and watched out the window as the taxi navigated the congested roads.

He didn't want to press Chad for any more information and risk being overheard by their driver.

When the cab finally pulled up in front of a brightly-lit

restaurant, Omar offered to pay the driver, and Jasmin thanked him. The restaurant was crowded, but her reservation got them immediately to a side table with four chairs.

As they perused the menus, Omar tried to keep his tone casual when he asked Chad, "Tell me about this woman of your dreams."

Chad set his menu down and leaned forward, an amused glint in his eyes. "Tell me about your girlfriend first. Mum says that you've asked her to marry you, more than once."

Omar tried not to let his cousin's statements annoy him. It was clear that if he mercilessly teased Chad, he'd have to take some ribbing in return. "I'm hoping the third time is the charm."

"Good for you," Chad said. "I didn't think you were the sort to give up easily on a quest."

If Chad only knew how true his words were, not necessarily in relation to Mia, but to the types of jobs he was assigned. Pretty much every situation was *do or die*. And more and more lately, he wished that Mia's job as an undercover agent wasn't equally dangerous. Worrying about her so much had clued him into the fact that he was treading dangerous waters. One of the first unspoken rules of working undercover was to avoid close relationships. It was simply too risky.

"Mia's worth waiting for," Omar said.

Chad nodded, and refrained from throwing out any more barbs. "Aamira has been pretty quiet about her family. She's the only daughter, and I know her family is fairly traditional Muslim."

Not traditional at all, Omar wanted to say. The Muslims he knew personally weren't involved in high-stakes, world-class art theft. "Traditional in what way? She wasn't wearing a headscarf."

"No, but I think her mother does," Chad said. "Not the full burka of course. Her parents were supportive of Aamira getting an education."

The waitress came and took their orders.

Chad continued when the waitress left; it seemed he was

quite eager to talk about his girlfriend after all. "She's the most amazing woman I've met, beautiful, too, of course," he said. "I noticed her much sooner than she ever noticed me. She was quiet and studious and took everything so seriously, that I guess I wanted to find out who she really was."

Omar nodded. "Does she mostly keep to herself then?"

Chad's brows drew together as if he thought Omar's question was odd, but he had no trouble answering. "She doesn't have any close friends. I guess I've fulfilled the role. She is willing to help anyone, but she spends all of her free time when we're not together doing homework."

"Tell him about how you're going to propose," Jasmin said, patting her son's arm.

Chad actually flushed red, and Omar stifled a groan. His cousin had fallen hard, but he couldn't let Chad propose to Aamira without knowing the truth about the Sayid family.

Rubbing his face, Chad said, "Tonight I'm going to ask Aamira to marry me. I've already set everything up with the DJ at the graduation party we're going to."

Omar arched his brows. "If she's from such a traditional family, don't you think you should speak to her father first?"

"Aamira told me her father's a hard person to get along with, so she's not close to him," Chad said. "He came to the graduation, and I saw him at a distance, but Aamira made me promise not to try to meet him yet. Besides, I want Aamira's answer first, and then I can plan something more formal."

"That's kind of a strange request from a woman who's supposedly in love with you—to not meet her father." Omar wished he didn't have to be the one to ruin Chad's conviction.

As expected, Chad didn't appreciate the comment. "She does love me. Not 'supposedly.'"

"Think about it, Chad," Omar said. "You're about to ask this woman to *marry* you, and she won't even introduce you to her father at graduation. You know she's from a traditional family, but they've allowed her to leave her country and attend the university. What do you really know about her background and her family?"

"Boys," Jasmin said in a strained voice. "Do you think this is all necessary?" She glared at Omar. "I don't know why you're so concerned over Aamira's family. She's a lovely woman, and Chad has made his decision. Let's enjoy our dinner, please."

"You're right," Omar said. "I apologize." He looked at Chad. "May I get your cell number? I'd love to keep in contact."

"So you can come to the wedding?" Chad asked, his tone hard.

"Yes, that's exactly it."

As soon as Chad gave Omar his cell number, Omar sent him a text that Jasmin wouldn't see. *I have important information on the Sayid family.*

After Chad read the text, he looked up at Omar, a question in his eyes. At least the hostility had faded.

We need to speak privately before you propose to Aamira.

Chad texted back: *Later.*

Their food arrived, and for the next half hour, the conversation was mostly between Jasmin and Chad. Omar kept silent, trying to keep himself from hauling Chad out of the restaurant and telling him all.

When the bill arrived, Omar insisted on paying. "It's the least I can do. Both in the form of an apology for berating Chad, and to offer my congratulations."

"Thank you," Jasmin gushed as they left the table. She hugged Omar. Over the top of her head, Omar met his cousin's gaze. *We need to talk,* Omar silently conveyed.

Chad gave him a slight nod, but then took his mother's arm and steered her out of the restaurant.

Omar watched them leave. Then, instead of returning to his hotel, he began to follow them.

CHAPTER FIVE

LONDON

"We'll pick you up at six thirty, and we'll all fly back together," Aamira's father said, as he pulled up to her apartment building.

She wanted to argue with him, to rage against this unexpected turn of events, but mostly she wanted to cry. Her plans for the next few days had disappeared with her father's pronouncement, and now she'd have to figure out a way to say goodbye to Chad. It was nearly 8:00 p.m. and the graduation party was well underway.

"I'll see you first thing in the morning," Aamira said, and climbed out of the car. She could feel her father's and uncle's eyes on her as she entered her building. Once she reached her apartment, she flipped on her lights. She was sure they were still looking up and watching her window.

She quickly closed the drapes, then opened the drawer where she kept the cell phone that Chad had given her. Her heart leapt when she saw that he'd texted her. And then she felt sadness. Starting tomorrow, she wouldn't have this way to communicate with him.

Just arrived, are you here? He'd texted.

Dinner took longer than expected. I'll be there soon, she wrote back.

While waiting for Chad's reply, she walked into her dark bedroom and shut the door so no light from the kitchen would reflect inside. She parted the drapes to see if her father was still below.

In the yellow glow of the streetlamps, she saw the black rental car parked in the same place. The windows of the car were cracked open, and cigarette smoke floated out in white wisps. Were they going to sit there all night, watching her apartment? She let the drapes fall back into place and turned on the bedside lamp. Let them think she was packing.

Hot tears burned as she quickly changed and slid her cell phone into a small purse that matched the blue dress she'd bought for tonight. Then, taking a deep breath, she left her apartment and double-locked the door. She headed down the back set of stairs.

The rain had stopped, and the night was cool and damp. She looked forward to seeing Chad, yet dreaded telling him her news. It took only about twenty minutes to walk to the party. Along the way, she passed many revelers and other apartments and homes lit up with ongoing celebration. She looked behind her several times to make sure the black sedan hadn't followed. And she hoped her father wouldn't get it into his head to come up to her apartment and knock on the door.

As she approached the walkway of the party house, light spilled from every window and music pulsed in the air. Aamira's heart rate quickened, and she took a deep breath before knocking on the door. She shouldn't have been surprised when no one answered because of the loud music. She turned the knob herself and pushed the door open.

A couple of people, beers in hand, greeted her near the entrance. Otherwise, no one seemed to notice her arrival. The front rooms had been cleared of furniture and a couple dozen people were dancing. Others lounged against the walls, in conversations that were probably barely audible over the thumping bass.

The kitchen was brightly lit and the counter and a table covered with all kinds of food. Aamira was hardly hungry, but she gravitated toward the kitchen anyway, looking for Chad, or for someone she might recognize.

She saw one woman she'd shared a few classes with and said hello. Then Aamira moved back into the main party space. A set of stairs led to the second level, but she assumed Chad wouldn't have a reason to go up there. In the corner of the dual room a table was set up with music equipment, and a thirty-something guy with black and blue hair was running the music.

Aamira saw Chad standing near the DJ. She met Chad's gaze and her heart tripped. He wore a pale green, open-collar shirt and dark pants. He wasn't drinking alcohol like the others, and his gaze was clear when he met her eyes. His dark, wavy hair was smoothed back from his face, and the dark stubble shadowing his jaw and chin told her he hadn't shaved since morning.

The moment he saw her, he started toward her, zigzagging around the dancers. He wore a slight smile. Heart pounding, Aamira started toward him as well, until they met somewhere in the middle of the dance floor. Chad didn't say anything, just pulled her into his arms. She slid easily into them, and the familiarity of his arms and body next to hers made her feel like her heart was breaking.

He started to sway with the music, although the beat was faster than his motion, and she moved with him. Her last dance with him. How could she say goodbye to him and leave England? How could she return to her city and her family and pretend that she didn't have dreams of another life?

"Aamira," Chad whispered in her ear. "I have something to ask you."

She looked into his hazel eyes and wanted to gaze at them forever. Pretend that the outside world didn't exist and that all she had to think about tonight was dancing in Chad's arms. "And I have something to tell you," she said.

But he didn't seem to hear her. He turned his head and nodded to the DJ, who stopped the music at once.

The DJ said into a microphone, "Sorry for the interruption, ladies and gents. One of our graduates has an important question to ask his lady."

The crowd of people around them oohed, and Aamira's face flamed. What was Chad up to? And then she made the mistake of looking into his eyes. She saw the depth and determination there. This was the man who had gotten through the death of his father, having to support his mother on his own, while getting a university degree. And a few weeks ago, this was the man who had said he loved her.

And now, she watched with widening eyes as he released her and knelt down on the floor. The crowd went absolutely silent, and all that Aamira could hear was a few whispered words over her rapid breathing.

"Aamira Sayid," Chad said in a low voice. "You have been an unexpected blessing in my life, and I want you to know that I'm in love with you."

No, Aamira thought. *Don't do this, not in front of everyone.*

Chad's face flushed, and he said, "I guess now everyone in this room knows how I feel about you."

Aamira didn't know whether to laugh or cry, so she settled for something in between, more of a choked sob. Chad reached into his pants pocket and pulled out a ring box.

"Aamira, you're the love of my life, and I'd be honored if you'd marry me."

Tears ran down her cheek, and she wanted to reach for him, to throw her arms about his neck, and to shout *yes* so that the entire room heard.

But she couldn't move, almost couldn't breathe. She knew what her father's face would look like if he could see this scene. He would disown her. She would never see her family again.

Aamira took a step back from Chad, bringing a trembling hand to her mouth. "I'm so sorry," she said in a choked voice. "I love you too. But I'm so sorry." She turned then, and headed straight for the door. The crowd parted.

She left the house, left the stunned silence, and what was surely the broken heart of the only man she'd ever loved.

The cool, damp air seemed to jump-start her breathing again, and she wrapped her arms about her torso and gasped. Had she just walked out on Chad's marriage proposal? Her mind felt numb, and she stepped off the porch. It was raining again, but she didn't notice she was getting wet.

As she knew he would, Chad came outside, hurrying down the stairs. She didn't know if she could look at him. But when she did, she didn't see the expected anger. It was much worse—his eyes were filled with pain. He'd folded his arms across his chest, and the wedding ring was no longer visible.

"I'm s-so sorry," she managed to say, another round of tears burning in her eyes. "I-I didn't know, I didn't expect—" She wiped at her cheeks and took a deep breath. "I need to tell you something, something I should have told you months ago."

Chad didn't move, didn't speak, just stood like a statue in the drizzling rain.

She looked toward the house. The front door was still open, probably letting much-needed cool air into the stuffy interior. But she and Chad also had an audience.

"Not here," she said. "Can we go somewhere?"

He looked at her, his jaw clenched.

"But not my place," she continued, knowing her voice was rising in pitch. "My father and uncle are watching my building."

Chad broke his silence. "What do you mean, they're *watching* the building?"

"I can explain," she said, and glanced again at the house. "Let's get out of here, though."

Chad shoved his hands into his pockets and hunched his shoulders. "We can go to my flat."

Aamira nodded and walked with him the few blocks in the rain. Both of them were getting wetter and wetter, but neither of them spoke. At his building, Chad let her inside, then led her to his first-floor flat.

She had been here a couple of times, briefly though, and one of the things that had drawn her to Chad was that he was a perfect gentleman. He unlocked the door, and the warmth of the flat was welcome after all the cold rain.

He flipped on the lights, then crossed to the bathroom. Coming out, he handed her a towel to help her get somewhat dry.

Chad disappeared into the bedroom and came out a few minutes later, changed into dry clothing. "Do you want some dry clothes?" he asked.

"No," Aamira said, her voice sounding hoarse. She cleared her throat. "The towel is fine." She rubbed it against her neck and then blotted her face.

"Have a seat," Chad said, motioning to the couch.

"I'll sit at the table so I don't get the cushions wet." She pulled out a chair, sat down and rested her elbows on the scuffed wood table.

"My family is very close," she began, and realized that she wasn't saying it quite right. "Maybe *controlling* is the better word."

Chad nodded for her to go on.

"I know I've told you they're traditional, but my parents also believe in education for women, and that's why I came here," Aamira said. "They didn't want me to become Americanized, so America was out. I guess England was acceptable."

She looked down at her twisting hands. "You see, the thing is . . . You were unexpected as well. I was foolish to think that I could return home after graduation and not hurt you."

"What do you mean?" Chad asked, his voice low and strained. "We could live wherever you want. Just because we've graduated doesn't mean we have to break up."

Aamira wiped another tear from her cheek. "I'm promised to another man, Chad," she whispered. "Engaged to be married. At least, that's what's expected of us. It's been arranged by our families. It's not love. Not at all."

His jaw worked as if he were trying to figure out how to react, what to say.

Aamira's heart felt as if it might swell right out of her chest with grief and regret.

Chad exhaled and scrubbed a hand through his hair. "So what are you going to do? Go home and marry him? Or break it off?"

"I don't have much of a choice," she said. "Breaking an engagement is not something that a woman does in the town I live in."

Chad stared at her. "You don't want to break it off?"

"He's my cousin, and our parents have been planning this since we were children," Aamira said. "My education is supposed to make me a better mother to his sons." Her voice dropped again. "It's expected of us. It's as good as done."

"What if you tell him about me?" Chad asked. "Won't he want to break the engagement?"

"No," Aamira said. "He's certainly not . . . faithful to me. Once we are married, that will change of course. We will both do our duty."

The anger now appeared in Chad's eyes. He spread his hands open. "If this is just an excuse, tell me the truth. I deserve at least that."

"I've told you the truth," Aamira said, her voice rising. She wished she could go back in time, to change the first time she'd met Chad. She'd known from the beginning that it could only bring pain. "And I was a fool to lead you on when I wasn't available."

The silence between them was heavy.

After several moments, Aamira stood. "Goodbye, Chad. The truth is that I really do love you."

She turned away when he didn't look up. When she reached the door, she stopped and inhaled deeply as a new round of tears started.

In a few hours, she'd be on a plane, leaving England and Chad behind. She had to find a way to survive her broken heart.

"Wait, Aamira."

She heard him scoot his chair back and cross to her. When his hand slipped into hers, she knew she would melt. She turned into him and buried her head against his chest, and his arms came around her, tight and protective.

"How can you resign yourself to an arranged marriage, Aamira?" he whispered, his breath hot against her neck. "Stay with me. Tell your family you've changed your mind. We can live in England. Marry me and become a citizen. You can use your education for teaching *our* sons."

Aamira's shoulders started to shake. How could she let this man go? She couldn't imagine herself in another man's arms, not Sadan's, not anyone's. She moved her arms up and around Chad's neck, pulling him closer.

"I can't let you go," she said.

"Then don't."

She kissed him then, and he kissed her back. She didn't want this moment to end, didn't want to say goodbye, didn't want to go back to Al Karak. Chad kissed her more urgently than he ever had, pressing her against the wall. She clung to him, wanting him even closer, yet knowing she needed to leave before she allowed it.

A knock sounded on the door, and Aamira jumped, a guilty flush spreading through her. She didn't want anyone to see her at Chad's flat.

"Open the door, Chad," a male voice sounded. "I know you're in there."

Chad released a sigh, and looking at Aamira, put a finger to his lips. He opened the door a crack.

"Is she here?" the voice asked, one Aamira didn't recognize.

Chad opened the door farther, and a dark-haired man stepped inside, soaking wet from the rain. He was in his thirties, good-looking but clearly stressed. His eyes flashed and his face was flushed livid red.

"Aamira," Chad said. "Let me introduce my cousin, Omar Zagouri."

CHAPTER SIX

LONDON

Omar had been waiting hours, but now that he was face-to-face with Aamira, he second-guessed his approach. She was not the sophisticated woman he had expected, but someone young and perhaps naïve.

It was just as well that both of them were here, inside Chad's flat; it would make this easier. Chad hadn't responded to any of Omar's texts, so he was left with having to confront him face-to-face. He wanted Chad to know exactly who Aamira's family was, and he wanted to see the woman's reaction to the news. It would tell him a lot about what she might be hiding.

"This is the cousin from Israel?" Aamira asked Chad, looking at Omar.

She was a beautiful woman, and that only added to Omar's curiosity. How had her parents allowed her out of Al Karak? Research on the Sayid family had told Omar that they were very protective. Not only that, she was engaged to be married to her cousin Sadan.

"Since you wouldn't answer any of my texts, I came to speak with you myself." Omar pulled the door shut behind him. "How did the proposal go?"

Chad's face reddened. "Not so well. What are you doing here? Want to give me grief?"

"If you'd answered my texts, we could have avoided all of this," Omar said.

"All of what?" Chad asked.

"Asking a Sayid woman to marry you," Omar said.

"What do you mean?" Aamira asked.

Omar pulled his cell phone out of his pocket then looked at Aamira. "Is your father Taheer Sayid and your brother Ehan Sayid?"

"Yes, but what does that have to do with anything?" Aamira looked at both men, then focused on Omar. "Or with *you*, for that matter?"

"We might want to sit down," Omar said, indicating the table.

Once they were all seated, Omar pulled up a couple of pictures on his phone.

One was a grainy, black-and-white picture taken by a security camera in the Museum of Fine Arts in Lyon, France. "Is this your brother?" he asked Aamira.

She was silent, but a look of trepidation had entered her eyes.

"Who's the man in the picture?" Chad asked, filling in the silence.

"Ehan Sayid," Omar said. "Ehan has been the main suspect in a chain of recent art thefts throughout England. Just tonight, we also traced him back to a stolen painting in Paris."

Aamira's gaze snapped to Omar's, and her mouth opened. "My brother wouldn't do that. How can you even say that?" Her eyes darted to Chad.

"Ah," Omar said. He tapped the picture on his phone to enlarge it. "So you've confirmed this *is* your brother."

Chad shook his head at Aamira as if to say he didn't know where Omar was going with this. He looked at Omar. "What are you doing?" he asked, his tone hard.

"I'm proving something to you, my friend," Omar said, as he tilted the picture toward Chad. "This man is your girlfriend's brother. Your girlfriend here is the eldest daughter of Taheer Sayid, and is part of the Sayid family, which has been running an underground operation for years. They steal priceless paintings, have them copied, then sell the copies as originals. It's quite ingenious, and has made the Sayid family into millionaires. It seems, though, they've recently been on a specific mission—confiscating paintings in a certain collection. Why, we aren't sure yet."

The room was absolutely silent. Aamira stared at Omar, her expression incredulous, as though she thought he belonged in a psych ward. "My father and his brother own the Bank of Al Karak," she said in a measured voice. "They're *bankers*, Mr. Zagouri."

"The bank is simply a front," Omar replied in an equally measured voice. "I can prove that too, but perhaps now is not the time."

Aamira brushed a strand of damp hair back from her face. "What you are saying . . . what you are accusing my brother of, that's criminal." Her voice started to shake, and Chad grabbed her hand. "And Ehan's a hardworking business man, *not* a criminal. He didn't even have time to come to my graduation."

"Of course he didn't," Omar cut in. He was losing patience. Could this woman be this naïve? Chad looked at him like he wasn't too far from punching him out. "Ehan's description has been announced on every police scanner in London. If your brother had attended your graduation, he would have been arrested."

Aamira released a shaky breath, and tightened her grip on Chad's hand. "Who is this cousin of yours, Chad?" Aamira hissed. Her eyes began to water. "How does he know all of this about my family?"

Chad exhaled slowly before speaking. "Omar works for the Israeli government. All I know is that he works in their historical preservation department." His gaze narrowed as he looked back at Omar. "You need to explain yourself."

Omar gave a brief nod. "My official title is the Director of the Preservation of Cultural Heritage and Ancient Artifacts

Division. Even though the Sayid family has been under investigation for months by different organizations, we didn't get involved until the crime ring came to London. Earlier today, Ehan attempted to steal a couple of pieces donated to the National Portrait Gallery by a prominent Israeli citizen."

"Crime ring?" Aamira said in a faint voice. She blinked rapidly.

"Ehan isn't working alone. We're not sure exactly how many are involved," Omar continued.

"What types of paintings have been stolen?" Chad asked. The earlier hardness in his voice now changed to alarm.

Ah. Chad was beginning to drill down to the important stuff. Omar pulled up a set of pictures on his phone. "Do you recognize any of these?" He tilted the phone toward the two across the table.

Aamira's eyes widened, but Chad shook his head.

Omar tried not to smirk at their opposite reactions. It seemed Chad didn't know his girlfriend too well.

"Those are . . ." Aamira began, wiping at the moisture on her cheeks. "Those are from the Passion of Nadia collection."

"And?" Omar prompted.

"My great-great grandfather Gorbat was an artist and painted a legendary family story," Aamira said, her voice still trembling. "The Sayid family threatened to disown him if he continued with those paintings. He claimed it was his calling to tell our ancestor Nadia's story through his art. When he died, the paintings were lost as well. But then years later, they were discovered and auctioned."

Aamira lowered her gaze as she spoke. "I didn't know the full story, and when I came to England for school, I spent an afternoon at the National Portrait Gallery to see the paintings for myself." She took a deep breath. "The plaques on the paintings are all wrong, though. I knew it the moment I read them." Her gaze lifted to Omar's. The tears had stopped but her eyes were red. "If my brother has done what you say he did, he has a good reason for it."

This was a new twist that Omar hadn't expected—Aamira defending her brother's criminal actions.

But Chad was already skipping ahead. "What does the Passion of Nadia mean?"

Omar folded his arms on the table and leaned forward. He was very interested in hearing Aamira's interpretation. He wondered how much it had changed through the generations.

Aamira released a shaky breath, her hand still gripping Chad's. "The story goes all the way back to the crusaders of the twelfth century, when Raynald of Châtillon married the French woman Stephanie of Milly and took over the Al Karak castle as well as other holdings. Stephanie's daughter Eleanor was a young woman at the time, supposedly betrothed to an Italian prince," she said. "But the story goes that one night, the son of the family's greatest enemy crossed into Al Karak and seduced Eleanor. He abducted her and forced her to marry him, changing her name to Nadia. Instead of converting to Islam, she took a dagger to her heart."

Omar was surprised he hadn't heard of Nadia's suicide before. He searched his memory for the studies he'd done of the crusader battles. "Which crusader enemy are you speaking of?"

"Salah ad-Din Yusuf ibn Ayyub."

"Ah. Saladin." Omar knew of Saladin—how could he not?—the Muslim hero who defeated the crusaders after decades on Muslim soil and liberated his people from the Christian tyrants. Raynald of Châtillon had been among the worst Christians. Of course, Saladin had been no angel either. Both had used brutal and violent means in the name of God.

Chad pointed to the painting displayed on the cell phone. The painting showed a woman dressed in warrior clothing, holding a sword over her head. "Is that Nadia, Raynald's stepdaughter, then?"

"Yes," Aamira said, her voice stronger now. "There are other theories as well. One is that the daughter did not kill herself, but fled the tribe after her Muslim husband was killed by Saladin."

"I thought you said Nadia's abductor was Saladin's son?"

"He was," Aamira said. "She married her abductor. But all records of the story and Saladin's son's name have been destroyed, so there is no proof. Another theory states that Nadia's husband was imprisoned for treason, and she escaped the Muslim warriors and joined up with another tribe. Her beauty was matched by none. The stories say she was like a temptress to all who met her. She used her sexual power to command men to do her bidding. She eventually raised an army and took her revenge on Saladin's family."

Omar's research of the crusaders and their wars came flooding back to his memory. He'd studied the Passion of Nadia paintings enough that he remembered their general compositions. "There's another theory."

Aamira looked surprised at this, so Omar continued. "Nadia went into hiding after her husband's death and joined a Bedu tribe. She must have married one of the men because she had several children, but she never forgot her experiences and created a secret organization to thwart the Saladin family in all things."

"By telling her stories so they could be painted?" Aamira scoffed. "That's just another wild theory." She'd relaxed her grip on Chad's hand and seemed to feel less threatened by Omar's presence. "I suppose no one will really know."

"You may have hit upon something," Omar said. "I think there's a good reason the paintings are being stolen. Perhaps they reveal things that your family is trying to keep secret since your family members are descendants."

"What are they trying to keep secret?" Chad asked.

"I don't know yet," Omar said. "But Aamira's great-grandfather must have painted them for a reason."

"Perhaps he was just a simple artist," Aamira said.

Omar looked from Aamira to Chad, then back to the woman. "Perhaps. But I think it's more complicated than that. We know that the descendants of Saladin split loyalties and now the various tribes compete over political and financial agreements in Jordan. There has been bad blood between these tribes for generations. The paintings are being confiscated by the Sayid family because somehow the information in the paintings will give the other tribes power over the Sayids. So the Sayid family is trying to keep their reputation clean."

"Saladin is a hero of the Muslim world," Chad said. "Why would his name need to be cleansed?"

"Because perhaps Saladin's Kurdish tribe people weren't the heroes everyone made them out to be," Omar said. "Some historians claim that the tribe operated under its own system of tyranny and deadly control. Granted, they are Christian historians, so their opinions would be biased. But one of the paintings depicts the execution of a Muslim man wearing royal robes. Some art critics believe the man being executed is Saladin's son and that Saladin killed his own son to preserve their heritage and expunge the marriage to the Christian woman."

"An *honor killing*?" Chad said.

"Yes, and Saladin kept a time-honored tradition alive," Omar said. "One that his descendants want to hide."

"What do you mean, 'time-honored tradition'?" Aamira cut in. "And how does any of this relate to me? I'm from the Sayid family, not Saladin's."

"Both families have a dark thread running through them," Omar said. "We've traced your family history, not through the men, specifically, but through the women. Do you know that there are eleven supposed suicides of women in your family in the past forty years, ages sixteen through twenty-two?"

Aamira's face paled and she blinked rapidly. "I didn't know. My aunt took her own life several years ago, but she was a very emotional person from what I remember, and was frequently depressed."

Omar lifted his shoulder in a shrug. "Perhaps she had mental health issues, but it's my guess that your aunt . . ." He opened a file on his phone where he kept his list of Sayid women. "Hana Sayid . . . It's my guess that her brother Kahul killed her for not agreeing to marry the man chosen for her. The family simply reported it as a suicide."

Aamira stared at Omar. "You're wrong," she finally managed to say. Her voice sounded hoarse. "My aunt was engaged, yes, but that just made it more of a tragedy."

"How old were you when she died?" Omar asked.

"About five or six."

"So your memories of her are from when you were a child," Omar said.

Aamira shook her head, then looked to Chad in desperation, as if she had to convince him as well. "It's not possible. My uncle Kahul is not a murderer. He still grieves her death. The whole family does, my father included." Her eyes snapped to Omar. "You're insulting me and my family in the worst way possible."

"Omar . . ." Chad said, releasing Aamira's hand and putting an arm around her shoulders.

She leaned into him and closed her eyes.

"I know this is hard to hear, Aamira," Omar said. "But your brother is a criminal, and it's my job to track him down. I need his contact information. Believe me, if he's innocent, then he'll be released."

"I—I don't have his contact information," she said in a faint voice. "I only get news about him through my parents." Aamira brought a trembling hand to her mouth, as if she were trying to hold back a sob. "I need to leave." She pulled away from Chad and rose to her feet.

Chad stood with her, grasping her arm. "Don't leave."

"I have to," she said. She held out her phone to him.

"No, keep the phone," he said. "In case you can find a way to contact me." He moved the phone to her pocket.

Omar sensed a lot more meaning to this conversation than the simple words they were speaking.

"Please let me go," Aamira whispered. "This is hard enough."

"I'll come with you," Chad said. "We can pack your things and you can leave with me."

"You can't come with me, my father might still be watching my place," she said. "And I have to be on that plane in the morning. Please, you have to understand."

She took a step toward the door, and Chad released her arm.

He watched her for a long moment, neither of them speaking. "When will I see you again?" he finally asked, his voice gravelly.

She shook her head, fresh tears tumbling down her cheeks. "I don't know. Maybe never."

"Take your phone with you. Hide it somewhere." He stepped toward her. Then he brushed his fingers along her cheek, absorbing the tears with his fingers. "I can send you money for a plane ticket, anything."

Aamira merely nodded, then kissed his cheek. Before Chad could speak again, she was out the door, shutting it behind her.

It took only seconds for Chad to join Omar at the table. "Tell me everything you know about the Sayid family," Chad said, his voice hard.

"I would have thought you'd know more about your own girlfriend," Omar said.

Chad's face flushed. "When I asked her to marry me tonight," he said, moving his fingers through his hair, "she told me about being engaged to her cousin. I don't know what's going on anymore. I mean, we've been dating for months, and this is the first I heard about her supposed engagement. What did she think we were doing? Having a fling?"

Omar rose to his feet. "It seems the Sayid women fall in love with the wrong men."

Chad gave a bitter laugh. "So what's going to happen now?"

Omar walked to the door and turned.

"Hey, where are you going?" Chad asked.

"I'm following your girlfriend," Omar said. "I want to find out if her father's watching her apartment to see how much he's willing to protect his daughter. It's time for the Sayid family to own up to their crimes."

CHAPTER SEVEN

LONDON

Aamira clenched her hands into fists as she hurried down the dark street toward her apartment building. Her mind reeled at all that Omar had said about her family, her history, and his accusations about her own brother. It couldn't be true, yet, the way her heart pounded with doubt had her questioning . . . questioning her entire family, her entire upbringing.

She came around the final corner to her building. The rented sedan was nowhere in sight, but she didn't dare take the risk of entering the front door. She found her way around the back and hurried up the stairs. She slipped inside her door and immediately knew something was wrong. Everything was still in its place, but it *felt* different.

Fear ebbed through her as she walked from the kitchen into the bedroom. Her lamp was still on, and her two suitcases open on the bed where she'd left them. She scanned for anything missing or out of place. Her closet doors were open—at least she thought she'd left them open—and her shoes were lined up in their usual rows.

Aamira exhaled. No one was in her apartment, and she had a plane to catch in a few hours. She didn't have time to cry over Chad or be angry about what Omar had said. She pushed her thoughts away and started to pack. She'd only take a few things because over the years she had collected clothing her family wouldn't approve of.

But each item of clothing that she did pack reminded her of Chad . . . What she was wearing when she'd first met him. What she wore on their first date. What she wore when he first kissed her. As she sorted through her clothes, tears streamed down her face, but it was no use wiping them away. They just kept coming.

When she finished packing and had boxed up everything she was leaving behind, only the cell phone remained on the bed. Chad had asked her to take it with her, as a means to contact him. Sitting on the bed, she scrolled through their texts. She'd saved every single one of them. For the next thirty minutes, she reread the first texts Chad had sent—and her cryptic responses when at first she worried that her father might somehow know she had a phone. Her father had her email passwords.

She was twenty-three and afraid of talking to someone her father didn't approve of. She knew from the beginning her relationship with Chad couldn't go anywhere, so why had she allowed it? Reading through the rest of the texts made that obvious. She'd wanted something, or someone, just for herself. She wanted to be happy, to feel free, to fall in love. And she had. But she knew what she had to do now, her duty to her family and community. It was time to say goodbye, to give up Chad.

She would erase the phone and leave it in a drawer. She slowly deleted each text message one by one, evaporating the memories click by click. She wished she knew her brother's phone number so she could call him. She'd only seen him during summers since she had started college, and it seemed each year they grew a little more apart. But surely he'd be honest with her and allay her fears.

A knock on the apartment door jolted her. She slid the phone and its charger underneath the mattress and went to look through the peephole. Her heart plummeted at the sight of her father and uncle. Then anger raced through her, hot and fast. "I'm getting dressed," she said. "Give me a moment."

She hurried back to her bedroom, not waiting to hear their

reply. Sliding out the phone and its charger, she unzipped one of her suitcases and tucked the phone into a sock, then rolled it and shoved it into a shoe. Then she zipped up the suitcase again and returned to the door to open it for the men.

Her father's gaze was hard as he studied her face. She tried to keep her expression neutral and pleased to see him. "Have you finished packing?" her father asked. "We need to leave now since the security at the airport is a mess."

Aamira stepped back. "I've finished packing, but I need to clean the bathroom."

Her father stepped inside and nodded to her uncle, indicating for him to retrieve the suitcases. Her uncle glanced around as he made his way to the bedroom.

"We'll pay the apartment superintendent to have someone clean the place up," her father said. "We can't delay."

"All right," Aamira said. She suppressed the trembling in her voice. She was really leaving the university, leaving Chad, leaving years of a life she'd never have again. She picked up her backpack she'd carry on the plane, and turned to scan her place one more time. A few more minutes alone would have been nice, but her father was holding the door open and her uncle was already carrying one of the suitcases down to the street.

The airport security check-in and the four-hour plane ride back were a blur. Whenever she tried to pause and watch one of the news programs on the airport televisions, her father drew her away. She wanted to see for herself her brother's picture on TV. Omar's accusations were still hard to believe. But if they were true . . . Omar's visit to Chad's place last night had been a shock, and now, with ample time to absorb all that he'd said, Aamira had a lot of questions.

But she had no way to contact Omar except possibly through Chad. Aamira focused on the fact that she'd brought the cell phone, and had a means of contacting Chad. Not that she would allow herself to, but it was a comforting thought all the same.

She kept her eyes closed most of the flight, pretending to sleep, although she was listening to the sporadic conversations between her father and uncle. Would they talk about her brother? Would they talk about the stolen paintings?

But they said nothing that connected them or Ehan to anything that Omar had talked about.

When they landed in Amman, Aamira's stomach started to cramp. Every moment, every hour, distanced her from her university life and brought her one step closer to her unwanted future with Sadan. At the baggage claim, her father said, "We have a small surprise for you waiting outside."

As a child, she might have been excited with this announcement. But she was far from that. She could only guess what her father might consider a "surprise." After retrieving her suitcases from the conveyor, they walked to the airport exit, and there, waiting at the curb in a white SUV, was Sadan.

He came around the front of the vehicle. He was taller and broader than she remembered. His mustache had grown in fully, and he smiled at her, his dark eyes full of anticipation.

She caught her breath. Sadan was a good man, wasn't he? She'd known him all her life, so what did she have to fear? It wasn't like there was any surprise about who her husband would be—there never had been. Chad was just an unfortunate detour of her heart.

"Aamira," Sadan said, when he reached her and bent down to kiss her cheek. He wore a tailored suit and smelled of expensive cologne.

"Hello, Sadan," she said, keeping a smile on her face and knowing her father and uncle—future father-in-law—were both watching.

"How was the flight?" Sadan continued.

She tried to relax. This was just Sadan. If he wanted to marry her, she could find a way to be a good wife. "It was nice. I got some rest." Which wasn't at all true. She hadn't slept the night before, and little the night before that.

Her father chuckled, coming to stand next to her and shake Sadan's hand. "She slept most of the flight," he said.

Sadan grinned. "Great. My mother is looking forward to seeing you. She's spent two days preparing food." He gave her a wink. "And your mother knows nothing about your early arrival yet."

Aamira said nothing, her throat suddenly tightening. She missed her mother, and she had even missed her aunt. How could she have even thought of letting them down by staying with Chad? Yet even as she thought it, she longed for him. Allowing herself to love him had been a mistake for them both.

Sadan opened the door for her, and she climbed into the back seat.

"I'll drive us back," her father announced. "You two can sit together and catch up on news."

Aamira settled into the back seat, hoping that Sadan wouldn't be too talkative. She could feel the adrenaline, that had kept her awake and packing and stressing out all night, was now starting to wear off. She'd fall asleep if she wasn't careful.

As her father pulled into traffic and began driving the hour-and-a-half journey back to Al Karak, Aamira stole a sideways glance at Sadan. He was messaging on his cell phone. She knew, as his wife, he'd probably get her a phone, but she also knew he'd have monitoring and security software on it.

She'd never really wondered why the male relatives in her family wore designer clothing, and drove new cars every two years. She had just assumed the banking business was lucrative. Now, after a few years at the university, she understood much more about economics and finances. Owning a small bank in a small town would provide a modest living for a family, but there were no large industries nearby that could support the lavish lifestyle her father and uncle lived. They'd changed her flight arrangements without thinking twice about the expense. Her father had paid for her university education in another country without complaint.

Running quick calculations in her head, she realized her university education had probably totalled a quarter of a million pounds. Her breath shortened at the realization.

"Did you see Ehan in England?" Sadan asked.

The question surprised Aamira. She glanced at her father's face in the rearview mirror to see his reaction, but he seemed focused on driving.

"No, he couldn't come to the graduation," she said. "Is he home yet?"

"Not yet," Sadan said. "I messaged him yesterday, but haven't heard back."

Finally, her father spoke. "Ehan is working on a delicate business matter and will be out of touch for a few days."

This was the first that Aamira had ever heard of him being "out of touch." "Is he working for the bank now?" she asked, and then wondered what the reactions of the men would be at her probing question. Women in her family didn't discuss business with the men.

"Not exactly." Sadan chuckled. "You're ready to talk business, are you? With that university education now?"

Aamira's face heated up. Sadan might be speaking lightly, but the old heaviness returned. This was how it was going to be. She would be shut out of any conversation about the family business. Yet, now that she knew it could possibly be a front for criminal activity, she wasn't going to be deterred.

"Maybe I could help out at the bank. You have female tellers, right?" she said.

The silence in the car was deafening.

"As my wife," Sadan finally said, "your focus will be on our home and our family."

"Of course," Aamira said. She smiled sweetly at him. "But until we get married, or even after we're married and before the children come, I could contribute to the family business."

Her father gave a choking sort of cough. "I don't think your mother would be very happy planning the wedding by herself."

Aamira knew that her mother would use a wedding planner, and had probably already booked her. She decided to change tactics. "When will Ehan return?"

Her father sighed, and Aamira wondered if it was with relief.

"Early next week, I think," her father said.

Aamira nodded, and all the men in the car seemed to relax. She flinched when Sadan reached across the seat and took her hand in his. He hadn't been affectionate before, and she wondered how he truly felt about her. He'd never declared his love or seemed to moon over her in any way. They'd both known their marriage was to keep the family line bonded.

For a moment, Aamira wondered if she'd been too harsh on Sadan. They were both in the same situation, had both grown up in the same type of family, and wasn't it better to stick together?

She let her mind rest and her eyes slide shut as the hum of the tires soothed her. She looked forward to seeing her mother and her aunt and other cousins. When Ehan returned to Al Karak, she would find a way to ask him some questions. In the meantime, she could look through the photo albums and family journals her mother kept to learn more about her extended family.

"We're almost there." Sadan's voice cut through her drifting thoughts. He squeezed her hand and let go.

Aamira opened her eyes just as the car arrived at her uncle's compound. He lived in a stately home that had been through a few generations of the Sayid family, and as they pulled through the high metal gates that connected the four-meter high walls surrounding the home, Aamira felt a bit of panic.

The walls were just another indicator of her disconnect from the outside world, from all that she had enjoyed at the university, and with Chad. Another layer of distance, another barrier, now stood between them.

Two women waited at the front door, holding it open. Sadan's mother and sister. Aamira couldn't help smiling and scrambling out of the car to greet them. She embraced both women and then turned to greet the small children at her aunt's feet. "You've grown so much!" she said, and the two little girls giggled. She knew that her aunt was happy with her girls, but desperately wanted sons.

It took only moments for Aamira to be swept into her relatives' home and kitchen, surrounded by love and food and laughter. She'd missed everyone, and when her mother arrived, she even cried tears of happiness.

CHAPTER EIGHT

LONDON

"You're kidding," Mia's whisper came through Omar's phone.

He hadn't been able to resist calling her. The fact that he'd spent part of the evening—well, about an hour in the middle of the night—with the most-wanted art thief's sister was too hard to keep completely to himself. Joseph and the big boss, Simon Greif, didn't count.

Mia was the love of his life, but also the most intelligent person he knew. She had a knack for discovering the smallest details, details usually crucial in bringing criminals to justice.

Omar had told Chad to call him as soon as he woke up, so they could go through all of Chad's messages and emails from Aamira over the past few months. Joseph had produced a couple of leads about Taheer and Kahul, but because they'd flown out this morning with Aamira, Omar considered them off the grid for now.

Omar gave Mia the rundown of the conversation with Aamira.

"So she claims she knows nothing," Mia mused. "Do you believe her?"

He hesitated, not wanting to admit that he might be a sucker. "I do."

"Me too," Mia said.

"Really? Why?" Omar asked, curious if Mia was going on her rock-solid intuition or knew some important detail he'd missed.

"She's a daughter of a prominent, but very traditional Muslim family," Mia said.

"Yes."

"And she would be kept out of the family business as much as possible, even after she's earned her college degree," Mia said.

"So we can assume Aamira's innocence is due to her gender," he said.

"Yes, more specifically, a woman in the Sayid family. But it seems this Aamira is smart and perhaps a bit rebellious. You said that Chad asked her to marry him, yet she turned him down. But the fact remains, she was involved with Chad, even if the outcome didn't result in a stronger commitment."

Omar wiped the prickle of sweat from his face. Here Mia was, casually speaking about marriage and commitment, when their own relationship had only recently progressed from dating to living together.

Mia broke into his roller-coaster thoughts. "Do you have a way to stay in touch with her?"

"Not directly. Chad might have some ideas. Oh. Wait. Just before she left, he told her to take the cell phone he'd purchased for her."

"She doesn't have her own?" Mia said, then continued before Omar could reply. "I'm not surprised, actually. Get her number from Chad and forward it to me. I'll contact her."

Omar straightened from the couch he was perched on. "What? Wait, I didn't call to get you involved."

Mia laughed softly over the phone. "Of course you didn't."

He found himself smiling. "At least that wasn't my intention when I called you."

"Why did you call me then, Omar?" Her voice was light, teasing.

He'd spent too much time dodging Mia's blunt questions

over the past year. So he decided to be direct, and take the punch as it came. “I miss you.” He hesitated, and when she didn’t reply, he added, “And you’re the best investigator I know.”

Her soft laugh was back, the one that tugged at his heart. “That’s better. Anyone can miss something, but I’ll take your compliment.”

“So, do you have extra time on your hands or something?” he asked. “I don’t want to piss off the boss and dominate your time.”

“My time has always been my own,” Mia said. “And helping you out would never be a waste.”

If Omar had a mirror, he knew he’d be glowing bright red. Not that he’d ever admit to blushing. “Thank you,” he said in a voice that wasn’t a hundred percent steady.

“Get that number, and then you can thank me,” Mia said. “Gotta go, babe. See you soon.”

Before Omar could say anything, maybe declare his love for her, she clicked off.

He stared at his phone for a moment, then scrolled through the incoming emails he’d missed during the call. Joseph had kept Simon Greif busy through the night, and it seemed those efforts were now paying off.

“Joseph!” Omar called. Footsteps coming from the other room sounded on the hardwood. Soon Joseph rounded the corner, a tablet in one hand and a phone in the other. The man was about twenty-four, fresh faced, but the circles beneath his eyes, the tousled brown hair, and a couple days’ growth of new beard told Omar that he’d been inundated during this “training.”

“Did you see these emails?” Omar asked.

“Just reading through them now,” Joseph replied, settling on the opposite end of the couch from Omar. “Looks like there’s a shared credit card account between Ehan Sayid and his father, which Taheer Sayid used to rent a car.”

“Yes, very sloppy of them,” Omar said, although it wasn’t

enough to actually track the man down. But they had a credit card number, so Omar told Joseph, "Start running the number and print off all the hits inside England over the past fourteen days. We need to find out if there's a pattern. Anything from yesterday might be one of the Sayid brothers."

"Yes, boss," Joseph said.

Omar didn't mind being called boss once in a while, but it made him feel a bit old and on the shelf when Joseph said it.

While Joseph ran the numbers, Omar called Chad's cell. He answered on the third ring, his voice scratchy.

"Are you awake yet?" Omar asked, holding back annoyance that his cousin had slept and he hadn't.

"I am now," Chad growled. "Do you ever sleep?"

"Sometimes," Omar said; now wasn't the time to discuss sleep schedules. "But not when we've had the biggest breakthrough on the case so far."

"And what would that breakthrough be?" Chad asked.

Was his cousin trying to be annoying? "Your girlfriend, Chad. I need her phone number."

Chad laughed. "You and me both. She's basically unreachable. All the eggs are in her basket, so to speak. If there's one thing I *do* know about her family, it's that they don't know anything about me, and to add another insult to my devotion, she's never given me her address or home number. I only have her university email, but that's probably closed out by now."

"I thought you gave her a cell phone," Omar said, cutting through Chad's bitter diatribe. Maybe he should have let his cousin sleep a bit longer.

"Yeah," Chad said, "but she didn't take it. She's worried her father would find it."

Omar didn't have time to debate schematics. "What's the number?"

"I don't think—"

"It's just for informational purposes," Omar said. "We want to see if she was contacted by her brother recently."

"But he didn't have her number, no one did," Chad protested.

"What's the number?" Omar asked again.

Chad recited the number, and Omar put it into his phone. While Chad continued to complain, Omar shared the contact with Mia.

"Meet me at my hotel café," Omar said, cutting Chad off once again. "Thirty minutes." He hung up before his cousin could start into another diatribe. Omar really needed coffee, and food, and it looked like Joseph would be dropping off to sleep at any moment.

Omar turned to the younger agent. "Anything interesting yet?"

"Just about to print off the transaction data now," Joseph said, as he clicked on his tablet. The printer on the kitchen table sprang to life with a series of lights and mechanical sounds.

Omar crossed to the kitchen and stood over the papers spewing out, and picked them up one by one. He was looking for a cluster of transactions in the same location—a location that might tell where Ehan Sayid was staying. At first, there was no discernible pattern, but then Omar lined up two of the pages vertically against the bottom of another page. He looked at the transactions top to bottom.

"He's living in Newbury Park," Omar said, mostly to himself.

Joseph joined him at the table and leaned over the printouts. He took a moment, then said, "You're right. Publix is a local grocery, and BP is a petrol station. He probably wouldn't buy groceries too far from where he's been staying."

"Agreed." Omar picked up a pen from the table and circled a few of the transactions. "After we meet with my cousin, we'll go to these locations and ask questions." He looked at Joseph's bleary eyes. "Get cleaned up first. You'll be asking the questions, and I don't want the store owners to think you're a druggie."

Joseph's face flushed, and he stammered, "Of—of course. Give me a few minutes."

Omar continued to study the printouts, reading through them more carefully this time. Spending money seemed to come easily to Ehan Sayid. Omar heard the shower water running, and hoped Joseph would be quick. He really wanted that coffee.

As he waited, he spent a few minutes tracing the bank that had issued the credit card, and found that it was an affiliate bank of Al Karak. At least the Sayid family hadn't used their own bank.

"Ready," Joseph said, coming down the hall.

Omar glanced at him. Now the man looked more awake.

Omar grabbed his jacket, sure that it would rain at some point while they were out. The sky was still a murky gray. He stepped outside with Joseph, and they took the lift to the hotel café.

Omar went ahead and ordered before Chad's arrival. By the time his cousin did show up, Omar was already on his second cup, and feeling better.

Chad shook Joseph's hand and sat at the table. He ordered a pastry and a coffee.

"Did you bring your laptop and phone?" Omar asked.

Chad nodded, pulling his laptop from a backpack and handing over his phone to Omar.

Omar gave the phone to Joseph and then he opened the laptop. After Chad entered the password, Omar began to run a mirror image of the hard drive, downloading it onto an external drive.

Joseph did the same thing with the cell phone.

"I don't have much hope of hearing from Aamira again," Chad said. "I mean, I gave her the opportunity to stay, and she still flew out this morning."

"You might be in luck," Omar said as he glanced at the text that had just buzzed into his phone. He held up the screen to show Chad. "Another agent . . . Mia . . . traced the cell phone that you gave Aamira to Al Karak. It appears that she took the phone with her after all."

Chad swallowed, staring at the cell phone screen. "How can you be sure?"

"I've learned not to doubt any information Mia collects."

Chad nodded. "All right, so she has the phone with her." His face brightened. "Maybe there's hope for us after all."

"Looks like it." Omar leaned back in his chair as another text buzzed in. "Mia wants you to try to text her. See what happens." He looked over at Joseph. "Almost finished with his phone?"

"It's done," Joseph said, and handed the phone to Chad. "I just copied over the text messages between the two of you." He looked from Chad to Omar. "And I sent you the file to review."

Omar picked up his own phone and clicked on the link to open the text message strand. He started to scan the messages, knowing he'd need to read them more carefully later.

"What should I say?" Chad asked. "I mean . . ."

"You need to be aware that although she took the phone with her, she might not be able to use it," Omar said. "Or someone in her family might discover it, and will read whatever you write to her."

"Yeah," Chad said, looking thoughtfully at his phone. "Good point. I'll just send a test text." He started typing, then said out loud, "I wrote: *I'm checking to see who this number belongs to.*"

"Good," Omar said. "She'll know it's from you, and then she can direct the conversation from there depending on her circumstances." He took a final swallow of coffee, then pushed back from the table. "When she replies, let me know as soon as possible. We're spending the day following other leads."

"All right," Chad said.

Omar stood and placed a hand on his cousin's shoulder. "And I am sorry for what she's put you through. It's not a nice surprise to find out those sorts of things about your girlfriend's family." He and Mia had been through plenty of ups and downs, including the discovery of some not-so-pleasant family secrets.

Joseph gathered up his things, and he and Omar said goodbye to Chad. Then they left the hotel to grab a cab.

En route to their first destination, Omar read through the texts between Chad and Aamira. They started out as friendly and informational. Then they grew more flirty. Aamira's texts were very short, as if she didn't really want to be texting. Chad's were much more revealing, but it wasn't the sort of information Omar was looking for.

"Here," Omar said, showing the phone to Joseph. "Read these few texts and tell me what you think." It was a late-night exchange between the two, and Aamira was telling Chad that she couldn't see him anymore. Dated two months ago, it seemed that Aamira's conscience had been bothering her, although she didn't give any specifics in her texts.

But the fourth text in the timeline strand said, *My family is very traditional like I told you, and very protective of each other. Even my brother checks up on me*.

"So her brother has been in contact with her—email? Phone?" Joseph asked.

"Possibly in person," Omar said. He glanced at the taxi driver and decided he wouldn't say anything else until they were in private. He was still reading the texts when his phone rang.

"We've found something," Simon Greif said.

Omar's boss rarely called; he usually sent orders through a series of commanding texts. So for him to call meant that whatever he'd discovered couldn't wait for a texted reply. "What is it?" Omar asked.

"The laptop imaging of Chad's that you sent over has security software attached to it," Greif said. Before Omar could ask him to be more specific, Greif continued, "The security software is registered to Taheer Sayid. This means that Chad's recent activity on his laptop has been monitored."

"What's the date of install?" Omar asked.

"Three days ago."

Omar exhaled deeply. That meant Aamira's father somehow suspected her of a relationship with Chad and was clever enough to install spyware. Omar's mind raced at how that all might have happened, but more than that, it told Omar that Chad needed to be careful. Omar had already known these were high-level criminals, and now tech-savvy proficiency could be added to their portfolio. And he worried about what the consequences might be for Aamira. Would her father punish her if he could prove she'd been involved with Chad?

He hung up with Simon and tapped the driver on the shoulder. "We're getting out here."

The driver looked back at him in surprise, then pulled over at the nearest open curb. Omar paid the man, then climbed out, Joseph following. Omar started walking briskly in the direction the taxi should have been taking them.

Joseph knew better than to prod Omar for information. It took only a few minutes for Omar to process his thoughts and come up with the next plan of action. "We need to contact Chad and tell him that Aamira's father knows all about him. In fact, he might even know about the marriage proposal if Chad used email or messaging to contact his mother about it."

Omar ran a hand through his hair. Out of all the women on the university campus, what were the odds of Chad meeting the one whose family could completely wreak havoc?

He sent a quick text to Mia. Less than a minute later, his phone rang.

"Yes?" Omar answered, as he and Joseph continued their brisk pace.

"I found something that may or may not be related to your search for Ehan Sayid," Mia said. She barely took a breath before saying, "First of all, I've made a discovery that I want to verify further, but it would explain why Aamira's father is monitoring your cousin Chad. What do you know about the Mika'il Order?"

Omar's breath stalled. "They've existed for centuries, since the time of Muhammad. Named after one of Allah's angels." His mind caught up with Mia's question. "Do you think they're connected to the Sayid family? Do you think they *are* the Mika'il

Order . . .?" He didn't need to finish the question. Of course she did, or she wouldn't have brought it up. "Wow."

"Yep," Mia agreed. "I've got to take a break from this for a few. Catch up on some sleep before I dive back in."

"Thank you," Omar said. "For everything." He clicked off, and stared straight ahead. If Taheer Sayid and his brother were members of the clandestine Mika'il Order, then Omar had a much bigger problem than bringing in an international art thief. "Damn, damn, damn."

"What's wrong?" Joseph asked. Now he was trying to keep up with Omar's torrid pace.

Omar didn't have time to explain. He had to take action now. He diverted into a narrow alley between a grocery and a restaurant. Thankfully, it was deserted with the exception of a few rubbish bins and a black and white cat napping in a spot of sun. He pressed Send on Chad's contact number and waited for his cousin to answer. Omar spoke. "You need to leave your flat right away. I'll text you an address of a safe house. Don't take anything with you. Leave your phone and any electronic device in your flat. Get a new phone and text me the number."

Joseph stared at Omar and his eyes widened.

Omar took a deep breath, then made an even harder phone call.

"Mr. Zagouri?" Omar asked, knowing very well that the man who answered was his father. But he couldn't be sure how secure his father's phone line was.

"How did everything go?"

"Listen, I need your help," Omar said. "I can't explain on the phone, but you need to get your sister to a safe place. Right now. Tell her to leave all of her electronics behind and to give you a new number to reach her. Then pass it along to me."

Dead silence on the other end of the line, and Omar found himself holding his breath, waiting for his father's reply.

"Are you sure about this?"

Omar rubbed the bridge of his nose. If Mia's hunch about the Mika'il Order was right, then his warnings to his cousin and aunt weren't a moment too soon, and trying to protect them and separate them from the Sayid family would save their lives. He drilled down into his subconscious and tried to listen to his deepest instinct.

"Yes," Omar said in a near whisper. "I'm absolutely sure."

CHAPTER NINE

AD 1187
ANCIENT KARAK

Eleanor stared at her stepfather, Raynald of Châtillon, former Prince of Antioch, and current Lord of Oultrejordain. His face was flushed red, his mouth edged with spittle, and his words were harsh. "By the flaming sword of all avenging angels, you will be a Christian woman who only associates with other Christians!"

Eleanor lowered her head and focused on the stone slabs that made up the grand courtyard of Karak Castle, which her stepfather had possessed upon his marriage to her mother. Eleanor was surrounded by her stepfather's soldiers who kept their hands on the hilts of their swords, as if they feared an aggressive attack from a woman of nineteen. Raynald had married her mother, Stephanie of Milly, the wealthy French heiress of Oultrejordain, eleven years before in 1176. And from the moment Eleanor was first introduced to her new stepfather, she'd known her life would never be the same. Eleanor's true father, Humphrey III, Lord of Toron, had died when she was a young girl.

The discovery that her handmaiden Zulla was a Muslim had enraged Raynald, and he threatened execution unless she renounced her god. When the handmaiden had refused to convert, vowing she'd rather die than worship the wrong god, Raynald carried through on his threat. At midnight, Zulla had been executed.

In the center of the courtyard to which Eleanor was now being summoned, Zulla had breathed her last. Eleanor blinked back her stinging tears and imagined Zulla lowering her head, exposing the slenderness of her neck, then falling to the stones as the executioner's axe ended her life.

Eleanor had never known anyone as religiously devoted as her handmaiden, and wished she had just a portion of Zulla's courage. Yet the woman was gone, and now Eleanor faced the continued wrath of a man who might be her stepfather by marriage, though she'd never felt anything but loathing toward this man who'd killed thousands in his role in the Second Crusade.

Being born to one of the wealthiest women in the world had been a curse.

"What do you have to answer for yourself?" Raynald roared. "You knew your handmaiden was Muslim, yet you kept it secret."

Eleanor knew better than to actually speak. Raynald would rage for a short time, and then another crisis would require his attention. And with the kingdom in flux, there was always something.

"Will twenty lashes make you understand what's expected of you?" Raynald asked.

Eleanor flinched, not able to help her physical reaction, even though she kept her answers to herself. She knew that for a bloodthirsty man like Raynald, twenty lashes was lenient. Even to a woman, and even to a stepdaughter.

"I will not have my daughter's skin marred," a woman's voice said.

Mother.

Eleanor lifted her head to see her mother, Stephanie of Milly, walk into the courtyard, accompanied by her guards and ladies.

Her mother continued straight toward her crusader husband, her chin lifted, without so much as a glance toward Eleanor.

The color of her stepfather's face muted from red to fleshy pink, and strangely enough, the hardness of his eyes softened.

Eleanor's mother had that effect on people.

"She will be meeting Azzo the Sixth of Este in a week's time, and I don't want her to look like a whipped dog." Her mother stopped before her husband, and to the discerning eye, it was clear who had the upper hand. Although her mother would never act as if she had the advantage over her husband in front of others, Eleanor knew her mother wasn't fooling anyone.

"Consider it, Rayn," she said, using her pet name for him. "Perhaps executing her handmaiden was a severe enough discipline."

Raynald blinked at his wife, then allowed a rare smile to grow on his face. Turning toward his advisors, he said, "Does anyone question why I married my dear Stephanie of Milly? She is a most brilliant advisor."

Advisors and soldiers nodded their eager agreement.

And then Raynald's gaze was on Eleanor. This time not as a wild avenger, but as a controlled disciplinarian. "You will return to seclusion until your presentation to Prince Azzo." He paused, and in that pause Eleanor found herself cringing. There was always one more thing with Raynald. "Your dancing had better be flawless. I'll settle for no less than a profitable marriage proposal."

Eleanor bowed her head, and before her stepfather could come up with any more orders or punishments, she turned and walked quickly away. Her new handmaiden fell into step beside her. The older woman, perhaps in her forties, had arrived the night before in Eleanor's bedchamber. It was then that Eleanor had known without a doubt that Zulla would never return. Eleanor had been so angry that she hadn't even spoken to the new woman, nor asked her name. Eleanor had no doubt there would be no friendship, nor foolishness, with the older woman.

As they left the courtyard, the soldiers stood to the side to let them pass, and Eleanor felt more than one pair of eyes on her. She kept her chin raised, her eyes straight ahead, mimicking the way her mother walked. Eleanor was considered an heiress, after all, and her status in Oultrejordain was no small thing.

Just as she exited the courtyard, a burst of hot wind pushed against her heavy velvet gown and stirred her long, dark curls from the nape of her neck. The season was turning hot, and it would soon be impossible to go outside without some shade. She would miss the nights that Zulla had let her escape her chambers to walk along the canal. She didn't know if the new pale-faced handmaiden would keep such secrets.

Eleanor stepped into the cool hallway of the castle, grateful for the change in temperature, as well as her mother's interference. At the age of nineteen, Eleanor was due for marriage.

She had never met nor seen Prince Azzo, but she knew that looks, or physical attraction, weren't taken into consideration with arranged marriages. Land and alliances were the bargaining considerations. Her older sister Isabella had married Ruben III of Armenia, and her brother Humphrey IV of Toron had married Isabella of Jerusalem. Eleanor's mother Stephanie had had two more children with Raynald, but Eleanor's half brother, also named Raynald, had died as a boy. Her half sister's name was Alix.

Upon her own marriage, Eleanor would miss her mother, but she would not be sorry to say goodbye to Raynald.

And she would not accept a handmaiden assigned by her stepfather.

Eleanor stopped on the steps leading to her chambers and turned to face the woman. "You are dismissed."

The woman's eyes widened, and it was then that Eleanor noticed the woman's eyes were different colors. One was hazel, the other a murky blue. The revelation made Eleanor hesitate. Women with different-colored eyes were said to be sorceresses. If this woman was such a creature, then Eleanor needed to take care, although she had always prided herself in reading people and glimpsing into the innermost chambers of their souls. In this case, the handmaiden's expression was innocent enough.

"His lord will not be pleased," the woman spoke in a raspy tone.

Another surprise from the woman. It was as if her throat had been scarred or injured. "I do not need a handmaiden. I'll be married in a short time, and my new husband will assign my household. In the meantime," Eleanor said, taking a great gulp of air, "no one can replace the loss of Zulla."

The woman's gaze was steady, although Eleanor was unnerved by the two eyes battling for attention.

"Zulla was a dear girl," the woman said, "and I am sorry you lost your friend."

If Eleanor could have predicted any sort of response from the woman, it wouldn't have been that. She looked deep into the woman's eyes then, seeing only compassion and years of wisdom that far outstripped her own.

"Thank you," Eleanor replied at last. "Her death was a tragedy."

The woman merely bowed her head.

"What is your name?" Eleanor asked, curiosity keeping her in the conversation.

"Miriam," she said. "Like the woman in the Bible."

"The sister of Moses," Eleanor replied.

Miriam nodded. "The sister who kept a secret for her brother for many years."

Eleanor's gaze locked on Miriam then, and although no words were spoken for several moments, it was as if an understanding passed between them. Eleanor could trust Miriam. And Miriam would protect Eleanor.

"I've changed my mind," Eleanor said in a hushed tone.

Miriam's mouth lifted into the faintest of smiles. "I am honored, Lady Eleanor."

"Follow me," Eleanor said, keeping the smile off of her face. She still didn't know Miriam. Tonight, after she ate supper alone in her room, she'd put Miriam to the test.

Anticipation caused the late afternoon hours to pass quickly, and when the servant brought in supper, Eleanor ate her chicken and rice eagerly. She didn't have to go through the formal motions of waiting for each course to be served. In the privacy of her own chambers, with only Miriam as company, Eleanor could eat in any order and amount.

"I will leave my chambers tonight," Eleanor said, noting how Miriam lifted her head to stare at her. "I'll wear a disguise and walk along the canal."

"You are taking a great risk, Lady Eleanor," Miriam said.

"Yes, and you will not call me Lady Eleanor beyond the castle walls." Eleanor smiled then. "It is part of the disguise, you see. I have walked along the canal for weeks now." She braced herself for an argument or an admonishment, or perhaps an outright refusal. If the women were caught outside the castle, surely Miriam knew her punishment would be far greater than Eleanor's. Miriam didn't have a royal mother to run interference.

When Miriam rose to her feet and crossed to the massive wardrobe, Eleanor was surprised. The handmaiden withdrew a selection of heavy robes and laid them out on the platform bed. "Do you think these are too elegant and will give you away?"

Eleanor had already thought of that, which only proved she'd been correct in keeping Miriam as her handmaiden.

"Zulla keeps the plain capes in the rear of the wardrobe," Eleanor said.

Miriam didn't seem surprised at the revelation. She crossed to the wardrobe again and pulled out two capes, one a gray wool, the other a dark blue. Miriam busied herself replacing the other garments and then turned to Eleanor. "How do you suggest we leave the castle?"

Eleanor's smile was full this time. "I'll show you."

After a servant returned the serving trays of leftover supper to the palace kitchen, it took only moments for the women to don their rough wool capes. Eleanor picked up one of the burning oil lamps and led Miriam to the large tapestry hanging along one wall. Lifting one side, she revealed a low wooden door. "Pagan the

Butler, Lord of Montreal and Oultrejourdain, built in a series of secret passages over fifty years ago," she said. "I don't think my stepfather knows, or else I would be moved from this room."

"Lead the way, my lady," Miriam said.

Eleanor decided that she and Miriam would become fast friends. The narrow passageways that wound throughout the castle, connecting random rooms, might have been used once. But now, they had long been neglected. Cobwebs and dust lined the dank stone walls, and the depths of the darkness always made Eleanor shiver.

In a short time, they exited into a grain storage room. One door led to the cooking rooms, while another led to a passageway that opened to a back courtyard. Eleanor knew the route well and continued to lead Miriam into the courtyard and through a locked gate. One she possessed a key for.

Eleanor smiled beneath her hood as she and Miriam strolled toward the canal. Others were out walking too, enjoying the moonlit night and the evening breeze, the break from the early summer heat. It was an innocent activity, at least for a regular citizen of Karak. But for a member of the royal family to walk unguarded among the laborers was unheard of.

A splash up ahead startled Eleanor and caught the attention of others walking along the canal. "My son!" a woman's voice screeched. "He can't swim!"

Eleanor and Miriam hurried to the edge of the deep canal to see a young boy, likely five or six, struggling to stay above the water. His crying and sputtering only seemed to make it worse, and the current had already dragged him to the center. Eleanor couldn't swim either, but surely she could fare better than a young child in the current. She removed her slippers and started to tug off her cloak, but Miriam grabbed her arm. "You will be found out."

"But the child—"

"Look, there's a man going in from the other side," Miriam said, pointing across the canal.

Eleanor lifted her gaze to see a man pulling off his own cloak and shirt. Other men stood above him on the bank, but this one man seemed determined to try what they would not. Within moments, the man plunged into the murky water and started swimming after the boy with long, sure strokes.

She watched the stranger swim, mesmerized by the way his powerful arms sliced effortlessly through the water. She found she was holding her breath as the battle between life and death played out before her. When the man reached the child and scooped him up with one arm, Eleanor gasped in relief. The man was now moving toward Eleanor's side of the bank, swimming upriver against the current, toward the hysterical mother.

Without realizing it, Eleanor had moved down the bank, near the water's edge, so that by the time the man came out of the water with the nearly drowned child in his arms, she caught a full view of the man's face beneath the moonlight. His eyes were dark and heavily lashed beneath prominent brows, and his face was angular, although his mouth was somehow full in appearance. Water dripped from his shoulder length hair, and his short beard was nearly as black as the night. His gaze swept past Eleanor, moving to the sobbing mother, but Eleanor knew he'd seen her. There'd been a fire in his eyes, a determination to rescue this child from a watery grave, that drew Eleanor to him as he climbed toward the mother.

Eleanor watched as the man deposited the crying child in his mother's outstretched arms, and after turning down any offers of promised gifts or money for saving her child, he moved back down the bank, as if he were intending to swim back across the canal.

With the child no longer in his arms, Eleanor caught sight of his full torso, lean and muscled. She knew instantly he was no Christian and probably belonged to one of the Muslim tribes outside of Karak. His arms were banded with thick ribbons of leather, and his bare torso had been striped with scars. Not just any scars, but deliberate carvings of his tribe.

The scars were formed into the design of a warrior horse, creating a tribal symbol.

Eleanor's breath left her chest as she realized she was staring at a member of the Ayyub tribe—the Kurdish tribe of her stepfather's greatest nemesis Saladin, or more formally Salah ad-Din Yusuf ibn Ayyub. And the appearance of this warrior along the canal leading to the castle could only mean one thing. War had come to Karak.

CHAPTER TEN

MODERN-DAY AL KARAK

Aamira gazed at the glowing screen of her cell phone while she lay in bed in her dark bedroom. The reunion with her family had been bittersweet, and now she was finally alone. The past twenty-four hours had been a whirlwind of extreme highs and lows, and she was completely exhausted. But still, she couldn't sleep.

With the house silent and her parents sleeping, she had slipped her contraband cell phone from her suitcase beneath her bed and turned it on. There was a text from Chad, and she couldn't understand it.

I'm checking to see who this number belongs to.

She frowned at the words. Chad very well knew this was her number; they'd been texting and calling for months. Had he tried to find the cell phone at her apartment and thought it stolen? Her finger hesitated over the text message app, wanting to reply to him. Wanting to tell him she was sorry, that she missed him, loved him, and that she didn't know if she could marry Sadan after all.

Hot tears spilled onto her cheeks. On a night like tonight, with so many things bothering her and discouragement settling deep, she normally would have called Chad. He would have listened and made her feel better. He might have even brought her flowers and pulled her into his arms until she could breathe freely again. But she was home now, and there was nothing Chad could do to change that.

Stay with me, he'd said. *Tell your family you've changed your mind . . . We can stay here in England. Marry me and become a citizen. You can use your education for teaching* our *sons.*

She blinked back her furious tears. How she wanted to go with Chad. To marry him. Her breath hitched at the thought—she had just realized she *did* want to marry Chad. She *did* want to become his wife and live her life with him. Not with Sadan.

Aamira passed on texting Chad; instead, she called him. Her heart thumped hard as she waited through the rings, hoping that he'd answer, yet hoping he wouldn't. Chad had never set up a voicemail—said that's what texting was for if someone wanted to leave him a message. She was about to hang up when the phone connected.

"Aamira?" Chad said in a voice that sounded like he'd just awakened.

"Hi," she breathed in a whisper. And then she started crying, audibly.

"Hey, what's wrong?" Chad sounded more awake now.

Aamira paused. "I've made a horrible mistake, Chad. I should have never come back home."

"What's happened?" he asked, anxiety in his voice clear.

"Nothing . . . I mean, I'm not with *you.* That's what's wrong," she said. She struggled to control her voice. "I'm so sorry. I just don't know how to get out of this."

"Out of your engagement to Sadan?"

Aamira didn't miss the hope in his tone. "Yes. I made the commitment to him before I met you, and it was expected of me, of both Sadan and me. He doesn't love me either. It's just that our families . . ." She took a deep breath. "It's what our families do. It's our tradition. And now I've hurt you."

"I'm not upset with *you,*" Chad cut in. "Even if you'd told me earlier, right when I met you, about Sadan, I still would have fallen in love with you. I wouldn't have been able to *not* notice you, or to not talk to you. I just didn't know I had this kind of competition."

A small smile helped ease Aamira's tears. "You don't have any competition—at least for my heart."

Both of them were quiet for a moment, and Aamira thought she heard a floorboard creak in the hall. She knew her father was gone overnight, and her mother had been asleep for over an hour.

"I should go," she whispered.

"Wait," Chad said. "I have to tell you something, but now's not the time. I'm getting a new phone, and I'll send you a text after I hang up. But listen, I can get you a plane ticket. Just tell me when. Come back to England, and we'll get everything worked out."

She wanted to say yes, but she was too scared. "I'll think about it," she finally said. Another creak, and her heart thumped. "Goodbye, Chad."

She hung up and powered off her phone, leaving the room absolutely pitch-black. Holding her breath, she listened for footsteps. Total silence. Perhaps she was paranoid, but if her father found the cell phone, she knew there would be plenty of consequences.

Still, she couldn't sleep, and when she powered on her phone again, there was a text from Chad with a new number. She saved it under a woman's name, and then sent a text to Chad confirming she had his new number. After deleting the copy of her own text, she turned the phone back off.

She closed her eyes and thought about what tomorrow would bring. Her mother wanted to meet with the seamstress, who was an exclusive wedding dressmaker in Karak. Aamira tried to imagine the cost but only knew it would be in the thousands of Jordanian dinars. Was running a town bank really that lucrative, or was her father in some other business—like the business Omar Zagouri had accused her brother of?

Aamira crept out of her bedroom to find the house completely silent. Using her cell phone light, she continued to the library where her mother kept journals and photo albums. She sat on the floor and pulled the albums out one by one, sorting through the pages to find a picture of Hana. She couldn't get Omar's implication out of her mind that her family had been involved in Hana's death. Going back more than ten years, Aamira finally located a few pictures at a second cousin's wedding.

Aamira's heart tugged with grief as she shone the light on Hana's smiling face. Hana had been a beautiful, vibrant woman, and her smile lit up any room she entered. She was wearing an elegant beaded gown, and smiling, but not directly at the photographer. Her eyes were looking past the photographer at someone else—perhaps someone behind him?

Aamira looked carefully at the other pictures of the wedding event. She could identify almost everyone, except for one tall man. She studied him for a moment, but couldn't place him. She used her phone to take a picture of the photograph, then turned the page. Her heart stilled. Aunt Hana was dancing with the stranger, smiling up at him. And if Aamira wasn't mistaken, he was looking at Hana as if she were the only woman in the world.

Aamira took another picture, and then before she could change her mind, she texted both pictures to Chad with a short message. *This is my Aunt Hana who took her own life years ago. I don't recognize the man in the picture*.

Pulse racing, Aamira continued turning pages of the album. The picture of Hana dancing with the man was the last one taken of her alive. Near the end of the album, Aamira's mother had taped in pictures of Hana's funeral procession and the extravagant displays of flowers at her gravesite.

Although it had been years ago, memories returned as Aamira sorted through the funeral pictures. The women had keened in mourning for hours after the men left the cemetery. Her mother had even pasted in a picture of the wailing women. Most of the main crowd had left, and only a few remained as the women, raising their voices together, clad in long, black robes, clutched each other near the freshly covered grave.

Aamira stared at the photo for a few minutes. Her eyes misted at the memory of her kind aunt, of a life lost too early, of the desperation and grief her aunt must have felt to commit such a heinous act against her own body. Then Aamira noticed an image she hadn't seen before at the edge of the mourners' photo.

It was the side view of a man just turning away so that only his profile showed. His arms were blurred as if caught in mid-motion as the picture was taken. Aamira pulled up the photo she'd just taken on her phone and lined it up next to the man at the funeral. Her breath stalled. The man her aunt had danced with months before at their cousin's wedding, a man Aamira had never met or knew anything about, had attended Hana's funeral.

Aamira closed her eyes, wondering what all this meant. She couldn't fathom the idea that her uncle or anyone in the family had killed Hana. Not their family. It wasn't possible. Yet the thick weight of doubt had entered her, making her stomach knot.

She put away the dusty albums and made her way back to her room. She put the phone under her pillow and closed her eyes, finally allowing herself to sleep.

When she awoke, the grayness of her room told her it was not yet dawn. Her eyes felt gritty and her mouth was dry, and as she rose to get a drink of water she heard the sound of a car pulling up to their home. Aamira lifted one of the blind slats and peered out into the early morning.

Her father's car was just coming to a stop in front of the house, and he was on his phone as he stepped out of the vehicle. Aamira watched him, wondering who he was speaking to at five thirty.

He looked tired and stressed, which only put Aamira on further alert. She let the blind slide closed as he approached the front door and unlocked it. Climbing back into bed, she wondered if she dared ask her father about Hana. How would she phrase it? She listened to his footsteps echo through the house, stopping in the kitchen. He must be getting something to drink, and then she heard the murmur of voices.

Her mother was awake, ready to serve her husband a meal. Sure enough, the smell of cooking soon reached Aamira, and then she heard water running in the pipes, indicating that her father must be showering.

She hurried to the kitchen to speak with her mother alone—a chance she might not have the rest of the day.

"Aamira?" her mother said, turning. "I thought you would sleep longer. You looked very tired last night."

Aamira crossed to her mother and kissed her cheek. Deena Sayid was still a pretty woman, although wrinkles had encroached on her smooth skin and her hair was now shot through with white strands.

"Can I ask you something?" Aamira said in a quiet voice. She didn't think for one second that if her mother knew about a crime within the family, she'd reveal it to Aamira. But Aamira could at least test her mother's reaction. "Did Aunt Hana really take her own life, or was she murdered?"

Her mother's eyes widened, and she shook her head, then turned back to her cooking. "Don't speak like that in my home," she hissed.

Aamira drew back, stunned at the vehemence in her mother's voice. She took a deep breath, then said, "I need to know, it's important. I understand that you might be keeping confidences that you can't betray, but I've come across some information—"

Her mother turned to Aamira and delivered a stinging slap across her face. "Do not speak of this again. Ever. Your questions disrespect our family and our good Sayid name. Go to your room. I don't want to see your face for the rest of the day."

Her mother's words were whispered but might as well have been shouted. Aamira felt as though she'd been punched in the chest. She took a step back, out of her mother's reach. Despite the fierce pain in her cheek and the subsequent throbbing, she stared, ignoring the tears burning in her eyes.

Her mother stared back, her own eyes rimmed in red, her breathing rapid.

The quiet of the kitchen was interrupted by the shutting of the bathroom door off her parents' master bedroom.

"I have one more question," Aamira said over the pounding of her heart. "Where's Ehan? And what is he really doing?"

Her mother momentarily flinched, but kept her locked-in gaze. Her lips pressed together as if she were trying to hold back a thousand words. It was too late. Aamira had seen it in her mother's eyes—there were secrets in this family. Secrets too terrible to voice.

Slowly, as if forcing her limbs to move, Aamira turned from her mother and walked to her room. She had no desire to encounter her father in the hallway. Once inside, she leaned against the door, and reviewed all that her mother had said. Aamira sank to the floor and leaned her head against the door as her father's murmured words sounded from the kitchen. Would her mother tell her father the questions she'd asked?

Would her father come flying into her bedroom, demanding an explanation? But as the voices continued, floating in and out of comprehension, there were no raised tones, only the clinking of silverware and dishes. And then finally, her father's footsteps retreated to his bedroom, followed by silence.

Aamira didn't know what her mother was doing. The house was silent. But Aamira did know one thing. She couldn't stay in this house of secrets any longer.

She powered on her cell phone and saw that Chad had replied to her texted pictures.

I'm forwarding these to O.Z. He'll be contacting you.

Another text had come in, from a number she hadn't saved. She assumed it was from Omar Zagouri when she read it: *When you're in a safe location, contact me. Delete this text as soon as you read it.*

CHAPTER ELEVEN

LONDON

As Omar and Joseph started up the stairs to Ehan Sayid's London flat, Omar already knew they were too late. More often than not, Omar could trust his intuition, and today that intuition told him that Ehan was long gone.

Especially if the Sayid family had been tracing Chad's phone or computer, they might already have Omar's name now.

"This is it?" Joseph said, coming to a stop in front of #18.

Omar nodded and pulled out his handyman knife. They wouldn't bother knocking. The lock was an easy pick, and moments later, Omar swung open the door, stepping inside first, gun drawn just in case his intuition proved wrong this time. He headed left and motioned for Joseph to go to the right. The front room was nearly empty, containing only a web-backed chair and a beat-up coffee table. It was as Omar suspected. They might be able to lift fingerprints, but they already knew Ehan had lived here. Unless he'd left behind a communications device, there was nothing worth recovering.

Omar took in a rose-colored glass ashtray, home to a few cigarette stubs, on top of the coffee table. He could still smell the cigarette smoke, and his throat felt suddenly dry. He'd given up smoking years ago, but that didn't mean the cravings had disappeared.

While Joseph entered the kitchen, Omar opened a closet door in the hallway. The shelves were empty except for a metal box.

Omar would come back to that later. He moved down the hallway and pushed open the bedroom door that stood ajar. The blinds had been left open, and the afternoon light warmed the empty room.

A mattress sat in the middle of the room, stripped of linens. Omar peered beneath the mattress and found a plastic bin. He pulled it out and popped the lid. He stared in surprise at the contents—multiple wires, a rusted car battery, and a couple of bottles of cleaning solution.

With a quick glance toward the closet to verify that was empty too, Omar backed out of the room.

His thoughts went to the forlorn metal box in the back of the closet that he'd bypassed. Seeing the makings of homemade bomb components in the plastic bin told him that the metal box might be wired.

"What's this?" Joseph asked from the hallway, reaching into the closet.

"Stop!" Omar said, lunging toward Joseph and grabbing his arm. Omar tugged the man back from the shelves. "That box might be a bomb."

Joseph's expression tightened. "What should we do? Call the authorities?"

"We're on the second floor of a five-story apartment building," Omar said. "If it goes off in here, there will be a lot of damage and possibly loss of life." He left the hallway and peered through the bedroom window that faced the back of the building.

Omar pointed past the greenbelt behind the building. "There's an empty lot. We can take the box there, then call the authorities." Joseph's face paled. But Omar knew it was either they move the box, or risk multiple lives.

"Wait here until I'm outside," Omar said. "If it blows, there's no reason for both of us to die."

Joseph opened his mouth to speak, but Omar didn't wait for further discussion. He moved again into the hallway and retrieved the metal box, being careful not to tip or shake it in any way. Joseph opened the door and Omar passed by.

He hurried down the stairs as fast as he could without jostling the box, then finally he was outside in the damp air. His heart started to catch up with his nerves, and it thumped erratically in his chest as he strode across the greenbelt. He set the metal box down in the middle of the lot that had once been paved. Then he backed away.

Either he was very paranoid or very smart. He turned to see Joseph waiting by the back of the building. Omar gave him a thumbs-up. Joseph nodded and placed a call to the local police, giving them the address of the apartment building.

Omar didn't know how long it would take for the bomb squad to arrive, but he'd have to stick around to make sure no one decided to cross the empty lot. He started walking toward Joseph when a terrific jolt knocked him off his feet. As he flew forward and knocked Joseph to the ground, he was numbly aware that the bomb had detonated.

He covered his face with his arms as he landed. He rolled away from the blast, fully expecting to be pelted with shrapnel coming from the metal box or glass from the building's windows. But there was nothing except dust. As far as homemade bombs went, it was only a minor explosion.

His ears rang and pain throbbed through his head and body. He coughed on the dust, then realizing nothing was broken, he rolled to his stomach and pushed himself up. Slowly, he climbed to his feet. "Joseph?" he said in a hoarse voice, looking around for the man through the billowing dust.

Joseph was crouched against the ground, his cell phone still gripped in his hand.

"Are you all right?" Omar asked above the ringing in his ears.

"Yes," Joseph said, then broke into a cough.

Omar walked to him, favoring his right leg. He reached for Joseph's hand and grasped it. Pain shot through Omar's hip as he helped Joseph to his feet. Joseph's face and clothing were covered with dust, and Omar supposed he looked similar.

"What set it off?" Joseph asked. He tried to wipe the dust off his face with shaking hands.

"Possibly heat-sensitive," Omar said, feeling like he was talking inside a tunnel. His hearing was off, and he gingerly touched the side of his face. "We're lucky it didn't go off sooner."

People began to emerge from neighboring buildings, some talking on their phones, others filming the bomb site. There was a small crater in the lot, but otherwise the major casualty seemed to be Omar's fuzzy hearing.

"You all right?" Joseph asked, peering at Omar. "Your cheek is scraped up."

Omar coughed. Several places throbbed and stung, and his ears were still ringing. "Yeah. I'm glad no real damage seems to have been done."

"If this had gone off inside, then all evidence of Ehan would have been destroyed," Joseph said. The wail of police sirens started up in the distance.

"I don't think there was anything in there to help us much," Omar said.

Joseph nodded. "We'll have to check for any new credit card purchases in the past couple of hours."

"Hopefully he's not already out of the country." Omar rubbed his forehead, and felt a bump starting to swell up.

A couple of ladies rushed toward Omar and Joseph, one of them calling out that she was a nurse and asking if they were okay.

Joseph verified that they were both all right as the police arrived on the scene. Omar let Joseph take the lead in answering the questions while he escaped from the chaos for a few minutes and made his way back into Ehan's flat. He combed the rooms as quickly as he could before he found a corner of the carpet in the front room that curved up instead of lying flat. He tugged at the corner, and the carpet came free off the floor. Nothing was underneath, but he wouldn't be surprised if Ehan had hidden something there.

Omar made another survey of the kitchen and paused when he found a plastic container in a lower cupboard. Gingerly, he opened the container, and pulled out several passports. A quick check told them they were all Ehan's, under different names with different associated nationalities.

Ehan would be sorely disappointed when he discovered he'd forgotten his fake passports. A fatal error. For now, Omar could run the different identities and put together a more complete profile. He hid the passports inside his shirt, then returned to the bomb site outside.

Joseph was still speaking with the police, and Omar circulated, asking the people if any of them had known the man living on the second floor in #18. Only one man said that he'd seen Ehan coming and going once in a while, but had never actually spoken to him.

"When did you last see him?" Omar asked.

"A couple of nights ago," the man said, adjusting his glasses on his thin nose. "He got into a cab in front of the building.

"Did you notice any strange behavior?" Omar continued.

"Are you with the police?" the man questioned.

"I'm with the international investigation office," Omar said, pulling out an ID that seemed to work when he needed it.

The man gazed at the ID, then back at Omar. "Very well, I did notice something unusual."

Omar waited, wondering if the man needed to be prompted, or even bribed.

The man looked away for a moment, then said, "He sometimes had a mustache, and he sometimes didn't. At first, when I noticed it missing, I thought he'd shaved. But then a couple of days later, it had fully grown back."

It was information that Omar could've guessed himself, especially since he'd discovered several passports. But it might be useful to keep in mind regardless. Omar thanked the man, and as soon as Joseph was free from his interviews, Omar motioned him over.

"They want your report as well," Joseph said.

Omar glanced at the officers, who were now speaking with a woman who seemed to have a lot to say.

"I'll catch them later," Omar said. "We've spent enough time here."

"You found something back inside, didn't you?" Joseph asked.

Omar flashed him a smile. "I think your training is starting to pay off."

Joseph chuckled, although it sounded a bit nervous.

The two remained quiet as they walked around the building, only to be stopped by a couple of curious onlookers who asked what had happened.

By the time they reached the road, a news crew had arrived. Omar steered Joseph away so they wouldn't be questioned. Their disheveled appearance made it clear that they'd been in the vicinity when the bomb went off. They walked two blocks and then hailed a cab.

"Now what?" Joseph breathed, as they settled into the back seat. He spoke in Hebrew so that the driver couldn't understand them.

Omar reached into his shirt and pulled out the passports. He handed them to Joseph and watched as he examined each one.

"What do you think of Ehan Sayid now?" Omar asked.

"Truth?" Joseph said. "This guy is really sure of himself, and I don't think he's left England. I think he'll stick around until he gets all the paintings he's after."

Omar gave Joseph a proud smile. "I agree. Nice work."

"Do you have the list of paintings from Simon Greif you can forward me?" Omar asked.

Joseph nodded, and within seconds, Omar had pulled up the attachment on his phone. He scanned through the names of the paintings and the various locations throughout the world. Five of them had been stolen: one from a Paris museum, two from a museum in Milan, one from a private collector in Istanbul, and the fifth from the Royal Academy of Arts in London. But according to Greif's research, there were still two paintings in London, both at the National Portrait Gallery museum.

"I don't think he'll leave without these," Omar said, pointing to the paintings. One was named Passion of Nadia, number 8, and the other was number 9. "These are the paintings he must have been after."

Joseph nodded. "What do you recommend? Stake it out?"

"That would be a start," Omar said. But they had to get closer, much closer. "We're about to become the newest hired security guards."

Joseph coughed into his hand. "How will we accomplish that? Can Greif hook us up?"

"It will take too long to get his approval," Omar said. "We'll have to go with my London connections."

Joseph raised his eyebrows but didn't argue.

The taxi pulled up outside their hotel, and after Omar paid the driver, they climbed out. "We need to run credit card checks on all of Ehan's aliases," Omar told Joseph as they stepped into the elevator. "Like you, my guess is that he hasn't left yet. He's definitely on the run now, so his heist could be as early as tonight. He wants those two remaining pieces in the museum."

"You want us in place by *tonight*?" Joseph asked, staring at him.

The elevator doors opened, and Omar stepped out, Joseph following. He stopped for a moment and held the door open for an elderly man who'd been waiting for the elevator. Half-way down the hallway to their suite, Omar said, "Start on the credit card research. I need to get hold of Chad to make sure he's still secure before calling in my favors."

But as Joseph opened the hotel room door, Omar's phone buzzed. It looked like Chad wanted to talk as well.

"What's going on?" Omar said into the phone.

Joseph glanced at Omar, and Omar motioned for him to close the door and get started on the next stage of research.

"I've made contact with Aamira," Chad said, his voice low and hoarse.

"Are you still in the safe location?"

"I am. I told Aamira that you'd be contacting her."

Omar exhaled. "I've sent a text, but no reply yet. What did you talk about?"

"Nothing about her brother, or family," Chad said. "Just about . . . our relationship. I told her I'd send her a plane ticket."

Omar moved to the tall windows overlooking the London road while Joseph plucked away at his laptop at the kitchen table. "What was her response?"

"She's open to it, at least she seems to be considering it," Chad said. "I guess I can see that in one of two ways."

"You're right," Omar said. He knew exactly where his cousin was going with this. "She either really wants to marry you, no matter the consequences. Or she's finding out her family is not who she thought they were."

Chad was silent. "You're kind of intense, you know."

Omar chuckled. "I've been called worse. But . . ." He lowered his voice to ensure that Joseph couldn't overhear. "I understand your frustrations to a certain extent."

"Mia?"

Omar didn't need to confirm.

"What can I be doing while we wait?" Chad asked. "I need to keep working, I can't let my financial situation get worse."

"We'll reimburse you for any lost income," Omar said. "As far as I'm concerned, you're under witness protection now."

"How did the Sayid family break into my computer in the first place?" Chad asked. "I mean, do you think Aamira knows more than she's telling us?" His voice sounded tired and defeated. "I don't want to think she's capable of this kind of deceit, but she didn't tell me something as important as her own engagement promise."

Omar looked outside and saw the clouds starting to build up.

It would be easy to accuse Aamira of being part of her family's crimes. But Omar had seen her and spoken to her and witnessed firsthand her surprise and denial of her family's involvement. He knew she was an innocent in all of this. Not that he could prove it quite yet, but he was willing to go with his instincts on this point. And it didn't hurt that Mia agreed with him.

So he told Chad, "I believe Aamira was just as blindsided as you were." Chad's sigh of relief was audible over the phone. "But you need to know something. By communicating with us, she puts herself in great danger. We have to make her understand that. She needs to know the risks she is taking, and that she still has a choice."

"How can I help her?" Chad asked.

"We'll do everything we can to protect her," Omar said, "*if* she wants our help. But if she doesn't, then you have to let her make that choice too."

"I know," Chad said in a near whisper.

Rain streaked the hotel window, and Omar stared down at the street below and the pedestrians on the sidewalk, some with their umbrellas open. "I don't want to worry you more, but I need to be up front."

"I'm listening," Chad said.

Omar's stomach tightened to the point that he wished he could have someone else deliver the news. "Because of the hacking done on your computer, the Sayid family will also have information about your mother. She's being put into a protection program as well."

"No," Chad breathed out.

"We hope this will all be short-term," Omar continued. "I have a plan, *we* have a plan, to upend Ehan Sayid's movements and apprehend him. Maybe as early as tonight."

"I want to help."

"We can't have you compromised," Omar said. "And there's one other thing I need to tell you. We've found a link between the Sayid family and the Mika'il Order."

"The Mika'il Order?" Chad asked. There was a brief silence. "What's—do you mean the tribe that broke off from mainstream Islam in the sixteenth century? That organization still practices honor killings, then sends out taped video recordings of executions. Somehow they've been able to evade government censure. Are you serious?"

"You know your history."

"They've been said to finance some of the major terrorist acts around the world," Chad said, his tone flat.

"Yes."

Chad went silent for so long that Omar wondered if they'd been disconnected. "If Aamira's father is a member, then she's as good as dead."

Omar hadn't said it—Chad had—but it still felt like a punch in the chest.

"Shit," Chad added.

Omar couldn't agree more.

Chad thumped the table. "We need to get her out of there." His voice rose in pitch. "You knew this all along, didn't you? That's why you brought up her Aunt Hana. Why did you wait to tell me? We should have never let her leave with those bastards."

"Chad," Omar cut in, but his cousin wasn't finished.

"What can *you* do?" he asked. "Whom do we need to contact?"

"It's delicate, to say the least," Omar said. "We have to come up with a concrete plan and make the right inquiries without raising suspicion. If we make the wrong move, the Sayid family could relocate, or even worse, kill Aamira prematurely."

"*Prematurely*?" Chad was shouting now. "As in, *they already have a plan?*"

"There will be no killing if Aamira goes forward with the marriage to her cousin," Omar cut in, matching Chad's volume in order to be heard. Or, at least, Omar hoped that was the case. If the Sayid family thought Aamira's reputation was already ruined, then she'd be killed no matter what.

Joseph looked up from his laptop. Omar waved him away, not wanting any interference.

"Do I tell her to marry her cousin then?" Chad's tone bordered on hysterical. "So that her father doesn't *kill* her?"

"Yes," Omar said. "That's exactly what you tell her until we figure out a way to get her the hell out of Karak."

CHAPTER TWELVE

AD 1187
ANCIENT KARAK

"There are deadly snakes in that canal," Eleanor told the dripping wet Muslim warrior standing in front of her.

His brows lifted above his very dark eyes, as if he were surprised that she had spoken to him in his mother tongue of Kurdish.

Languages were Eleanor's only real accomplishment in her nineteen years. She'd prided herself on learning Arabic and French. She'd also learned some of the dialects of the surrounding Muslim tribes. This was done in secret of course. Kurdish was one of those secret deviations.

The Kurdish man had revealed his Muslim tribal affiliation in order to save a young boy from drowning, and now he surely knew that the citizens of Karak would not let him escape, not an enemy as foreboding as he.

The man was silent as he scanned Eleanor from her uncovered head to her bare feet. She'd taken off her slippers and started to remove her cloak in order to go in after the boy herself, but her handmaiden had stopped her. Now, Eleanor felt exposed beneath the man's gaze.

"Do you not speak Kurdish?" she asked, then switched to Arabic. "I thought all Sunni Muslims knew their core language."

"I am trying to understand how *you* know Kurdish," the man

answered, speaking in plain Kurdish himself. His voice was deep, yet soft like the velvet blackness of the night surrounding them.

"I know many languages," Eleanor said, trying not to be bothered by the way this warrior gazed at her.

"Do you swim?" the man asked.

Surprised at the question, Eleanor merely shook her head.

The darkness of the man's eyes seemed to lighten, and those full lips twitched. Was he amused? Did he think her a fool?

Eleanor's face heated, and even though she was protected by the night's concealing darkness, she tugged her hood once again over her head.

The man released a quiet laugh.

"You dare to laugh at me?" she asked, in a low but threatening tone. The mother with the crying boy had moved up the bank and far enough away that the crying seemed distant. The man's friends were still on the other side of the bank, and they wouldn't be able to overhear a quiet conversation. Still, Eleanor was more than wary of this Kurdish man. The scars on his chest were in the shape of a stallion, inked in to create a permanent and intimidating image. Around his neck he wore a thin leather band.

When he said nothing, but continued to watch her in amusement, his eyes scanning her body, as if he could see right through her cloak, she only became more angry.

Not knowing where her bravery came from, she stepped closer to the man until he towered over her. "Do you not know you are in enemy territory? One word from me and you will lose your head."

"I've no doubt," he said, his eyes holding hers.

He said the most unexpected things, and it only confused her because his very presence was unexpected as well. "Do you know the dangerous position you're in?" she asked.

"I know that I'm standing upon the land of my people, and it's currently occupied by a traitor and murderer," he said, his voice slow and firm. "I know that there's a beautiful but angry woman standing before me. One who is educated in languages, whose hands are not calloused, and whose rough woolen outer cloak doesn't hide the fact that her skin is soft and fair." This time he took a step closer, lowering his voice even more. "I don't know who you are, my lady, but based on your clothing and your fair complexion and the castle you now stand in front of, you can be nothing but a mortal enemy."

Eleanor stiffened, feeling as if she'd been slapped. How dare this man call *her* an enemy? *He* was the enemy; *he* was the one trespassing. *He* was the one in danger. "What is your name?" she said coldly, refusing to move back from him, even though he was close enough that she could feel the warmth of his breath as he looked down upon her.

The edges of his lips lifted ever so slightly. "I am who you think I am."

"You're with the Ayyub tribe, a follower of Saladin?"

His mouth turned up more, although now Eleanor thought his expression more of a sneer. Was he challenging her?

"I am," he said. He watched her carefully to gauge her reaction.

"You are a follower of Islam, then?" she asked, unable to stop herself from glancing down, along his torso, at the painted horse on his chest.

"Yes." His answer was simple, yet the way he watched her told her he was not afraid to state his conviction. Just like Eleanor's former handmaiden Zulla, who had died rather than convert to Christianity. The fire and determination in this warrior's eyes told Eleanor that this man was no different.

"If you value your life," Eleanor started to say, then glanced across the canal to the men still waiting for their friend, "and the life of your comrades, you should leave Karak now. Never return. Tell your leader that Raynald will never give up, will never back down. Nothing will stop him." These were the most loyal words she'd ever spoken of her stepfather. And she cared very little for him. But something about this tall warrior standing before her, scarred and painted in honor of his tribe, made her want to scare him away. To protect him. To warn him.

"Raynald?" the man said. "You call the terrorist crusader *Raynald*?"

Again, Eleanor was confused. She didn't understand why he was questioning her in this manner. Had he heard nothing she'd said? And then his mouth dropped open as if he were about to speak, but no words came. His eyes widened, and she wished she could know what he was thinking. Why he looked so stunned.

"I should have known," he said, his voice a whisper now. "The way you stand, the way you have no fear, the way you speak, the way you . . . look."

Eleanor's stomach felt as if it was slowly being turned inside out. "*What* should you have known?" she demanded, although her tone didn't sound demanding at all. If anything, it was a plea.

"You are *Eleanor*," the warrior stated, her name like a drop of poison on his tongue.

She'd given herself away, and she'd told a dangerous enemy, a strong and lethal warrior, who she was. How could she have been so foolish? For an instant, she wondered if he'd pull out a dagger from a hidden place on his belt and plunge it into her heart. All of the surrounding Muslim tribes would celebrate. This day would become their new holy day.

But the warrior did no such thing. Instead, he bowed before her. This time Eleanor's mouth parted in surprise.

When he straightened and again met her gaze, he said, "It is an honor to meet you, Lady Eleanor. My name is Jed al Ayubi, son of Saladin, and I am here to assassinate your stepfather."

A dozen moments, or perhaps two dozen, passed before Eleanor could respond. This warrior's father was Raynald's greatest enemy, which should make him hers. Saladin had besieged their palace during the marriage ceremony of her brother Humphrey and his betrothed child bride, Princess Isabella, daughter of Baldwin IV of Jerusalem. Eleanor's mother had sent a messenger to Saladin, begging him to cease his attack because of the wedding. Saladin agreed to leave only the wedding chamber alone.

Constant battles and broken truces littered the relationship between Saladin and Raynald. Saladin would attack, Raynald would counter, and the conflict continued. And now this man, this warrior, was standing like a free man inside the Karak borders. Eleanor not only had her stepfather and mother to worry about, but her innocent half sister, Alix.

When Eleanor finally did respond, it was as if someone else was speaking with her voice. "Your words are bold, but assassins don't identify themselves to the family members of their intended victim."

Jed threw his head back and laughed.

Everything in Eleanor's body burned with indignation.

When Jed ran out of breath and stopped laughing, he grasped Eleanor's hand. She tugged hard against his grip, but he held fast.

"My lady," Miriam said behind Eleanor.

Eleanor had almost forgotten her new handmaiden was with her. It was some comfort that Miriam had overheard Jed's confession. Now she'd have a witness. Although his confession hadn't struck fear through her, didn't send her running, or turn her into a quivering mess of nerves.

"Let me go," Eleanor told Jed, her heart speeding up as he drew her hand upward until he'd pressed it against his lips. The action was so astounding that she didn't even react.

"Tonight has been unexpected," Jed said.

Eleanor could say the same, but probably not for the same reasons.

"I meet the most beautiful woman I've ever seen only to learn that she is the daughter of my father's greatest enemy," Jed continued. He still held her hand, lightly this time, but for some reason Eleanor couldn't bring herself to draw away from his warmth.

"Stepfather," she whispered. "Raynald is my stepfather."

"Eleanor," Miriam's voice cut through Eleanor's trance. "Soldiers are coming."

Jed released her hand and stepped back as she looked toward the top of the bank. A half dozen of Raynald's soldiers were moving swiftly along the path edging the canal bank. They seemed to be looking for someone. Eleanor drew her hood more fully about her face and turned to tell Jed that he should hide himself.

But he was already gone. She stared in disbelief at the spot where he'd just stood. Then her attention was caught by a soft splash. Jed was swimming across the canal to where his friends waited. They greeted him and tossed a cloak over his wet body. Eleanor looked to see if Raynald's soldiers had spotted him. But they continued forward, apparently intent on another mission.

"Where are they going?" Eleanor asked Miriam. The soldiers couldn't possibly know what, or who, they'd bypassed. Whatever was requiring their attention, surely the son of her stepfather's greatest enemy warranted inspection.

Then another group of soldiers exited the castle. "Something's happening," Miriam whispered, tugging Eleanor up the bank. "We need to get back inside."

As Eleanor watched, a detachment of cavalry came out of the castle. They rode toward the trails leading off of Karak's plateau. Having listened to more than one banquet conversation on military strategy, she knew there were camps of soldiers surrounding Karak. Were they expecting an invasion? Or were they preparing to waylay a caravan on the Muslim trade routes?

It was her stepfather's favorite activity.

Eleanor's gaze was drawn again to the other side of the bank where Jed had rejoined his comrades. They were no longer in sight.

The commotion outside the palace might serve as distraction for Eleanor and Miriam to hurry by unnoticed. Yet it was also a risk if someone recognized them. But Miriam was right, they couldn't expect to be protected if they remained outside the walls. The other people who'd been walking along the canal were fast disappearing. Even the mother with the crying son had left the scene.

"Let's go," Eleanor said, linking her arm through Miriam's. It would look less like they were lady and handmaiden that way. They climbed the rest of the way up the bank, and then started toward the castle. To Eleanor's dismay, another soldier came out of the castle—and this one she recognized. Her stepfather was dressed in his military uniform of a chain mail headdress and a long belted tunic. Even in the moonlight, there was no doubt of his identity. Several men carrying torches accompanied him.

One of the soldiers held the reigns of a thick-muscled Arabian horse, and within moments Raynald had mounted the beast and was handed a long sword.

"Raynald is on a mission," Eleanor whispered to Miriam. "And a deadly mission at that." They could no longer continue toward the castle or they'd be spotted. "This way," Eleanor said, tugging Miriam upriver. There was a bridge not too far away and they could cross it and wait on the other side until Raynald left the plateau.

Miriam hurried with her, and Eleanor hoped they'd look like any other two women fleeing the scene of men preparing for battle. They crossed the bridge, their footsteps on the wooden structure echoing the thumping of her heart. On the other side of the bridge, Miriam said, "Let's move down the bank, out of sight."

Eleanor nodded, and they started down the bank. A crouched figure rose in front of them, and before Eleanor knew it, someone grabbed her from behind and covered her mouth with a strong, warm hand.

Eleanor would have screamed, but she didn't know which was worse, alerting her stepfather whom she'd disobeyed, or being abducted by . . .

"Hush, it's Jed," the whisper sounded in her ear. "You need to get out of sight. My guard, Kazbech, will keep a lookout."

Next to her, Miriam had been stopped as well, and Eleanor

allowed herself to be pulled beneath the side of the bridge, well out of sight of any soldiers.

Miriam sat next to her, deeper under the bridge, with Jed on the other side. The man whom Jed had called Kazbech returned to his crouched position that gave him a view of what was happening near the castle.

"Are they looking for you?" Eleanor demanded of Jed.

"Hush!" he said, "or I will have to gag you."

Eleanor closed her mouth and blinked up at the man. Why was a warrior hiding beneath a bridge like a coward? She was about to ask him when he slid his arm around her and pulled her tightly against him. At least he was wearing his cloak now, since Eleanor didn't want to know what it would have felt like to be pressed against his bare torso.

She struggled to get free, wondering if she should scream after all, when she heard the sound of footsteps on the bridge. Miriam was leaning forward, her head buried in her hands, her knees drawn up to her chest, as if she could make herself smaller and therefore invisible.

As the footsteps moved directly overhead, Jed pulled Eleanor off the ground until she was sitting on his legs, completely out of sight if someone should look over the side of the bridge.

She didn't dare breathe but didn't dare let herself feel safe in the strong arms that wrapped around her. This warrior might be hiding her for now, but what would happen next? He was her family's enemy. And her stepfather's soldiers would kill him if they found him.

The footsteps continued across the bridge until they left the wood planks. Jed didn't release her, and she didn't want to move until she was sure she wouldn't be seen. After several moments, all conversation between the soldiers faded, drowned out by the sound of the flowing canal and the breathing of Jed and Miriam's whimpering.

When Eleanor felt Jed's hold on her relax, she moved off his lap. Miriam was shaking, and Eleanor wrapped an arm around her.

"We're all right," she said in a hushed voice. "We'll make it back to the castle soon and we'll be safe."

Miriam wiped tears from her face and nodded. Then she stood with Eleanor's help, and they walked out from under the bridge. The night air had grown cold and sharp, but it was a welcome change after huddling beneath the bridge in fear.

"Wait," Jed said, coming up behind them. He once again grasped Eleanor's arm.

It seemed he had no problem ordering her around.

When she looked up into Jed's dark eyes, her heart shifted into a new place she didn't recognize.

"When can I see you again?" he asked.

Eleanor stared at him, and then gave a short laugh. "You're my enemy, Jed al Ayubi, son of Saladin." She leaned toward him, whispering, "You are lucky I don't strike you dead right now."

One of his brows lifted, but he didn't look afraid. "Do you have a weapon?" he asked, perfectly serious.

"My voice is my weapon," she said. "One word from me and you'll be surrounded by my stepfather's guards. And he will not be merciful once he learns who you are."

Jed watched her for a long moment, the intensity of his gaze seeming to reach directly into her soul. "But you are not like your stepfather, are you?"

She didn't know how to respond, so she simply stepped back. To think clearly, she needed more space between them.

"Come, Miriam," Eleanor said, reaching for her handmaiden's arm. They started up the bank together, and Eleanor sensed that Jed wanted to follow, perhaps question her. Perhaps ask about the castle and to see what she might tell him. Although she didn't care for her stepfather, she would not betray him. Because then she'd be betraying her mother also.

Eleanor walked quickly away from the Ayyub warriors and their secret plans. Raynald's soldiers who'd come so close to discovering them were now gone.

Eleanor kept her head lowered and stayed close to Miriam when another group of soldiers exited the castle. She and Miriam sat on the ground and held out their hands like beggars as the soldiers passed. The soldiers paid no attention to the begging women. Then the women rose to their feet and hurried back the way they'd left the castle. Through the gate and the back gardens, and then inside the castle walls themselves, they hurried until they reached Eleanor's chambers.

Once they were securely in her chambers and saw that the only change was the low-burning oil lamp burning even lower, Eleanor allowed Miriam to take her cloak and conceal it in the back of the wardrobe. Then Eleanor removed her overdress and soiled shoes. They were ruined from traipsing so close to the water of the canal.

While Miriam cleaned her overdress, Eleanor crossed to the high window that overlooked the canal. From this distance, she couldn't make out any faces of those outside beneath the moonlit night.

"I've never met a man as strange as Jed al Ayubi," Eleanor said, mostly to herself. "How dare he ask when he might see me again? Does he not know it would result in his death? Luck cannot be cheated twice."

"You would do best to stay inside the castle until we know the outcome of why your stepfather set off with his army tonight," Miriam said.

"Yes, you're right," Eleanor said, continuing her study of the canal and the moving figures below. She wondered if one of them were Jed and if so, when he would leave. Because the sooner he left, the better.

CHAPTER THIRTEEN

MODERN-DAY AL KARAK

Aamira might have been grounded, restricted to her room by her mother, but she was also a twenty-three-year-old, educated woman. She should have been able to ask her parents questions and not face discipline because they didn't want to give her answers.

Using her cell phone, she logged into the home Wi-Fi which her father had installed for Ehan's studies. Aamira had memorized the password long ago and now discovered it hadn't changed. One point for her. She started doing searches for the name of Hana Sayid, death, obituary, Karak. A few links came up, and Aamira clicked on each one, reading the newspaper accounts of Hana's tragic death and the statements of disbelief and grief shared by her father Taheer and uncle Kahul. She even found a write-up about the funeral, which mentioned the Karak town officials who'd attended, but all the names were familiar to Aamira.

There was absolutely nothing about the man Hana had danced with and who later attended her funeral.

Aamira had yet to hear back from Chad or Omar on the pictures of the man she'd forwarded, but she did run them through a search engine. Though the matches that came up were close, Aamira didn't think any of them were a true match.

She had to find another way to get information. Although it had been years since Hana had died, Aamira knew that her father still kept boxes of her belongings in storage. Her mother and father had once argued about it, but her father had insisted he wanted the things saved, just not opened or used.

"It brings a bad spirit into the house," her mother had argued. "Hana took her own life, and she should not be remembered."

It was the way of their family, Aamira knew, and those in their town. Suicides were considered cowardly, abhorrent. The deceased would be erased from all memory. In fact, Aamira was surprised her mother still had Hana's pictures in those albums.

A text came through her phone, and Aamira's heart jolted when she saw that it was from Chad. He had found out the man's name. Naser Ali. Aamira stared at the spelling of the name, to see if it triggered any memories. But there was nothing.

She typed it into a search on her phone and watched as a lot of hits came up. Naser Ali was quite common. Then she typed in Naser Ali and Hana Sayid. Two hits. Opening the first one, she discovered they'd gone to the same school. So Hana had probably met him there. The second link was on a blog by Naser. Hana had made a comment.

This surprised Aamira. First, that her aunt had enjoyed enough liberties in her home to read and comment on blogs, and second, that the blog was still active. The most recent post was yesterday, and it seemed to be written by Naser himself. Aamira clicked on the "About Me" and started to read.

Naser lived in Amman, where he was a professor at the University of Jordan. There was only one picture of him on the blog and no mention of a wife and family. Aamira began to scroll through previous blog posts, and stopped when she reached a post about a program that Naser was part of: one that opposed violence against women. Aamira knew there were plenty of organizations out there that made grand statements, but little actually happened. Break the Silence was apparently associated with a university.

Since this man had known her aunt well enough to attend her funeral, Aamira couldn't ignore the connection. The date of the blog post was about five years old, well after Hana had died. Aamira typed in a new search on the organization, and a website came up with some testimonials and a "Donate" button. She clicked on the "About the Founders" link and was shocked when a picture of Hana appeared, standing with two other women.

When Aamira's heart slowed, she took a picture of the photograph and sent it and the website link back to Chad. She then texted him Naser's blog link, as well. Her aunt had not only been good friends with a man other than the one she was to marry, but she had also been a founder of a women's organization. Aamira didn't need to speak with her mother or anyone in her family to know that both activities would have been considered disgraces to the family.

Then, taking a deep breath, she set up an email account and texted the email address to Chad. Opening Naser's blog window again, she clicked on the Contact Me form and typed in her new email with the message: *I must speak with you asap on an urgent matter. Please contact me.*

It was three hours before she heard the stirrings of her father, and she listened for his telltale footsteps as he prepared to leave for an afternoon at the bank. Or at least Aamira assumed he was going to the bank. Now, she couldn't be sure what he did during the day, or the night. Was he in communication with her brother? Directing him to his next "job"? Was her brother really a thief posing as a collector?

Aamira bit her lip as she heard the front door shut and the car engine start. In a matter of just a few hours, she'd had her entire view of her family shattered, and now the new thoughts tumbling around in her head were overwhelming. Had nothing been as it seemed when she was growing up? Every memory—of the aunts and uncles and cousins and family members—was now tainted.

She listened for any sounds that her mother was making, but only heard the quiet drone of the DVD her mother was watching. Her father didn't allow mainstream television, but purchased DVD movies that he'd pre-approved.

Aamira climbed off her bed, dressed, then lined up her pillows vertically on the bed and threw her quilt over them. A quick glance into her room would make it look like she was sleeping. Then she crept out of her room and down the hall. She paused outside her parents' room. Her mother seemed to be settled in. Aamira made her way to the front room where her mother kept the family scrapbooks. She scanned the dates and names on the binders. She took the one that included Hana as a youth.

Aamira hurried back to her bedroom and leafed through each page carefully. But there was nothing in the few months leading up to Hana's death. Either Hana or her mother had put in the usual milestone pictures and school awards and certificates. Then Aamira stopped at a middle school photograph. It was a class picture with about two dozen preteens in it. Someone had drawn a circle around a young man's face. About two students down from Naser stood Hana herself.

Hana was looking at him when the picture was taken. Aamira didn't need to pull up the picture on her phone to know that the young man was Naser. She released a sigh. Another link that strengthened the connection between her aunt and a man she wasn't betrothed to.

Aamira tucked the scrapbook under her mattress where she could return to it later, and was surprised when she looked at her phone again to see the email icon with a notification next to it. She released a shaky breath when she saw that it was from Naser.

He'd simply written, "I'm happy to help."

Aamira started typing. "My name is Aamira Sayid and Hana was my aunt."

Moments later, he wrote, "I remember you."

"I don't remember you," she wrote. "But I found your picture in a couple of places. I have some personal questions that I can't ask my family." She exhaled and decided not to wait any longer. "Do you know who killed my aunt?"

"Her family claims it was suicide."

"What do you think?"

"It wasn't."

Aamira stared at the two words, her stomach twisting with nausea. "Tell me what happened."

"Can you call me?" He wrote his number.

Aamira closed her eyes. The sound of the TV still droned. Her father wouldn't be back for hours. "Yes," she typed back. Then she locked her bedroom door, and went into her closet, closing that door as well to muffle any sound she might make.

Then, by the light of the glowing phone, she placed the call.

Naser's voice was deep, yet had a soft quality that Aamira hadn't expected. As Naser spoke, she realized it was a sad tone, and that this man was still grieving.

"Before I say anything," he said, "tell me how you found my information and why you're contacting me."

She told him about doing a search on his name and her aunt's name and finding the blog. Then she told him about her recent graduation and about Chad and how his cousin had accused her family of terrible things. She didn't go into detail about that, but told him that he had said some disturbing things about her aunt and how her death wasn't a suicide. About how there had been many women killed in her family's history.

Naser sighed. But when he didn't say anything, Aamira continued, "I decided to see what information I could find about Hana. I asked my mother and she became livid. Sent me to my room—although I'm twenty-three years old. I looked through photo albums and scrapbooks, and that's when I found your picture. I sent the picture to Chad, and he was able to come up with your name."

"I guess with technology, I shouldn't be surprised," Naser said. "But I need to warn you, Aamira, that this type of research into your family could be very dangerous for you, and for Chad."

She had to ask. "How?"

"Because your aunt didn't commit suicide. And that's the reason I now live where I do," he said. "I've broken off all contact with Karak and my family there. I haven't spoken to them in years."

Aamira wished she didn't believe what Naser was saying about her aunt, but she knew it was true. Her mother's reaction had been too extreme. Aamira thought of the mourners—the keening women during Hana's graveside service. Had they known too?

"Does your family know what happened to Hana?"

"I don't know," Naser said in a quiet tone. "I'm assuming they do, and that's why they haven't contacted me."

"Tell me about Hana—how you knew her and the work you were involved in together."

A soft chuckle sounded over the phone, but it sounded more sad than happy. "We met in school. You probably found our class picture. We became friends first, and then we fell in love."

The similarity of Naser's story to her own story with Chad sent a rush of conflicting emotions through her.

"We knew it was doomed from the start, well, at least that's what I assumed," Naser said. "When Hana told me her family wanted her to marry someone else, someone approved by the family, I told her we had to break off all contact. I couldn't be with her anymore, knowing that we were counting down the time before she'd be married to someone else."

Aamira found herself gripping the phone tightly against her ear, listening intently to each word.

Naser continued, "Hana didn't want to break it off. She told her father that she refused to marry the man the family had chosen. She told him she was in love with another man and that she would leave the country if the family didn't support her decision."

Aamira was absolutely silent. She remembered Hana as a fun-loving, sweet woman who brought treats every time she visited. Aamira could only imagine a Hana who stood up to her father in such a way. Aamira's grandfather had passed away a couple of years before, but he had been a stern man with a soft spot that only came out around the young grandkids. Was he responsible for his own daughter's death?

"Around that time, Hana invited me to one of her cousin's wedding celebrations," Naser continued. "I didn't want to go. It was a blatant rebellion against her father to have me there. He didn't know my name before then, but after the wedding party, we'd danced enough times together that it was pretty obvious to everyone that Hana was in love . . ." His voice trailed off.

"I remember that wedding party," Aamira said. "I don't remember you specifically."

"You were pretty young," Naser said, his voice sounding strained as if he were battling the emotions of painful memories. "You wouldn't have noticed that type of tension." He paused, then said, "That night her father beat her for the first time. He broke her nose and her wrist."

A gasp pushed its way through Aamira's chest. Domestic violence was never spoken of in her town, but she knew it happened sometimes in homes. To think of her dear aunt with a battered face and broken wrist at the hands of her own father made her heart break.

"I didn't hear from her for a week after the wedding party," Naser continued. "When I found out what had happened, I told her I'd help her in whatever way she wanted. If she married her relative, I'd disappear and never bother her again. If she wanted to leave, I'd find a way to get her out."

"What did she say?" Aamira asked in a horrified whisper, certain she already knew the answer.

"She left home and went to a women's shelter in Madaba," Naser said. "Her father found out and somehow talked her into coming back home. He told her he wouldn't force her into an engagement for at least a year, that she could do online college classes. It was then that she started the women's organization, raising money for abused women. She found ways to sneak back to the shelter, where she and a couple other women put together details of their organization. Her idea was to create a fund that would help abused women relocate and find homes and jobs in other cities."

"That sounds like a huge undertaking," she said.

"It was like she found her calling in life, if you want to label it," Naser said. "I helped out where I could, creating the website and setting up the fund at an out-of-town bank since we couldn't use the Sayid bank."

"Of course," she echoed. With each word from Naser, Aamira felt more and more sick. The fact that Hana had fled to a women's shelter sent goose bumps along Aamira's skin, and that her father had talked her into returning made Aamira feel even worse, especially knowing the end result.

Aamira tried to calculate the time between the wedding party and Hana's death. Nearly nine months, Aamira realized. Even though she was sitting in a dark closet, she closed her eyes, battling the emotions of anger and disbelief coursing through her.

"Her father found out about her trips to the women's shelter," Naser said. "He canceled her online classes and disconnected the internet service. I realized something was wrong when she didn't reply to any of my messages. I was afraid he'd beaten her again, and I wanted to call the police, but I didn't know if that would make things worse."

Aamira listened, speechless, trying to imagine what Hana had been going through at that time.

"When she contacted me, it was through a telephone call," Naser said. "She'd sneaked out of her room and was at a friend's house. Of course that house wouldn't have been any protection against her family since every person in town had ties to the bank. She told me that she'd been cut off, but that our website was still safe. Her father hadn't beaten her that time, but had commissioned her brother to keep her locked in her room. And we started to plan an escape." He took a breath. "She'd continue acting the part of the obedient daughter. She'd find a way to sneak out in the next week, I'd pick her up, and we'd take the next bus out of town. We couldn't get tickets in advance because we couldn't leave any sort of trail for her father to follow."

Aamira waited, not asking any questions, wanting to know where it all went wrong.

"It was perfect, or so we thought," Naser said in a low voice. "It took me a long time to find out everything that had happened, but eventually I was able to piece most of it together. Her family either caught her in the act of escaping, or they'd already planned that same night to kill her."

Aamira could barely breathe as she listened to Naser's story.

"Her father didn't kill her, that I'm sure of," he said. "In the research that Hana and I had done, we learned that families who condone honor killings often choose a young male in the family, someone who is a minor. This makes the crime harder to prosecute."

"Was it one of her brothers, then?" she couldn't help but ask. Was it *her* father? Her eyes burned with tears at the thought.

"I think it was her brother Kahul. He was the younger one, and would face lesser consequences if caught."

She closed her eyes. Kahul was supposed to be her future father-in-law. What had he done to his sister? What had her grandfather ordered to be done?

"Her death was never investigated as a crime," Naser continued. "They said she threw herself down the stairs, but I think she was already dead before she was pushed down any stairs."

Aamira listened to herself breathing in the closet.

"I waited for two hours for her to show up at our meeting place, then I figured that she wasn't able to meet for some reason, and we'd try the next night," he said. "When I returned home, there was an email waiting for me that said, 'In case our plan doesn't work.' It wasn't until the afternoon of the next day that I found out she was dead."

"What was in the email?" Aamira asked in a quiet voice.

"She'd sent a bunch of scanned files of her family records," Naser said, "and she had circled the names of all those who'd died mysteriously. Most of them were women, but there were a few men as well. All young. It seems that she'd been doing research on her lineage and discovered a long tradition of honor killing. She'd started researching each name and included a file with her notes. She'd gotten through four names and had documented all of her research. It took me a while to read through them and to understand what she was trying to do." He paused, then said, "Aamira, she was trying to bring her entire family down, both past and present."

Aamira's breath stalled. Hana was not the woman she remembered. It seemed that she didn't know her at all. "Do you think people in my family knew all the investigating she'd done?"

"I'm not sure," Naser said. "But I made plans to leave Al Karak right after the funeral, and I haven't returned since." His tone became sharp. "You're playing with fire, Aamira. If you think you can dig into your family history without consequences, you're wrong. If you're willing to live by your family rules, then stop your questions. If not, then—"

"I need to leave Karak too," she said, knowing that although the thought terrified her—uprooting everything, never seeing her family again—she couldn't live with their lies. "I know that now. I want to finish what my aunt started. Email me all of her files, and I'm going to forward them to some people who can help me build a case."

Naser spoke very deliberately. "Aamira. Your aunt wouldn't want you to take this type of risk. Even though your grandfather is gone now, the Sayid men are still a danger. You need to get out of Al Karak. When you're safe and away from your family, then I can help you more."

Aamira wanted to scream, then remembered she was in the closet trying to keep quiet. He was right. "I want to know why," she started. "Why do they feel they can take a human life? Control another person in this way? Make decisions that only Allah should make?"

Naser was quiet for a moment. "It's complicated," he finally said. “Very, very complicated. And believe me, I’ve wondered the same thing. My only answer is fear and pride. And this fear causes people to act irrationally when they fear the outcome of a loved one’s action, or fear what their neighbors or other families might think if their secrets are discovered. Pride comes in and stirs everything up to a boiling point.”

“It’s one thing to want to protect a family member, or to be disappointed, even hurt and angry when they make a wrong choice. But to *kill* them?” Aamira’s voice was a little hoarse. “We are all precious in the eyes of Allah. We’re all trying to live truth and obtain entrance into Paradise. When we take that right from someone else by cutting short their life’s journey and their chance to become who they are meant to be, we sin against Allah himself.”

“Yes,” Naser said, his tone subdued. “You’re quite the philosopher, Aamira. But you have witnessed for yourself the heat of angry blood that pulses through someone whose pride has been wounded.”

“Pride that is sinful,” Aamira countered.

“Yes,” Naser repeated.

They were quiet for some time before Naser spoke again. “If I could help you, I would. At my own risk, in memory of Hana. But I no longer have trustworthy ties to Karak.”

“My boyfriend said he would help me, and his cousin—he’s an intelligence officer of some sort,” she said. “When you send me Hana’s files, I’ll have a place to start.”

“I’ll send the files once you are safe, but even then, please be very careful,” Naser warned again. “You need to dig down deep to know who to trust, and you also need to know that everyone you involve will also be in danger. Make sure you password-protect every file, delete every email, and always delete the browsing history on your phone. Your family will search. Any link to me will surely be a death sentence.”

His words made the darkness complete. The weight on her shoulders seemed to grow heavier. Listening to Naser had confirmed one important thing. She could not reconcile herself to a life in Al Karak. She could not become Sadan's wife. She would rather meet the same fate as Hana than live within her family's web.

CHAPTER FOURTEEN

LONDON

The night watchman opened the well-oiled back door of the National Portrait Gallery, and led Omar and Joseph along an interior hallway until they came to the security office door. Inside, the watchman showed them their uniforms, and when he left, the two men quickly changed. As Omar buttoned the final button, he decided that the less the big boss knew in advance, the better. Timing was paramount. If they were able to apprehend Ehan tonight, then of course the entire story would come out. If not, then Omar and Joseph could go to their backup plan and start tracking the traditional way.

"Ready?" Omar said, looking at Joseph. He hoped their ill-fitting uniforms wouldn't give their identities away. As it was, Omar reached for one of the name badges on a shelf along the wall. Tonight he'd be Raul.

"Ready," Joseph confirmed.

"Let's get to our positions," Omar said. He grabbed two electronic tablets from the shelf, per museum protocol, and handed one over to Joseph. They left the room and made their way back down the hallway. They'd already determined that if Ehan used his usual method of breaking and entering, he'd remotely switch off the electronic security system. Only this time, the security guards would be there to stop him.

Omar stationed Joseph at the front desk, and made his way to the ground floor gallery that housed the two Passion paintings. He paused at the archway leading into the room. All was quiet and still, and the only illumination came from the dim night lights that ran along the floor. Then he moved to an adjoining, smaller gallery. His impulse was to pace, but he wanted to avoid detection by anyone possibly hacking into the video security system.

From this location, he could make it to the main gallery in seconds. Waiting, he replayed his conversation with the museum director. He'd known Mrs. Shira Moberg for many years, and she'd always been quick to help. At first, she wanted to bring in several armed policemen, but Omar knew that the arrival of police at the museum would be leaked throughout the police department. And it was possible that the Sayids had at least one accomplice, as evidenced by Ehan's earlier escape from the museum. So, at Omar's request, Mrs. Moberg had contacted the head of security and informed him that two men would arrive and need uniforms.

Omar patted the stun gun in his pocket and withdrew a Glock from the strapped holster inside his shirt. He turned on the tablet he'd taken from the security office so that he could watch the rotating security cameras and survey the empty rooms. He leaned against the wall, settling in for what might be a very long night with no action, or perhaps a night of bringing down Ehan Sayid and beginning the task of breaking apart a criminal organization. Omar was looking forward to it.

More than two hours passed before Omar heard the sound of breaking glass. He checked the tablet. Each room showed empty, and because he didn't have time to wonder why, he set down the tablet and moved toward the corridor connecting the main galleries. The breaking glass might be a decoy, but he was still going to check it out.

The dim night lighting hadn't been altered, but Omar sensed something was different. The quiet atmosphere had suddenly grown tense. Keeping his back to the wall, Omar crept down the hallway until he rounded the corner that opened to the front lobby where Joseph was supposed to be.

Joseph wasn't at his station. Before Omar could take another step, a dark form came hurtling toward him. Omar barely had time to lift his stun gun and press the trigger before the person plowed into him, pushing him backward into the wall.

The impact of his body hitting the wall momentarily disoriented him, but then he realized that his attacker wasn't moving. The full weight of the man's body on top of Omar wouldn't have been that hard to lift, if it weren't for the way Omar's arm had been twisted and pinned behind him.

Jolts of pain shot from his hand up into his shoulder. He drew up his knees and pushed the man off him, but before he could stretch out his arm and climb to his feet, he heard Joseph shout from somewhere in the room, "Watch out!"

Omar ducked instinctively and heard the bullet hiss past, and he knew his life had been saved. The next bullet grazed his thigh, and he reflected that it wouldn't be nearly as devastating as a bullet to the head. He had to find the silver lining. Then he lost his balance, and he tried to stop his fall, but the polished floor did him no favors.

Omar heard a thump from the direction of Joseph's yell and guessed that his partner had just been knocked out.

The man Omar had stunned was moving again, and Omar twisted away from his grasp, only to be paralyzed by the pain in his thigh.

A second assailant grasped his already sore arm and wrenched it behind him, then cuffed both of his hands behind his back.

Omar arched backwards, trying to head-butt the man's nose, but he met with empty space. The sound of electric clicking made him still. An instant later pain shot through his body as his own stun gun was used on his upper chest. Omar cried out as the pain flashed then numbed. One of the men yelled at him to shut up. In Arabic.

Omar knew Arabic well enough to know that the accent was

Jordanian. What the hell was going on? And who were these men? Omar could only assume they were with Ehan, but as he was half-dragged, half-carried through the broken glass door of the museum, he tried to get a look at his assailants.

There were four men, all wearing masks, but their dark olive skin color and rapid Arabic gave them away. If Omar had to judge Ehan's dialect by his sister's, none of these men were Ehan.

That left only one answer. These men hadn't crashed the museum to steal priceless artwork. They had broken in to kidnap him.

And now he and Joseph were being carted off by a group of Jordanians to who knew where, and Simon Greif had no idea what they'd been doing that night. He wouldn't even begin to know where to look. Omar thought briefly of Mia. She could look up the location on his phone, but she probably wouldn't do that in the middle of the night, especially if she didn't know there was something wrong.

By the time anyone suspected that he and Joseph were missing, Omar was sure their cell phones would have already been confiscated and destroyed. He winced as a cry of pain erupted from Joseph. A door opened up ahead, and Omar was dragged out one of the museum's back doors onto a loading dock. Parked next to it was a utility van. Joseph was shoved into the back, and the next moment Omar found himself landing on the hard metal bed of the van, next to his companion.

Omar's thigh pulsed in pain, and a rush of dizziness passed through him. He gritted his teeth against the throbbing in his leg, trying to stay conscious. Two of the masked men climbed in after them, and the other two must have gone up to the driver's bench. Then the engine roared to life, and the van peeled away from the back of the museum.

The assailants settled on opposite sides of the van, each of them keeping a firm grip on their Kalashnikovs.

"We should knock the other one out," one of the men said in

Arabic, tugging off his mask. He had the most complete unibrow Omar had ever seen.

The second man, who had rather large ears, said, “I got him good with the stun gun. If he rouses, then we’ll stun him again.”

The shock of the stun gun began to wear off, and Omar tried to calculate which direction they were headed. He opened his eyes a slit, taking in as much as he could see in the dark interior of the van. It was still night, and the sun wouldn’t rise for hours. Turning his head with the motion of the van, he saw a metal box near his head. It rattled as the van made one turn after another. Omar hoped there were tools inside and that he’d get a chance to use them. It wasn’t the first time he’d been abducted, and he intended to make this a short stint.

Joseph had been unnaturally quiet, and the assailants continued arguing whether they should stun Omar again. They hadn’t handcuffed Joseph; apparently they’d only reserved the privilege for Omar. But this was an opportunity that Omar planned to take advantage of. If Joseph was alert, Omar didn’t think it would be too hard to distract them, and Joseph could snag one of the rifles.

But how to disarm these guys? He’d definitely need Joseph’s help. Omar could kick the gun from one of the men with his good leg, but then the second man was certain to react before Omar could do much else. And because he was handcuffed and probably still bleeding, he was more incapacitated than he wanted to be.

“Should we tie him up?” Large Ears asked. “What if he bleeds to death?”

“He’ll live,” Unibrow said in a sharp voice.

Omar took the opportunity to pretend he was waking up and groaned. Then he said in English, “Does Taheer know where you’re taking us?”

Large Ears narrowed his eyes, but said nothing. It wasn’t until Omar repeated he question in Arabic that he got their full attention. Large Ears leaned closer, his foul breath on Omar, who continued in Arabic: "Our last instruction from Taheer was to get the paintings out quickly since Ehan has been compromised."

Unibrow tightened his grip on his rifle just as Joseph opened his eyes and looked around in confusion. When he saw Omar tied up next to him, his vision cleared, and Omar could see his panic set in.

"Welcome back," Omar told Joseph in English. "I'm going to get you out of here in a few minutes. Call Simon and Mia and let them know what happened. But don't try to come after me yourself. These guys aren't worth both of us."

Joseph opened his mouth as if to say something, but only a garbled gasp came out.

Omar turned his attention back to the assailants. "Taheer would not be happy you hurt his pretty boy."

Large Ears pressed his stun gun against Omar's chest, while still gripping his rifle in his other hand. "You're a liar," Large Ears said. "We were warned about you."

Omar didn't know whether to be flattered or slightly afraid. These guys were professional and ruthless, which made for a lethal combination.

"Shut him up," Unibrow growled. "Taheer said not to let him talk."

Omar barked a short laugh. "Taheer is always joking. Did he tell you about the time we—" An electric charge zinged through him, making his teeth clack together. He narrowly missed biting his tongue, and his body arched out of control, thudding back hard against the floor of the van.

This time Omar didn't pretend to go unconscious. As the stun finished its circulation, he smashed his good foot against Large Ears who'd pointed the rifle at him, sending the gun spinning out of his hands. The man cried out and scrambled for the weapon. This gave Omar the opportunity to drive his shoulder into the man's side.

Then it was full chaos. Joseph grabbed the fallen rifle and

pointed it at one of the men, while Omar fought his way toward the van doors. He managed to kick them open before another shot rang out. Omar had no time to figure out who shot whom, but he turned so he could grab Joseph's legs with his handcuffed hands and tug him toward the wildly swinging door. The van hadn't slowed down yet, but Omar knew it would be a matter of seconds before the driver clued into the disturbance.

"Remember what I told you," Omar said, and shoved Joseph out of the van with his good foot.

Joseph had enough sense to wrap his arms about his head as he tumbled to the pavement. He'd earn a few bruises from the fall, but he'd live.

The van started to slow, and Omar was about to roll out himself, when a hand grabbed his arm and dragged him back into the interior. Omar fought against Unibrow, trying to get him to let go, but Omar's leg injury and the handcuffs made it difficult.

"At least bind up my leg," he spat out. "Or Taheer will have your heads."

Laughter was the last thing Omar heard before he passed out.

CHAPTER FIFTEEN

AD 1187
ANCIENT KARAK

Eleanor's stepfather Raynald didn't return for two days, and she had nearly warped the floorboards of her chambers with her pacing. It wasn't because she feared for Raynald's life. She couldn't stop thinking about Jed and where he'd gone and if he was fighting against Raynald's soldiers.

When she was awake, she saw Jed's dark eyes and heard his direct words that had seemed to cut into her soul. But when she slept, she remembered his strong arms around her, keeping her out of sight of her stepfather's soldiers and protecting her from being discovered. The past two days, she'd tried to forget him asking when he could see her again. Did he not understand the very idea was impossible?

Still she thought of him, and still she paced.

Miriam watched her, saying little. The woman was becoming a true friend. In the two days since meeting Jed, Miriam could have informed Eleanor's mother of what had happened at the canal, but she had kept quiet.

Eleanor felt fortunate that she'd found another loyal and trustworthy handmaiden so soon after Zulla's death. In the past two days, Eleanor had had Miriam obtain as much information as possible about Raynald's mission. A caravan had been spotted, and the clothing of the guards traveling with the caravan was synonymous with the Ayyub tribe, Saladin's people. Jed's people. She didn't know whether or not Jed had made it off the Karak plateau alive. At this very moment, he could be engaged in battle with Raynald's soldiers.

A knock at the door interrupted Eleanor's thoughts. She remained in place while Miriam went to unlock and open the door. Quiet words were exchanged before Miriam shut the door and locked it, all without revealing who the messenger had been.

When Miriam turned to face Eleanor with a dusty scroll in her hand, Eleanor knew the sender before opening it. Miriam handed it over without a word, and Eleanor turned away from her handmaiden and settled on the low bench near the window overlooking the canal.

The script was Arabic written in the Kurdish language, and Eleanor read every word slowly. There was no signature, but she had no doubt who'd written the looping words.

I cannot stop thinking about you. I will be waiting.

Nothing else was written. And Eleanor realized she didn't need anything more. She brought the parchment to her face, smelling the faint trace of wood and pine. She closed her eyes, imagining him bent over the parchment, writing the words, thinking of her.

Eleanor opened her eyes. She was a foolish woman. In five days, Prince Azzo would arrive at the castle. Eleanor was expected to make a strong impression on him and subsequently earn a marriage proposal. She could not let her imagination distract her. She would not meet Jed tonight. That was impossible.

"I hear horses," Miriam said, rising to her feet from across the room where she sat stitching. She crossed to the window, and Eleanor rose to join her.

Dozens of soldiers on horseback were cresting the plateau. Raynald rode at the front of the militia, carrying a victory flag.

Eleanor's heart plummeted, and she gripped the windowsill to steady herself. What had happened? The scroll from Jed gave no clue as to when it was written. It could have been more than a day ago, it could have been last night, or more recently. She watched the approaching horses and soldiers and the triumph in their expressions as crowds of people followed and called out congratulations.

"I need to hear the report," Eleanor said. She moved toward the wardrobe.

"But your stepfather's orders are for you to stay in your chambers," Miriam began. "He will not be pleased."

Eleanor turned to face Miriam. "He's just had a victory. He will not notice me above the reveling. If you fear for your position, you may remain here."

Miriam didn't hesitate. "I will come with you and accept my fate."

Eleanor wanted to embrace the woman, but instead she gave a regal nod. She let Miriam choose a gown of deep blue and a matching cloak. The handmaiden plaited Eleanor's long hair, then pinned it up.

Pulse racing and palms moist, Eleanor stepped out of her chamber for the first time in two days. She walked the corridor as fast as her heavy gown would allow and started down the winding stone steps. When she reached the landing at the bottom, she was nearly swept into a tide of people rushing to the grand hall of the court. The crowd parted before her, giving her room to walk, their gazes more than curious.

Every step brought Eleanor closer to discovering the outcome of the battle against Jed's tribe. She wondered if she'd hear his name. She wondered if she possessed the last words he'd ever written.

Once inside the main hall, Eleanor was grateful that it was teeming with people, and hoped to keep out of direct sight of her stepfather. But he seemed to have an eagle's eye and called out over the murmuring crowd, "Eleanor, I was about to send for you."

The throng hushed, and everyone turned to see Eleanor

standing just inside the entryway. Her mother was by Raynald, wearing a deep purple gown. It was early in the day for such formal wear, but then Eleanor realized that on her stepfather's other side stood a tall, angular man dressed like royalty, wearing a white tunic embroidered in gold thread. She knew that her life was about to change drastically.

"On our way back from our little raid," Raynald started, laughing to himself. Others in the room chuckled along with him as if they were in on a great joke. "We met up with Prince Azzo. He's arrived a few days early, and your mother and I couldn't be more pleased." He turned and actually bowed to Azzo. "Prince Azzo, this is my stepdaughter Eleanor."

Azzo bowed in return to Raynald, and then turned his full attention on Eleanor. If she had been feeling generous, she might have said the prince had a pleasing face. His hair was mahogany brown, his face a bit red—most likely from the sun and wind—but his jaw was strong, though his lips were so thin as to be almost nonexistent. Otherwise, he was certainly of European blood and most certainly nothing like Jed.

The fact that she was still thinking of Jed and wondering if he were still breathing should have distressed her. But in truth, her secret meeting with her father's enemy gave her the courage to lift her chin and face Prince Azzo directly. "Welcome to Karak." She bowed her head. "I hope your journey was safe."

What she really wanted to ask was, *Tell me everything about the raid. Did you come across a warrior named Jed? Is he alive?* But she kept her expression calm, and when the prince smiled at her, she smiled back, though it seemed her heart was starting to tear.

"We've had two victories today," Raynald announced. "We've turned down Saladin's request and driven back his warriors, and we have Prince Azzo with us to celebrate."

"Saladin's request?" Eleanor found herself saying out loud. Everyone looked at her, including Raynald. She regretted having spoken, but it was too late.

Raynald chuckled, looking at Eleanor and speaking for everyone to hear. "Saladin had the gall to send his warriors with a request." Raynald's gaze shifted to the others in the court to command their attention. "When we defended ourselves against Saladin's sister's caravan last year, we might have confiscated some of their valuables as payment for trespassing on our land."

Eleanor knew that the caravan had been traveling on the international trade route. Raynald had attacked and plundered it, leaving a few dead, but mostly taking jewels, silks, and spices.

As Raynald spoke, he twisted a jeweled ring on his finger. "Saladin's request was that I return the valuables to his tribe." He laughed long and hard, and others in the courtroom joined in. "He expects me to say, 'Very sorry for taking your things. Here's everything back, and you're welcome to cross our lands at any time, leaving polluted wells and long trails of animal dung.'"

The people around Eleanor laughed.

"And what happened?" Eleanor asked, her mouth feeling dry.

"I said *no*," Raynald said, his gaze moving back to Eleanor. "And I was ready to fight to prove my point, but the messengers ran away." He shook his head. "Some warriors they are."

So, no bloodshed? Eleanor thought. She tried not to look happy about that bit of news. She glanced at her handmaiden as Raynald accepted congratulations from those in the court and called for a banquet. Miriam's flashing eyes told Eleanor they shared the same thought. Jed was still alive. He might be on his way to join up with Saladin, but he was alive.

She thought of the scroll now hidden in her clothing and Jed's words to her. After failing at their mission, there was no reason for them to stay near Karak, within range of Raynald's troops.

As the banquet began, the lute musicians started to play a lively melody. Eleanor sat among a group of women, but she barely paid attention to their gossip. One of the women, a Muslim who'd converted to Christianity and renamed herself Agnes, was young and beautiful with smooth olive skin and raven dark hair.

She caught all the men's eyes, and tonight it seemed Raynald was watching her as well.

The dancing began an hour later, and the ladies sitting by Eleanor stood one by one, invited by the men onto the floor. The dancers formed a circle, linking hands, and stepping together to the music. Eleanor felt Azzo's eyes on her more than once, and she knew it was only a matter of time before he invited her into the dance circle. It would delight both her parents if she received a marriage proposal soon from this man.

As Eleanor gazed along the banquet table, she once again saw her stepfather's eyes on Agnes. The heat of embarrassment swelled within Eleanor, and she looked over at her mother, who seemed oblivious to the attention Raynald was giving this woman.

Eleanor looked beyond her mother to the other guests. There were plenty of former Muslims in the court, ones who had pledged their loyalty to Christianity and were happy to pay the levies and taxes to Raynald. In return, these new, prominent Christians were welcomed at court, and some had even been granted positions.

So it was not a surprise when a young man, dressed as a Christian, but who must have been another convert from Islam, asked her to stand up with him. Eleanor didn't catch his name as he spoke in a low, accented tone, but he looked familiar. And she assumed that he belonged to one of the more prominent families of Karak.

Azzo's eyes were on her as she danced. Her mother would certainly be pleased by this attention, but in truth, Eleanor's thoughts were far away. She wondered where Jed was now, and which direction he was headed. Was he traveling to meet his father and deliver the news of Raynald's rejection?

The man she walked with onto the dance floor spoke little and kept a pleased smile on his face. They linked hands, then began to move in the dance circle with the other guests. She didn't notice how far from the main banquet table they'd moved until another man appeared in front of Eleanor, speaking in broken French to Eleanor's partner.

He held out his hand to Eleanor, with barely a glance at her partner.

Eleanor looked up at the intruder and nearly gasped out loud. Although the man was dressed in clothing much like the other nobles in the court, there was no doubt she was staring at Jed Al Ayubi. He was alive. Until this moment she hadn't realized how worried she was about him. One part of her knew it was irrational to be so concerned about a man who was a stranger and a Muslim, the other part of her rejoiced that he was standing before her, unharmed.

She couldn't speak, and was barely aware that the man she'd been dancing with had now released her hand.

"How are you here?" Eleanor whispered, hoping that the tremble in her voice wouldn't betray her emotion. Jed took her hand and joined in the dancing circle. His fingers linked through hers, warm and strong. His touch seemed to spread through her whole body. She was drawn to him more than she had been in the darkness of the night she'd first met him, and she couldn't keep her eyes off him. In the light of the court, he was more handsome than she'd realized beneath the moonlight. His eyes were as black as his thick lashes when he gazed at her. The color of his skin was a golden caramel, and his shoulders were broader than she remembered.

She tried to look away, but soon was drawn back by his eyes. After they'd mindlessly danced for several moments, Jed tugged at their clasped hands and pulled her away from the circle. "Did you get my letter?" he continued in his pathetic French. The circle continued on without them.

Eleanor wished she could switch to his native language, but others around them might hear. She reluctantly pulled her hand away from his. She didn't want anyone to pay attention to their closeness. "I read the letter, but I thought you'd left. I thought something had happened to you. My stepfather said—"

"I was there when he spat on the ground and laughed at my

father's offer of a truce," Jed said, his dark eyes growing darker, his voice harsher. But then his eyes shifted and softened, and he stepped very close to Eleanor to whisper in her ear. "You were worried about me?"

She swallowed against the tightness of her throat and nodded.

He exhaled. "Come to the canal tonight."

She drew back quickly, afraid to look at him, afraid that someone might see her standing so close to this man. "I can't," she started, even though the pull toward him was stronger than ever. She was relieved he was safe, but now new danger had arisen. "I cannot put your life in danger," she said.

He gazed down at her, and Eleanor's heart fluttered at the deep intensity she saw in his eyes. Without saying a word about her feelings, she knew that he sensed something was growing between them.

"Prince Azzo has arrived," she whispered. "We are expected to be betrothed—"

He brought a finger to her mouth and stopped her from speaking more. Then he dropped his hand and turned.

Without another word, he moved through the milling crowd, instantly swallowed up.

She wanted to follow him, but knew it would be a disaster for both of them if she did. She couldn't do that to him. No matter that he was a stranger—yet he was no stranger to her heart. It seemed that his presence had filled an emptiness that she hadn't known was there.

The music thrummed around her, mimicking the beats of her heart. And soon another man stood in front of her, asking her to join in the dance circle. It was Prince Azzo. A thread of panic shot through her as she wondered if Azzo had seen Jed. But Azzo's gaze held no suspicion. He offered his hand, and Eleanor took it, telling herself not to look behind her for Jed. Had he left? Or was he still in the room, hidden someplace, watching her?

Azzo led Eleanor through the dance formations. He made an

elegant figure, while she felt that she was perspiring through her underdress and breathing too hard for poise. Raynald's and her mother's eyes were on her now, their faces flushed with anticipation and pleasure. It only made her feel hotter. She had to get out of this room, leave the dozens of pairs of eyes that were watching her, speculating, anticipating, planning.

But Azzo was speaking to her, asking questions about Karak, and she had to force herself to listen to him and pay attention so that she could give him the proper response. He spoke of his home in northern Italy, and Eleanor tried to listen attentively, but her thoughts were distracted by what Jed had said to her about his father's truce offering to Raynald. And the vehemence in his voice. And how he'd asked her to come to the canal. How he didn't wait for her to turn him down. Had Jed seen Azzo coming through the crowd? Had he decided to leave before there was any sort of confrontation?

Wasn't Jed worried that someone in her stepfather's court would have recognized him? Dressed as a Christian or not?

Servants brought in desserts and more wine, and people returned to the banquet tables. Entertainment started with a female dancing troupe taking up the space of the dance floor. The women wore low-hipped, flowing pants and small bodices that barely concealed their breasts. As they moved and swayed to the slow music, Eleanor felt more and more stifled in the crowded room. But she couldn't leave the entertainment without drawing notice. And Azzo was now sitting next to her, leaning toward her every so often to make a comment that Eleanor was expected to laugh or smile at.

The music sped up, along with the speed of the dancers' gyrating hips, and Eleanor felt she might not make it one more moment in this room without screaming. Perhaps she should have listened to Miriam and remained in her chambers, although she knew that with the arrival of Azzo, Raynald would have called for her anyway.

As the belly dancers entered their finale, the court guests stood and clapped, and Azzo grabbed Eleanor's hand. She was so surprised that she almost pulled away. He smiled and brought her hand to his mouth and pressed a slow kiss to the top of her fingers.

"You are lovely," he said, his eyes gleaming in a way that nearly turned Eleanor's stomach. She should have been pleased with his attentions. It was what Raynald and her mother wanted, and what *she* should want. It should have been a lovely conclusion to the evening.

"May I spend time with you tomorrow—in quieter circumstances?" Azzo asked, with a smile.

She returned the smile, although there was a sharp ache in her heart. Azzo was not Jed. Her heart knew it. She could practically feel her mother's eyes burning into the back of her head, watching her every move. "Yes," Eleanor said, wanting to swallow back the word the moment it left her lips.

"Until tomorrow then," Azzo said, as he held her gaze.

Eleanor had no choice but to look pleased. Inside, fear had built. Fear of taking this next step, fear of what Saladin might do when he received Raynald's edict rejecting Saladin's request, and fear of never seeing Jed again. This was the most crippling of all. But what did she expect? They were as different as a man and woman could be.

"Come, Miriam," Eleanor said. "We will retire for the evening. Tomorrow I have important plans with Azzo." She gave him a final smile, then turned away from the table.

She didn't know if he watched her leave the room, although she knew there were plenty of people watching her departure, most certainly Raynald.

Once she reached the staircase leading to her chambers, she felt her emotions start to break. But she could not allow herself to cry now. There were still guards to pass, and she could not give the court anything more to gossip about.

But with each step closer to her chambers, Eleanor's heart

rate increased, and she knew that she could not let this night pass without making contact with Jed again. She had to warn him, to make him understand once and for all. And mostly, she needed the chance to bid him a final farewell.

Miriam unlocked the door. Eleanor stepped inside and quickly cast off her overdress.

"What are you doing?" Miriam asked in a quiet voice.

Eleanor turned to the woman. "Are you loyal to me and none else? Tell me now or I will dismiss you this very moment."

"I am loyal to you, Lady Eleanor," Miriam said. "I've proved that to you more than once."

Eleanor thought of the events at the canal two nights before, and about the scroll that Miriam had delivered to her. Neither had been reported to her mother or stepfather. "You have proved loyal." She looked down, inhaling sharply, then raised her gaze to meet Miriam's. "I apologize for my suspicions, but I haven't been able to trust many people in my life."

"I understand," Miriam said simply.

"Tonight, I will go to him," Eleanor said. "I will meet Jed at the canal, and I can't promise your safety if you come along."

Miriam didn't blink. "I will come."

"Why?" Eleanor asked. "Why are you so quick to follow me? Do you not know the dangers?"

This time, Miriam's gaze faltered.

"Tell me what is going on," Eleanor said. "Tell me how you were chosen and why you are here."

Miriam crossed to the window and looked out into the darkening night. "Before I converted to Christianity, I was an outcast in my tribe. They called me a *djinn*, and even the children were afraid of me."

Eleanor stared at the older woman. She'd known of djinns since she was a child. Some called them sorcerers, others called them genies, while still others didn't think they were human at all but evil spirits that took on human form. Her mother had employed djinns before she'd married Raynald. When Raynald found out about their powers of sorcery, he'd had them all banned.

"Does my mother know what you are?" Eleanor asked.

Miriam met Eleanor's gaze. "She's the one who brought me to court. But your stepfather has no idea."

"What are you doing here then?" Eleanor asked.

"Your mother wants me to protect you and to inform her of any stirrings of evil fate."

Eleanor sank onto the edge of her bed. Her mother was hiding this behind her stepfather's back. Eleanor didn't know how to react.

"What is your prediction about my life?" she asked, half in jest, half in bitterness. Her stepfather would call for her execution if he knew she was entertaining the prophecies of a djinn.

Miriam took a moment to answer. "That you will die if you remain under your stepfather's care."

CHAPTER SIXTEEN

MODERN-DAY AL KARAK

An entire day of confinement in her room passed for Aamira. She and Chad had periodically texted, so when her phone buzzed, she fully expected a text from Chad or possibly a message from Naser. But she was surprised to see that it was from Chad's cousin, Omar. He introduced himself and told her to delete each text she sent and received as soon as possible.

We're putting together a plan to get you out of there. We don't believe you're safe.

Aamira's breath left her as she read his words.

You think my father will turn against me? she wrote.

He's been tracing Chad from early in your relationship. He can't be happy with it, and he won't let it go. Not as a member of the Mika'il Order. They don't let anything go, even if they take months or years to act. Remember Hana.

Aamira's hands trembled as she read Omar's text again, then deleted it. Omar had said they were going to get her out of there . . . that she was in real danger. But she didn't know how they'd rescue her. She checked the lock on her door, then climbed into bed. Instead of sleeping, she reviewed her childhood memories, and tried to piece together everything she knew about Hana's life.

When Aamira's mother knocked on her door in the morning, Aamira was ready. She opened the door and startled her mother with a pleasant smile.

"I'm very sorry, Mother," Aamira said. "I hope you can forgive me."

Her mother's eyes widened, and she said, "I—I do. I—Where are you going?"

"I hoped that we could meet with the seamstress today for my wedding dress," Aamira said, trying not to dwell on how wrong the words sounded inside her head. She had once entertained girlish dreams of the happy day when she and her mother met with a seamstress to make her wedding dress. Now she watched her mother carefully, and wondered how much her mother knew about Hana's death. How much she'd hidden all these years.

Her mother nodded, and her eyes lit up with new hope. "Yes, that would be fine. Let me make a phone call."

While her mother prepared, Aamira made sure she hid the phone charger deep inside one of her drawers behind clothing. Then she went into the kitchen and opened her mother's address book. With her phone she took pictures of the names and numbers and addresses on each page. When she'd nearly finished, she heard her mother coming down the hallway. Aamira hid the phone inside her blouse and moved to the refrigerator, pretending to get a jar of iced tea.

"Have you spoken to Ehan lately?" Aamira asked her mother casually. "I wanted to tell him about my graduation."

Her mother's face seemed to close down. "He's very busy and will call when he has a chance."

She followed her mother out of the house, and they walked the few blocks to the seamstress's shop. Aamira thought of her brother and how they used to tell each other everything when they were young. He'd been close friends with their cousins, Kahul's sons, as well. Had her brother known anything about Hana? Did other men in the family know about her death? Had any of them tried to stop it?

The seamstress's shop was filled with the fragrance of flowers and spice. They were ushered in by a petite receptionist and offered tea and pastries. After another customer left, the seamstress came out of the back room. She was older than her mother, with fine wrinkles about her eyes. Aamira couldn't help but wonder if this woman had known Hana too.

"Welcome to my humble shop, and please call me Parvina," the seamstress said, grasping Aamira's hand. "You'll make such a beautiful bride. Come in, come in."

Aamira smiled at the seamstress's enthusiasm. She and her mother followed Parvina into the back room where several dress forms lined the wall. In the center of the room was a raised platform. Aamira stood on the platform, and Parvina took her measurements, then she brought out partially finished dresses, and pointed out what she wanted to create.

Aamira smiled and nodded, agreeing with all of her mother's opinions. Aamira needed to be in her mother's good graces in order to carry out the rest of her plans that day. They settled on a white gown with a high-necked bodice, sleeves fitted to the wrists, a lacy head scarf, and a short train. Once the tasks of measuring and fabric selection were complete, they walked back home. They passed a few others walking, women with other women, or women with one of the men in their family. Greetings were brief.

At home, Aamira helped her mother prepare rolled grape leaves and rice, and then she said, "I'd like to look through the family scrapbooks and put together an invitation list of those to invite to the wedding. I'd also like to see if I get any ideas from the other weddings in our family."

When Aamira was sure her mother was settled again in her room, Aamira took out several photo albums and scattered them across the desk in her father's library. Then she powered on the ancient computer. She and her brother had once played games on it, and she didn't know if her father even used it anymore. But at the time of Hana's death, Aamira was sure this computer had been in full use. If her mother came in, Aamira would tell her she was designing the wedding invitations.

Once the computer was on, she typed her father's old password. It was still the same after all these years. She began to search through the files, one by one. Her father kept rather good records, and this surprised Aamira. She had expected that he kept all of his records at the bank office, but the records on this computer included the monthly household budget. The most recent ones were dated five years earlier, before Aamira had left for the university. But it was interesting to see all the items that had been budgeted for and paid for over the years. Aamira stopped on one line, a jewelry box, her birthday present when she turned fifteen.

She continued opening files, looking for anything that didn't seem to fit in with regular household expenses, until she reached the year of Hana's death. She didn't know if her father would have recorded anything related to his sister's death, but it was worth checking out.

Aamira stalled on a few lines that detailed a wedding gift to the cousin who had married. The same wedding that Hana's boyfriend had attended. The gift was a set of silver platters. Aamira read more slowly, analyzing each expense, but seeing nothing. And then she read the expense records on the day that Hana had died and the several days that followed. The only thing different from the week before was a gallon of carpet cleaning solution. Aamira's heart thumped. Had the cleaning solution been meant to clean up after Hana's death? If Hana had truly fallen down the stairs, would there have been a lot of blood? Or was Naser's theory correct, that Hana had been killed in another way? A messier way?

Aamira took a picture of the records that listed the cleaner. Then she searched the rest of the computer files and found that many of them wouldn't open. They had either been deleted or were old temp files.

Then she closed down the computer and crossed to the closet where her father had stored some of Hana's things. She remembered the arguments between her parents over keeping the boxes. When she was young, she had heard repeatedly to stay out of this closet, and she couldn't remember the last time anyone had opened it. Turning on the closet light, she was surprised to see only one box on the shelf. Below the shelf, a few jackets were hung up, but otherwise the closet was bare.

She reached up and pulled down the single box. It wasn't heavy, and she set it on the floor and lifted the top off. The first thing she noticed was the musty smell that rose and made her nose itch. Aamira was expecting to see a few pieces of jewelry, maybe a framed photograph, or even a childhood stuffed animal. Instead, folded neatly in the bottom of the box was a black burka veil.

The women in her family rarely wore burkas. The only time her mother did was when traveling to another city with her father. Otherwise, in their hometown, most of the women kept their faces uncovered.

Aamira lifted the burka from the box and held it up. The dark folds unraveled and hung stiffly against the floor. For some reason, the fabric gave off a floral scent in combination with the dustiness. She wondered if Hana had worn perfume.

Aamira drew the burka closer and began to examine the seams and the fabric. It was then that she noticed the discoloration. As though the fabric had been stained, and someone had tried to get the stain out.

Near the back of the head portion, the black had faded to a gray-brown color. And the scent was stronger closer to the fading. Aamira brought the faded portion up to her face and inhaled. What she thought was perfume earlier now seemed to smell like floral-scented bleach. Had her father kept the clothing Hana had worn when she was killed?

Aamira's stomach dropped. Why had someone tried to bleach out a stain in Hana's burka? A stain that would have been over the back of Hana's head if she'd been wearing it. Aamira dropped the burka back into the box as if burned by the fabric. Her mind raced, imagining Hana trying to sneak out of her home, wearing her burka. And then her father catching her, and perhaps hitting her over the head, striking her dead. Or someone had waited for Hana to leave her room and struck when she came out. Then they dragged her to the stairs and tossed her down.

Aamira tried to imagine the terror and confusion in Hana's mind. Had Hana known who hit her?

The door to the library opened, and Aamira startled at the sudden noise. She turned around to see her father standing in the doorway. Her breath stalled. She hadn't heard him enter the house. His eyes went from her to the box on the closet floor.

"What are you doing?" His voice was calm, but Aamira recognized the steely control behind it.

She wanted to tell him the truth, to tell him that she knew about his sister's death. She wanted to question him, confront him, but the darkness of his eyes told her he was already suspicious. If he could cover up the murder of his own sister, then Aamira wasn't safe either.

"I—I was looking for photo albums," she started to say, not liking how breathless she sounded. "Mother and I are making the wedding plans, and I thought—"

He held up his hand, and she stopped talking.

For a moment, he stared at her, his jaw clenched, his silence more painful than his words.

"Where is your mother?" he said at last.

"In her room," Aamira said in a near whisper.

When her father left, she exhaled and quickly lifted the burka again and took several pictures of the fabric contrast. With shaking hands, she folded the burka in the same way she'd found it and set the box on the shelf.

It was then she heard the argument break out between her parents. Aamira didn't have to listen at the door to know that they were talking about her. She moved back to the desk and replaced all of the photo albums, then left the library. On the way to her bedroom, she passed her parents' room.

Her father was railing about keeping their daughter in line, the need to uphold the family's *honor*. The words sent a shudder down her spine, and Aamira hurried to her room and shut and locked the door. If her father came to speak with her, the locked door would probably make him even more angry. So she unlocked it and sat at her desk with her back to the door. She texted all of the pictures to Chad, then she emailed them all to Naser, telling the men that the pictures were of Hana's burka, the one she might have been wearing at the time of her death. She wanted them to have evidence in case her father decided to destroy anything.

And then she texted Chad: *My father's yelling at my mother right now for letting me have access to the library. I don't know how this will end.*

As soon as the message sent, she deleted the text receipt and the sent files from the email account. Then she closed the browsers on the phone and deleted all of the browsing history. Next she turned off the phone and tucked it inside her shirt. She didn't want to hide it in her room in case she needed to leave immediately.

Finally the arguing stopped, and it was plain that her mother was crying.

Next her father's footsteps left his bedroom and started down the hallway. Aamira held her breath and waited, not moving.

Her father opened the door, and Aamira stayed seated at the desk, waiting for him to speak first. She didn't move, hardly took a breath, and so when he did speak, it was like his voice was on a speakerphone, sounding loud and far away.

"Your mother said that you asked about Hana's death," he said.

She turned to face him. His eyes were dark and hard and his face red from the argument.

"Why would you ask her such a thing?" he asked. "Why would you bring back pain into the family?"

At that moment, Aamira realized she'd heard these words before. Others had brought up questions, and she'd overheard other conversations through doors and down corridors, soon after

Hana's death. Her father might have kept boxes of Hana's things, but Aamira had been told more than once not to speak of her aunt. It brought too much pain. And her mother had used the same argument as her father about keeping Hana's things in the closet.

Her father wasn't going to make any sort of confession. He was going to use the same answer he'd given anyone else who brought up Hana or questioned her death and why she supposedly took her own life.

Aamira knew she needed to answer him, to come up with an excuse that he would fully believe. She thought of the files that Naser had sent over—Hana's own research into their family lineage and the deaths of some of the women, all presumed accidents or suicides.

"At the university, in one of my classes, we discussed honoring our lineage and learning about our ancestors," she began, surprised at how easily the lies came once she started. "As I was reading the birth and death dates, I found out that there have been quite a few women in our family who died at a young age."

Her father didn't move, didn't even blink.

"I wondered if some people in our family have a mental disorder, one that causes depression," she said, watching him closely to see if he was buying it.

His face was unreadable.

"I wanted to find out more about Hana since I don't remember a lot about her," Aamira said.

"What was the class?" her father asked.

Aamira thought fast. "Communications. We studied about how families communicate, and we did a unit on passing along the way we communicate from one generation to another."

Her father's gaze was impassive, and Aamira wondered if he was looking at her or through her.

"I don't want you in the library," her father said, his eyes finally showing a bit of emotion, a mixture of determination and a strange sort of regret. "There are many memories stored there that I don't want to open."

A twinge shot through Aamira. Even if he knew about his sister's murder, perhaps he truly had nothing to do with it. Perhaps he missed his sister and still grieved her death. Perhaps, as twisted as it was, he regretted his sister's death.

There were always two sides to a story, but this was one that Aamira hadn't considered. What had her father's childhood been like growing up with a parent who would order the death of one of his children? How deeply did the betrayal run? For a moment she saw her father, not as a beast who might participate in the death of another, but as a man growing up in a family of terrible secrets.

She looked down at her clasped hands, feeling she'd just escaped an explosive situation. Her father stood in the doorway for a few moments longer, then left, shutting the door behind him.

CHAPTER SEVENTEEN

JORDAN DESERT

The room Omar woke up in was hotter than midday in the Rub' al Khali desert. The space was not much larger than a closet, and the sense of claustrophobia overtaking him didn't help as he tried to come up with a logical escape strategy. Omar lifted his head and groaned. His arms and legs were shackled to the hard cot with thick plastic ties, and every part of his body ached. It looked as if the wound on his thigh had been taken care of. A hole had been cut in his pants, and a tight bandage wrapped around his leg. What he wouldn't give for a drink of water and a place to piss. And a handful of ibuprofen.

He examined his surroundings more closely in the dim light. At the foot of the cot was a wooden door. A couple of high windows had been covered with thick paper, letting in some light. Omar guessed it was late afternoon, maybe only one day after his abduction. But he had little hope for that. The smell of his own body told him it had been at least two days. No flies or bugs seemed to be in this godforsaken room, and he couldn't smell anything besides his own sweat. He vaguely remembered someone escorting him to a toilet a couple of times.

He closed his eyes, listening to the sounds around him. *Laughter.* That he wasn't expecting, and then he realized there was a television program running on the other side of his wall. The audience laughter faded to muted conversation, followed by another burst of laughter. Omar kept his eyes closed, trying to hear beyond the sounds of the television. Probably more significant was what he couldn't hear. No cars or trucks, no rushing river or the sound of crashing waves of an ocean, and no birds in trees.

He was either in the middle of a closed industrial park, or a desert. Omar opened his eyes and lifted his head again to look at his limbs. The plastic ties were not grocery grade; they were plainly industrial. It would probably take bolt cutters to get them off. Omar strained against the ties about his ankles, but there was no give. The same result for his wrists. The ties were snug, and no matter how much Omar twisted in them, they held fast.

He hoped that Joseph had done as instructed, and decided that there was no use delaying the inevitable. He shifted his weight on the cot, making the cot thump against the wall. The television muted, and a moment later the door to his room opened. He recognized one of the men from the museum immediately. Unibrow. The one with little compassion. The second man who entered his room was clearly someone with authority. He wore an expensive watch that flashed in the dim light, and his teeth were white and even. Perhaps a dental plan was part of his benefits package.

"Good afternoon, nice to see you again," Omar said to Unibrow in Arabic. "Where's our friend?"

The man's face flushed, but he said nothing.

Gold Watch stepped fully into the room, eyeing the ties around Omar's wrists and ankles, as if to ensure they were still in place. Then he looked at Omar's face. "We have instructions to keep you quiet."

It was then that Omar saw the stun gun in his hand.

"Not again," Omar muttered. "I'll be quiet after I answer all of your questions."

Gold Watch seemed confused for a moment; he very well should be since Omar was doing his best to confuse him.

Then Gold Watch gave Omar a slow smile. "You think we have questions for you? And that's why we went to all the trouble to break into a high security museum and bring you here alive?"

"That's usually how it works," Omar said. "I'm quite popular among the kidnapping crowd. Practically irresistible."

Gold Watch's face didn't soften; Omar needed a better audience.

"We can settle everything right now if you get Taheer on the phone," Omar continued. "I'd call him myself, but I don't know what happened to my cell phone." He could very well guess it was in the next room somewhere, probably downloaded onto one of the abductor's laptops. And if they were running sophisticated software, they'd at least get his contacts off the phone, although his main files were encrypted.

"Tape his mouth shut," Gold Watch said, and Unibrow grinned as if he'd been waiting for that particular order all day.

Seconds later, Unibrow was back in the room, tearing a piece of silvery duct tape from a thick roll.

"If you tape my mouth, then I won't be able to tell you where the treasure is," Omar said.

Unibrow actually hesitated. "Treasure?"

"Or the seven virgins," Omar said.

Gold Watch moved forward so quickly that Omar thought he was going be struck, but instead, Gold Watch took the duct tape himself and strapped it across Omar's mouth.

"That's better," Gold Watch said. "Now you're going to listen to us." Another look at Unibrow. "Untie him."

This is interesting, Omar thought. *And unexpected.* He would have bet that they'd leave him tied up for the duration, until whatever happened that they were waiting for.

Just as Omar suspected, it took a bolt cutter to sever the plastic ties. Once they were cut, Omar sat up, his head pounding with the sudden movement.

"Not so fast," Gold Watch said, holding up the stun gun.

Omar flinched, waiting for the impact, but it didn't come.

Gold Watch stared at him until Omar lay back down on the cot. His gaze went to the door where Unibrow had disappeared with the bolt cutters. Omar wondered how many men were in the house, and if he'd be able to wrest the stun gun away from Gold Watch without it going off and causing more damage.

Unibrow came back in the room with a new man. This one was short, with a neck like an ox. His dark eyes stared at Omar intently. "Lead him out and sit him down at the computer."

So maybe they weren't in the middle of a desert.

Unibrow and the new man walked to either side of the cot and grasped Omar's arms. They hauled him to his feet, and Omar's legs felt strange bearing weight again, not to mention the tender wound on his thigh and other various bruises from the previous night's abduction.

He didn't resist, since he was more than happy to leave the small room, and they led him into the next room. This room was larger than he expected, and he was surprised to see a long table with several computers set up, making the place look like some sort of command center.

Another man sat at the table in front of one of the computers, and he looked up as Omar walked in. Omar recognized the man by his ears—his very large ears. He'd been the one in the back of the van helping transport him.

Omar was at a distinct disadvantage, not being able to talk his way out of whatever they wanted him to do. They sat him down in front of a computer, and then Gold Watch leaned against the table, facing him. "You're going to call all the dogs off and erase all of the evidence against Ehan Sayid."

Omar stared at Gold Watch. The man couldn't be serious. Even Omar's boss, Simon Greif, couldn't do that. If Omar didn't have the tape over his mouth, he would have been more than happy to explain.

Gold Watch powered on the computer and pulled up a browser, typing in searches for Ehan Sayid. "All of these are lies, listing him as a person of interest," he nearly growled out. "And we need to protect our tribal name." He clicked link after link, randomly pulling up news articles, most of them out of the UK.

"Our tribe is a sacred culture, and if one of our members is dragged through the mud, we will do anything to stop it." He brought his face up close to Omar's. "You tried to capture Ehan Sayid. You were trying to stop his divine mission. Because of that, you will now make recompense, and then Taheer Sayid will decide your fate."

Omar's head and body already hurt, but now fear entered the game. Not necessarily fear for his own life, because he'd worked on dangerous projects for years, and knew that one day his number would come up. But fear for what someone like Gold Watch could accomplish, what sort of crazy action he could start, and how many casualties there would be in the end. Omar recognized the false beliefs of a man who was convinced his ways were right and his words were truth.

Gold Watch pulled up a second file, a list of names and phone numbers. "These are the people you will call. One by one. You will explain that everything has been a mistake, that Ehan Sayid is working undercover for your government, doing research on the corrupt pursuits of the Janin tribe."

As Gold Watch spoke, Omar scanned the list of names in front of him—department heads of universities, curators of museums, high profile art collectors, and a few names that he knew from shadier deals in the antiquities world. Whoever had put this list together had pretty much covered every angle. But at the mention of the Janin tribe, his gaze snapped to Gold Watch. The Mika'il Order and the Janin tribe were notorious enemies in Jordan, fighting over government positions, and now the Mika'il Order wanted to scapegoat the Janin for the Order's crimes.

"Ah, I see you know who I'm speaking about," Gold Watch said. "I hope we are in agreement." He lifted the stun gun and gestured with it.

It was odd that Gold Watch didn't feel the need to threaten Omar with a rifle. Perhaps the man had a stun gun fetish.

Gold Watch reached over and tore the tape off Omar's mouth

in one easy motion. The burn seared across his mouth and chin, but he was grateful to have it gone. He was about to tell his tormentors that making the calls wouldn't change the manhunt for Ehan Sayid. In fact, the calls would only increase suspicion. Omar didn't have the security level or the political influence to accomplish what Gold Watch expected him to. But if Omar told him that, then there was no telling what might happen.

It was better to go along with Gold Watch, and then watch the Mika'il Order's plan implode. Whatever happened to Omar, he wouldn't let this become political mayhem between the two tribes. Enough lives had been lost over the years in various skirmishes. Recently, he'd read an article about how the Janin had protested the Jordanian king's appointment of a member of another tribe to a government position. The action had taken place during one of the king's scheduled departures to another country, and the king's guards had ended up shooting several protestors.

Which had only further strained the relationship between the two tribes.

"I'll do it," Omar said, rotating his jaw.

"You're a smart man," Gold Watch said, then nodded to Unibrow. The man produced a cell phone, and Omar took it, surprised that it wasn't a burner phone.

"You expect me to make calls on an iPhone?" Omar asked, as if it were the worst thing that could have possibly happened to him that day. "This can be traced at least a dozen different ways."

"The SIM card is not registered, and we'll destroy it after you use it," Gold Watch said.

"That's not good enough. Any government can petition Apple and get the location records at the time the phone was used." He set the phone on the table, trying to keep his face a picture of innocence. "We need to set up an anonymous Skype account. If someone tries to trace us to the computer's IP address, it will only tell them the owner of the computer, not our location."

Gold Watch stared at Omar for a moment, then looked at Unibrow. "You idiot. Are you trying to ruin this whole operation?"

Unibrow shook his head emphatically.

"By the way," Omar said, "since we'll be working together for the foreseeable future, I think introductions are in order." He extended a hand toward Gold Watch. "I'm Omar Zagouri. My friends call me Omar."

Gold Watch took a step back, keeping his stun gun at the ready. "Don't touch me, and don't try to touch any of my men. Next time, I use this."

"Call me Zagouri then," Omar said with a mock shake of his head. "Can I open the browser and download the Skype software?"

"Yes," Gold Watch said. He nodded for Unibrow to take a seat across the table, and Gold Watch stayed near Omar, watching every move.

It was annoying as hell.

Omar downloaded Skype and went through the motions of creating an anonymous account. When there were a few seconds of Gold Watch glancing over at Unibrow and telling him to make coffee, Omar logged into his own account, conveniently named Anonymous. He'd call down the list from his account and blind-conference Mia into all the calls. Even if she didn't pick up at first, he could turn on a recording feature that would record the conversation that she could download and listen to later. She'd have total access. And with any luck, she'd start tracing the IP address of the computer he was working from.

"Are there headphones?" Omar asked.

Gold Watch chuckled, a low raspy sound. "You'll put it on speaker so we can all hear."

The first phone call was to the National Portrait Gallery curator, Mrs. Shira Moberg. Omar was pleasantly surprised when she answered on the second ring.

"Mrs. Moberg, this is Omar Zagouri," he said in a smooth British tone.

"Omar," Shira said, her voice sounding alarmed and relieved at the same time. "We heard that you—"

He cut her off before she could say anything too revealing. "I'm sorry about the damage that was done to the museum, and we'll pay for all repairs. I need to speak with you about something extremely important and confidential."

"Of course," Shira said, her voice sounding more business-like now, but wariness had also crept in.

Good for you, Shira. Don't sound the alarm, though. "A lot depends on you getting the right information to those who are asking questions," Omar said, "whether it be the police or newspaper reporters or other media inquiries. Lives may depend on how closely you listen to me."

Gold Watch narrowed his eyes, and Omar gave him the thumbs-up sign.

"It's come to my attention that I wasn't cleared for the highest security level and—" Omar started. "Can you guarantee confidentiality?"

"Of course," Shira said, her voice even and calm now. She was definitely onto him.

"Ehan Sayid is an undercover agent," Omar said. "He's been transferred recently from working for the Italian government and is now on the case of exposing criminal activity by the Janin tribe. In fact, he's been working undercover in the Janin for nearly three years. He has been copycatting other art thefts in order to bring out the real culprit, whose name and identity I'll get you as soon as I have clearance to do so." He paused. Gold Watch was still watching him closely, but approval marked his face.

"I understand, Mr. Zagouri," Shira said, sounding completely official now.

"The media can't know that Ehan Sayid is an undercover agent, of course," Omar continued. "But we need to clear his name with the authorities. You're my first phone call, and I'll be contacting all the police departments in the area and airport security officials. Do you understand the sensitive nature of this information?"

"Yes," Shira replied, her voice coming through clearly. "Are you all right, Mr. Zagouri? We were worried about you, and there've been a lot of questions and speculation by the police."

Omar didn't need to see the warning glare by Gold Watch."I am as well as can be expected in this type of crisis. I'll be much better if you agree to cooperate."

"Of course I'll cooperate," Shira said. "Can I expect an in-person meeting soon to further explain the details?"

"I'm out of town right now," Omar said. "We'll be in touch later."

Gold Watch stepped closer, the stun gun lifted.

Omar had held Shira on the line long enough for Mia to trace the call, and he hoped she was listening now. Omar hung up with Shira and dialed the police chief's number at the London station. Gold Watch had to know that Omar was only buying Ehan a little more time to go dark. Most of the people he was asking Omar to call would be suspicious.

Omar relayed the same information to the officer he was able to reach. Apparently, the police chief wasn't accepting unscheduled phone calls. But there was no way the officer would be able to read into what Omar was telling him. With each call, he kept Mia's number linked, and with each passing moment, he hoped she was working to trace him.

Within two hours, Omar had completed the calls. One bonus was that Gold Watch rewarded him with a cup of coffee. He could have used some food too, but would wait a little longer to make demands. The coffee was lukewarm, but strong, and Omar appreciated every drop.

When he hung up with the final person on the list, Omar stretched his arms above his head. Gold Watch remained in the same place near Omar, stun gun at the ready.

"I'm buying lunch," Omar said, lowering his arms and patting the pockets of his pants. "Anyone seen my wallet?"

"Take him back to the cot," Gold Watch said to Unibrow.

“Don’t I even get a treat?” Omar asked. “That was a lot of work.” He closed down the Skype program, not able to check whether Mia had been logged on during any of the calls.

Between linking Mia into the Skype calls and hoping that Shira Moberg understood the trouble he was in, he was depending on his girlfriend, on another job in another country, and a British museum curator.

He’d done all that he could do for now. Any rescue mission would come at the complete mercy of others. Again.

CHAPTER EIGHTEEN

ANCIENT KARAK

Eleanor was sneaking out of the castle again with her handmaiden Miriam because of the woman's prediction. Miriam's former tribe believed she could prophesy the future and cast curses on people. Eleanor's circumstances inclined her not to discount any warnings, and she wasn't about to turn away a woman who'd become a loyal friend and protector. She'd never needed an ally more than now.

Jed would be waiting for her by the canal, of that she was sure. She couldn't deny his intensity earlier at the court celebration—a celebration rejoicing in the fact that her stepfather had refused to negotiate a truce with Jed's father. In the morning, she would face a proposal of marriage by Prince Azzo. The very thought of it made her want to pack her things and flee. But that was foolish. She couldn't allow herself to be ruled by her heart.

Tonight she'd meet Jed, yes, but she would tell him what she had failed to communicate earlier at the celebration. She'd tell him to leave Karak for good, to return to his tribe, and that they would forever be separated by opposing loyalties. She'd tell him that if he cared for her at all, he would choose to live rather than the certain death coming to him if he continued to contact her.

The air was surprisingly cool as Eleanor and Miriam stepped outside. They walked slowly together, their heads bowed beneath the hoods of their cloaks. They appeared to be a couple of old women seeking the cool night air.

Eleanor felt Jed looking at her before she saw him. He was across the canal, near the bridge. Her face warmed, even before she could see him clearly. Eleanor tightly gripped Miriam's arm against her, and together they crossed the bridge.

"Good evening," Jed said, his voice quiet.

"How did you get past the guards?" Eleanor asked him. He was wearing Christian clothing still, but it didn't fool her. He looked like a tribal warrior through and through.

One side of his mouth lifted into a half-smile. "Can we walk?" he asked.

Eleanor knew she should say no because time with him alone would likely crumble her resolve. It would be much easier to tell him here and now that they could no longer speak or see each other. "Yes," Eleanor said. Her mind was no match for her heart tonight.

Eleanor slipped out of Miriam's linked arm, and soon found herself walking side by side with Jed, away from the castle, along the bank of the canal. They didn't link arms, didn't touch, but Eleanor could nonetheless feel the heat of his body as if he were brushing against hers.

"You are taking a great risk to come out here," Jed observed. "I wondered if you'd truly come."

Eleanor let a laugh escape. "Your risk is greater than mine. It seems you went through a lot of effort to speak to me in a court full of Christians," she answered. "Which means whatever you have to tell me must be important. Besides, any information I can gather about my stepfather's enemy might prove to be valuable."

This was a good plan, Eleanor decided. Don't speak about *them*, but speak about what information could be traded. And then they would part.

"Ah." Jed stopped and turned toward her. "That is good news."

"Why?" Eleanor asked. Miriam had fallen behind, waiting some distance away.

"I'm now your *stepfather's* enemy, which means I am no longer yours," he said, his dark eyes holding hers.

Eleanor tried not to get lost in those eyes. She had to keep reason about her. "Why did you come back?" she asked. "You are the one who's risking too much."

"For a beautiful woman, it is but a small thing." His gaze moved from her eyes to the rest of her face.

"There are many beautiful women," Eleanor said, breathless at his words. "So many, it would be impossible to count. Will you risk your life every day for one of them?"

"Ah, you think I'm trying to flatter you." Jed moved a step closer.

No, she knew this was more than flattery. She'd never felt this way in her life. She'd never cared so much for another person's well-being.

"Yes, there are many beautiful women," Jed continued, "but only one Eleanor."

She wanted to lean toward him and smell the scent she was becoming too familiar with. "You hardly know me," she argued, as much for herself as for him, "so I can only conclude you are a great flatterer."

At this, he raised his brows. "You think I hardly know you? What kind of man would I be if I didn't know all about the family of my father's greatest enemy? Do you not know that a man's most vulnerable weakness is his family?"

Eleanor took a deep breath. "Raynald is my *stepfather*. Did you know that he confined me to my rooms for protesting the execution of my handmaiden?" She expected him to laugh or to refute her claim. Instead, his expression went sober.

"I am sorry about your handmaiden," he said. "I heard of her execution."

This surprised her. "How?"

"I told you, I know all about you, Lady Eleanor," Jed said. "I know about your brother Humphrey and your sister Isabella. I know that your mother has been widowed twice. I know that your handmaiden took the name Miriam upon her conversion." He lowered his voice. "I know that you watch out your window many times a day, gazing at the canal and the desert beyond the plateau."

As he spoke, Eleanor found herself mesmerized by his soft voice and the way that he barely touched her hand, brushing the tips of their fingers together. She should have kept Miriam with them. Allowing him this near was a mistake.

"And now that I've met you, and touched you, and danced with you, I know you even better," Jed said.

Eleanor stepped back. She needed the space. "What does this all mean?" she asked, a little more demanding than she'd intended. "Are you here to abduct me? To instigate another war between our fathers?"

Jed moved close again, erasing the distance she'd put between them. "It's already been instigated," he said, moving his hand up her arm and causing her to shiver with warmth.

She knew she needed to step away again, distance herself from his touch, but she couldn't bring herself to do so.

"I've come to warn you, Lady Eleanor," Jed said. "There will be a great war soon. My father is gathering forces of tens of thousands. They plan to wipe out all the crusaders. My people are determined to take back their lands, and they are willing to give their lives."

It was a pretty speech, Eleanor knew, but didn't Jed know the crusaders were ruthless and had better weapons and more soldiers? There was a reason that Jerusalem fell before them in the first place.

"War is not exactly new," Eleanor said, trying to concentrate on their conversation and not how much she was craving more of his touch. "All my life, war has surrounded me."

"There has never been a call such as this," Jed continued, his hand on her shoulder, barely resting there. But Eleanor felt the warmth throughout her entire body. "Your stepfather again turned down our pleas for a truce. Did you know that he also turned down Guy of Lusignan's request for a truce with Saladin?"

Guy of Lusignan was the new king of Jerusalem. His court was divided, and the crusaders were trying to earn his favor. Raynald hadn't seen fit to obey a newcomer from a castle in Oultrejordain. At the time, Eleanor believed Raynald was a fool, but what could she do? She was simply expected to obey her parents and the protocol of the new kingdom.

"So there will be another battle," Eleanor said flatly.

"Not just a battle," Jed said. "A war, and your stepfather will be forced to fight if he wants a chance to hold onto Karak. It's come down to my father or your stepfather."

Eleanor nodded, although everything Jed was saying made her feel numb.

"What do you think will happen if your stepfather is defeated?" he asked.

"I don't know," Eleanor admitted. "He will go into exile until he can organize another army."

"No," Jed said. "He will be executed. My tribe will not stand for his continued threat. My father has sworn to his death."

Eleanor didn't care for her stepfather, but since he'd married her mother, Eleanor was dependent on his protection so long as the crusaders were conquerors. And here was a man telling her, no, threatening her, with her stepfather's death. She could call for guards right now, expose him, and let him meet his fate. She didn't know this man, and he might be feeding her false information just to get her to say something to her stepfather.

"I am telling you this for your own protection," Jed continued, when she didn't reply. "You must flee this place and take refuge."

"Even if you were speaking the truth, and did care about me for some strange reason to warn me, I cannot leave Karak on my own," she said. "My mother would never come with me, and what sort of life would I have as a refugee?"

"You would be alive, that's what," Jed said.

Eleanor turned away from him then, looking toward the castle. Battles and wars were fought all the time in these desert countries. If it wasn't between the crusaders and the Muslims, it was between neighboring tribes. Someone was always fighting someone. Even if she did move on, or her mother agreed to take her somewhere, they'd probably land in the middle of another battle between other antagonists.

"Come with me," Jed said, his fingers brushing hers again.

Eleanor would have laughed, but he turned her toward him, and she saw the seriousness in his eyes. "A Christian woman traveling in a Muslim tribe? Do you think that won't incite a war?"

"Keep your disguise on," Jed said. "I can tell them you're mute." He glanced over at Miriam who still stood several paces away. "Your handmaiden may come as well."

Eleanor straightened, still feeling small next to Jed's tall frame. She had to be strong, no matter how tempted she was. "Thank you for your concern and your offer. But I'm not about to leave my home and my mother and live as a nomad. Tomorrow I'm meeting with Prince Azzo, who I expect will offer marriage. That is the life I've been born into, and that's how my mother brought me up—to tend to my obligations. Fleeing Karak because of an impending war is a coward's way. And if there's one thing I've never been, it's a coward."

Jed didn't seem surprised at her frenzy of words. His hand wrapped around hers, and she found herself having trouble breathing.

"Don't come as a Christian refugee," Jed said in a low voice. He leaned down and whispered in her ear so there was no chance of Miriam overhearing. "Come as my wife."

Eleanor couldn't have been more surprised. She immediately pulled her hand away from Jed's. He released his hold but remained staring at her.

She held no illusions that Jed was in love with her, no matter how much he claimed to know about her, or how strong the attraction between them seemed to be. It was impossible to be in love with someone so recently met. Wasn't it? "You think an alliance between our fathers will save your people's lives?" Eleanor asked.

Jed shook his head. "I don't think our people will ever truly reconcile. There may come a time when there is more peace than war, but as long as they both want the same piece of land, there will always be tension while they believe in different gods." He held up his hand as Eleanor was about to refute. "The fact that your stepfather is a crusader tells me that he agrees with my statement. It's why he forces the members of his court and the soldiers in his armies to convert to his religion. But," his words dropped to a whisper, "no one should ever be forced to convert to a religion they don't believe in."

Eleanor looked at Miriam. She'd been a black mark and an outcast in her own tribe; had she seen Christianity as a way to start a new life? Or did she truly believe in Jesus Christ and his apostles?

"Why would I come with you?" Eleanor said. "Our people will continue to battle until one side kills more of the other side. There can be no benefit in me leaving. If I stay, I'll carry on the royal legacy of my birth when I marry Azzo."

"Those are powerful reasons to stay," Jed said.

His acknowledgement wasn't what Eleanor expected.

"But I'm not asking you to be my wife in order to offer you protection," Jed continued. "I want you to be my true wife. Our children would be born into the most powerful tribe in Arabia—"

"How many wives do you have, Jed?" Eleanor cut in.

A smile lifted his lips. "You would be the only one," he said.

"Until you find another beautiful woman." She shook her head, needing to convince herself, as well as him. "We are not the same, you and I. You are a tribal warrior, and we obey different gods. It could never work, even if each of our parents did bless the union." She arched a brow at him. "Have you considered how your father will react to you bringing a French woman into your tribe?"

"I am my own man," Jed said, but his tone had turned wary.

"Are you?" Eleanor asked. "What if your father forbids our

marriage? What if your tribe detests me? What if the women won't accept me and our sons grow up ostracized?"

"When you convert, my father will accept you. The tribe will also accept you," Jed said. "They will offer us respect because they'd know their lives depend on it."

Eleanor's smile was sad. "And so we continue our traditions of fear and threats and ultimatums until we are just ghosts of who we were when we came into this world. I have lost my father already. My two siblings have married and live in different countries now. When I marry, I will finally have something of my own—a husband and children. I do not want to bring more chaos into the world by going against my family's expectations."

"Eleanor," Jed said, moving closer. "I haven't been able to sleep since I met you. I can't stop thinking about you. As sure as the moon hangs in the sky above, I know that I want no one else in this world to be my wife." He leaned down and kissed her cheek so lightly that she barely felt it.

"I'll be here tomorrow night, waiting for you," Jed continued in a whisper. "If you don't appear, then I'll know your answer."

She could only stare up at him, feeling the tears burning in her eyes, but unable to speak. His words had shifted something inside of her, and she knew it wasn't because he spoke flattery. She'd felt his sincerity deep inside. But how could she leave with him? She'd simply be trading one side of the battle for another. The son of her stepfather's greatest enemy had just asked her to marry him. Eleanor couldn't fathom what Raynald's reaction would be to all of this. He'd probably hunt down Jed himself and cut his throat, leaving him to bleed out on the night sand.

Jed strode away, and Eleanor watched him go. She watched him until he disappeared down a trail that led off the side of the plateau. She still didn't know how he came and went without being stopped by soldiers. It was as if he were a shadow that no one but she could see. Perhaps he was her imagination after all, but when she turned back to see Miriam's wide eyes beneath the moonlight, Eleanor knew she hadn't imagined Jed for one moment.

He had been as real as anything else in her life to this point.

When Eleanor returned to the castle, instead of going to her rooms and waiting for the next day to approach, she made her way to her mother's chambers.

The hour was late, and when the handmaiden let Eleanor inside, she found her mother sitting at her vanity table while a second handmaiden was unpinning her hair. Stephanie's golden-brown locks tumbled down and rested on her shoulders.

"You made a nice impression on Azzo tonight," her mother said, a pleased smile on her face.

"We are meeting in the morning, privately," Eleanor said, coming to stand by her mother. Eleanor clasped her hands together, making her image in the brass mirror seem calm. Inside, she was anything but.

"Ah, as I had hoped," her mother said, reaching up to pat Eleanor's arm. "He will make a fine husband, and you'll live a life of privilege and security as his wife."

Eleanor found herself nodding. Her mother spoke the truth. But what would she think if she knew that her daughter had received another proposal tonight? One from a Muslim warrior? One that Eleanor found was tempting her more and more by the moment? It was foolish and completely unreasonable, that she knew, but the idea wouldn't leave her mind.

"Mother," Eleanor said in a soft voice. "As a woman now, one about to be betrothed, I need to ask you something."

Her mother's pretty smile curved. "Anything."

"Did you ever marry for love?"

Her mother arched her thinned brows. "Love?" She released a quiet laugh. "In our world, a woman cannot afford to marry for love. If she wants love, she risks a life of insecurity." Her eyes met Eleanor's in the mirror. "And if there is one thing you'll desire above all else when your first child is born and placed in your arms, it is for that child to be safe."

Eleanor knew her mother was right. Azzo would offer her

that. He'd take her to Italy, and she'd live out her days behind a walled fortress with soldiers and guards and handmaidens to protect her and her children at all times. With Jed . . . there would be nothing but open desert and the emotions of men, rising and falling on the wind, to dictate her fate.

CHAPTER NINETEEN

MODERN-DAY AL KARAK

At some point in the early evening, Aamira fell asleep. When she awakened, it was dark outside and the house was silent, not even the television was on. She peered at the glowing clock by her bed and saw that it was nearly 2:00 a.m.

She climbed out of bed and sipped at the glass of water she'd left on her desk. Then she removed her phone from beneath her mattress, wondering if there were any messages from Chad or Omar. Her heart stilled as she saw three missed calls and one urgent text from Chad: *Call me asap.*

The phone rang twice before Chad answered.

"Are you all right?" he asked.

"Yes, what's going on?" Panic pulsed through her as she thought of all the possibilities. Had her brother been captured? Had her father found out more about her romance with Chad?

"Omar's gone missing," Chad said. "I was contacted by Joseph, a man he works with, a couple of hours ago. He asked if I had any way to track him down."

Aamira felt cold all over. "What do you mean *missing*?"

Chad hesitated. "Joseph told me that they were trying to track down your brother, waiting for him at a museum they suspected he'd break into. Both Joseph and Omar were attacked and dragged out. Joseph managed to get away. Omar was taken by some men—we haven't identified them yet."

"They must be connected to my brother," Aamira said in a horrified whisper. "Why would my brother do that?" Her question was mostly to herself.

"Joseph didn't see Ehan, although he thinks that either your father or brother ordered the capture."

Aamira squeezed her eyes shut against the anger and frustration building inside of her. She felt betrayed, like she'd witnessed the death of someone she loved, and discovered that person hadn't been who she thought he was. How could her family do these types of things? How could they be like the monsters she read about in the crime section of the newspapers?

New thoughts crowded in as she wondered what her mother knew and what she might be hiding. What would it take to get her mother to talk?

"What can I do?" she asked Chad.

"Sit tight for now and wait for instructions," Chad said.

"But I can't just sit and wonder."

"Aamira, listen to me," he said. "You're already in enough danger as it is."

She remained quiet for a moment, then Chad said, "I love you, and I'll message you as soon as I get more instructions. Hopefully it will be within the day."

Aamira's heart twisted with longing and with missing him and with sorrow over the situation they were now both in.

"I love you too," she whispered, then hung up the phone. She deleted the evidence of the incoming calls and the earlier text sent by Chad.

She stared into the darkness. If her brother was involved, was her father? She listened to the sounds of the house. All was quiet except for the thudding of her heart.

Maybe she could sneak into her parents' room and check her father's phone records. Find out who he'd been calling or texting recently. She stood and crossed her dark bedroom.

Once in the hallway she paused, listening to the sounds of the house. The refrigerator kicked on, emitting a low hum. Aamira stopped outside her parents' bedroom door. It was partially open, and she listened for sounds of breathing or snoring. Hearing nothing, she pushed open the door a little way.

As her eyes adjusted to the shapes and dim light in the bedroom, she could only make out one form in bed. On her mother's side. Aamira watched for a moment, listening and waiting to see if her father might be in another part of the house. She continued along the hallway, but the library was dark as well. Finally she looked out the back door and discovered her father's car was gone.

She moved back to her parents' room, turned on the lamp by her mother's bed, and shook her awake.

Her mother flinched and opened her eyes. "What is it?" she immediately asked in a panicked voice.

"Where's Father?" Aamira asked.

Her mother moved up in bed, half-sitting. "He had to leave town for a couple of days on an urgent business matter."

"Did he say where he was going?" Aamira pressed.

"I'm not sure," her mother said. She narrowed her eyes against the lamp. "Why are you doing this in the middle of the night?"

"Some terrible things are happening, Mother," Aamira said. "I need you to be honest with me."

At that her mother scooted back from Aamira. "This isn't about your aunt again, is it? I told you not to speak of her."

"It's more about Ehan," Aamira said. She decided to take the plunge. Aamira would be gone before her father returned. "And Father. What they are doing. The crimes that Ehan is committing, and how Father is helping him."

Her mother stared, and Aamira met her stare, refusing to break eye contact.

"Ehan is an art thief, and the authorities in England are hunting him down," Aamira said. "In school, I became friends with a man named Chad, who's related to one of the agents looking for Ehan."

Her mother's eyes widened, and Aamira didn't know whether her mother was more shocked to hear about Chad or Ehan.

"Chad's cousin made the connection between me and Ehan when he came to the graduation," Aamira rushed on. "He told me things about our family, things I didn't believe at first. Terrible crimes, including theft and murder."

Her mother looked away.

"And now Chad's cousin, the agent, is missing," Aamira said. She told her mother about how Chad's computer activity had been traced and how she'd been doing research into their family records and discovered that Hana was in love with another man. And how Hana had run away from home, only to have her father bring her back from a women's shelter. During all of this, her mother cried silently, but Aamira didn't know if it was from guilt or from the shock of learning so much.

"Look at me, Mother," Aamira said, grasping her mother's clenched hands. "Tell me what you know. This has to stop. It's wrong, and you know that whatever Father or anyone else in the family has told you, Allah would not approve."

Her mother pulled her hands away from Aamira and climbed out of bed, wiping at her eyes. Then she crossed to her bureau and opened the bottom drawer. From inside, she withdrew a small lacquered box that looked several decades old. She lifted the lid and pulled out a necklace with a pendant at the end of it. The long gold chain was thick and glinted in the lamplight. She turned, holding the necklace up.

"This was given to me on the day after my wedding, and it was then that the significance of it was explained to me," her mother said in a quiet voice. "The pendant has the symbol of an angel, representing my father's tribe, the Jibreel tribe, named after one of Allah's angels. Our tribe was the main branch that started the Mika'il Order. Your father's tribe was accepted in when his grandmother became one of the favorite wives of our tribal sheik."

Aamira stared at the swinging pendant. She'd heard of her mother's tribe, but hadn't connected it with the Mika'il Order. She realized now that Jibreel and Mika'il were both angels of Allah, also called Gabriel and Michael. Her skin felt cold as her mother walked toward her, holding out the necklace.

Aamira took the necklace in her hands and brought the pendant closer to the light. The angel, Mika'il or Jibreel, was holding a sword. This was not the image of an innocent cherub but of an avenger. At the university, they'd done a unit on tribal families and tribal laws. Some of the other students had been able to name the ancient tribes they'd descended from. When Aamira told a couple of people the name of her mother's tribe, one of them had looked surprised, but she'd thought nothing of it.

Until now.

"Tell me about the Mika'il Order," Aamira said.

Her mother dropped her gaze. "It's hard to explain to someone who's on the outside. These things are not explained to unmarried women."

"I'm your daughter, and my aunt was wrongfully killed."

Her mother's face flamed red.

"Don't deny it," Aamira said. "I know the truth. I've spoken with Naser Ali."

Her mother's eyes widened. "He was the cause of all of it," she said in a fierce voice. "Hana was warned many times, and so was Naser."

"So you just killed Hana? Took another person's life for not agreeing to marry a person not of her choice?"

"The purity of the bloodline of the Mika'il Order is more important than one person's lusts," her mother said in a slow voice, her eyes a hard, glittering black. "Naser wasn't descended from an acceptable tribe. By marrying him, Hana would have spoiled the purity of her ancestry. But more importantly, as a member of our family, it was not acceptable to go against her father's wishes. A daughter needs to respect her parents, the ones who gave her life, and the ones who have cared and provided for her."

Aamira felt sick to hear her mother's fanaticism, even though she could have guessed. When she was able to form a coherent sentence, she said, "How many women have died this way in our family?"

"Been punished because of their disobedience?" her mother said.

"How many?" Aamira held her breath, waiting for the answer.

"I only know of three," her mother said, "but there have been many throughout the generations. You would think that each generation would grow stronger and more obedient. But it seems that there are always those who have to be taught a lesson, those who are too stubborn to learn in this life and must depart for the next in order to learn a higher lesson."

Aamira set the pendant and its avenging angel on the bedside table, glad to have it out of her hand. Her mother was no better than the men in the family who had committed horrible crimes. "Is stealing artwork from museums part of the Mika'il Order's moral code as well? How does the Jibreel tribe justify that, Mother?"

Her mother didn't even blink. "Those pieces of art belong to our tribe, to our people. They are rightfully ours."

Aamira rose from the bed and walked to the door. "Goodbye, Mother," she whispered, then turned away. Her final image of her mother was of the dark-haired, petite woman staring after her with a confused look on her face. It was as if her mother had been programmed to believe everything about the Mika'il Order. She didn't question anything. She didn't feel any guilt over her knowledge of Hana's death. Like everyone else, she had covered up Hana's death.

Back in her room, Aamira texted Chad. *I just spoke to my mother, and she confessed to knowing about what happened to Hana. She's part of the cover-up. She'll tell everything to my father, too, so I'm not safe here any longer.*

Aamira paced her bedroom as she waited for Chad's reply.

Her nerves hummed, and she was sweating. She had to leave. Tonight. Her mother might call her father at any moment. It was a long fifteen minutes before Chad texted back. *Get out of the house for now, and I'll text you details as soon as I can.*

Okay, Aamira wrote.

Her hands shaking, she packed a single bag with only a few necessities. Tears pricked her eyes as she looked around her childhood bedroom before turning off the light. This was probably the last time she'd be in her home—a place that was feeling more foreign to her by the moment. She settled the bag over her shoulder and turned off the light. And then she saw the beam of the headlights flash across her window.

She hurried to the window. Her father's car had just pulled up. Aamira backed away slowly. Had her mother called him already? Or had he just shown up by chance? She quickly arranged her pillows lengthwise beneath her quilt as she had on other occasions.

She moved into the hallway and walked toward the kitchen, then through the washing room until she reached the back door. When the sound of the front door opened, she used that noise to mask her actions.

Aamira closed the door as silently as possible behind her, and she walked into her mother's herb garden. The multiple fragrances rose around her, making her remember the many family meals she'd helped her mother cook, but she couldn't let herself dwell on memories now. She moved deeper into the garden, along the winding path that she'd helped to weed throughout her childhood.

She stopped by the gate and turned back to look at the house. All of the windows were dark, which she thought was odd. Her father hadn't turned on any lights.

She turned back toward the road and watched as a car slowly drove by. She didn't recognize the car, but her heart sped up when the car stopped a few dozen paces down the road from her house, near an empty field. The hair on the back of her neck rose as two men stepped out of the car and turned toward her house and started walking. Fast.

Aamira shrank back into the cover of the trees, knowing that if the men got much closer, they'd be able to see her beneath the moonlight. She crouched down, hoping to stay out of sight. Perhaps the wall separating the garden from the road would provide enough cover. She didn't want to be questioned. But who were these men, and why were they headed this way? Her house was the last one on the block and backed up to a high traffic wall that separated the neighborhood from a busy street.

Her phone buzzed, and she held her breath hoping that the sound hadn't carried into the night air. Hoping that she wouldn't be discovered by the two men. She couldn't risk looking at the text and creating a spot of light. So she waited until she could no longer hear the men's footsteps as they continued past her house, going who knew where.

She exhaled in the stillness and then withdrew her phone and turned it on to see the text. Chad had sent an address that was on the other side of town. *This is a safe location, and they will hide you until we can make transportation arrangements.* Aamira wasn't familiar with the exact neighborhood, but she had no other choice but to trust the information Chad had given her.

She darkened the phone again and tucked it inside her shirt, then stood up, listening carefully. She'd have to walk since she didn't dare spend the small amount of money she had on a taxi and risk one of the drivers knowing her family.

Aamira crossed to the gate and unlocked it from the inside. She wouldn't be able to reach over and relock it, so it would be obvious how she left the house. But she couldn't worry about that now. She pulled open the gate, wincing as it gave off a light screech. She slipped through the narrow opening that she allowed for herself, then pulled the gate shut, wincing a second time as it squeaked again.

She almost wished there were no streetlights so that she could travel in complete darkness. As it was, she decided to skirt the brightest spots on the pavement and hoped that no cars would stop to find out why a woman was walking through the neighborhood alone at night. She turned away from the gate, and that's when she felt a heavy hand land on her shoulder.

CHAPTER TWENTY

JORDAN DESERT

The smell of acrid cigarette smoke startled Omar out of his slumber. He'd fallen asleep since there was nothing else to do but wait and stare at the walls and pray that the cockroaches scuttling about didn't start climbing onto the cot. His mouth was dry, his head hurt, his stomach felt hollow, and a cigarette would be very welcome right now. Might help with the headache.

Omar heard voices through the thin walls. At least they hadn't tied him up again, though they'd made it clear they were ready with their stun guns and rifles at any moment. The coffee had given him a temporary boost, but now he felt weak with hunger. When he heard one of the male voices say "Taheer's daughter," all thoughts of hunger fled.

He climbed off the cot, careful not to make any noise. He listened at the door. The conversation in Arabic sounded as if the person speaking was on the phone. "Yes, I understand. We'll make sure there is no media surrounding the execution. Taheer's daughter will only serve as a private example to the Mika'il Order."

Omar tensed at the words. Aamira was in grave trouble.

"The camera crew will be carefully selected," the man said. From the voice, Omar guessed it was Gold Watch. "I'll film it myself if I have to. But then I need to get rid of Mr. Zagouri first."

Ah. Mr. Zagouri sounded so professional.

Another pause, then Gold Watch said, "All of the calls have

been made, and we're watching the news feeds to confirm that our orders were taken."

Someone actually laughed. Was it Gold Watch? It didn't sound pleasant.

When Gold Watch started speaking again, Omar knew he couldn't stick around and wait to be rescued. Gold Watch and whoever he was speaking to were planning an honor killing.

Omar turned from the door and looked for anything he could use for a weapon. The only object of substance was the cot's metal frame. Breaking it down would make noise, so he'd have to be quick. And it was best to do it while Gold Watch was focused on his phone conversation. He didn't need to try the door knob to know it had been locked. He'd have to worry about that later.

Omar picked up the cot and turned it upside down. The hardware holding the frame together looked relatively simple, and instead of smashing anything, he used the edge of his shirt as a grip and twisted all the nuts off the bolts. With the frame in pieces, he picked up one of the shorter metal rods. Perfect. And he hadn't made any sound.

He eyed the high window and knew he wouldn't fit through it even if he could somehow hoist himself up there. Omar wasn't tall, but his broad shoulders would be a problem. And since he didn't have the time to dig a tunnel through the wall, his only choice was to get through the door. He tried the knob. Yep, it was locked.

There were at least four men on the other side, unless someone else had shown up unbeknownst to Omar. Four against one weren't the worst odds, and Omar did have a weapon. But he needed some sort of distraction. He looked around the room again. The dismantled cot, the thick cement walls, the cot bed made out of rough canvas stiff with age, the dust.

Gold Watch's voice continued to drum from the other side of the door, accompanied by another waft of cigarette smoke. A chain-smoker was in their midst, or two of them were puffing away. Omar closed his eyes, imagining the white cigarette on the other side, burning down smaller and smaller.

He needed chaos and confusion. If only he had a lighter. He picked up the discarded cot canvas and moved to the far corner of the room, where he scraped the metal against the cement wall, hoping for a spark, for anything that might be strong enough to light the aged canvas on fire. He had to be quick. The men would hear the scraping.

Last year, he'd been abducted in Yemen by a group of tribesmen. He'd escaped then, and he intended to escape now. With the metal rod gripped in his hand, he hurried to the door, ready to pound on it and shout "Fire!" Sometimes saying it was just as effective as the real thing.

The door burst open as he reached it. "Get him out of here!" Gold Watch shouted. And that's when Omar heard the helicopter.

CHAPTER TWENTY-ONE

ANCIENT KARAK

Morning came too swiftly, and if Eleanor had possessed the powers of nature, she would have delayed the arrival of the sun as long as possible. Dressing for her private meeting with Prince Azzo, she felt Miriam's silent questions rising, one after the other. She was grateful for Miriam's silence. This morning, of all mornings, Eleanor did not want to explain herself.

She'd made a decision. One that would change the course of her life forever.

Once she was dressed and her hair coiffed, Eleanor gazed at her reflection. She saw a petite woman, fine-boned, blue-eyed, and pale-skinned, looking back at her. Satisfied, she turned and crossed the floor of her chambers, then walked through the door that Miriam held open.

Walking down the stairs and through the corridors until she reached a private garden where she'd agreed to meet Azzo felt like some sort of a farewell march to the castle. The castle walls had provided security, but that would no longer be the case.

Azzo was already in the garden when Eleanor stepped outside. He turned to greet her, his dark brown hair gleaming beneath the warm sun. He smiled, and Eleanor felt a well of sadness open up inside her, its depths seemingly bottomless.

"Eleanor," Azzo said, her name a caress on his lips.

She smiled, but it was not a true one. Perhaps one day Azzo

would know the difference between her smiles. "Good morning, sir," she said.

"I trust you slept well despite all of the celebrations into the night?" he said. "You left the banquet early."

Was that suspicion in his tone? "The day was long for me also, and I wanted to be refreshed for our meeting."

Another smile from Azzo, and then he took her hand and led her to a garden bench. They sat together beneath the pomegranate trees and while the birds chattered and the bees droned, Azzo regaled Eleanor about his childhood in northern Italy, his upbringing, his conquests at war, his current lands and holdings.

She widened her eyes at the appropriate moments and smiled at others. Once she even laughed. So by the time he knelt before her on the stone walkway, she'd convinced him that she would be an eager wife.

"It would be my honor to ask for your hand in marriage, dear Eleanor," Azzo said, looking up at her with those light brown eyes.

She held his gaze with the barest of hesitations, and then said, "I would be honored to be your wife, Azzo. Yes, I'll marry you."

He was on his feet in an instant, pulling her up with him, and crushing her into his embrace. His mouth found hers and moved against her lips, hot and demanding. Taking her breath away, but not exactly in the way she'd imagined being kissed. This man would be her husband, and she would have to be satisfied with that. The passion was all from his side, but eventually, she might learn to care for him.

He drew back, his face flushed, his eyes on hers. "We will marry Friday and then travel back to my home."

Friday was only a few days away. "We have to speak with my parents first," she said.

Azzo's smile was back. "I don't see why there'd be any objections," he said. "Times are volatile, and the sooner I have you settled on my estate, the better." He moved closer, leaning down and whispering in her ear, "Besides, I can't wait to make you my wife in all things."

Eleanor felt herself blushing, but not in the way that she blushed around Jed. Azzo's eyes were hungry, demanding, and she wasn't sure about sharing the wedding bed with him. She supposed that was why so much wine was drunk at weddings.

He tried to kiss her again, but she pulled away.

"We are expected at the morning meal," she said, "and we can announce our happy news."

He seemed pacified by that, and she disentangled her dry hands from his moist ones. Eleanor bade him farewell, and walked toward Miriam, who waited by the castle entrance. By the time she reached Miriam, Eleanor was shaking. "I don't know if I can do this," she whispered.

They entered the castle and turned down the corridor leading to the morning room where the meal would be laid out.

"You've made your decision," Miriam said. "You now need to live with it."

"I know," Eleanor breathed. She blinked back the tears forming in her eyes. There was no time for hysterics now. She'd made the right decision, the only sane decision. Weeks or months from now, she'd wake up one morning and know she'd chosen wisely. It was getting through this week, and the months to come, that would be difficult.

She lifted her chin as she stepped into the morning room, leaving Miriam in the corridor.

Her mother sat at the table, picking at her food. Eleanor was surprised by the swollen redness of her mother's eyes. "What is it, Mother?"

Stephanie brought a hand to her heart. "Raynald is calling together all his soldiers. We are marching to battle."

Eleanor felt cold and hot rush through her at the same moment. Jed's warnings of the night before came to mind. "How many soldiers?"

"Thousands," her mother said. "Only a few hundred will be left behind to protect Karak."

Both women knew what that meant. If Raynald left the castle vulnerable, any Muslim tribe passing through might take advantage of its weakened defenses.

"Word has returned to Saladin about Raynald's refusal to sign a truce," Stephanie said, spreading her hands. "A messenger arrived early this morning. King Guy of Jerusalem claims his position has been made precarious because of Raynald's rejection. Jerusalem is fully surrounded by Muslim states, and now King Guy is furious with us. Saladin amassed forces at the southern edge of the Sea of Galilee with thousands of soldiers. Two days ago, Saladin crossed the Jordan at Sennabra. Half of his army is at Kafr Sebt. And his other soldiers have taken Tiberias."

Eleanor stared at her mother. Raymond of Tripoli lived in the castle at Tiberias with his wife, the Countess Eschiva. Raymond was a nephew to King Guy through marriage. "What about the countess?"

"She is holding out, and King Guy has called a council to decide what to do," her mother said. "But Raynald wants to start his march to join up with Guy. Raynald is determined to win back Tiberias."

Jed's description of an impending battle seemed modest compared to what Eleanor's mother was telling her. She sank into a chair on the other side of the table.

Her mother continued, "We are not safe here, just as the countess is not safe. We'll be traveling with the army. Raynald will assign us our own guard, and just before we reach Tiberias, we'll split off and travel to the sea, then take a ship to Italy with Prince Azzo. I assume he has proposed by now?"

Eleanor couldn't have been more astounded by her mother's quick change of subject. "Yes, and I have said yes. He wants to marry Friday."

"Yes, that is what we expected. The marriage will need to take place in the prince's country now. There will be no time before we leave. And we cannot send you off with him from here with our enemies gathering up their armies," her mother said. "The servants are packing now, and the militia are preparing the horses. Your brother and stepfather have already issued commands. We leave tonight beneath the light of the moon."

"Already?" Eleanor said, mostly to herself. Even Friday had seemed soon, and now that timeline had been shortened once again.

Her mother rose to her feet, her height making her appear elegant and regal. "Prepare your things. Your stepfather is meeting King Guy and Raymond of Tripoli to drive out Saladin and take back Tiberias. Depending on the outcome of this war, we may never return to Karak."

Eleanor shuddered at Stephanie's words. And as she left the morning room, without eating anything, she had the feeling she'd made more than one mistake.

Over the next few hours, getting everything ready left Eleanor little opportunity to dwell on how her life was changing. By the time the wagons and chariots and pack horses were ready, the main body of the army had already started their march. They'd travel through the night to avoid the fierce heat of the Arabian sun.

Eleanor didn't see Azzo among the travelers, but her mother told her that he was close to the front, next to Raynald. It was for the best, Eleanor decided, since her emotions swirled about her like a windstorm. The only anchor she had now was the quiet steadiness of Miriam. Eleanor's mother stayed busy overseeing the loading of the bundles and wooden chests. And as the moon rose high in the sky and Eleanor looked back at the canal, possibly for the last time in her life, an overwhelming swell of sadness enveloped her.

The canal flowing beneath the moon and the stars reminded her of Jed. She knew she missed him, but she couldn't allow herself to yearn for him. He was likely leagues ahead of Raynald's army, hurrying to join Saladin's warriors. How had this all happened? How had she come to meet a man such as Jed al Ayubi, a bitter enemy who'd turned out to be a friend? And now, how could she only think of his well-being and what this war might do to his tribe?

The caravan slowly started to move forward, with a squad of fifty soldiers following behind as a protective escort. The desert wind was cool, and the cloud cover obscured the moon. Eleanor pulled her cloak around her as she sat inside the litter with Miriam. Her handmaiden had been quiet, and Eleanor was grateful for that, but now she wanted someone's opinion on all that was happening.

"Do you think we'll be safe?" Eleanor asked. If an enemy got through the soldiers, she had no way to defend herself. She might be a master in languages, but she was no female soldier. She had more than one reason to ask Miriam in private what she thought. If the handmaiden truly had prophetic powers like the fabled djinns, perhaps she would know something.

But when Miriam lifted her gaze, Eleanor immediately knew that what she was about to tell her was not good news.

"Raynald will fall," Miriam said in a whisper, so soft that Eleanor had to lean forward to catch the words.

A shiver climbed up Eleanor's back. "How? What happens?" She couldn't quite believe that she was asking someone to forecast the future. "What about my brother, Humphrey?"

"He will live." Miriam shook her head. "I do not know any more details, and if I did, I could not disclose them. It's very dangerous to try to change the future."

Eleanor's pulse drummed. "Can you tell me anything more? When will Raynald fall?"

"Soon," Miriam said. "That is all I can say."

Panic gripped Eleanor. Here she was, in an enclosed litter, traveling toward a battle that even her mother was afraid of. They would break off the main army before Tiberias, but until then, anything could happen. Eleanor opened the curtain of the litter and tied it back to let in the night air. Although it was getting cold, she'd rather see what was going on. The clouds had moved, and now the moonlight spilled across the desert floor, illuminating man and beast alike.

Her mother's litter was several paces ahead of Eleanor's. She still hadn't seen Azzo since before their departure, but then suddenly she saw a man on a horse coming toward her, moving in the opposite direction of the caravan. It was Azzo. As he rode nearer, his eyes scanned the travelers until he finally picked out her litter.

He approached, a smile on his face. "You are well, I see," he said. He commanded the young men who were carrying the litter to stop. The rocking motion halted, and Eleanor sat up straight.

"You know the plans, right?" he asked.

"I do." Eleanor knew she should be pleased by the prince's attention, but his eyes were wild, his voice unsteady.

"We need to discuss them further," he said, and looked over at Miriam who sat across from Eleanor in the litter. "We'll need privacy."

Miriam climbed out of the litter without a word, and Azzo climbed in, then commanded the carriers to start moving again. Just before Azzo untied the curtains and let them fall into place, Eleanor saw Miriam walking alongside some other servants.

"Eleanor," Azzo said, in a soft voice. "We should take our vows right now, just between you and me."

"Our marriage vows?" Eleanor said. "Have you spoken to my parents?"

"They will understand our need for urgency," Azzo said. "We don't know what will happen in the next day, or the next few hours. We could encounter danger before we reach your departure point, and I will have to fight."

Eleanor narrowed her eyes. Azzo didn't seem particularly afraid of engaging in battle soon, but she couldn't miss the strange look in his eyes. He was gazing at her like she was some sort of delicious meal after a long day of labor.

"We'll pledge our vows to each other now, and then

consummate our love," Azzo said, taking her hand and drawing it toward him. He kissed the top of her hand, then moved his lips to the inside of her wrist.

Consummate? Here, in the litter? Without a proper wedding? Eleanor pulled her hand away, and fire leapt into Azzo's eyes. "You are mistaken about my parents," she said. "I am not a servant girl, and I will not be treated in such a manner." Her pulse raced at her own boldness, but this man to whom she was pledged had lost his senses.

Then she realized that he really was afraid for his life. The fire in his eyes concealed his true emotions—fear.

She made a motion to lift the curtain and call the carriers to stop again, but Azzo grabbed her wrist tightly. "Tomorrow I may die," he said in a harsh whisper. "Tonight may be the only time I can leave a legacy with my name. As my wife, you'll be taken care of through my wealth, and if you carry my child, my name will live beyond my grave."

Sweat beaded on his forehead, and he leaned forward, gripping her knee.

"If God could be so cruel as to separate us days before our wedding, then we must live with God's will." She shoved Azzo away and lifted the curtain. "Stop the litter," she called out in a shaky voice.

Azzo tugged her back against him, and just as she was about to scream, another cry went up. Both Eleanor and Azzo froze.

"They're coming!" someone shouted. "Prepare yourselves! Step into your formation."

Azzo scrambled forward and pushed back the curtains. Over his shoulder, Eleanor could see the guards on their horses forming a protective circle around the part of the caravan that contained the women and servants.

Beneath the light of the moon and tapestry of stars, the forms of galloping horses topped by warriors streamed down the nearby hills. As the thundering cavalry neared, the raised swords and bows became visible. Fear shot straight to Eleanor's gut. "Saladin's men," she whispered. "*Jed.*"

"Do you know those warriors?" Azzo asked.

But Eleanor didn't take the time to explain. She pushed past Azzo and jumped out of the litter, falling to the ground on her hands and knees. She quickly recovered and ran toward her mother's litter, which had already stopped.

Miriam was suddenly at her side, and the two women grasped hands. "It's them," Miriam said. "Saladin's warriors."

"Yes," Eleanor said. "We must warn Mother."

Miriam tugged on Eleanor's hand. "Look at me," she said. "He's coming for you."

Eleanor stopped dead. "What do you mean?"

Miriam seemed to look right through Eleanor. "Jed's coming to send you a message."

Panic jolted Eleanor to her very bones. "How can that be? I . . ." She followed the direction that Miriam was pointing. There, on the ridge of the nearest hill, stood a horse with a man atop it. He was holding a banner of sorts, and even at a distance, Eleanor knew it bore the likeness of an Arabian horse.

"I don't understand," she finally said.

"See where the warriors are heading?"

Eleanor watched the horses approach the middle of the procession. Not the rear where the women traveled, or the front, where Raynald and the captains rode.

"He's scattering everyone, creating havoc," Miriam said. "If Jed wanted to engage in battle, they would have already destroyed us with arrows. They are just making noise right now."

And she was right. As Eleanor watched, the warriors circled the caravan, riding hard and fast, not attacking.

"It's a warning," Miriam said. "They are telling us that if we don't turn back, there is much worse to come. Raynald will see it as an antagonism, though, not as a warning."

Eleanor was mesmerized by the scene. Now Raynald's

archers started to send volleys of arrows at the Muslim fighters, but none of them hit their moving targets. Saladin's warriors screamed their battle cries, but stayed just out of range of Raynald's army. It was a strange sort of desert game.

Her gaze returned to the lone man on the ridge. He didn't move, and Eleanor wondered what he saw. Could he see the litters that carried her and her mother? Did he know that she'd been thinking of him nonstop since their last meeting at the canal?

And then it was over, almost as soon as it started. The warriors turned away from the caravan, regrouping and riding as a great mass back up the ridge. Their battle cries faded, and the thundering of their horses' hooves turned to a faint rumbling. The warriors rode past the still figure of Jed.

Eleanor couldn't tear her gaze away from him, even as she heard her mother call out orders to the surrounding soldiers to tighten their ranks. It was as if Eleanor didn't hear any of the melee about her, fixated entirely on one man. Jed had come to warn them. Eleanor knew her stepfather would not slow his pursuit. Death lay ahead for many of them. Eleanor and her mother and Azzo would be long gone before Raynald entered the battle. So why did Eleanor feel the rising panic that if she didn't act now, she'd regret it for the rest of her life?

Miriam stood silently beside her, also watching Jed.

Eleanor turned to her handmaiden as horses and soldiers jostled all around them, the two women quite forgotten as new traveling formations were called out.

"The crusaders will be defeated, won't they?" Eleanor whispered.

Miriam shook her head. "Even I could not predict that."

But Eleanor felt it in her bones. She was marching toward her death, and at the same time marching away from a man she might never see again.

"Miriam," Eleanor said, as she fumbled to find her handmaiden's hand. "I've changed my mind."

CHAPTER TWENTY-TWO

MODERN-DAY AL KARAK

Aamira was too shocked to scream. The hand dug deep into her shoulder, and something was slipped over her head, making everything go black. "Don't make a sound," a voice said, and Aamira sagged against the man behind her.

The voice belonged to her brother, Ehan.

What was he doing home, and why had he put a bag over her head? She tried to twist out of his grasp, but he was a strong man now, no longer the skinny boy of his youth.

"Keep moving," he said, propelling her forward.

She nearly stumbled as she figured out how to walk without being able to see anything. Her breathing became rapid. The dark didn't bother her so much as the cloth touching her nose and mouth. She wondered if her breath would be cut off soon. If Ehan was here, who was the other man?

They reached the street, with Aamira noting the change in the terrain beneath her feet.

Where was Ehan taking her? She didn't want to reach for her phone, to give away the fact that she had one.

She released her breath as Ehan steered her to a stop. She heard a car door open, and was forced into what she assumed was the back seat of the car she'd seen earlier. So the car had been for her, and the men coming out of it had instructions to bring her with them.

She had to find a way to talk him out of doing this. "Ehan," she said after the car door shut.

"I said *shut up*," he growled.

Aamira stiffened at the menacing tone of his voice. She wanted to pull the bag off her head and confront her brother. He pulled her hands together and wrapped something around her wrists.

"What are you—?" She started, and something hard drove into the side of her face.

Aamira gasped and hunched forward, bringing her tied hands up to her covered face. Her brother had just hit her. A sob strangled her throat. The car started to move, and Aamira was rocked back with the motion. She could see nothing, no shapes, no colors, and her entire body was trembling.

She tried to twist her hands out of their bindings, but then Ehan hissed a warning.

No, she pleaded silently. *Don't let this be happening.* She hoped this was a terrible dream, that she'd wake up soon and find she was still in her bedroom. But the car turned, and she swayed with the movement, with nothing to hang onto. The car turned again, then picked up more speed. They were on a main road now.

The men in the car didn't speak, and the silence brought out subtle sounds that she probably wouldn't have noticed if she'd been able to see. The driver had a nasally rhythm to his breathing, as if he had allergies or a cold and had to breathe through his mouth.

Her brother was fidgeting, and she heard some soft clicks. She stiffened with fear. Did he have a gun? She wanted to ask him questions and wanted him to tell her he was taking her to safety. That he wasn't a criminal, and that she would be fine in his care.

But as the car gathered speed and barreled down an unseen road, she knew that her brother wasn't taking her any place safe.

When the car came to a stop, she was surprised they'd arrived so soon. She'd expected hours of driving, perhaps even crossing the Jordanian border to get her far away from anyone who might know the Sayid family.

Ehan shifted on the seat next to her, sliding away and opening the door. Then he grabbed her upper arm and half-dragged her out of the car. The motion made her bump her knee hard against the car door. She cried out, but Ehan only tightened his grip. And then they were walking again, swiftly, over dirt and gravel. Aamira stumbled more than once, and if it wasn't for Ehan's iron grip, she would have fallen. This did not bode well, and she couldn't help but think of Hana.

Where they stopped, the air was cooler and the wind stronger. Aamira sensed they weren't in the main part of town any longer, but someplace out in the open.

Then they were inside a building, by the feel of the smoother surface beneath her feet. The scents changed again, to dry and musty, mixed with a chemical odor she couldn't identify.

The ground had changed from dirt and rocks to hard cement, and then it changed again to carpet, probably industrial. The lights must have been bright inside because Aamira could see a filmy gray, although she still couldn't make out any defining shapes.

"Sit here," Ehan commanded. He tugged her down until she came in contact with a hard chair. Then he used something that felt like a belt or a thick strap and wrapped it around her waist, then tied her to the chair.

She bit back a cry, not wanting to make a noise and be hit again. She felt sick to her core. How could this be happening? To her? Was this how her life was going to end?

And then Ehan pulled the bag from her head, and she didn't know if it was better to be blind or to see. She was in a warehouse of some sort, one she didn't recognize. A desk sat in one corner, and a couple of crates in another. The lighting overhead was spotty fluorescent tubes, flickering at random.

Ehan leaned over, his eyes intent on her. "Don't move and don't make a sound," he ground out.

It had been months since she'd seen her brother, and he'd changed, yet hadn't changed. His mustache was thicker and darker, and his eyes seemed to have new lines on the edges as if he'd aged a few years instead of a few months. She looked for the Ehan who was her friend, but she only saw a man she didn't know. A man whose face was dark with anger and whose eyes were filled with hatred.

She felt as if she'd been slapped again. Her mouth moved, involuntarily, but no words came. It was as if she couldn't formulate a question because she couldn't comprehend how she'd incited her brother's wrath. The expression on his face told her this was no game.

Her gaze slid to the other man in the room, the one who'd driven the car. She recognized him as a friend of her father's, which only frightened her more. She wasn't sure of his name, and she didn't like the way he was leaning against the wall, watching her with a sneer on his face.

Her brother straightened, apparently satisfied that she'd keep quiet, and crossed the room to speak with the other man. They started talking in low voices while they consulted Ehan's phone.

Desperation pulsed through Aamira, and she knew she couldn't stay in this place any longer. She didn't know what her brother thought he was doing, but she had never been so scared in her life, and all her instincts told her to flee.

She surveyed the room and tried to locate the exits, any windows, any place she could run and hide. First she'd have to get free, but it would take a distraction to allow escape. Propped up against the wall in front of her were several paintings. Some were wrapped in thick cloths, others were uncovered, their frames glinting in the dim light.

Aamira nearly gasped when she recognized one of the Passion paintings, perhaps the original. Which meant that it had been stolen from one of the museums Omar had told her about. This painting was familiar, yet new. Now that Aamira had heard

Omar's words about her family, she looked differently at the image of the woman—Nadia—flanked by two men. In the scene of the painting, Nadia was depicted in the middle of a desert, wearing a deep red tunic, the wind tugging at her clothing. Two men were also in the painting. One of them stood a fair distance behind Nadia. The other man was kneeling, closer to Nadia, but turned away from her.

A chill spread through Aamira. Nadia's hands were outstretched, one toward each man, although it was clear that the man kneeling closer to her was the only one she saw, as her head was turned in his direction and her eyes on him.

Aamira gazed at the three people in the composition. The woman in the painting was being pulled in many directions, as her outstretched hands indicated. Her shapely body was outlined by the clothing she wore, and it was clear that the wind was doing the rest of the work, as it also lifted her hair from her shoulders. Aamira studied the painting carefully, trying to make out the faces of the men. But their features were nothing remarkable, although distinctly Middle Eastern.

Who were these two men? Aamira remembered Omar's theory that Nadia had married again and bore many children. Would it make sense that she still thought of her first husband, even though he'd abducted her? Or had she loved him? Was the story that Aamira had originally been told wrong?

Aamira sensed that the man farthest from Nadia represented much more than a person whom Nadia might have fallen in love with. The painting suggested that he represented a life that was out of reach, that was too far to connect with, and that was part of her past. But the second man, the one she was looking at, was the one of her future. What did he represent?

The chill spread across Aamira's limbs, across her entire body, and she felt at one with the woman in the painting. Many legends surrounded Nadia, and Aamira didn't know for herself what had truly happened. Had she been killed or taken her own life like some of the stories said? Had she escaped and lived under another name, found happiness? Raised a brood of children?

Whatever happened to Nadia, Aamira knew without a doubt that Nadia had felt betrayal, fear, and sorrow at the deepest level. It was history being repeated. Terrible history.

She looked at Ehan again. Did he not see the irony of his sister tied to a chair in this large warehouse, with the painting of their abducted ancestor facing her?

Her brother looked her way, sharp and knowing. She didn't want to guess what he was thinking, but she couldn't stop herself from feeling the adrenaline shoot through her. She wanted to break the ties that held her in place and fight her way out of this building. Do whatever it took, harm anyone who stood in her way, and run outside, taste freedom. Get away from here.

Ehan looked back at his phone, and the second man spoke to him in a low voice. She couldn't hear their words. Leaning forward slowly, she tested the strength of the bands. They held fast, but if she had time, and if the men weren't paying attention, she knew she'd figure out how to free herself.

She turned her head, looking for anything that might help her. Then she froze at what she saw on a table behind and to her left. Several weapons were laid out. A couple of rifles, two handguns, and a heavy axe, lined up neatly. Her body went cold all over as perspiration broke out on her skin. She could no longer stop the panic building inside her, and she started to gasp for air.

Ehan crossed to her and gripped both of her shoulders, his strong fingers digging into her flesh and creating painful bruises. "Stop, Aamira," he said. "Don't make a sound and don't move."

It was then she saw a flicker of something other than hardness and anger in his eyes—it was as if he were warning her. Was he trying to tell her he'd find a way out of this? Would he save her in the end?

The second man walked toward them. "There's a problem."

Ehan released Aamira and straightened. "What is it?" he asked in a tight voice.

“The video camera has been damaged, so they’re trying to find another one,” the man said.

Aamira didn’t know what was so important about a video camera, but her skin began to crawl. She looked at the man, and he gave her a half sneer.

“Did you tell her what’s going to happen to her?” the man said.

Ehan paled and took a step away from Aamira. “Not until the others are here.”

The sound of an engine sounded outside, and the second man said, “I’ll go check it out.”

When he was gone, Aamira turned to her brother. “What’s going on, Ehan?”

He glared at her and shook his head.

Aamira pulled at her bands, twisting against them as hard as she could. But they wouldn’t break.

Ehan’s eyes were on the door that the other man had exited through.

She wanted to scream at him and make him answer, but she also didn’t want to be backhanded again. The answer was obvious anyway. Why else would her brother abduct her and bring her to this place? “Are you going to execute your own sister?” she asked in a trembling voice. “Is this what type of person you’ve become?”

Ehan stepped toward her, fire in his eyes. He gripped the upper part of her neck with one hand, choking off her windpipe. But Aamira continued to whisper, “You’re better than they are, Ehan. You don’t have to prove yourself in this way—to kill a defenseless woman? Is that what will make you a respected man?”

“Shut up,” he growled. He released her neck, but grasped her arm. His eyes flitted from her to the door again. The second man was still outside, and taking his time.

“Do I deserve death for having a boyfriend?” she asked. He tightened his grip, until a hot, burning pain started to numb her arm. “Is that how little my life is worth? How little I mean to you as a sister?”

Ehan's eyes were back on her, his grip bruising. "You don't know what you're saying," he said. "You're to blame for this! For all of this!"

"Let me go, Ehan." Aamira was pleading now. "Untie me, and I'll disappear. You won't have to see me again. You won't have to be shamed by a sister like me."

He looked at her then, really looked at her. "I was never ashamed of you." Then his eyes went hard again. "If you understood anything, you would shut up."

"I *have* shut up for my entire life," Aamira said. "And look at me now. Look at you. It's time I spoke up, even if it's too late for me, maybe it's not too late for *you* to change."

At last, Ehan released her arm. He stepped back as the door opened.

Needles of pain shot through her arm, and the muscles throbbed where he'd held her. Footsteps sounded behind her, and she knew more than one person had entered the warehouse.

Aamira had no idea what the next moments might bring. So she spoke fast. "They know all about you and all about Father," she told Ehan. "You're on every policeman's radar, and every undercover agent has your profile. They know you by all of your alias names."

His eyes locked onto Aamira's despite the approaching people.

"You might get away with killing me, my brother," Aamira said in a voice stronger than she thought possible. "But you will never be safe on earth, and you will burn in eternal hell."

Before Ehan could answer or try to choke her again, a man's voice spoke behind her. "Oh, good, she's talkative. We'll start recording soon, since we want her alert."

Aamira didn't have to turn her head to see who was speaking because within moments he stood directly in front of her. He wore traditional, and expensive, robes. His thick beard was peppered with white and his mustache impeccably groomed. He was a heavyset man, but moved with grace, as if he were half the size of his bulk.

"I am Yamil," the man said. His deep brown eyes pierced her.

Aamira wondered what his penetrating gaze saw. Was it a tired young woman with bruises on her face, neck, and arms?

"Did your brother explain to you what's happening?" Yamil asked.

She opened her mouth to reply, but no words came. She shook her head.

Yamil's smile was broad. "Ah, it will be my pleasure then." He looked over at Ehan. "Thank you for your service, I will take it from here."

Aamira recognized the look of annoyance on Ehan's face, although he covered it quickly. It seemed Ehan listened to this man, perhaps worked for him as well. She didn't know Yamil. He crouched in front of her at eye level, his robe billowing about him. "Four witnesses are all we needed to obtain an order for your punishment." He smiled again. "The fourth one signed earlier tonight, and so we are prepared to proceed."

"Four witnesses to what?" Aamira asked, finding her voice at last.

"To your infidelity," Yamil said. "In the Jibreel tribe, we take the morality of our members very seriously. Our bodies and actions should always be sacred, and when a person goes outside the approved tribe, the bloodline becomes tainted. We won't risk anything that compromises our alliance with the Mika'il Order."

Aamira fought to breathe evenly. "I have been unfaithful to no one. I have not started any bloodline."

Yamil's eyebrow lifted. "Even thoughts can taint a bloodline. We know you have been in a relationship with a man in London. We have more than enough evidence, and we have witnesses who have testified against you."

"My parents can disown me; they can send me away," Aamira said, desperation in her voice.

"It's not that simple," Yamil said. "If one person gets away with disgracing the tribe, then others will follow. We can't allow any infraction. You will be an example to the rest of the tribe."

Aamira felt as if the breath had been knocked out of her. Even though Ehan was on the other side of the room, she could feel him listening and watching. "How?" she whispered.

"You will confess your guilt on camera," Yamil said. "And then your execution will also be recorded and used as a lesson for others in the tribe who might be wickedly tempted as you have been."

Aamira didn't know if she was really hearing this. It was a terrible dream. But her brother, the young man she'd grown up with, wasn't denying it. She'd been abducted from the garden of her home. And there was a table full of weapons a few meters away.

"What does my family get out of this?" she asked.

Yamil looked startled for a moment, so Aamira pressed on. "Is this like a suicide bomber agreement? My family will be praised and heralded as heroes once they are rid of me? Will they receive money?"

"No," Yamil said, his thick brows drawing toward each other. "No one wants this. You've made your choice, and this is simply the consequence. We all need reminders from time to time about how to make good choices. Your parents view this as a tragedy, but it's a necessary one to restore our tribe's honor and keep our bloodline pure."

"My parents have agreed to my execution?" Aamira said, hardly believing she was speaking these words aloud.

Yamil's expression took on a gentleness one might see in a kind doctor. "Your father put in the order."

CHAPTER TWENTY-THREE

JORDAN DESERT

Gold Watch dove toward Omar before he could react to the arrival of the helicopter outside. Omar didn't know if those flying the helicopter were friend or foe, but Omar's first priority was to elude Gold Watch's stun gun. He jumped over the man, who seemed intent on tackling him, and was set to run out the door, but then bullets ripped through the windows of the hideout. Omar dropped to the ground, covering his head with his hands as he shimmied toward the long table holding the computers. Two other men were already under the table by the time Omar reached it. Gold Watch had elected to make his way into the smaller room that Omar had just left.

The firing bullets stopped almost as soon as they began, and the silence deafening in the aftermath.

Although Omar was dizzy and slightly nauseous, he scrambled for the stun gun that Gold Watch had dropped. Unibrow made a move for it too, but Omar was able to strike him viciously with the metal rod from the cot frame. As Omar's hand closed around the stun gun, he turned toward Unibrow just as the man grabbed his leg. Omar twisted away, aiming the stun gun at Unibrow at the same time. The man writhed as the electrical current pulsed through him, and Omar scrambled out from under the table.

He reached the door and yanked it open. Before he could

make out what was going on in the billowing dust and rotor noise beyond the entrance, someone slammed into his back. Omar pitched forward and tried to break his fall with his hands. His palms scraped dirt and small rocks as he skidded a couple of meters. Omar had no doubt it was Gold Watch who'd shoved him. Omar turned with a groan, unable to see much with all the dust the helicopter had stirred up, and delivered a solid kick to the dark figure looming above him. Gold Watch grunted and staggered backward, dropping his stun gun.

Dirt and other bits stung Omar's skin as he tried to get on his feet before he was attacked again. The helicopter was too close, and its whirling rotors were deafening.

Just as Gold Watch recovered from Omar's kick, Omar reached for the dropped stun gun, but Gold Watch got there first. In what seemed a slow-motion arc, Omar dove for Gold Watch just as Gold Watch lunged forward. The collision was ugly, each of their stun guns shocking the other person. The jolt of fiery electricity swept through Omar, sending him backward and snapping his head against the ground. Omar tried to curse but had lost the power of speech. His hearing still worked, though, and he heard someone shout his name.

That could be good or bad, but the good won out as Omar realized he was being called from the direction of the helicopter. And it was a voice he recognized. "Joseph?" Omar croaked.

He tried to turn, but there was still no feeling in his body. It seemed only his neck worked, and he craned his head to see the approaching man. Through the dust, Omar couldn't see much, but the figure had the shape and presence of Joseph. Omar's limbs started to tingle back to life, and all he could think about was that he needed to attack Gold Watch before the man regained the use of his own limbs.

Omar shoved himself off the ground, gritting his teeth as pain ran through him. He'd definitely need a massage after this, maybe a whole week's worth.

He picked up the stun gun and backed away from the hideout building, keeping his gaze trained on Gold Watch's inert form. It seemed the man wasn't as resilient against electrocution as Omar was. Perhaps Omar had developed special immunities to the pain, if such a thing were possible. It was a good thing Gold Watch hadn't brought out a rifle. But who knew when the other men would come out of the hideout.

"We've been looking for you!" Joseph called out, jogging toward him, emerging from the cloud of dust.

"Took you long enough," Omar said. He checked Gold Watch's position again. The man still wasn't moving.

"We've got to get out of here," Joseph said, his voice rising in panic.

Omar looked up. Joseph's forehead was grimy with dirt and sweat. "I'm coming," Omar said.

He was unsteady, but the distance to the helicopter was short. Just as he started to turn toward the chopper, a spray of bullets erupted around Omar's feet. He didn't need to look back to know they were being pursued. Omar started to run, Joseph along with him, and as they hurled themselves into the helicopter, Omar said, "Who'd you get to co-pilot this thing?"

"Hey, babe," a woman's voice said, over the thundering wash of the helicopter blades.

Omar turned to look into Mia's eyes. He'd never felt so relieved in his life. "Mia?" He dragged his seatbelt across his chest as he crammed himself into the small backseat space. "I guess you got the Skype recordings?"

She flashed him a smile and put on her headphones as Joseph took over the pilot controls and powered the helicopter upward. Several bullets pinged against metal, but they'd already gained enough altitude to escape any lethal damage.

Omar put on headphones too so he could communicate without shouting. "I'd offer to fly this thing, but I need a few minutes of recovery," he said, keeping his gaze on Mia. She wore a simple T-shirt and loose-fitting, khaki pants, and her dark curls were pulled back into a messy ponytail, but she looked like a saving angel.

"It looks like you went down pretty hard," Mia said, turning in her seat. "You all right?"

"I will be. It was only a stun gun."

She shook her head. "Only you would say that. What's the bandage on your leg?"

Omar looked down. "Oh, this? Bullet graze, but it's been cleaned."

"Wow, but okay," Mia said. "We didn't know if we should interrupt you, since it seemed like you were handling things all right by making all those prank calls."

"Yeah, it was a real party in there," Omar said. "I'm going to miss my new friends."

Joseph laughed.

"Where are we anyway?" Omar looked out the window. But just as he spoke, he recognized the terrain. "Jordan?"

"Home sweet home," Mia said.

And she was half right. A couple of years ago, Omar had spent weeks in this area, trying to infiltrate an archaeology ring that was selling artifacts on the black market.

"I won't miss this place," Omar said. "Good thing I was passed out when they carted me here or I would have made them drop me off at the local hotel." He gave a mock shudder. "Still trying to forget the cockroaches."

"I don't think any hotel around here would be cockroach-free," Mia said.

"You're probably right," Omar said, then clapped a hand on Joseph's shoulder. "I'm glad they're insisting that all undercover agents have a helicopter pilot license now. Helps out guys like me when we've been electrocuted."

"Mia told me about your piloting escapades," Joseph said. "And Simon Greif gave me strict orders to keep you out of the pilot's seat."

"I can still fly from another seat," Omar said. "I'm pretty flexible." Mia looked at him again, and he gave her a wink, and she actually blushed through her scowl.

"So what's going on?" Omar asked. "Did any of my phone calls create havoc?"

"Oh, it's all over the news and the Internet, if that's what you're asking," Mia said. "You did your job well, although I did receive a call from Shira Moberg, from the museum in London. The anonymous Skype call had a Jordan prefix number. That was when Joseph and I decided to catch a plane to Amman, hoping it would give us a head start on nailing down your location."

"Shira's a smart lady," Omar mused. "I'm glad she answered her phone."

"She told me about your call on Skype, and that's why I logged in when I did," Mia said. "You'll have to thank her for your rescue."

Omar shifted in his seat and brushed his fingers along Mia's shoulder. "I have a lot of people to thank. I was getting really hungry in there, and you know how that makes me cranky. Their watered-down coffee was an abomination."

Mia cracked a smile as she grabbed a backpack next to her seat. "Eat to your heart's content," she said, handing it over.

By the weight of it, Omar was hopeful there might actually be something good inside. All he found were protein bars and a couple of water bottles. "That's it?" he said, but he ate two of the bars anyway.

"So what's the agenda?" Omar asked Joseph, although he was looking at Mia.

"You're the boss," Joseph said.

"Brown-noser." Omar grinned at Mia. "Let me be more specific. Where's the last known location of Ehan Sayid?"

"We lost him," Joseph said. "But Simon's working on some leads."

"I'll bet he went back home," Omar said.

"How do you know?" Mia said.

“That’s where his sister is,” Omar said. “He sent his thugs to capture me and Joseph, to get us off his trail. Where else would he be hiding? Did Chad give us anything more about Aamira?”

When Joseph and Mia exchanged glances, Omar said, “What’s going on? Tell me now.”

Joseph seemed to hedge, so Mia answered, “We both reached out to Chad before we left to get you. No answer yet, though we haven’t exactly been in cell phone range. But if you think that Ehan went back to his hometown . . .”

Omar didn’t need her to finish the sentence. He couldn’t shake the feeling that Ehan had returned home, probably at the request of his father. And that didn’t bode well for Aamira. Omar tried not to get overheated. This was exactly what he was afraid of. Chad’s involvement with Aamira and the Sayid family leading to tragedy. There were too many honor killings actively going on to dismiss Aamira’s situation. “It looks like we’re going to Karak. At least we’re close.”

Joseph turned to stare at him, but Mia didn’t seem fazed. “You heard me,” Omar told Joseph. “There’s been a change of plans.”

“We’ll take the helicopter to the Dhiban airport,” Mia said. She read off the new coordinates to Joseph, and he banked the chopper toward their new destination. They flew toward a narrow valley that ran between two mountain ranges.

“I didn’t know there was an airport in Dhiban,” Omar said.

“It’s more of a stopover,” Mia answered.

By the time they landed on the sand-drifted runway that was more of a landing strip, Mia’s phone had started buzzing with messages.

“Not good,” Mia said, as Joseph powered down the helicopter.

Omar wasn’t seeing any planes on the tarmac. Only a single cinderblock building. Was the airport closed? *Did* airports ever close? He wasn’t sure what Mia’s texts said, but they might have more than one problem on their hands.

Mia handed Omar her phone instead of explaining. The first message was like a punch in the gut. Chad wrote: *No communication with Aamira for hours. I've tracked her phone to Al Karak. I'm going to find her.*

"When was Chad's text sent? Just now?"

"I don't think so," Mia said. "It just downloaded when we came into range of a cell tower. It could have been sent anytime in the last few hours."

"Damn." Omar started scrolling through the next texts. They were all from Chad, requests that Mia return his calls. To let him know what was going on with his cousin, Omar. To contact him with any advice on his travel plans. "My advice would be for him *not* to go," Omar said. "This situation will be dangerous enough without a lovesick boyfriend panicking on the sidelines."

"Hey," Mia said, her voice sharp enough to capture Omar's full attention. "Give your cousin more credit."

"I can't," Omar said. "My cousin *and* my aunt are both in danger. I can't let my family get mixed up in this."

Mia grabbed his hand and held on. "They're already mixed up in this, and they were before you found out Chad's connection to Aamira. I agree that he needs to stay safe in England, but by those texts it looks like he's already on his way."

Omar scratched at his dirty scalp. What he wouldn't give for a shower, a decent meal, and of course a massage right now. But it looked like they were continuing on to Karak, to somehow save a woman's life and protect his cousin all at the same time. At least, he hoped Aamira was still alive and that they could indeed rescue her. But they couldn't land a helicopter in a small town like Al Karak. That would be like sending out a news broadcast about their arrival. And by the looks of it, Mia was coming too—which had both pros and cons. Pros because she was the smartest woman he knew, and cons because the more serious their relationship grew, the more he hated her line of business.

Omar turned back to the phone and called Chad. It rang four

times then went to an automated voice mail. He hung up and dialed again. Same result.

He looked up at Mia and Joseph. "We need a vehicle."

"Agreed," Mia said, unlatching her seatbelt and popping open the door. Omar followed her out of the helicopter and looked around. The runway was in poor condition, and the flight tower looked abandoned. The setting sun had turned everything orange and gold. Now it seemed they were working against the final hour of daylight.

"How much fuel do we have?" Omar asked Joseph as the man joined them.

"Not much," Joseph admitted. "The detour used up what would have gotten us back to Amman."

"Give it to me in kilometers."

"Two hundred fifty, maybe two seventy-five."

Omar gave him a quick nod. They needed more fuel, and there wasn't a petrol station in sight. Perhaps there were extra gas cans in the airport tower.

He set off toward the cinderblock tower. "I'll be right back," he said over his shoulder. As he neared the building, a rush of foreboding passed through him, strong enough that he slowed his step. He didn't often hesitate going into an abandoned building, but the combination of shattered glass on the ground in front of the door and the stench seeping through the cracks gave him pause.

"What is it?" Mia's voice reached him from where she stood in the helicopter's shade.

"Do you have a gun?" Omar asked.

She jogged over to him, Joseph following close behind. "I don't see what you're . . . oh." She stopped, covering her nose with a hand. "That's putrid."

"Yeah," Omar said. "Gun?"

She handed him a small pistol. Not a powerful thing, but it offered a layer of protection that Omar wished he'd had earlier.

"There's something, or *someone* dead in there, Omar," Mia said. "We should stay out."

"We probably should, but we need more fuel," he said in a slow voice. "And if there's something wrong here we need to report it as well."

Mia grabbed his arm, her eyes full of warning. "We should leave." She tugged Omar with her as she took a step back, then another step.

He held his ground. "I can't leave without checking."

Mia closed her eyes for a moment. Then she released Omar's arm and let her hand drop. "What if there's a trap? Or a bomb rigged?"

Omar glanced over at Joseph. "You in?"

Joseph's face was pale as he swallowed nervously. "Sure, boss."

"Wait here," Omar told Mia.

She didn't say anything, just folded her arms and stared at him, telling him with her expression that he was making a mistake.

But Omar couldn't walk away without investigating—not if there was a crime scene inside the tower that should be reported to local authorities. And if there wasn't anything to be reported, he still hoped to find a couple of gas cans. He strode to the door, gun in hand, and turned the handle. He didn't know if the fact that the door was locked was a good sign or bad sign. Taking a step back, he lifted his leg and smashed his foot into the door, feeling the ripple of pain all the way into his leg muscles.

As the door caved forward, his first thought was that it wasn't rigged with a bomb, but the smell that hit him might as well have been an explosion. Omar staggered backward with his hand over his nose and mouth and tried not to puke.

The dim interior delivered sobering news. There were several bodies inside, all in various states of decomposition. Omar pulled up the collar of his shirt over his mouth and nose and moved toward the entrance again.

He took a single step inside, and as his eyes adjusted to the dim light, he found himself wishing he'd listened to Mia.

The bodies were a tangle of severed limbs, scattered and

jumbled, and Omar couldn't make out which body parts belonged to whom. He estimated five or six men, two women, and two or three children. The smell made it hard to count. The checkered cloth headscarves of the men were all the same black and red pattern. That was a small but important detail.

Omar couldn't remain inside this building much longer as bile burned in his throat. Going further inside made no sense; there were no survivors. And pictures would only defile the scene more. He pulled the door shut and walked rapidly away from the building. He turned toward Mia and Joseph who were covering their own mouths and noses.

"It's a massacre," Omar said. "At least ten people. Possibly from the same family, but definitely from the same tribe."

"Tribal war?" Mia said, lowering her hand and looking at the surrounding cliffs. Her face had paled. "This airport might be the location of a border fight."

Omar gave a slow nod, and continued to walk away from the building. Suddenly, everything felt eerie, and the desert airport was way too silent. Even if an airport was closed, wouldn't there be some passing traffic on the road running alongside it, people traveling from one town to the next? It was like there was some invisible barrier as far as they could see, empty of human life and activity.

"Omar," Mia said. "Do you feel it?" She grasped his arm, and it was one of the few times that he'd ever seen his girlfriend fearful. "I think we're being watched."

His heart hammered. Mia was rarely wrong, and her assessment made perfect sense. If this airport strip was a battle line between tribes, then that was why it was devoid of life, and why there were desecrated bodies in the building—as a warning. A warning to keep away, and Omar and Joseph and Mia had just violated that warning.

"Get in the helicopter, now!" Omar yelled, as he started to run. Joseph and Mia were right behind him.

Then the first bullet struck.

CHAPTER TWENTY-FOUR

THIRTY-TWO KILOMETERS NORTH OF ANCIENT KARAK

Eleanor counted on the cover of night as she pulled on Miriam's cloak and drew up the hood over her head. She and Miriam had switched their clothing in the litter. As the clouds moved in front of the moon again, Eleanor silently weaved her way through the soldiers and horses. Thankfully, Eleanor hadn't seen Azzo since the first battle cry had been raised. And right now, Eleanor didn't want anyone to discover that a handmaiden sat within the moving litter, while Eleanor fled the caravan. She'd asked Miriam to come along, but Miriam refused and said that she'd be able to delay the search if she remained behind. It was not lost on Eleanor that Miriam might very well be sacrificing her life.

Eleanor forced back the rising emotion in order to continue on her quest. She looked toward the ridge to see that Jed still waited on his horse. When she reached the farthest group of soldiers, she kept pace with their cantering horses for a moment. But when another mass of clouds shifted, plunging the desert into near blackness, Eleanor started to run away from the caravan, toward the ridge. She didn't turn to see if Miriam had obeyed her and stayed in the litter. Eleanor couldn't let anything or anyone slow her down.

Holding up her skirts, she cursed the heaviness of her gown and cloak, but she pressed on, running along the hard, upward slope of the desert floor, her legs and feet burning with the exertion.

As the clouds moved and the moonlight once again shone through, Eleanor dropped to the ground and remained curled up, waiting for darkness to return. Moments passed, during which Eleanor listened to the sounds of the moving caravan mixed in with the hiss of the desert wind and the clicking of a nearby insect.

Tonight she loved the wind. She prayed that it would continue to blow the clouds in front of the moon. And when it did, Eleanor rose to her feet and started to run. As the caravan receded and the ridge drew closer, she slowed her pace, trying to catch her breath. The desert seemed inordinately silent as she started up the ridge, as if the sand was holding its breath, and watching for what might happen next.

When she next looked to where Jed had been, she only saw dark sky. His silhouette was no longer visible. She desperately scanned the ridge. He couldn't have disappeared when she was so close. And then a movement to her left caught her attention. Jed was on his way down the ridge, heading for her.

"Eleanor?" His voice was quiet, but urgent.

"Jed." She said his name like a sigh. She'd finally reached him and hadn't been discovered by her people.

When he drew nearer, she saw his expression wasn't as pleased as she'd hoped it would be. His eyes flashed with anger. "What are you doing?" he said, closing the final space that separated them and grasping her shoulders.

"Is it true?" she asked. "Were you sending a warning to Raynald?"

Jed's eyes widened as if he were surprised by her question. "It's true," he said, after a moment.

"Why would you warn him?"

His gaze was steady when he replied. "He won't survive this war, Eleanor. And I couldn't bear for you to be associated with him. My father has sworn either his own death or Raynald's death by the end of the battle."

"My mother and I were to turn off just after Tiberias with Azzo," she said in a quiet voice.

"Yet, you are here, while your caravan moves farther away by the moment," he said. "Do you know what you've done?"

"I—I," she started to explain, but faltered when she couldn't understand why he was so angry.

"You must return now," he said through gritted teeth. "Take my horse and catch up with your caravan. It's not safe for you out here alone."

Finally, Eleanor realized Jed had no idea why she was coming to meet him. "I've left my people," she said. "I've changed my mind about Azzo."

He stared at her for a long moment, his grip still tight on her shoulders. "Did Azzo not ask you to marry him?"

"He did," she said. "And I accepted, but it was a mistake. I knew it was a mistake from the beginning. I could never give him my heart."

Jed released a breath and eased his grip on her shoulders, but only slightly. "You accepted his proposal; that makes the two of you betrothed, which means he has full claim on you."

"Not anymore," Eleanor said, feeling the burn of tears in her eyes. "I've left him. I've left my family. I cannot go through with a charade."

At that, he raised his brows. "What charade do you speak of?"

She lifted her hands and grasped his fingers, tugging them away from her shoulders, but keeping her hands on his. "The charade of marrying one man when I want to be with another."

His eyes were dark and intense. "Do you know what you speak of?"

Eleanor gave a slow nod. "I know I cannot marry Azzo. I cannot follow my stepfather into a war we have already lost. I cannot watch my mother become a widow for the third time. You are all I can think about, day or night." She paused, blinking away the tears in her eyes. "Jed al Ayubi, I want to be with you."

He pulled away from her and turned to face the caravan that

was disappearing into the distance. It was moving fast, no longer on a slow march.

"There's still time," Jed said, as if he hadn't heard a word she'd spoken. "You can easily catch up with them on my horse. Tell them you fell behind, that you found a discarded horse and decided to ride it. Then warn them of the terrain up ahead. Once they join up with King Guy, the road to Tiberias is without water. My father has poisoned the wells along the way."

Eleanor closed her eyes. "It's too late for me," she whispered. When she opened her eyes again, she found Jed watching her. "I am no longer a part of them. They will have to fight their own way through."

She stepped toward him and touched his arm, and felt his warm skin through his sleeve.

His eyes searched hers. Then he lifted his hand and brushed his fingers along her cheek, her jaw, then traced down her neck. "You are staying." It was a question.

"Yes."

He took a moment to respond. "You've captured my soul, Eleanor, and I was not lying when I told you I want to make you my wife."

She smiled up at him, yet found that his gaze was still serious, his tone somber.

"You do not know what you are committing to," he said, dropping his voice to a whisper.

She moved closer until their bodies were nearly touching. The warmth of his skin seemed to radiate against hers. "Tell me then, dear Jed, of my commitments."

"You'll need to convert to Islam," he said, watching her closely.

She leaned into him, her body against his. "What else?"

His brows shot up. "You would convert to Islam to marry me?"

"Yes," she said. With that word, she felt the conviction even more strongly. "There is much truth in all religions. Embracing Islam would be my honor."

He inhaled her scent, and his eyes seemed to soften, losing their intensity.

"You would never see your family again," he said. "You would have to change your name so that our marriage doesn't incite further battles."

"I will already be taking your name as mine upon marriage," she said, sliding her hand up his chest.

He stiffened for a moment, as if he couldn't believe her boldness. But Eleanor had already been bold from the moment she switched cloaks with Miriam. Now she was acting on her natural inclinations. She wrapped her fingers around the back of his warm neck, feeling the pulse of his skin. Then she moved until her face brushed against his skin as she inhaled his desert and pine scent.

She wanted to kiss him, she wanted to taste him, but she knew his traditions would not allow such things until they were married. He was different than Azzo in that way.

His arms wrapped around her, pulling her close, but still he did not lower his mouth to hers. He simply held her securely against him as the wind tugged at their clothing and the clouds moved again over the moon.

"Are you sure about this?" he whispered.

"I'm more sure of this than anything else in my life."

He didn't move for a moment, then he drew away, releasing her a bit at a time. "We have a hard ride ahead of us. There's no telling when your absence might be discovered, and I want us to be married by the time it is."

She looked up at the man she was falling in love with. "What will you call me, Jed?"

He studied her for a moment, then said, "Nadia. You'll be my Nadia."

"Nadia," Eleanor repeated.

Jed caressed her cheek, then looked over his shoulder at the receding caravan. "We must leave," he said. "I will not rest until we've rejoined my tribe." His eyes were intent on hers again. "Are you sure, Eleanor?"

"Call me Nadia."

He nodded, then grasped her hand. They hurried together up the ridge to where he'd left his horse, and after helping her on, Jed vaulted up behind her. His arms encircled her as he gripped the reins and called out, "Aiyah!"

Eleanor had ridden horses before, but never a war horse, never one this strong. The horse was all muscle and strength, stretching its legs out across the sand. Jed's arms tightened about her as he urged the horse faster. They accelerated across the flat of the ridge, then traveled down the back side. Eleanor held onto the horse's saddle even as she felt the solidness of Jed's chest against her back. The wind picked up, pushing through her hair and against her clothing.

Once the terrain smoothed out, Jed pushed the horse even faster, and they were soon galloping at a pace Eleanor could not have imagined. They traveled for an eternity it seemed, until she saw a glimmer of light in the distance.

"Do they have a cooking fire?" she called over the driving wind and thud of the horse's hooves on the hard sand.

Jed grunted. "They aren't supposed to—surest way to be spotted."

As they neared the camp, Eleanor saw more details beneath the moonlight. There were rows of tents made out of black goat hair, much like those used by roaming Bedu tribes she'd seen pass by Karak. Guards were stationed about the perimeter, and they recognized Jed and his horse because he approached with no resistance.

"Put your hood on," Jed said in a quiet voice. "And say nothing."

She lifted her arms and tugged her hood up over her hair and down so that it concealed her forehead.

They passed by the guards, and Eleanor could feel the

soldiers looking at her. One even grinned up at Jed with a knowing smile.

Jed said something dismissive, and the man laughed and looked away.

Eleanor wanted to turn around and ask the soldier what he was laughing about, but Jed's hold tightened on her.

When he reached the first row of tents, he reined in the horse and brought it to a halt outside one of the tents. Then he quickly dismounted and held out his hand to Eleanor. She took it and moved off the horse. Jed's other hand went to her waist, and by the time her feet landed on the ground, she was in his arms. He released her immediately, put his finger to his lips, then motioned for her to go inside the tent.

She had so many questions, but she obeyed. The interior of the tent was nearly black, although she could make out the forms of a low table and a row of cushions. Voices came from outside, and Eleanor recognized Jed's. He was speaking Kurdish, telling someone to make sure the cooking fire was extinguished on the other side of the camp, and then he asked the other man to bring the allamah. Eleanor knew an allamah was the Islam holy man, like a priest.

The second man seemed argumentative and wanted an explanation.

"Bring the allamah, and I will tell you," Jed said in a sharp voice. "And wait, Kazbech . . . I also need Commander Bahar."

Eleanor remembered Kazbech, one of Jed's guards who had been with him at Al Karak. The tent flap lifted, and Jed stepped inside. She couldn't see his face, it was too dark for that, and he didn't say anything to her. He moved about on the far side, and moments later, light cut through the darkness from an oil lamp. Jed looked across the tent space and met her gaze. "Are you all right?" he asked, and Eleanor realized that she was shaking.

"I'm all right," she said, although she suddenly felt cold. The interior of the tent was rich with thick furs on the ground and cushions of heavy velvet. This place was meant for an important tribal member. A selection of robes made of fine cloth with intricate embroidery of silver and gold thread at the hems and neckline hung from a hook lashed to the interior tent wall.

"Is this your tent?" she asked, although she already knew the answer. He was Saladin's son, and it only stood to reason that he was a leader in his own right. Eleanor exhaled a shaky breath.

"It's your tent now, too." Jed crossed to her and cleared her tangled hair from her face. "Kazbech is bringing the allamah to guide you through the conversion," he said. "But I won't force you. I'll take you back to the caravan if that is your wish."

She looked into his dark eyes for more knowledge, and although she was in a foreign soldier's camp surrounded by her family's enemies, she didn't want to leave him.

"I'll go through the conversion," she said.

Relief, mixed with pleasure, crossed his features. He stepped closer, and she caught his desert pine scent again.

"Is your father here?" she asked. "Or other family members?"

"No," Jed said, looking away. "They occupy other fronts. Once this battle is over, I'll take you to our permanent camp, where my father's wives and younger children live."

Eleanor put her hand on top of Jed's, and he gave the barest of shivers, which made her smile. "Remember you promised I'd be your only wife."

"I remember." He leaned down, and for a moment Eleanor thought he might kiss her after all, but he merely paused, before speaking again.

"Are you willing to accept Islam as your one, true religion?" he asked.

Eleanor nodded and whispered, "Yes."

"The allamah will ask you to state your beliefs—the principles of Islam," he said, watching her carefully. "It's a simple conversion process, but an important one to accept with your heart and soul."

She nodded again, her heart thumping in anticipation.

"The principles are the belief that the Holy Quran is the literal word of God," he said. "Belief that the Judgment Day is true and will come. Belief in the prophets that God sent and the books He revealed. Belief in His angels. And a commitment to worship only God."

"Yes," Eleanor said. It was as Zulla had believed, and what she had died for. And it would be what Eleanor believed—no, Nadia believed—and would marry for.

Jed still watched her closely, as if he wondered that she was about to change her mind. "And finally, he will ask you to recite the Shahada, which is a testimony of faith." He recited it to her as she tried to remember all the words. When he finished, he said in an even voice, "We will marry tonight, right after you convert."

"So soon?" she said, suddenly breathless. *Tonight?* She'd be a married woman before the sun rose.

"It's better that way since the guards already think I've captured a prostitute."

Eleanor shouldn't have been surprised at the revelation, but a hot burst of indignation swept through her.

Jed's mouth lifted into a small smile. "In the morning, every man in the camp will know you are my wife, and they will not even dare look at you, or I will take their life."

"Jed," Eleanor said, her own anger softening. "That would be very extreme."

"No, it wouldn't be," Jed said. "It would be a fair punishment."

The tent flap moved behind Jed, and they looked over to see an older man step in. He had probably once been tall and broad, but his body had lost the battle against age, and he walked with stooped shoulders and a slow gait.

"Allamah Raahil," Jed said, "Welcome. This is Nadia, and she is to be made my wife this evening. But first, she will convert to the one, true religion so that we might unite our fates for eternity."

The allamah looked at Eleanor, and his clear gray eyes seemed to find the depths of her soul.

She didn't know if she should be afraid of what he might understand about her.

He crossed to her, stopping in front of her. "Who is your family?"

"Jed al Ayubi," she said, meeting his gaze. Her throat was dry, and she wondered if the allamah would somehow turn her away.

"Do you believe in the principles of Islam?" he asked.

"I do," Eleanor said. Jed watched and listened intently.

"What are your beliefs?" the allamah asked, clasping his hands in front of him.

She repeated the words that Jed had taught her, and as she stated each belief, she felt something shift inside. She might not be internalizing this new religion yet, but she was devoting herself to this marriage. By accepting Islam, she knew she was becoming one with the man she was about to marry. She was turning herself over to him, and he was turning himself over to her.

Allamah Raahil nodded as she spoke. "Do you accept Islam as your true religion?"

She glanced at Jed and saw the softness in his eyes contrasted with the strength of his jaw.

"Recite the Shahada," the allamah said.

Eleanor thought of the testimony of faith that Jed had shared with her. "I testify there is no true god but Allah, and I testify that Muhammad is the messenger of Allah," she said. She felt breathless, but she also felt exhilarated. A joy she'd never felt before seemed to encompass her. She didn't know if it was from the recitation or from the fact that she was, for the first time in her life, doing something wholly by her own volition.

When Allamah Raahil nodded his approval, Eleanor smiled. She looked over at Jed, and her heart soared at the pleased look on his face, and something else . . . pride. They were really doing this. They *had* done this.

"Thank you," Jed told the allamah. "And now you will join us as husband and wife."

The allamah's brows shot up. "You are to marry this woman without your father here?"

"We will have enough witnesses," he said, then crossed to the tent flap and lifted it. "Come in," he said.

Two men entered the tent, their eyes alight with curiosity. The first, Kazbech, she recognized. He was as tall as Jed, but more broad and muscular. His face was square, like a block of wood, and if it weren't for the crook in his nose, he would be a handsome man. Despite the curiosity in the new arrivals' faces, she could also see that they would not question their leader, the son of Saladin.

"Nadia," Jed said, using her new Islam name, "This is Kazbech, and Commander Bahar. They will be witnesses to our marriage."

The men nodded. Commander Bahar was a short, wide man, with the eyes of a hawk. Jed turned to the allamah. "It would be our honor for you to marry us tonight."

Allamah Raahil looked at all three men, as if he wanted to say more, but when he met Jed's determined gaze, the allamah's expression reconciled.

"Bring the loaf of bread," he said.

Jed moved toward the low table in the corner. He unwrapped a loaf of flatbread and brought it over, handing it to the allamah. Then Jed withdrew a dagger from his waistband. In a single stroke, he sliced the flat bread in two.

He took the bread from Allamah Raahil and handed half of it to Eleanor. She took a bite from her half of the bread, and Jed took a bite from his.

Then Kazbech stepped forward with a goatskin of wine. He handed it to Jed, who took a drink straight from the top, then handed the goatskin to Eleanor. She took her own swallow. The wine was strong and sweet, and she almost coughed when it went down her throat.

She wiped her mouth with the back of her hand, and then returned the goatskin to the commander.

The allamah turned to Jed. “Do you take this woman, Nadia, as your wife?”

“Yes,” Jed said without hesitation.

Allamah Raahil looked at Eleanor as the shadows from the flickering oil lamps danced about them in the tent. The wind outside had increased, beating against the paneled walls, and causing them to billow inward. But Eleanor felt cozy and safe. She was here with Jed, surrounded by his warriors. There was probably not a safer place on earth.

“Nadia,” the allamah said, using the Muslim name that Jed had given her, “do you take Jed al Ayubi as your husband?”

Eleanor knew not to answer yet. The allamah would ask the question three times before she answered, and then on the third time, she replied, “Yes.”

She felt Jed’s smile before she met his gaze. He nodded to her, grasped her hand, then squeezed it.

“Thank you for your service this late at night,” Jed told the allamah. He released Eleanor’s hand and crossed to the two other men and thanked them for their service as witnesses. Jed walked out with the men, and Eleanor was left alone in the tent, the oil lamps casting shadows high and low.

The commander had left his goatskin of wine, and Eleanor picked it up and took another swallow of the vintage. She needed the extra courage. She’d completely changed her life in the past couple of hours. Left her home, her family, her mother, her betrothed, and even her god. Excitement, nervousness, and curiosity all blended together inside of her. She looked toward the tent flap that started to snap with the increasing wind outside. It seemed a storm might be coming after all.

And then she heard it, quiet but sure. Jed was arguing with someone outside, and it sounded like Commander Bahar. She moved toward the sound, trying to make out the rapid Kurdish language. She could follow most of it, but not all. The man told Jed he'd made a terrible mistake marrying a woman outside his tribe, outside of his religion. And that's where Jed stopped Bahar's complaints. "She is as much a part of Islam as you and me now. She's made the exact same promises and commitments. And she will be the mother of my children and the grandmother of my grandchildren."

Commander Bahar wasn't finished, though. "What about Dahma? She was promised to you since you were a boy."

"Dahma will find another man to promise herself to," Jed said. "We were never formally betrothed."

Eleanor held her breath. Of course she should have known that Jed had been intended for someone else—a woman in his tribe.

"I haven't seen Dahma for two years," he said. "She might have changed her mind."

"No, Jed, you know that hasn't happened," Bahar said. "I'm worried about your safety. What will your father do?"

Jed released a short, bitter laugh. "Nothing. My father can do nothing. I have two witnesses to my legal marriage. I am my own man and make my own decisions. I have married the woman I love."

Eleanor inhaled sharply. *The woman I love.* Did he truly love her? It was hard to believe after such a short acquaintance, but she felt the same way about him. With Jed on the other side of the tent walls, she wanted nothing more than to be with him, to have him return to her.

But was the commander right? Would Jed's family reject her? Would they annul the marriage because she wasn't born into their tribe? Would they send her back to her people, or would they keep her as a prisoner of war?

A breeze rushed into the tent, and Jed stepped in, closing the tent flap behind him.

His eyes were hooded as he looked at her, and she felt unsure for the first time since she'd switched clothing with Miriam. Had her marriage to Jed put him in mortal danger? Jed crossed to the oil lamps and blew out all of them except one. The weak yellow glow didn't even make it to the tent walls, keeping its light confined to a small patch on the rug and nearby cushions.

"The storm will be a fierce one," Jed said, straightening and turning to face her.

His face was in shadow now since he stood out of reach of the oil lamp's glow.

"Is it a sandstorm?" she asked in quiet voice.

"Not so rough as that, but there's a chance that some of the tents will blow over and we'll be rounding up tent stakes in the morning." His voice sounded light, but Eleanor still didn't know what to make of the argument she'd overheard.

"I heard what the commander said, and I want to know if it's true," she said. "Have you made a terrible mistake? Will I be cast out?"

Jed stilled for a moment, and Eleanor wished desperately she could read his expression in the dimness. Perhaps he hadn't heard her above the increasing pitch of the wind.

But then he strode across the space and stopped right in front of her.

He gazed down at her, a mixture of incredulity and intensity in his eyes.

"You are not a mistake," he said, his voice low and hoarse. "The commander is only afraid for himself, as if he has any control over my actions, and that he'll somehow be punished for my decisions."

"Will he be?" Eleanor asked in a whisper.

"It's of no concern to me," Jed said. "When we said our marriage vows, you became my primary concern." He leaned down, his breath warm on her skin. "And you are now my wife. Nothing or no one can ever change that."

He was so close, yet she wanted him closer. He still hadn't kissed her, and now there was nothing stopping him. She wondered if he'd make her his tonight, or if he'd wait until he had his father's approval of their marriage. A child born to an annulled marriage would be disastrous for both of them.

"Eleanor," he whispered, using her Christian name. "Do not be afraid. I will always take carc of you."

She nodded, closing her eyes, and that's when she felt his lips on hers. Her eyes snapped open.

His smile was soft when he whispered, "May I kiss you, wife?"

She literally had no words, but she didn't need them. Eleanor moved her hands up his warm, hard chest, and wrapped her arms about his neck, tugging him toward her.

He chuckled and ran his hands down her back, stopping at her hips and pulling her close. Jed pressed his body against hers, his mouth finding hers again. This time the kiss was stronger, more sure, and possessive.

Eleanor couldn't help but think Jed kissed differently from Azzo. The prince had made her want to squirm and turn away. Whereas Jed was like drinking from the deepest well of the purest water—water she'd never tire of. Jed made her feel different; he made every part of her body crave his touch. His touches were gentle, and she kissed him back.

His mouth moved from her lips to her jaw line, and he trailed kisses along her skin, hot and sweet. Then he was kissing her neck, and she let her head fall back as sensation after sensation traveled from her head to her toes.

"Eleanor," he whispered, "I've fallen in love with you."

She raised her head and opened her eyes, even though her body was buzzing with a pleasant numbness. "I love you too, Jed."

He smiled at her, and Eleanor didn't need any more light from an oil lamp to show her what his gaze meant. He scooped her up in his arms and carried her toward the cushions.

CHAPTER TWENTY-FIVE

MODERN-DAY AL KARAK

The agonizing minutes ticked by, and Aamira's bound wrists throbbed. Her head hurt and her mouth and throat were parched. She wondered about other hostages who'd faced what she was facing, and if their executions had actually been a relief.

Yamil had answered some of her questions, but as she tried to continue the conversation, he grew silent and then threatened her each time she spoke.

The quiet was such that she could hear the buzzing of the overhead lights and occasional bursts of wind outside. Once she heard a faint clatter and deduced it was a soda can blowing down the street.

And then, finally, Ehan came back into the warehouse. Aamira watched as he exchanged a few quiet words with Yamil.

Yamil grunted, and then nodded toward Aamira.

She had no idea what they were talking about.

When Ehan headed in her direction, his rifle slung over his shoulder, she didn't know if she should be relieved or afraid. Her brother was not the man she thought she knew. What had happened to the boy who had played childhood games with her?

"Ehan," she croaked out, her throat barely able to push out the word. "I am not going to marry outside of our tribe." The words were desperate, but she hoped she could convince him. No matter what, she couldn't let these men win. She'd say whatever she had to in order to survive. Later, much later, she would find a way to escape.

Ehan didn't break his stride, but his brows lifted. More in amusement than surprise. He stopped in front of her and swung the rifle around so that it was in his grip, the trigger within easy reach.

"Tell our father that he's right," she said, her voice sounding hoarse in her ears. "We need to keep the bloodline pure and keep the integrity of our tribe. I never intended to marry outside our tribe, even though I made some mistakes in England. I never intended to break my betrothal to Sadan." She choked on the sudden tears of anger and fear. She hoped her brother would think them sincere and contrite. "Sadan and I are destined to be together, and what I might have done in England was only a young girl's foolishness."

Ehan raised his free hand and slapped her across the face.

Aamira was so stunned that she didn't speak for several moments. "I deserved that," she finally whispered. "I have hurt the family. But I ask for your forgiveness, and I ask for Father's."

"It's too late for that," Ehan said, his tone hard. "You have ruined yourself. You are soiled and no longer pure."

"We never—" she started to say, but stopped when Ehan raised his hand again.

"Even if Sadan forgave you and took you back, he would always be looked down upon by others in our tribe," Ehan spat out, his eyes dark with fury. "The sacrifice must be made not only to keep our bloodline pure but our hearts pure. Whores like you do not deserve to carry our name."

The insult hurt deeply, but coming from her brother, it dug even deeper. She had to find a way to unlock her brother's sentiments. Get him to calm down. Surely he could be reasoned with. "Tell me about the paintings," she said. "Why are you taking them?"

His eyes flashed with suspicion, but he said, "Ten years ago, a collection of her poetry was found. The documents were shared in secret circles and have caused women and men to rebel all over the world. Muslims are converting to Christianity. They're marrying into other cultures. They're producing crossbred children."

"Because of the writings of our ancestor, Nadia?"

"Yes," he said. "We've collected and destroyed all of the manuscripts we could locate, but copies have likely been made. We want to know if you have any of the copies."

"I've never seen her poems, and this is the first I've heard of any of this," Aamira said.

Drawing his eyebrows together, he said, "You're lying."

"No," Aamira insisted. It was the first time she saw a flash of doubt and insecurity in her brother's eyes.

"Father said you had," Ehan said in a slow voice. "He said that Nadia's writings gave you the idea that you could enter into a relationship with a man not of our tribe."

"I've never read her poetry. I've only heard about her through family or history lessons. But I don't understand why her writings are so taboo. Nadia was Muslim," Aamira said. "If the theory of her suicide is false, then she lived among Muslims her entire life."

"She was *Christian*," Ehan cut in. "She converted to Islam, but it was only to gain power. She was a radical until her death. We just discovered that some of her more suggestive poetry was secretly passed down, and Gorbat hid some of the documents between the canvas and backing of the Passion paintings. So I need you to tell me where any other copies might be."

Aamira shook her head. "I swear that I've not seen any poems by Nadia, copies or originals."

Ehan chuckled, but it wasn't a pleasant sound. "How ironic." He raised his rifle so that the barrel was level with her eyes.

Aamira drew back against the chair.

"It looks as if we're about to have a little poetry reading," Ehan said. "When Father arrives, I don't want you telling him some story about never having heard of Nadia's writings." He crossed to the stack of crates near the hanging painting and cracked open the one on top. After shuffling its contents around with the barrel of the rifle, he glowered, then moved the crate to the floor. He popped open the second crate and pulled out another, smaller wooden box.

With a sneer, he carried the box to where Aamira sat. Then he pulled up a chair and picked up the box again, setting it on his lap. When he opened it, a distinct, musty smell reached Aamira, and she watched, fascinated, as Ehan pulled out a glass jar. Inside were scrolls. He fished one out of the jar and said, "This set of poems was discovered behind one of the canvases. Although they've all been translated, I wanted you to see the original."

He rolled the scroll open and turned it toward her. She could see the broad, elegant lettering of another language, which she wasn't sure of at first. But upon more careful study, she realized it was an older version of Arabic. The lettering was beautifully formed and well-preserved. From her position and because of the dim light, she could only make out a couple of words.

After a moment, Ehan replaced the scroll inside the jar and packed it into the box.

Then he pulled out his phone and tapped a few keys.

"You have it in your phone?" she asked, incredulous.

"The translator emailed them last month," Ehan said. "It was then that we decided to recover all of the paintings and the original poetry hidden between the canvases and the frames."

He held her gaze for a moment, and Aamira tried to search the depths of her brother's eyes to see why and how he had turned into a criminal.

"When I read the first poem to you," Ehan continued, "you'll understand why we need to destroy this. It's completely anti-god. I'll read the phrases that our tribe is very concerned with."

"I have dreamed for many years of a nation and a people who can coexist in peace and tranquility," Ehan started, gravity in his

voice. *"The color of our skin, the god we kneel before, or the language upon our lips, should not determine how we treat others."*

Aamira nodded. These were all truths.

He continued to read. *"Our hearts should be taught to love purely and not be dictated to . . . Marriage is a sacred covenant that should be entered into with deliberation and care with a person to whom we promise love and faithfulness."* Ehan looked up from the text. "As you can see, this preaches against obedience and family unity."

"No," Aamira said. "I don't see it that way at all."

Ehan frowned. "Of course you don't. You and Nadia seem to think that if we put our mind to it, we can be like little children running through a field of flowers, with not a care about our future." His eyes clouded. "But there is no such thing as utopia. We must stand with our own people and unite against outsiders. If we contaminate our lineage, then we are no better than our enemies."

"This is not the crusaders' time, Ehan," she said.

"Is it not?" he asked. "You saw plenty of media and news in England. We are still at war, centuries later, and it will never change. Our only choice is to protect our own families and traditions. That's all that matters," he growled. "Family and tradition. And you've become a traitor to all of us."

"I haven't," Aamira said. "I'm as loyal as ever. I love you and Father and Mother. I would never want anything to happen to any of you. I told you I was willing to make any sacrifice, and I am being truthful. I'll marry Sadan. We'll raise a fine family we can all be proud of." She hoped her words didn't sound desperate, because that was exactly what they had become.

A cell phone rang, and Yamil answered it. His voice was low when he spoke into the phone, but Aamira could decipher plenty. Her father was coming.

"It's time," Yamil said, after hanging up. He turned to Ehan. "Put everything back how it was."

Ehan nodded, picked up the box and returned it to the crate.

"Where's the extension cord?" Yamil barked.

Ehan replaced the lid of the crate. "By the door," he said.

Yamil crossed out of Aamira's view, but soon he walked in front of her, carrying a digital video camera and a tripod.

The blood drained from her face as she watched him set up the camera and tripod only a few feet away. Yamil then ran an extension cord to a power outlet.

"Don't worry," Ehan said, approaching the video camera. "It will all be over before you know it." He turned on the video camera and adjusted the lens so it pointed directly at Aamira. "You will be required to make a confession, and I don't recommend giving Father a hard time about that. If you do, then we'll be sure to track down your beloved Chad as well."

Her brother was stone-cold crazy. Or, at least, Aamira wished that insanity was the reason he would kill his own family member and film the process. The problem was that Ehan was not insane. A shudder rippled through Aamira as she recognized her brother was much more dangerous because he truly believed he was doing a noble thing and preserving his lineage.

She had to find a way out. With more men on the way, she knew the odds against her increased. If she stood any chance at all, it was with only two men to contend with. Ehan and Yamil had moved off to the side of the room, deep in conversation, while Yamil smoked. Aamira looked around the place. She couldn't see anything to be used as a weapon, nothing that could gain her freedom.

Then her gaze stopped on Yamil and his cigarette. He held the lighter in his other hand. It was practically dangling from his fingers. With a lighter, she could start a fire. There was plenty of litter on the floor that would burn easily. But first, she had to get a hand free. She strained at her bindings, but they only seemed to grow tighter.

Frustrated, she stared ahead at the video camera. The tripod was long and narrow and thin. But was it strong enough to knock someone out? She strained again, turning her arms at the same time. Something gave, and she was able to get some movement. Encouraged, she put all of her strength into twisting out of her ropes.

"What are you doing?" Ehan spoke sharply.

She turned to look at him, ready to give an excuse, but he was already in her face, leaning down. And at that moment, with a desperate effort, she propelled herself forward and fell, with the chair, against the video camera. The equipment toppled and smashed. Aamira's momentum continued as she and the chair pitched forward. She turned to avoid a face-down landing, and took the blow on her cheek and shoulder, crying out at the impact. But in the crash she managed to wriggle one arm free of its binding.

She reached for the tripod, and swung it with all her might at Ehan.

He easily stepped out of the way. Yamil arrived and wrenched the tripod from her hand. She snatched the lighter from his other hand. Before he could get his bearings, she flicked it on and touched it to a nearby crumpled newspaper. This ignited swiftly, and Aamira twisted away from it.

"What are you doing?" Ehan shouted, stamping out the burning newspaper with his feet. He grabbed her free arm and yanked her up from the ground, chair and all. She cried out at his brute force as he twisted her arm behind her back. He ordered Yamil to bring him another rope.

"Stupid girl," he said. "Did you really think you could get away? Just hope the camera still works, or Father will be furious."

Yamil appeared with a rope, and Ehan grimly tied her other arm securely behind her back. Then he stood back, lifting his rifle, and said, "If you try anything else, we won't wait for Father."

Yamil set the video camera upright, and the red light blinked on. "It still works," he said, casting a glare at Aamira.

She touched the edge of her lip with her tongue. It was bleeding and starting to swell.

There was the sound of an automobile pulling up outside the warehouse. The two men and Aamira stared at each other in silence as two car doors slammed, followed by footsteps. Moments later, the warehouse door clicked open, followed by the sound of footsteps. Aamira knew without turning her head that her father had arrived.

"What is this?" her father's deep voice boomed in the warehouse.

Ehan spoke first, "She started a fire."

Her father walked around her chair, stopping in front of her. His gaze seemed to grasp hers and hang on.

"A fire?" he said, but it was clear his mind was on other things . . . things like carrying out the execution of his disobedient daughter.

Aamira should have prepared herself for this moment, but she didn't expect the flood of emotions that burst through her. Tears burned in her eyes, and spilled onto her cheeks, no matter how hard she tried to blink them back.

The man staring back at her couldn't be her father. Yet it was his body and his face and his eyes. She wondered how many people in the world had a chance to see their murderer before they died. And how many of them knew their killer? How many of them loved their killers and prayed for their welfare?

"I've written out your confession," her father said. His voice sounded distant, as if he were speaking through a phone.

Or perhaps it was her hearing. She had hit her head pretty hard. Her father held up a piece of paper showing a typed message. The words shifted and blended together on the paper, and she couldn't read it.

She started to speak, started to apologize, but her father lifted his hand. "There is no turning back from this, Aamira," he said in a firm voice. "You've deceived us long enough, and now it's time to put a stop to your lies. I would prefer that you simply read this confession when prompted, and say nothing else."

If she didn't read the confession, what would happen?

Another man came into view, one she didn't recognize, but before she knew it, she was surrounded by four men. Yamil held a pistol.

She blinked rapidly, and her father held the confession closer.

"Read it out loud so that I know you understand," he said.

Opening her mouth, she started to say the words, but they came out as a hoarse squeak. "To my family, I have committed a grievous act. To my people, I have betrayed you—"

"Louder!" her father said.

She started again, but kept her voice soft, hoarse. "I—Ehan choked me. I can't speak louder."

Her father's gaze cut to her brother. "Bring her a drink of water," he ground out.

Yamil took the order. He walked away, and moments later returned with a water bottle half covered in dirt. He handed the water to Aamira's father, and after forcing her to guzzle several stale swallows, he said, "Start again."

She started to say the words as slowly as possible, as if her throat was in great pain.

Yamil stepped forward and placed the barrel of the pistol against her temple.

"Louder," her father said, his eyes blacker than Aamira could ever remember.

She closed her eyes, then opened them again. She cleared her throat and made a great show of wincing. "I—I can't," she whispered. "My voice is getting worse the more I try to speak."

Looking up into her father's eyes, she hoped he would show mercy, even if just for a short time. The longer she could stall them, the better chance she had of surviving.

But there was no mercy in her father's hard gaze. When his hand swung out to strike her, the last thing she remembered was her neck snapping back and her head hitting the chair.

CHAPTER TWENTY-SIX

JORDAN DESERT

The bullet missed Omar, but Joseph wasn't so lucky. Omar rightly guessed there were caves in the cliffs above the airport, because caves were everywhere, and the men firing at them had high-powered rifles. Before Omar could shove Joseph behind the small airport building, he went down like a discarded toy thrown by a toddler. In addition to a bullet wound, which Omar could only hope wasn't fatal, Joseph would have a nice case of road rash.

"Get to the chopper," Omar shouted at Mia. "I've got him!"

Omar tugged Joseph to his feet. The man's leg was bleeding, and it buckled beneath him. Joseph cried out in pain, but this was no time for sweet-talking. The airport building would offer them protection for only so long. They'd be sitting ducks. Omar bent forward and lifted Joseph over his shoulder. Fortunately, Joseph was on the thin side.

Omar started toward the helicopter, knowing his life might be measured in seconds. It was only a few meters to the helicopter now, and nothing motivated Omar more than being shot at by an unseen assailant. Correction, plural assailants. Another bullet whizzed past and ricocheted off the helicopter. Whoever the shooters were, they weren't half-bad.

The blades were spinning by the time Omar hauled Joseph into the helicopter. Mia reached over and helped tug Joseph into place behind the pilot's seat. Another bullet came close, actually creasing Omar's pants. He hopped up, pulled the door shut, and locked it tight. Then he reached for the controls.

Warning lights flashed, and the chopper blades powered down. He stared in disbelief as the fuel gauge sank to zero. "Dammit. They've hit the fuel tank," Omar said. "We're not going anywhere."

"What do you mean?" Mia started to say, then she saw the warning indicators.

The helicopter would repel bullets for only so long. If the snipers could hit the fuel tank, at some point they would penetrate the glass. As if the snipers were reading his mind, a bullet pinged off the windshield.

"Someone's coming," Mia said, grasping Omar's shoulder.

He looked up to see a truck barreling toward them. It looked like there was a solo driver and he wasn't shooting.

"Get Joseph's wound tied off, in case we make it out of here. He was hit in the thigh," Omar said, reaching for his gun.

As the truck grew closer, Mia shuffled through items in her backpack and came up with a tourniquet from her first aid kit. Omar wasn't surprised at her efficiency.

"He's stable," Mia said. "But we'll have to get the bullet out soon."

"Let's hope this guy can be bribed," Omar said. His heart thudded as the truck screeched to a stop next to the helicopter. The driver waved frantically at Omar.

"He's not going to shoot," Mia said. "Open the door."

Omar wanted to ask how she knew, but he also knew they were desperate. He popped open the helicopter door.

"Get in the truck!" the man shouted in Arabic. He looked like he'd been in a fight or two. His wide nose gave way to a crooked scar running the length of his cheek and disappearing into the folds of his red-checked khafiyah. "*Yallah*!"

Omar didn't need to look back at Mia to know she agreed.

Another bullet hit the helicopter. It was now or never. With

Mia's help, he turned and dragged Joseph out of the back seat, and within moments, they'd loaded him onto the rear bench of the truck with Mia beside him. Omar climbed in by the driver.

"You picked the wrong day to visit our village," Scarface said, stepping on the gas and throwing them all back against their seats.

"Village?" Omar said, switching to Arabic.

"We live over the ridge, and we're in a war with the Dahi tribe who now control this airstrip."

Scarface sped up, the airport receding in his rearview mirror. The truck slammed through interminable potholes.

"Where are we going, and why are you helping us?" Omar continued.

"Anyone with a helicopter has money," Scarface said. "How much are you willing to pay for a drive to the hospital in Amman?"

"I'd need to make a phone call," Omar said.

Scarface nodded. "Then I'll keep driving."

"We saw the people in the airport control tower," Omar said. "They were of your tribe? We pray that Allah will bless them in the afterlife."

"Thank you," Scarface said. "They were killed more than a week ago. I've been watching the airport to find a way to fetch the bodies and give them a burial."

"Were they your family?" Omar asked.

Scarface was quiet for a moment. "Not directly. The party was made up of our sheik, and the women included his second wife and her sister and one of his daughters engaged to be married. They were traveling in the middle of the night to meet her fiancé's family. Trying to pass by the airfield undetected."

"But they were hijacked anyway?" Mia asked in a quiet voice.

"Yes." Scarface said, glancing back at her.

"What started this feud?" Omar asked.

"About two years ago, they abducted two of our girls—young teenagers. When we discovered what had happened—we were only suspicious at first—we tracked down the two girls. One had been killed, the other was married and pregnant with one of their own."

Scarface shook his head and continued, "The Dahi tribe is sanctioned with the desert laws; they fulfill positions in the Jordanian government. If we had complained, there might be an investigation, but nothing more than a hand-slap would have been issued. And our tribe would pay even more for our complaints."

"So what *did* you do?" Omar asked.

"We cut off trade with them, and some of our younger people organized protests when one of the Dahi received a government promotion," Scarface said. "Two of our boys were killed in the protest by government police."

"It just never lets up, does it?" Omar said.

"It gets worse every day," Scarface said. "There are no peacekeeping rules in place any longer."

"What's that?" Mia asked, pointing ahead. A gray cinderblock building sat next to the road, and three men with rifles stood close by. Lights from inside glowed against a darkening sky.

"That," Scarface said, "is the Dahi border check. We won't get past it alive, so we're about to take a detour."

CHAPTER TWENTY-SEVEN

ANCIENT DESERT CAMP

Eleanor nestled against Jed's bare chest as he held her in his arms. She was a married woman, through and through, and whatever might come her way, today, tomorrow, or the next day, she would face it as Jed's new bride. It was time to put away her old name, Eleanor, and embrace her new name, Nadia. Her new life had already begun. The flickering shadows of the tent had long since faded as the oil lamp burned out, and now dawn's gray light came in through the seams between the tent panels.

Jed slept, his arms heavy and solid about her, but Nadia had been awake for hours. She may have not even slept, especially after Jed showed her the wonders of the marriage bed. It was amazing to think that a child might be the miracle result of their coupling. She inhaled Jed's familiar scent and wished the sunrise could somehow be delayed, that they might stay secluded in this tent a few more hours.

The wind had finally died down, and Jed said there might be plenty of damage in the morning to repair, but their tent was strong and had held up well against the storm. As Jed's even breaths sounded in her ear, she thought of her mother and of Miriam. Soon her mother would know of Nadia's escape, if she didn't know already. There was no way that Miriam could maintain her disguise through the morning meal.

For a moment, Nadia wondered if Raynald would turn back

for her, or send a search party. But the more she thought about it, the more Nadia believed Raynald would use her disappearance as another grievance against Saladin. It would be her mother who would send out the searchers. This thought brought Nadia to full awareness of her surroundings and her location. Surely a camp this size wouldn't be hard to discover for the trained desert men in Raynald's company.

Jed must have sensed her tension because he lifted his head and blinked his eyes open. But his smile was lazy when he looked at her. "Good morning," he said, then kissed her, long and hard.

She became tangled up in his limbs and his kisses, and the longing from the night before returned with a new fierceness.

"What are you worrying about so early in the morning?" Jed asked, breaking off their embrace for a moment.

"About everything, but you make me forget quite completely," she whispered. She traced the inked stallion tattoo on his chest, then leaned up to kiss him again.

He reciprocated, then drew away, his eyes sober now. "We have overslept, my dear."

"What do you mean? Are we going somewhere?"

He trailed his fingers along her shoulder, then down her arm. "This camp is only a temporary stop. My father is waiting for me to bring the legion I oversee with Commander Bahar."

Shock ran through her. "We're going to war? Against Raynald?"

He nodded. "As my wife, you are now a member of the Ayyub tribe. I don't want you out of my sight, and you will travel with me and my warriors. I'll ensure that you are protected at all times."

A shiver passed through her, but she didn't know if it was because dread was forming a hard rock in her stomach or because of the way Jed was pulling her close to him again.

"You'll wear a headdress and veil," he whispered between kisses. "No one will recognize you as the lost woman from Karak. Until we meet with my father, no man will see your face."

She kissed her new husband back, becoming lost in his touch and his love. When a shout arose outside and Jed pulled away from her, it took her several moments to bring her mind back down to earth.

Jed was already dressing by the time she sat up and looked around the tent's dim interior. The sun would not rise for a couple of hours.

"What is it?" she whispered.

He turned, his dark eyes meeting hers. She didn't like the worry she saw there.

"Stay here and get dressed," he said. "There's clean water in the basin, and you'll have to wear the clothing you arrived in. I'll find out what's going on."

Before Nadia could ask anything else, he'd crossed the rug and untied the tent flap, then pushed his way outside. By the stillness of the tent walls, Nadia knew there was no wind this morning. She rose, keeping the woven blanket around her to cover her nakedness even though she was alone in the tent. She worried that one of Jed's men might come in unexpectedly.

She washed her face and hands and the rest of her body as best as she could, then used the blanket to dry herself off. She pulled on her undergown she'd discarded the night before, then the overdress she'd swapped with Miriam, and finally her cloak. She didn't have a veil and would have to ask Jed about how to get one. Surely there were other women in such a large camp as this.

It was then that she smelled something cooking, no, burning. She wasn't sure of the scent, and perhaps it was a common smell in a Muslim military camp.

She moved toward the tent flap, then hesitated. Jed had ordered her not to leave the tent. She could at least look out, though. So she lifted the flap, and almost wished she hadn't. Not far from Jed's tent a group of men was dragging another man by his arms. His clothing was torn and soiled, and he looked like he'd been badly beaten.

She watched with horror as the soldiers pulled the man to his knees, then tied his hands behind his back. They forced him to bend forward until his forehead was against the ground. A crowd of soldiers had gathered to watch, and Nadia could see Jed among them.

And then another soldier stepped forward, sword in hand. Nadia's breath stopped. This was an execution. She turned away just as the soldier raised the sword over his head.

Releasing the tent flap, she moved back inside. She took several deep breaths. This was like her handmaiden's execution. The man had been found guilty of something and punished right away.

The shouts outside continued, and Nadia sank onto one of the cushions. She wondered if her life would always be surrounded by soldiers and wars and executions.

"Nadia?" Jed's voice cut into her thoughts.

She hadn't even heard him come in. He crossed to her and grasped her hand. "You're crying?"

She wiped her cheeks with her other hand. "I didn't mean to. Who was that man?"

"A spy," he said, bitterness in his voice. "He was caught delivering our military strategy to a crusader."

Nadia wanted to ask which crusader, but something told her not to. She was no longer a part of Raynald's crusade. She was now Nadia al Ayubi.

"He's not worth crying over," he said, running his thumb along her cheek and soaking up the moisture. Then he leaned down and kissed her softly, and lingered as he inhaled. "I regret that our privacy has been intruded upon. When this war is over, we will find our own oasis." His arms wrapped around her, and she leaned into him, feeling his warmth and strength and the beat of his heart against her.

"When are we leaving?" she asked.

"We're leaving now, before the sun can rise," he said. He released her and pulled out a piece of flatbread he'd tucked inside his tunic. Then he handed her a few dates. "Eat what you can. I don't know when our next meal will come."

She took a few bites of the dry bread, but she had no appetite after what she had seen. She tucked the dates into the pocket of her cloak.

Jed handed her a filmy piece of black fabric. "You must wear this veil at all times when we are outside our tent."

She lifted the veil with trembling hands and draped it against her face, then tied it behind her head, leaving only her eyes showing. She pulled her cloak's hood up to secure the veil in place.

Jed gazed at her for a moment, then nodded. "Come, my horses are ready. You'll ride next to my man, Kazbech."

"I am a novice rider," Nadia said.

"You'll become expert in no time. My horse can't carry the both of us too far for too long. And a litter would only slow everyone down. The only other choice would be to leave you here at camp, but I won't risk that either. Kazbech will tie your horses together, and you'll be protected no matter how fast you ride."

Nadia's throat swelled with emotion, both at Jed's concern and for the fact that she'd be going toward the battle after all.

"Let's go," Jed said, and took her hand.

By the time they stepped outside the tent, the crowd of soldiers had dispersed, but the decapitated body still lay on the ground. The man's head had rolled a few paces away. Jed's hand tightened on hers as they walked past the gruesome scene and Nadia attempted to avert her eyes. They passed other tents until they reached a large open area of the camp where the horses were corralled.

Other soldiers were already riding out, and Jed stopped to talk to several men on the way, answering questions. It was clear he was a revered leader, and the military commanders listened to him carefully.

Jed led Nadia into the corral, still keeping a firm grip on her hand, which in and of itself caused her heart to race. Did Jed trust his own soldiers so little? He stopped before a gray mare that wore a deep brown saddle. "This is Faekah, she'll take good care of you."

He turned toward her, and helped her mount the horse.

"Easy, girl," Jed said, as the horse began to prance. "Lean down and introduce yourself."

Nadia grasped the reins of the horse and leaned forward. "Hello, Faekah. I am . . . Nadia. Nice to meet you." She looked at Jed.

Remarkably, the horse settled down, and Nadia breathed easier. Jed guided the reins until they reached the horse he'd ridden the night before—a big, rangy stallion that eyed Nadia with a bit of panic in his eyes.

"Come on, boy, it's just Faekah and Nadia," Jed said. He mounted the stallion, then reached for Nadia's reins and led her horse out of the corral.

They rode through the camp to where soldiers were forming up into groups. The wind was a gentle, warm breeze now, dispelling the early dew of dawn. Jed continued past all of the units until they reached the front where the flag bearers waited atop their horses. The flag with the outline of the stallion flapped in the breeze.

When Nadia looked behind her, she was amazed to see the mass of soldiers and horses, now in regular formation. Within the camp, she would have guessed a few hundred men. But at the front of the army, there were maybe a couple thousand.

"How many warriors follow your father?" she asked, as the wind tugged against her veil.

Jed's smile was brief. "I don't think my father has ever disclosed such numbers to me," he said. "I would estimate over thirty thousand."

Nadia gasped. "That's nearly twice what the crusaders boast."

Jed nodded. "Now you know why we warned Raynald's army. He won't make it past the Horns of Hattin."

"How can you know?" Nadia didn't want to argue, but she was genuinely curious about Jed's proclamation.

"Because," he said, releasing her reins and tightening his own. "We are bringing up the rear, and Raynald will be trapped."

"You will spare my mother?" she asked in a quiet voice.

His gaze held her for a moment. "I will ensure her safety if at all possible." He turned his head and whistled.

A horse with a rider started toward them, and Nadia recognized the allamah.

"He's riding with me?"

"We need our religious leader as much as our warriors in battle."

Allamah Raahil neared them and nodded his head to Nadia. He pulled his horse alongside her gray mare and tied her reins onto his horse's saddle.

And then suddenly everything happened at once. Jed rode ahead and met with the row of commanders. Flanking them were the flag bearers, their crimson flags waving in the wind.

Jed raised his fist, mimicked by the commanders, and a hush fell over the thousands of soldiers almost instantly. Somehow the horses understood they were to still their movements as well.

Then Jed opened his mouth and shouted, "Allegiance to Saladin!"

Following his single shout, an echo from the soldiers bounced back as they repeated the shout. Nadia's ears rang and her heart thumped. Then Jed lowered his fist and wheeled his horse around in tandem with the other commanders. As one moving mass, the horses and their riders started forward, hooves digging into the sand, robes billowing in the wind, and shouts of "Aiyah!" went up as the horses broke into a run.

Nadia's mare jerked in the commotion, but soon was running smoothly beside the allamah's horse. She leaned into the wind, her veil nearly tugged off, and all she could do was concentrate on holding the reins and keeping her balance.

All around her the riders plunged forward, horses panted as their nostrils flared, men shouted commands at their beasts, and the wind roared past. Nadia was in the middle of it all, but the warriors were gaining speed, their horses flying past Nadia and the allamah.

Within minutes, they were riding toward the back of the group. They weren't the last ones, and Nadia suspected there were soldiers who had been ordered to provide a rearguard escort. She'd seen no other women from the camp during this mad dash across the desert. They had stayed well hidden inside whichever tents they occupied.

She thought of her mother, of Miriam, and of the soldiers. With dawn still a promise against the eastern hills, her mother would be splitting off from the main army about now, in flight from the impending battle. The main army would be tired, hungry, and looking forward to a much-needed rest. Were they camping yet? Had they discovered the poisoned wells?

And here Nadia was, riding along with the warriors who were about to block the crusaders from fleeing Saladin's main force of thirty thousand. If her heart was pounding hard before, now it was ready to leap out of her chest.

The sun finally tipped the horizon, its yellow color bathing the rocks and stretches of sand in a bright morning glow. Stretched out before them, the sand seemed to sparkle and move as they rode. With the rising sun came the heat, slowly at first, then more fierce.

But the wind blowing through Nadia's clothing and against her veil kept her skin dry. She was glad she'd eaten very little of the morning meal Jed had brought her. The movement of the horse she rode was brutal on her stomach.

The warriors began to ride up a ridge, and then down the other side. As Nadia reached the summit behind almost everyone else, she could see the narrow valley spread before her.

The allamah slowed their horses together, then stopped. "We will wait here," he said. "We'll be able to see the success of the battle without risking your life."

Nadia heard his words, but she couldn't fathom a reply. Spread before her was King Guy's sleeping camp. Tents had been erected to protect the tired soldiers and travelers from the morning sun. Bedrolls had already been situated, and it looked like many in the camp were still asleep. These soldiers had no idea what was about to befall them. They were her people. Or had been.

One part of her wanted to run down and warn them. Tell them to wake up and defend themselves. The other part of her wanted to find Jed and plead with him to flee this place. No woman should have to choose between her own family and her husband's family, but that was exactly what she'd done. For better or for worse.

The day promised plenty of heat, and if what Jed said was true about the poisoned wells, the soldiers and horses would soon be suffering. Beyond the rocky hill on the other side of the camp, two summits rose.

Watching her eyes, the allamah said, "The Horns of Hattin."

She understood now how the land formation received its name. The two summits indeed looked like horns of a beast, rising high into the air, at least thirty meters, maybe more. And beyond, the terrain sloped toward a village and a blue lake.

The vision of fresh water had Nadia's mind turning, for situated in the valley between the crusaders and the lake stretched Saladin's army. Nadia stared at the masses of soldiers, and her heart sank, betraying even herself. The Muslims seemed outnumbered, but they had the advantage of freshly watered horses and men on their side. If she could cast lots and choose a winning side, she knew she would choose Saladin, simply because it meant choosing her husband and her future.

The heat of the early sun intensified, parching Nadia's own throat, and she knew that water would be the premium commodity in this battle.

And then she saw the commotion beyond King Guy's camp. Raynald had arrived with his army. Her gaze swept past the horses and riders and flag bearers and servants to the colorful litters for the women. Her mother was in one of them, and Miriam perhaps in another. The women in the camp consisted of only her mother and the handmaidens along with a few other servants. But why hadn't her mother's litter turned away yet? Hadn't she left with Prince Azzo?

Jed's warriors had halted, facing the camp, too far away to raise an alert just yet. Nadia's blood chilled. Surely the crusaders could see the peril they were in. But the camp seemed quiet.

"Why have the crusaders stopped here?" Nadia called over to the allamah. "There is no oasis."

"There's a well," the allamah said. "One that has been dry for years. It only fills up during the rainy season, and is quickly depleted by the animals. And the water is too fetid for humans to drink." The allamah nodded toward the camp. "They would have found out about the empty well upon arrival, but it appears they decided to camp here anyway. Foolish. Now Saladin's men will surround them."

"Do they not understand their peril?" Nadia asked. The sun had fully broken above the eastern hills. Dawn was starting to surrender to full morning. "They are not stirring? It only seems as if a few guards are awake."

The allamah chuckled. "They've been kept awake all night by the prayers and songs of the Muslims. Now look."

Nadia watched as a few crusader guards broke from the camp, riding hard toward the lake, trying to skirt the massive Muslim camp.

Arrows flew from unseen assailants, and the crusaders fell off their horses, one by one.

Nadia covered her mouth. She'd seen death before, but standing on this hillside beneath the glaring sun, with thousands of men in the camps below, brought it thudding into her soul.

Smoke billowed from the dry scrub along the hills. She grasped the allamah's arm and pointed. "There's fire!" Even worse than a few dead soldiers was a wildfire in the desert.

The allamah didn't seem surprised. Did he not know that a desert fire could wipe out both armies? Jed's warriors weren't moving. They simply watched the smoke increase and creep toward the crusader camp.

"What's going on?" Nadia asked, and could almost taste the acrid smoke even though it was so far away.

"Saladin set the fires," the allamah said. "The crusaders have no way out now."

The people in the camp below began to stir. Some came out of their tents and saw the smoke. The soldiers started to take down tents and shelters and repack their horses.

Nadia felt rather than saw the moment when the crusaders noticed the silent army of warriors guarding their path away from the smoke. Then the entire tone of the camp went from hurried motions to outright panic. The guards started shouting orders, and several ran toward Raynald's army. But Raynald was trapped too.

"Will they attack now?" Eleanor asked. Judging by the momentum of Jed's warriors, she knew the Muslims had the advantage , though the crusaders might still put up a fierce fight.

"No," the allamah said. "Jed and his father always give a surrender option. It will be up to King Guy if he wants to take it."

The disdain in his voice was plain, and Nadia was glad the allamah didn't know her true identity. But how could she watch the events unfold below her without being affected by them?

The main mass of Muslim warriors stopped several hundred paces from the camp and formed a line. A small group of six warriors continued toward the camp. One of them was undoubtedly Jed. Nadia wanted to run to him, to tell him to stop, not to fight against the crusaders. To negotiate a peace treaty. To avoid so many lives lost.

But as Jed and his party advanced, Raynald's soldiers were forming into a line with their long spears extended.

And then the young man who carried the Al Ayubi flag spurred his horse forward, and galloped ahead of Jed and the others. He flew across the sand until he was a mere dozen paces away from the front line of soldiers. Reigning his horse to a stop, he lifted the flag, and shouted.

"What is he saying?" Nadia asked the allamah.

"He asks in their own language if they surrender Jerusalem back to our people."

Nadia knew that would never happen. One of the crusaders threw a spear. Its tip ripped through the cloth, and the flag fell. Time slowed to a standstill as the flag fell to the ground in a billow of scarlet and black while all eyes watched its progress. But before the cloth had imprinted itself on the curves of the sand, an earsplitting cry went up from the crusaders, and as a single horde they leapt forward and started to run, spears horizontal for the kill.

Jed's warriors responded in kind. The front rows dropped to their knees and staked their spears in the ground in vicious rows, waiting to gut the runners. A volley of arrows flew from the short bows of warriors in the second row. Crusader soldiers began to crumple, and when they did they fell screaming to the ground and were trampled by the men behind them. Despite the numbers of soldiers falling, they kept coming.

Nadia lost track of Jed's location. He'd been at the front in the emissary group, but where was he now? So much action, so much carnage made it hard for her to follow any single thing. She searched for Raynald or any of the women who'd been in his group.

But then another horror appeared, and Nadia felt the blood drain from her face.

"Oh, no," she choked, and grabbed the allamah's arm so she wouldn't fall off her horse. Through the billowing smoke, a second army came into view, riding up from the village by the lake. It poured over the ridge like a swarm of desert beetles.

"Saladin has arrived," Allamah Raahil said. "If King Guy and Raynald don't surrender now, only the women will be spared."

The words rocked through Nadia, and when she swallowed, it felt like a knife in her throat. She knew King Guy and Raynald would not surrender. There were more crusaders, after all, but at this moment the Muslims had the advantage. The dust of battle rose up to engulf both Christian and Muslim armies.

Somewhere, down there, was her husband. And caught in the

middle of the Muslim pincer movement were her mother and brother and Miriam.

The sun cleared the horizon, and perspiration pricked the back of her neck. The crusaders were pushing their way up the slope of Hattin, but the Muslims drove them back, time and time again.

The crusaders had now divided, fighting on two fronts, then three, then four, ragged bands splitting up as the Muslim warriors began to slice and dice them.

Nadia could no longer watch. She slid off her horse and curled up on the ground. The sounds of men yelling, of horses screaming, the smells of smoke and sweat and blood filled her body until she could barely breathe. She was dimly aware of the allamah standing next to her, his hand on her shoulder as the mayhem unfolded below.

"I cannot watch," Nadia whimpered. "Tell me, does Jed yet live?"

"Yes," the allamah said. "The crusaders are making a second effort to take the high ground, but the Muslims are driving them back. The flames are higher now, and many of men have succumbed to smoke."

He was silent for maybe half a minute. "The crusaders are falling in great numbers," he continued. "The smoke only multiplies their dehydration. Their horses are collapsing. Saladin is also taking many prisoners."

When he grew silent again, Nadia said, "Talk to me."

"A group of crusaders is begging Muslim soldiers to take their lives, to end their misery."

Tears streamed from Nadia's eyes. "What about the women?"

"Saladin is merciful toward women," the allamah said in a soft voice. "Always." A pause. "Ah, the fools."

"What is it?" Nadia asked.

"The crusaders are moving King Guy's red tent to the summit," the allamah said. "The king himself rides to the top, surrounded by his knights. But it will not last long. It cannot."

Nadia kept her eyes squeezed shut.

"Ah."

"What?" Nadia almost opened her eyes, but dared not.

"The Bishop of Acre has been killed," the allamah said, reverence in his tone. "The Holy Cross which he bore is now in our hands. And the red tent is being torn down."

Nadia concentrated on breathing. It was over. Even she didn't need the allamah to tell her that. Saladin was victorious. Jed was victorious.

And then the allamah's pressure on her shoulder increased. "They are chasing Raynald."

Nadia wiped the tears from her face and opened her eyes. Her throat nearly closed off when she saw the bloody mess spread below. She looked until she found Raynald in the scrum. He rode toward their ridge on his horse, and in the gray smoke cut by the golden light of the morning sun, he looked as powerful as ever—a commanding leader rising above an epic war that undulated all around him.

He rode hard, straight for the ridge where Nadia waited.

Only a moment passed before another man could be spotted in pursuit.

Nadia didn't need to ask who chased her stepfather. It was the hound on the rabbit. The man was tall on his horse like Jed, but even from a distance, Nadia could see his gaunt face and lean body. He was a true desert man, used to surviving on very little food when necessary, someone who drove his body in extreme conditions. Hunting down a crusader would be no hardship for a man like Saladin.

Raynald looked behind him, and Nadia immediately knew that action was her stepfather's downfall—he now knew how close the enemy was.

And by the way Saladin rode after Raynald, Nadia was certain only one man could survive.

CHAPTER TWENTY-EIGHT

OUTSIDE AMMAN

Omar grabbed the dashboard as Scarface veered off the road a couple hundred meters before they reached the border stop. If the potholes were bumpy, the unpaved terrain was worse.

"Watch out," Omar said as Scarface plowed into a ditch.

The truck stalled, and Scarface started to curse in a panic.

"Let me drive," Omar said. He got behind the wheel while Scarface clambered over him to the passenger side. Omar pumped the gas pedal a few times, and the ignition turned over. Just then a bullet struck the back window.

"Go! Go!" Mia screamed.

Omar stepped on the gas and peeled out on the dirt and rocks. A couple more bullets hit the passenger side of the truck before he could get up any speed.

"They're in a Jeep," Mia said.

A glance in the rearview mirror confirmed that the border guards were closing in on the truck. The Jeep's headlights blazed in the desert darkness.

Mia turned to face the shattered back window, took out a pistol, and laid down a line of fire at their pursuers' vehicle.

"You can join up with the road over there," Scarface said, pointing to the right.

Omar detoured right, praying he could reach the road before any more bullets flew, hoping he wouldn't crater the truck in a ravine.

“They’ve turned off their headlights,” Mia said.

Omar looked into the rearview mirror. It didn’t take much observation to see that the Jeep was now running dark. Omar turned off the lights of the truck.

“Are there any other escape routes?” Omar asked.

Scarface kept his gaze forward. “Not for several kilometers. For now, stay on the road up ahead.” Scarface picked his rifle from the floor, then climbed into the back seat next to Joseph and fired out the shattered back window.

The Jeep seemed to slow, and there was no return gunfire.

“Did you hit the driver?” Mia asked.

“I don’t think so,” Scarface said. “But it’s hard to see. Backup is coming, though.”

Omar’s gaze jerked to the rearview mirror again. Now two vehicles followed them. And simultaneously, they flipped on their headlights. “Where did that truck come from?” Omar asked.

“Not sure.” Scarface spoke to Mia. “Aim for the tires.”

Mia turned toward the back window again, put in a new clip, and resumed firing.

They finally reached the road, and the drive smoothed out, but only just. Omar accelerated.

“Slow down,” Mia said.

“What?” Omar threw a backward glance at her.

“We need to get in range,” Mia said. “We’re wasting ammo.”

“Then they’ll be in better range too,” Omar said.

“Just do it,” Mia said.

It didn’t make sense, but for Mia he could prove his obedience training. “Here we go,” Omar said. “You’ve got about fifteen seconds, then I’m speeding up.” He hit the brake, and Mia and Scarface started shooting in earnest.

Omar watched the road ahead as he counted down, then floored the gas pedal. The rearview mirror told him that the two vehicles had separated, each driving on the edge of the rough road, and they were firing back.

“Go, go, go!” Mia shouted, ducking down by Joseph. A bullet

shattered the side mirror at Omar's left elbow. Scarface ducked too, and Omar's only option was to floor the gas pedal.

He slouched in his seat, hoping to take himself out of target range. But that didn't ease his fear. Up ahead, he spotted a turn off the main road. "Where does that side road lead?" Omar shouted back to Scarface.

"I don't know," Scarface said. "There are many side roads, and most of them join back up."

"Great," Omar said. "I guess we'll find out." He wrenched the wheel left, and the truck careened around the corner. He leaned forward, intent on the curves of the rough terrain. It was barely a road at all.

One of the vehicles followed, while the other continued on the main road. Omar's heart sank. If this road joined up with the main road soon, they might be blocked off by the second vehicle.

Then he heard Scarface tell Mia, "Stay in here. I need to get closer." He climbed out the back window and landed in the bed of the truck with a thump.

Omar glanced behind him to see Scarface setting himself up to shoot, using the tailgate as his cover. Scarface fired one shot. The pursuing Jeep swerved, nearly flipped over, then skidded into a full circle. The spinout would keep the vehicle at a safe distance if it continued to pursue them. *One down,* Omar thought, feeling triumphant. He continued to drive as fast as the truck would allow. They were nearing the main road again, and now the second vehicle was speeding parallel to them.

Omar reached down to the floor with his right hand and picked up the rifle that Scarface had brought for him. He aimed it out the passenger side window, and drew a bead.

Steady now.

"Hang on." Omar jerked the wheel so that he pulled directly in front of the vehicle, nearly crashing into it. Then with the muzzle of his rifle aimed directly into the cab of the vehicle, he pulled the trigger.

The vehicle immediately slowed, and Omar knew he'd hit the

driver, although he didn't know if it was fatal or not. Scarface fired into the cab as well, and Omar glanced back to see the result.

"They're stopping," Mia said in a breathless voice. She clasped Omar's shoulder. "You did it."

Omar could only nod.

"We all did it," Scarface said. "We've won this round."

"Is Joseph all right?" Omar asked.

"He's stable," Mia said. Moments later she climbed into the front seat. She sat close to Omar and rested her head on his shoulder.

Omar could feel her tension slowly ebb as they drove into the night. He linked his hand with hers, their fingers interlocking, and reveled in the warmth of her touch. If only this desert drive was a little less treacherous and they weren't traveling with an injured Joseph in a shot-up truck toward a distant hospital.

It was quiet on the road, a nice change from the car chase.

"There it is," Mia said in a soft voice. She lifted her head from his shoulder. The road started to descend into a valley, and lights beamed up from the low buildings. Civilization was a very welcome sight.

Scarface directed them to the hospital in subdued tones, and when they arrived he entered the building to alert a nurse. Soon two aides came out with a wheelchair. Mia handed a debit card over to Omar while the aides rolled their injured friend inside.

Omar didn't need to ask what it was for since his own wallet had been confiscated by Gold Watch. "I'll be in soon," Omar told her, leaning down to kiss her cheek.

She said goodbye to Scarface, and he gave a dignified bow. "Thank you for your help."

"I am getting your payment," Omar told Scarface after Mia had gone inside the hospital.

Scarface raised his hands. "If you insist." Then he grinned.

Scarface followed him to the ATM in the hospital lobby, and Omar used the debit card to pull out the daily limit. He handed over the cash.

"May Allah bless you," Scarface said.

"Thank you," Omar said. "You're a good man."

Scarface gave a small nod and walked out of the lobby. Omar watched him through the glass doors as he climbed into the truck.

Omar hurried to the waiting room and found Mia in a chair. He sat by her and asked, "How's Joseph?"

"Stable," Mia said. "But he'll likely be here for several days." She handed over her phone without Omar asking for it.

"Are you sure?" he asked.

"Of course."

She looked tired, but her eyes were bright and her expression calm. "We can't let a little detour slow us down."

Omar slid his arm around her shoulders and drew her close. For a moment, he breathed her in, then he called Simon.

"I see you're in Amman. A car will be there in an hour," Greif said.

"Thanks for asking how we're doing," Omar said. "We're alive, but just barely. Joseph is on the mend but will be here at least a week."

"When your call came through, I had no doubt you were alive," Greif said drily. "Besides, who else would call me at three in the morning?"

Omar looked up at the clock. "Sleep is for the bored," he said.

"So you've told me," Greif said. "There will be a new phone as well with the car. I assume you lost yours?"

"Stolen by a nice group of guys with an affinity for prank phone calls. Does the car also have a shower and a hot meal?"

"I'm afraid you're on your own for that one," Greif said. "I'll text you the location of the Sayid compound in a couple of hours. For now, just head toward Al Karak."

Omar nodded. "Any updates on Chad? Where is he?"

"Your cousin is a pain in the ass," Greif said. "Must be related to someone I know. With Joseph out of commission, and Mia now babysitting you, I don't have anyone else to send in to stop Chad. You're on your own. I hope your cousin knows what he's getting himself into."

"He doesn't know," Omar said, "and that's what I'm afraid of."

Greif was silent for a moment. "Look for my text in a couple of hours. We're sending for Joseph tomorrow and will relocate him if he's stable enough."

"He's stable," Omar said. "Just has to toughen up."

Greif chuckled. "I'm sure he'd wholeheartedly agree with you."

"Might have to wait for that pronouncement when he's back to work," Omar said, imagining the lift of Greif's thick eyebrows.

"Get yourself some food and drive safe," Greif said. "Oh, and don't make Mia save your life again."

It was Omar's turn to laugh. Greif was actually in a friendly mood. A good sign that Omar might actually get his request granted. "We need weapons, Greif, and not stun guns."

The pause was longer than Omar wanted. "The police are ready to act."

"We just spent three hundred rounds of ammunition trying to cross one tribal border," Omar said. "How many borders on our way to Karak?"

Greif didn't need to count; they both knew Omar was right. "I'll start working on it."

CHAPTER TWENTY-NINE

HORNS OF HATTIN

Nadia didn't realize she was still clutching the allamah's arm until he drew both of their horses back. "We might need to return to Jed's camp," he said, and it was the first time Nadia had heard alarm in his voice.

She'd observed Saladin's chase after Raynald. But then both horses and their riders had disappeared in the fray of fighting and smoke. She wondered what might happen when the two enemies met face to face.

Nadia looked at Allamah Raahil to find that he was studying her carefully. Although only her eyes and part of her forehead showed through her veil, she knew the allamah was an intelligent man and likely guessed there was more to her story than the official version that Jed had told everyone. The allamah had presided over her conversion to Islam, after all, which obviously meant she hadn't been Muslim in the first place.

Nadia averted her eyes from the allamah's gaze. It was hard enough to sit waiting on the ridge while her mother and handmaiden Miriam were below, about to be taken prisoners of war.

As Nadia watched, a small group of riders left the main camp, heading almost straight up an embankment. She found she was holding her breath. A woman was among the riders, and she'd seen her mother ride more than once. Stephanie was escaping with someone, and to Nadia's amazement, no one stopped them. Nadia wanted to ask the allamah about it, but he spoke first.

"Those women might escape for now," he said, "but where will they find refuge?"

Nadia knew exactly where, but she held her tongue. For she also recognized Azzo and knew that he'd take her mother and the others back to his kingdom. It was a small comfort, one for which Nadia knew she'd be eternally grateful. She didn't regret her refusal of him, for if she had stayed in the camp, she could very well be dead now, or captured, or fleeing desperately into the unknown.

As groups of crusaders surrendered, Nadia could only hope that her mother and Miriam had escaped safely. Some crusaders on horseback who had been unhorsed by the Muslim archers continued to fight on foot. At one point she thought she saw Jed, but couldn't be sure. Her heart leapt with hope regardless.

But the horror of the battle sickened her. She didn't know how anyone survived this kind of savagery. The crusaders had banded together on top of the plateau, and the number of men falling to their deaths by Muslim arrows and spears and swinging swords continued to mount. As the smoke dissipated, the outlines of the piled-up bodies began to emerge. She took a drink of water from her goatskin.

"We will have victory soon," the allamah said in a quiet voice. Even he sounded more somber than victorious.

Nadia could barely move, barely watch anymore. A few remaining crusaders on the Hattin plateau were still putting up resistance, making a last stand. But even with her untrained eye, Nadia saw that the crusader loss was too great, and the Muslim forces too overwhelming in numbers.

Then a cry went up among the Muslims. The remaining crusaders had sunk to their knees and dropped their weapons. Another cry went up among Jed's warriors and Saladin's men. This was the shout of victory. Nadia wondered about specific individuals: how Jed was doing, was Raynald captured, had her mother escaped?

"Come," the allamah said, dismounting his horse. "It will be some time before anyone arrives to fetch you. We will give our horses a rest."

He helped her down from her horse, and she asked, "Do you think Jed is all right?"

"Allah willing," he said in a quiet voice.

Nadia nodded, and felt the tears prick her eyes again. She turned away from the allamah and sat down on a rock next to a scraggly pomegranate tree. She was hungry and thirsty and tired, but she had no cause to complain about her physical well-being when spread out in the valley were so many corpses of soldiers who would never draw another breath.

Hours passed as she waited with the allamah, yet she barely noticed the time. She felt numb, and her mind replayed the dying horses and falling men. The way the smoke had infiltrated Raynald's camp. Her mother's flight. Saladin chasing Raynald. The crusaders beaten down on the slopes of the plateau. Their surrender.

When the sun reached its zenith, the allamah spoke at last from where he reclined near the rock where she sat. "Someone is coming," he said.

Nadia brought her hand up to shield her eyes from the sun's glare. Two men rode toward their ridge. The larger man, the taller of the two, had to be Jed. She rose from the rock and ran down the ridge. The allamah walked behind her.

"Jed!" she called, even though she knew he couldn't hear her yet. He'd taken off his headdress, and his shoulder-length hair streamed behind him. His movements were sure and strong as he guided the horse up the ridge. But most of all, he was smiling. Her heart thumped as she took in the sight of him. Healthy and alive.

This was her husband, and he was coming to fetch her.

"Jed," she said again, softer this time. She stopped and waited for him.

When his horse neared, he reined it to a stop. She didn't recognize the other rider with Jed, and Jed made no introduction. He slid off his horse, then took the remaining strides toward her.

"You're . . . alive," Nadia said, staring into his dark eyes. His face was caked with dirt and sweat, but there were no serious wounds on his body that she could see. His arms and hands showed scratches, and there was some dried blood on his clothing mixed with dirt and sand.

He pulled her into his arms, nearly crushing her against him. She clung to him to stay upright.

"We have been victorious," he said, his voice full of elation. Then he drew back and gazed at her. "You will meet my family now, and we'll have a true wedding celebration." He waved his hand toward the plateau. Already, a new royal tent had been erected—that of Saladin.

Nadia was unable to stop her tears. She wanted to ask him so many questions, but now, as his wife, she knew nothing mattered more than he. "Are you hurt?" she asked.

"A few bruises," he said, cradling her face with his hands.

Despite the presence of his guard and the allamah, he leaned down and kissed her. His lips were hot and his kiss demanding, triumphant and possessive. She kissed him back, but her heart thumped more with fear and uncertainty about her future than with desire for her husband.

"You'll ride with me," Jed said.

She could only nod, her emotions too raw to speak. He helped her onto his horse, and then he swung up behind her. She leaned against him, and one of his arms tightened about her, keeping her securely against him.

Was it only last night that they'd ridden through the dark night together? And now they were husband and wife, riding past the tragedies of the battle.

"We'll set up camp in the valley by the lake," Jed said. "My father is taking care of the punishments of the crusaders. When he's finished, I will take you to meet him."

"What about Raynald?" she couldn't help but ask.

"He will be banished."

Nadia stiffened, and Jed leaned close to her ear. "Thousands have died because of your stepfather's refusal to keep his truce. My father and your stepfather cannot coexist. One of them has to leave, and since we won the battle, it will be your stepfather." His words were firm. "Do you understand?"

"I understand," she said, knowing her voice sounded weak. It was the way of war, the way of men, the way of survival. Raynald had lost.

"And your mother escaped with a few others," Jed said. "I watched them go and prevented anyone from following."

"Thank you," Nadia managed to say.

Jed's arm tightened about her waist, and they continued to ride. Jed kept the horse away from the greatest destruction on the battlefield, and Nadia closed her eyes and relied on Jed to get her to their next destination.

"We're here," Jed said, slowing the horse to a stop.

Nadia opened her eyes. They'd reached the other side of the plateau where several tents had been put up. It was clear which one was Saladin's—the largest tent, and one fit for royalty.

Soldiers crowded around the tent, and it looked as if Saladin was holding some sort of court hearing inside. "What's happening?" she asked Jed as he helped her dismount.

"It's Raynald. This is the official surrender," Jed said. He led her into his tent before she could see much else.

The tent was bare except for a couple of bedrolls. Minimal comfort, and not nearly as settled as the one at the other camp.

"We'll only be here for a day or two," Jed said, reaching toward her and removing her veil. "You must promise that you'll stay inside the tent until I can introduce you to my father. I need to go and take part in the council now. Don't worry about the women captives of your camp. They will be taken care of. But I don't want you to leave this tent for any reason."

"What if I wear my veil?" she asked, and looked around. She didn't know how long she'd be able to wait in the tent alone, especially when the council was deciding the fate of her people.

"Nadia," he said in a soft voice, and she looked back up at him. "After war, many men are still full of passion and bloodlust. I do not want any of them to see you. Even the ones who know we are married may not let that deter them."

She felt her skin grow cold.

"My guard will remain outside the tent," he continued. "So you will be safe. Just wait here for my return."

She nodded, suddenly feeling exhausted. "How long will you be gone?"

"I hope not too long," he said. "I'll bring back some food, too."

"All right," she said.

"Nadia," he began, as if he wanted to tell her something else. But instead, he leaned down and kissed her softly, lingering until she couldn't stop her arms from encircling his neck. She kissed him back, wanting to drown out all that she'd seen and heard that morning. She wanted to forget the terrible images.

Jed's breathing deepened, and he drew her closer until no more space divided their bodies. "I very much look forward to spending the night with you."

Her face heated, and she knew she was blushing. Jed reached up and smoothed her hair from her face and neck, and she let her eyes close at his touch.

"Are you happy you decided to marry me?" he asked in a low voice.

His touch was making it hard for her to think, to believe that there was death all around them, that the crusaders' fate had been changed forever on this very battleground.

"If only the world could disappear," she whispered against his lips, "and it could be just the two of us for a time."

She felt him smile.

"Soon," he whispered back. "We'll have our time together

without thousands of soldiers surrounding us." His arms pulled her against him again, and just when she thought he might change his mind about joining Saladin's council, he released her.

"I'll return as soon as I'm able," he promised, and then he left.

Nadia felt his absence even more keenly than when she had watched him ride with his warriors against the crusaders. This tent had nothing of *him* inside of it. For a moment, she remained where Jed had left her, standing in the middle of the tent, and remembered his whispered warnings and the way his kisses had warmed her entire body.

With Jed gone, she had too much time to think about her family. What had happened to her stepfather? Had her mother truly escaped? What did her mother think of Nadia's betrayal? Her throat felt tight; she knew she'd never see her mother again.

And was Miriam a prisoner now? Nadia's stomach ached at the thought of any harm coming to either woman. Jed had promised that any captured women would be treated well, but then why couldn't Nadia leave her tent? Tears welled up in her eyes, and she knew that if she let a single one escape, she'd break apart.

So she set herself to task and turned toward the bedrolls. In order to occupy her mind, she unrolled them and positioned them on the opposite side of the tent flap. As she worked, she allowed her thoughts to stray to the intimacies she'd shared with Jed the night before on their wedding night. They were truly husband and wife, although she had yet to be introduced to his family. She could only hope that they would welcome her, for she had left behind everything to marry Jed. Not only her mother and heritage, but also her name.

"Nadia," she whispered to herself. She was starting to think of herself as "Nadia al Ayubi." No longer as Eleanor.

She sat down on one of the bedrolls and listened to the sounds and movement of the camp outside, trying to ignore the creeping loneliness taking root. Mostly she heard male voices, but occasionally she thought she heard a woman's voice. She decided she was tired and imagining things.

Reclining on her bedroll, she closed her eyes and wished for sleep to numb her. Yet she heard a woman's voice again: "You must protect yourself."

Nadia's eyes flew open, but there was no one inside the tent. Was someone standing outside? "Hello?" she called out in a soft voice. "Is someone there?" No one responded, but the more Nadia considered the voice, the more she thought it sounded like Miriam.

Again, the whispered words. "All is not as it seems. You must protect yourself."

"How?" Nadia said aloud. "How do I protect myself? I'm a woman in the middle of a war camp."

But the voice didn't speak again, and Nadia couldn't see any shadow of a person outside her tent. She listened closely, but heard no retreating footsteps.

And then a sound drew her attention to the tent flap. It quietly lifted, and Nadia thought her heart might stop when a dark-clad figure stepped inside carrying a satchel.

"Nadia," the man said.

"Jed," she said, relief replacing the fear. She rushed to him and grabbed his hand. "Was there a woman outside the tent just now?"

"No," he said, setting down a goatskin and satchel. "What's happened?"

"Nothing," she said. "I thought I heard someone speaking."

He studied her for a moment. "Your mother has been located, and Saladin wants to strike a truce with her."

Nadia's breath rushed out. "Is she all right? Can I see her?"

"I'm sorry," he said. "I can't allow that. She's a political prisoner right now, with your brother Humphrey. But know," he touched her chin and lifted her face to meet his gaze, "they will not be harmed."

Nadia noticed his exclusion of her stepfather. "Will Raynald be spared?" she whispered.

Jed paused. "He is inside my father's tent now, with King Guy and the other dignitaries."

Nadia stepped close to Jed and buried her face against his chest. His arms came around her and pulled her close. "You were right," she said. "This war has been devastating. What will happen to my family?"

"Despite what you've seen, Saladin is a man of mercy. The fate of your mother and brother is in their hands. I cannot speak for your stepfather, though."

"Do you think once your father knows about me, he'll be merciful to my family?" she asked.

Jed drew away and looked her in the eyes. "There will never be true peace between Muslims and Christians. They both believe they are right in the eyes of their respective gods. Until the day I die, I know I will not see peace between the two peoples." He ran his fingers along her jaw, then down her neck. "You are my wife now, and our marriage will be one of harmony. It is the only peace that I expect to witness."

He leaned down and kissed her softly, not passionately as he had the night before, but as if he treasured her, cherished her, and knew she was fragile.

"Peace takes great sacrifice, and it is impossible for mankind to achieve that type of selflessness in their natural state," he continued, then kissed her again.

Nadia wrapped her arms around his neck and pulled him tightly against her. For now, for this moment, they were both alive and healthy. They were together.

"I must go," he said. "I've brought food in the satchel, fruit and bread. Again, do not leave this tent."

"I want to come," Nadia said. "I want to witness what your father hands down to my stepfather."

"I can't risk taking you. My father will ask about you, and it's not a good time to meet him," Jed said. "I am hoping for tomorrow, after the negotiations are completed with your mother and brother."

Nadia knew he was right, but as he left, she couldn't sit, she couldn't stay still. She paced the length of the tent repeatedly, like a caged animal. She ate some of the fruit that Jed had brought. Then she secured her veil to conceal most of her face, and lifted the tent flap. Kazbech stood guard and turned to her immediately. If Nadia hadn't known how loyal he was to Jed, she might have been intimidated by him.

"Kazbech," she said. "Take me to Saladin's tent. I must know what's happening. I'll stand where no one will notice me."

But he was already shaking his head.

"Please," she said. She grasped his arm.

His brows lifted in surprise at her boldness.

"Raynald is . . . my stepfather."

This time, Kazbech didn't show surprise. Perhaps Jed had told him or perhaps he had guessed.

"It may be the last time I see him," she said.

Kazbech's light brown eyes seemed to darken for a moment, then he said, "I will take you to the perimeter, but do not leave my side."

"Thank you," she whispered.

He nodded, but said nothing else as he led her through the camp to the makeshift court of Saladin.

CHAPTER THIRTY

MODERN-DAY AL KARAK

"This is the place?" Omar asked. He squinted into the darkness of the Bedu camp that was situated a few kilometers from the city of Karak. Simon Greif had said that Chad would be there waiting for them, and it was also a place where they could obtain weapons.

"Yes," Mia said. She looked at her phone. "I hope they're expecting us."

"Not a friendly tribe?" Omar asked, slowing their rented Jeep as they approached the guarded outpost.

"Depends on who you are." Mia turned off her phone and pulled on a scarf to cover her hair. "If Simon did his job, they're expecting us and already have our names."

"What's the status about getting into Al Karak and finding the Sayids?" Omar asked.

Mia shook her head. "The same. Simon wants us to lie low until morning. We can stay at this camp under . . ." She paused to read the name on her message. "Badawi. Or we can stay at the hotel in Al Karak."

"I don't like any delay," Omar said. "Nothing feels good about this situation." He brought the Jeep to a stop. "Tomorrow might be too late. But if everything goes as planned, at least Chad will be here."

The three men who stepped out of the guard post with AK-

47s pointed at the Jeep didn't quell any of Omar's worries. They all wore white gallabiyahs and red and white checked headdresses. Omar guessed them to be in their twenties, young enough to take insult, old enough to shoot straight.

Omar produced one of his IDs, holding it up so it was the first thing the guards would see.

One of the men approached, his gaze swinging from Omar to Mia. Wearing a scarf over her head was a good choice. These Bedu desert dwellers were more traditional than those living in the cities. It wasn't worth offending the guards before conversation started. The guard took Omar's ID, and then Mia's.

"Omar Zagouri?" he said.

"Yes," Omar said. "I'm here to meet with Badawi."

The guard didn't respond, but continued to look the IDs over.

"They're legitimate," Omar offered, wondering why the man was studying them for so long. With all the fake IDs Omar had used in his career, this one actually contained his real name.

"The woman is with you?" the guard said at last.

"Yes, she works with me," Omar said. "Has our partner Chad arrived?"

"No one else has come yet," the guard said. Just then a pair of headlights swung up behind them.

Omar turned to look. The dark SUV stopped, and the other two guards approached it. The tension in the air increased several notches. The passenger door opened, and a man stepped out of the vehicle.

Omar was relieved to see his cousin. "That's Chad," he told the guard. "He's with us and will be part of our meeting with Badawi."

The guard next to Omar said, "Get out of your Jeep. We'll walk you into the camp for your meeting."

Omar slipped the keys out of the ignition. He didn't trust any of these guards to leave the Jeep alone, although taking the keys wouldn't guarantee anything either. He and Mia climbed out of the Jeep with the guard pointing his rifle at them.

"Chad," Omar said. The other two guards escorted his cousin toward the outpost. The SUV turned around and drove back down the desert road.

"It's good to see you, Omar," Chad said in English as he drew closer.

"You don't look too good," Omar answered. "When's the last time you slept?"

Chad rubbed his neck. "I'm not sure," he said. "What about you? You don't look so great yourself."

"Hostage situations aren't flattering to my looks," Omar said, and flashed a smile. "Fortunately Mia appreciates me for my charm."

"Is that what you call it?" Mia asked.

"Stop speaking English," one of the guards barked in Arabic. The three of them fell silent as the guards led them inside the Bedu camp. The sun had long since set, and all that remained was the blackness of the sky above, interrupted by its thousands of stars.

Omar had a number of questions for Chad, about how his mother was doing, and why he was being so bullheaded. And why he had to go and fall in love with the wrong woman in the first place.

They passed a few tents lit from within by lanterns. It seemed quiet in the camp, but Omar wasn't fooled. The Bedus were listening to every step and every word.

The guards stopped before a tall tent that was easily larger than Omar's apartment in Tel Aviv.

"Omar Zagouri and his two comrades are here," one of the guards called out.

"Have him enter," a voice said from inside.

The guard parted the tent flap, and Omar stepped inside, followed by Mia and Chad.

A couple of lanterns cast warmth and shadows across a rather opulent interior of thick rugs and fat cushions.

A thin man with a long, graying beard sat behind a table. On its surface lay two rifles and one of the burning lanterns.

"*As-Salaamu-Alaikum,*" the man said.

"*Wa-Alaikum As-Salaam,*" Omar replied. "Thank you for your hospitality, Badawi."

The Bedu man looked as if he'd seen happier times, far removed from the present. Omar crossed to the table. The two rifles Badawi had on display there were rusted and scuffed, to say the least.

"These are well used," Omar commented.

Badawi shrugged. "They are reliable. No flaws."

"How much?" Omar asked

"Four hundred dinars."

Omar winced. He knew the price would have been half on the regular market. Badawi was asking for roughly six hundred dollars. But with Simon Greif's involvement, Badawi saw an opportunity. He knew Omar was desperate, and had priced his weapons accordingly.

"I'll need three rifles," he said.

Badawi chuckled. "You shoot with both hands?"

Omar glanced at Mia. "My partner also needs one."

"These aren't built for women," Badawi said in a flat tone. Omar knew the man wasn't insulting Mia's gender, just stating a fact.

"She can handle the weapon better than most of your men," Omar said. "How much for all three?" Omar gazed into the man's narrowed eyes, framed with deep wrinkles.

Mia sighed. He was just as anxious as she, but he also wasn't going to get swindled by some desert opportunist. He didn't want to show any desperation. If Badawi thought Omar could find a better deal, he'd lower his prices.

"One thousand dinars for three rifles," the man said, rubbing his forehead. More wrinkles seemed to appear with the action.

Omar glanced back at the tent entrance. Two of the guards remained there, and they were keeping a close eye on Omar, Mia, and Chad.

“Let’s see the third rifle?”

Badawi reached beneath the table and brought out a third weapon, setting it on the surface. Like the other two, it showed a lot of wear and tear.

“Can we test these out?”

Badawi laughed heartily. “Not unless you want to disturb the entire camp and put thirty men on high alert.”

Omar looked at Badawi. “What’s your best deal?”

“One thousand dinar for three.”

“Omar, we should pay it,” Mia said in English, so that she wouldn’t sound like she was overriding the male authority in the tent.

But it seemed Badawi understood English perfectly. “She’s a smart woman,” he said.

“All right,” Omar told Mia. “But I gave all my cash to Scarface.”

Mia dug into her pack and pulled out some bills. She counted them out and placed them in Badawi’s outstretched palm. Then Omar bargained for some ammunition and Mia counted out more bills.

Mia picked up a rifle and slung it over her shoulder, then handed one to Chad.

“Do you know how to use it?” Omar asked Chad in English.

“No, but I’ve watched a lot of movies, and of course played video games.”

Omar might have laughed at Chad’s comment, but the man’s pale face told him he wasn’t too excited about being entrusted with this kind of firepower.

Picking up his own rifle, he said to Badawi. “Before we leave, can you tell me what you know of the Sayid family?”

The Bedu’s brows lifted. He didn’t make an effort to hide his surprise at the question. “You think you can take three rifles into Al Karak and contend with the Sayids?” Badawi asked, a chuckle in his tone.

The two guards at the tent entrance laughed.

Omar felt his face grow warm. "You told me these rifles are in good shape."

"Oh, they're excellent rifles," Badawi said, although it was probably what he said about all the weapons he sold or traded. "No one goes against the Sayid family. They own the bank, which means they own most of the town. If you upset them, your business will fail."

Omar decided it was a good thing his job wasn't dependent on getting a bank loan or establishing financial credit.

He was running out of time. "Is that why you live the life of a nomad, instead of in the modern part of Al Karak?" Omar asked Badawi. "Have you been crossed by the Sayid family?"

The Bedu hesitated. Then he shooed the two guards away after a bit of protest. When they were gone, Badawi stepped closer to Omar and Mia, and looked at them. "Take my rifles with you, but know that if you die in Al Karak, I am not to be blamed."

"Why are you afraid of the Sayid family?" Mia asked.

"Tell me why you're seeking them out," the man said.

"Fair enough," Omar said. "We're trying to stop a terrible crime from happening. My cousin has unfortunately gotten himself mixed up with the family."

Badawi gave a short nod. "We took in a member of their family many years ago who was trying to leave their tribe," he said. "They would punish us if they knew we had helped."

"Was it in connection to an honor killing?" Omar asked. He knew it was a risk to ask, but this man didn't seem friendly with the Sayids.

Badawi didn't seem at all surprised at the question. "You mean the killing curse?"

"What's that?" Chad asked.

"The killing curse is what we Bedouins call those born into the Sayid family or anyone in the Jibreel tribe," Badawi said. "The tribe is exclusive, and any disobedience or deviance is punishable by death. They are their own government and social system."

"Do the police know about this killing curse?" Omar asked.

Badawi laughed. "Some of the Sayids *are* police." He shrugged and set three ammunition clips on the table. "Unfortunately, the Sayids are like royalty at Karak. No one goes against them, although they try hard to make all of their actions look legal."

"How can you make an honor killing appear legal?" Mia asked.

Badawi faced her. "To the world, it's another tragic suicide or terrible accident. To the tribe, it's a warning to keep quiet and obey the tribe leaders, or else it will be their turn next. To the authorities, money can keep any mouth shut." He picked up one of the ammunition clips. "Fifteen dinars each for these."

"We need three times that," Omar said.

"But we want a good deal," Mia said, stepping forward, a smile exclusively for Badawi. "After all, we might be doing you a favor if we take down the Sayid family a notch or two."

Badawi nodded. "Ten dinars then."

Mia grinned, and Omar scowled. "Favoritism," he said. Mia handed over more money.

Badawi produced several more ammunition clips, and Omar and Mia packed them up. Mia handed one extra clip to Chad.

Omar wasn't finished asking questions. "Do you know this location?" he asked, telling Badawi the address that Simon had texted over.

"Yes, it's the Sayid home, a couple of blocks from their bank," Badawi said. "You're going to show up at their doorstep?"

"No," Omar said. "Where would they conduct business they want to keep secret?"

Badawi straightened, his eyes moving from Omar to Chad. "What is it that you are planning, Omar Zagouri?" he asked in Arabic.

"Chad was recently in contact with the Sayid daughter, and he has every reason to believe her life is in danger." Omar glanced at Chad, but the man knew little Arabic.

"What does he know?" Chad asked in English.

"That's what I'm trying to find out," Omar told Chad. The last thing he wanted was for Badawi to become impatient. He said to the Bedu, "Can you give me a location?"

Badawi was silent for a moment, then said, "I can give you a neighborhood. But know that it's based on rumors only. Nothing has been proven. My men go into the city just to purchase supplies. We try to stay out of the politics."

Omar waited. Letting Badawi give them information at his own leisure was the best method.

"There's a warehouse district," Badawi said at last. "The last execution by the Jibreel took place at a warehouse there. I don't know which one." He looked at Chad, switching to English. "If what you say is true, then the Sayids might have taken the woman to one of those buildings."

"Where?"

Badawi drew out a knife from the folds of his gallabiyah and stabbed it onto the table. "We are here," he said, then traced his finger along the grain of the wood. "Al Karak's main entrance is here. Turn here and continue until the road ends. Four buildings are in this area. Start looking there."

Omar nodded. "Anything else we should know or prepare for?"

Badawi glanced at the rifles over their shoulders. "I hope you can all shoot straight."

CHAPTER THIRTY-ONE

MODERN-DAY AL KARAK

Aamira didn't know how long she'd been unconscious. The blow from her father's fist had knocked her out cold. Her head throbbed, and the side of her jaw was swelling.

The men had spent a while talking to each other by the desk, but they were finished now. Yamil walked over to her, pistol in his hand. Her brother and father were close behind.

"You will read this confession," her father barked, holding up the paper once again. "With or without your confession, in exactly three minutes, you will die."

Yamil stepped forward, and pressed the barrel of the pistol against Aamira's temple. She read the words of her confession in a tremulous voice. It was over, and she knew it. She could no longer delay them. Tears streaked her cheeks. She stared into the video camera with its blinking red light. She couldn't bear looking at her brother or father. They had betrayed her in the worst possible way. Even after she'd begged for her life and promised to marry Sadan and be a faithful wife, they had declared her sins unforgivable.

Had it been so terrible to fall in love with a man not of her tribe? Had her father set her up all along—sending her to a place where she was sure to meet other men and women that her family didn't approve of? And where was her mother in all this? How much did she know, and how much was she allowing to happen?

Aamira thought of the women in her family history, her own relatives, who had died young, in their late teens or early twenties. Was it possible to have several deaths in the family and not be suspicious? Perhaps that was what the men of her family feared more than anything. Exposure as criminals. Yet they were not only criminals in this; they were criminals in their business dealings, as well.

It seemed they'd created a female member of the family who was too smart for their own good. And now she was paying the ultimate price. At least the family tradition of control over her would end with her death.

"Put the camera on me," her father said, and Ehan aimed the lens toward their father.

"You have heard my former daughter Aamira confess her sins," he said. "I will keep our tribal covenants and demand a pure bloodline not only of myself but of everyone in our tribe. Aamira is no longer my daughter, not after becoming a traitor to our family and our name and our tribe. Her choices have grieved me." Here he paused, as if trying to overcome sudden emotion. But Aamira knew it was only for effect. The man who had fathered her was nothing but a cold, empty husk of a man, capable of heinous acts.

"Don't let Aamira die in vain," he continued, his voice lower now, harsher. "Let her death be a lesson to us all. A recommitment to our priorities and our beliefs. Aamira's choices have had grave consequences for her and my family and the innocent man she was engaged to, but now the consequences of her choices become an example to us all."

Her father stepped back, out of the camera's view range, and he said, "Yamil."

Yamil inched closer to Aamira, his gun still pressed against her temple.

Everything seemed to slow down at that point, and Aamira could hear Yamil exhale, the beating of her father's heart, the thick swallow of Ehan's throat, and the shuffle of the other man's feet.

The video camera's low humming noise seemed to surround her—this small mechanical device that would broadcast her death to the world.

Aamira looked up into Yamil's face. His breathing was rapid, and she smelled his dank sweat staining his shirt. She closed her eyes, unable to look at him anymore, unable to see her father's and her brother's faces any longer. Silently she prayed to Allah, asking for mercy, pleading for a miracle.

"What's that?" her father said, and at first Aamira imagined it. Why hadn't they shot her yet?

"Did you tell anyone else to come?" her father spoke again.

Aamira opened her eyes to find the men staring at each other.

Yamil spoke. "No one else." The barrel of the pistol pressed against her head moved slightly as if he was undecided about what to do.

"Turn off the camera and see who it is," her father told Ehan. "If it's the police, we won't have time to clean up if we shoot her right now."

Ehan stepped away from the video camera, his face pale. He walked behind Aamira, and everyone listened to his footsteps. Then he switched off the lights and opened the door.

In the new darkness, Yamil stood in place, his pistol still aimed at Aamira. But her father moved away, his own pistol at the ready.

"There are two vehicles," Ehan said into the quiet. "One is a Jeep—I don't recognize it. The other is about a hundred meters away. If it's the police, the vehicles are unmarked."

Her father said, "Are you sure you didn't tell anyone else about tonight?"

"No one knows anything," Ehan said.

"Everything has been kept secret," Yamil added. "Unless your daughter alerted someone."

Aamira held her breath. There was no way she'd confess to being in contact with Chad. But no one questioned her because in the next moment the shooting started.

Aamira twisted her head to look toward the door and saw her brother dive to the ground.

"Get down!" one of the men shouted.

Aamira pushed off the ground with her feet and winced as her chair toppled over. She landed on her shoulder and left hip, trying to keep her head from hitting the ground again.

The gunfire continued, although now it came from the men inside the warehouse. Someone shouted outside, but the noise of the guns drowned out the words. Aamira struggled against her ropes, twisting her arms and wrists to loosen them.

A bright light flashed, filling the entire warehouse and momentarily blinding her. She closed her eyes against the light as darkness took over again. Then she felt someone's hand on her arms, and the touch jolted her. She screamed.

"Don't move," the person said in a harsh command. He started to untie her ropes. "Are you hurt?"

"No," she managed to gasp, although every part of her body was throbbing. She wanted to get out. More bursts of gunfire peppered the air, and she didn't know who was still in the warehouse, or who might have been hit. She opened her eyes, but she couldn't focus on the person bent over her. "Who are you?"

"Omar," he said. "You need to listen to everything I say and follow my directions."

Omar was here. That had to be a good thing. She wanted to believe that was a good thing, but there were too many variables.

"We're going out the back entrance," he said, hoisting her to her feet.

She winced at the movement, and said, "There isn't a back entrance."

But Omar wasn't listening. "Stay low and run with me. We don't want to draw attention."

He gripped her hand and tugged her along, while in his other hand, he carried a rifle. She looked toward the front door of the warehouse and saw two silhouettes. One man was lying on the ground, motionless.

She forced her legs to keep up with Omar even though she felt stiff and bruised. They were halfway across the warehouse floor when an explosion shook them. Aamira's entire body jolted, and her ears felt punched. Then she couldn't hear anything at all. Everything moved in slow motion. She was falling, then she realized Omar was pulling her to the ground. She landed hard, and Omar covered part of her body with his. She couldn't see; she couldn't breathe, and when she finally gasped for air, she choked on smoke and dust.

"Come on," Omar said, his voice sounding far away. He grasped her arm and tugged her upward. "We need to get through the hole first."

Aamira lifted her head, blinking against the dust in her eyes, and saw that indeed there was a hole in the wall. A back entrance. Sounds returned, although muted, and she felt like her throat was on fire, but she forced her legs to carry her forward. Omar guided her over the rubble caused by the blast, and soon they stepped outside. Aamira breathed in the cool night air and tried not to let panic overtake her. She was alive and she was out of the warehouse, although there were still many unanswered questions. What had happened to her father and brother?

Gunfire started up again inside the warehouse, and Aamira began to tremble. She wanted to drop to the ground and cover her head.

But Omar took a firm hold of her arm. "Come on," he said. Then she was getting into a Jeep. "On the floor and don't sit up until you hear from me or Chad. Do you understand?"

"Chad's here?" Aamira asked. Had he been in the warehouse? Was he the man lying inert on the ground?

"Where is he?" she rasped. "I need to find him."

"No, you're staying in the Jeep." Omar all but forced her inside and shut the door and left.

The sounds of the burning warehouse and gunfire dimmed with the shut door. She wedged herself between the front and back seat and looked out the window, trying to see through the smoke. Orange flames were coming out of the building now, and dark silhouettes moved about. Aamira strained to make out the figures, but it was impossible. She wondered about Chad's weapons training. Had he gone to the shooting ranges at a young age, like the men in her family? Another explosion rocked the Jeep back and forth, and Aamira emitted a startled cry. This felt like a war zone, and Aamira didn't know how much more of it her heart could handle. She burrowed down on the floor in front of the backseat, making herself as small as possible.

When the sound of sirens pierced the air, relief flooded through her trembling body. The police would straighten everything out. The shooting would stop, and no one else would get shot. Yet a new horror dawned. What if the police had been sent by her father? She flinched when the Jeep door swung open, and Omar climbed in. Alone.

"Where's Chad?" Aamira asked, her voice high-pitched with fear. "Is he all right?"

"We're going to get him now," Omar said, as he started the engine. The Jeep lurched forward and roared down the street, then it came to a sudden stop, and Omar jumped out.

Aamira moved onto the seat and looked out the window. They were behind the warehouse now, and Omar and a woman were carrying a body toward the Jeep. It had to be Chad. Her stomach flipped over.

She grasped the door handle and opened it. "Chad!" she cried, as she scrambled out of the Jeep. Police lights flashed from a couple of vehicles that had arrived at the front of the warehouse. The gunfire had stopped, but the fire in the warehouse was still burning, and black smoke continued to billow from the building.

"I told you to stay inside!" Omar barked at her.

But Aamira ignored him. She had to know Chad's fate. "Is he alive?"

"He's breathing," the woman said in a much calmer voice

than Omar's. "We have to get out of here," she continued. "Then we can see what the damage is."

Aamira helped them load Chad into the backseat of the Jeep. His eyes were closed, but he was breathing.

"Sit up front," the woman told Aamira. "I need to check his vitals."

Aamira nearly stumbled getting into the front seat of the Jeep.

Omar climbed in beside her and gunned the engine. "Get down, everyone!" he shouted.

He slouched over the steering wheel as he turned the Jeep back around and headed for the main road. Gunfire erupted around them, plinking on the Jeep doors, and Aamira ducked and covered her head. The police didn't seem to be taking Aamira's side. The Jeep swerved and picked up speed, and the bullets stopped. Aamira lifted her head to see that they were driving out of the town, toward the desert.

"Are you all right?" the woman asked Aamira.

"I think so," she said.

"Aamira, this is Mia," Omar said.

"Nice to meet you, Aamira," Mia said, her voice firm. "We'll take you someplace safe where your family can't hurt you."

"Thank you," Aamira whispered. The woman's calm made Aamira feel steadier. The past few hours seemed like a terrible dream now, and she wouldn't have believed it if she hadn't just lived through it. "Do you . . . do you know what happened to my father and brother?"

"They're both alive," Omar said beside her. "We'll turn their names into the Jordanian authorities. Our priority tonight was getting you out of there before—"

"Before they killed me," Aamira said. "They'd already recorded my confession while Yamil held a pistol to my head."

Mia handed her a jacket and said, "Here, put this on." To Omar she said, "Can this thing go any faster?"

Omar pressed harder on the accelerator, but the Jeep had already found its maximum speed.

"How's Chad now?" Aamira said, turning to look at his slumped form.

"Still breathing," Mia said. "I can't find any bullet wounds, at least not any that are visible."

Omar reached into his pocket and handed a small flashlight to Mia. She turned it on, and Aamira watched as she examined Chad more closely for wounds. His eyes were shut, and his face seemed pale and lifeless. Aamira felt the panic rising.

"He needs a hospital," she said.

"We'll get him help," Mia replied.

"But the hospital is the other way," Aamira said, looking behind them at the receding buildings of the city.

"Al Karak is out of the question," Omar said. "Your father would find out, and he'd come after you both again, including Chad."

"Can you find anything?" Aamira said, watching Mia's examination.

"Not yet," Mia said.

"My ribs hurt," Chad said, his eyes fluttering open.

Aamira stared at him. "You're awake?"

"You guys are making it hard to rest," he said, a slight smile lifting his lips.

Aamira reached back and grabbed his hand. He squeezed back. She covered her mouth with her other hand as new tears spilled out. "Check his ribs," Aamira said.

"I am." Mia lifted the bottom of his shirt to reveal a nasty wound on his left side.

"That's it," Chad said with a groan.

Mia used her flashlight to get a better look. "It's not a bullet wound," she announced. "Probably shrapnel from the bomb."

"Get the first aid kit from the jockey box," Omar told Aamira.

With shaking hands, she complied and opened the glove compartment. "What do you need?" she asked Mia.

"The cleanser, gauze, and the Ace bandage for now," Mia said.

Aamira handed her the items. Mia worked quickly, and Chad closed his eyes, keeping his groans quiet.

"All finished," Mia said, giving Aamira a triumphant look. "Your boyfriend was lucky tonight."

"*I* was lucky tonight," Aamira said, meeting Mia's gaze. "Thank you. Thanks to all of you. I can't believe you risked your lives for me."

Chad opened his eyes. "I told you we'd get you out."

Aamira reached back and squeezed his hand. "You did, although I wasn't sure how. I can't believe you came all the way to Al Karak. How did you find the warehouse?"

"We looked for the building with the lights on," Omar said. "We didn't think they'd videotape in the dark."

Aamira felt sick. "Now what?" she said in a quiet voice.

"We're taking you and Chad into protective custody," Omar said, glancing over at her. "Until your family is in prison, you aren't safe."

She nodded. Chad was looking back at her. He threaded his fingers through hers. "We'll figure it out," he said, and she knew she could believe this man. Could always trust him.

As they drove deeper into the moonlit desert, Aamira also knew that she was lucky to have escaped with her life. That life would never be the same again. Nor would her name. From this moment on, she would forget she had been born a Sayid.

CHAPTER THIRTY-TWO

HORNS OF HATTIN

The glow of torches lit the way as Nadia walked with Kazbech toward the makeshift court of Saladin. A row of warriors encircled the open-faced tent, standing guard to protect their leader. Crusaders stood clustered and tied together, guarded by the Muslims. The crusaders' spears, swords, and bows had been cast into a pile, and their clothing was soiled and blood-stained. Saladin sat upon a dais before the crowd. In one hand he gripped what looked to be a crusader sword.

Kazbech led her to the outer reaches of the gathering. Nadia's heart thumped as she watched the crusader leaders turn over their weapons then drop to their knees in obeisance before Saladin. They were making pledges, although Nadia couldn't hear their words. After their pledges, the Muslim warriors slashed off their white outer-tunics sewn with the holy cross in red.

Then Nadia saw Raynald. He sat on the other side of King Guy, who was seated immediately right of Saladin upon the dais.

Raynald stared out at the gathered crowd, his clothing filthy, his gaze defiant.

"What are they saying?" she whispered to Kazbech.

"They are pledging their loyalty to Saladin, and converting to Islam," he said in a quiet voice.

These men were switching allegiances to stay alive. Nadia thought about her conversion to Islam and knew it was different.

She hadn't converted to save her life, but rather to live the life she wanted with Jed.

And then it seemed as if the world went silent. The crusaders and the Muslims all listened to Saladin as he spoke to King Guy. Saladin handed the king a goblet and said, "This is rose water, kept cold by the snows of Hermon."

The king accepted the goblet and drank long and deep.

Nadia's heart soared. Saladin had offered the king hospitality, which meant his life would be spared.

Then King Guy handed the cup to Raynald, who also drank. As he did, Saladin said, "Tell the king that I am not the one who gave Raynald the drink."

Nadia glanced at Kazbech. "Why did he say that?"

Kazbech hushed her.

Saladin turned his full attention to Raynald. "Since the day you stepped onto my people's soil, you have brought only death and terror. If that is what your god demands, then today you will pay for those demands."

"I am a follower of Jesus Christ," Raynald spat out, "and not even the loss of all my men will make me bow to a devil like you."

Saladin leapt to his feet, his sword gripped in his hand. He lunged for Raynald, and before anyone could move or think, he swung the sword and sliced completely through Raynald's neck.

Nadia's knees gave out, and Kazbech grabbed her before she sank to the ground. Her stepfather's headless body toppled forward, blood spurting across the dais. Someone screamed, and Nadia wondered if it was she. But the others in the gathering cheered.

Nadia steadied herself by grasping Kazbech's arm, and he held her securely upright. "Let's go," he said in her ear.

But she was transfixed. King Guy's face had blanched, and he brought a trembling hand to his own throat.

Saladin turned to the king and barked out a laugh. "I will reassure you now," he said. "A king does not kill a king." He threw a cursory glance at Raynald's inert form. "But that man's insolence went too far." Saladin turned toward his soldiers and the cowering crusaders. "None of the barons will be executed, but those that Raynald led, the knights of the military orders, will all be put to death before the sun sets."

Kazbech tugged Nadia away from the crowd. Though she must have walked with him back to the tent, she couldn't remember doing so. Her mind was numb, her body trembled, and her thoughts were spinning under the shock of what she had just witnessed.

She stumbled into the tent alone. Her stepfather was dead. She didn't know how long she lay curled up on her bedroll before Jed returned. The inside of the tent was nearly dark, and only the faint glow of the torches outside provided any light when he opened the tent flap.

"Nadia," Jed whispered. "You shouldn't have gone to Saladin's court."

She awakened more fully then. "I had to know Raynald's fate."

Jed said nothing, just held her tight. "Word has reached my father about our marriage," he said. "He has asked to meet you tonight."

"Tonight?" she said, drawing away from Jed, her heart hammering. "Did he see me at the execution?"

"No," Jed said. "Commander Bahar told him; I'm sure of it." He paused. "I wanted to be the one to tell him so that I could present it properly. Come," he continued, "my father is not a patient man. We will dine with him in his private tent."

He rose to his feet, then held out his hand. Nadia grasped it and stood. Her breathing felt jagged as she anticipated meeting the man who'd just killed her stepfather. She pulled on her veil and walked out of the tent with Jed. Kazbech stood outside the tent, keeping guard, and Jed nodded to him to follow them.

Although it was deep into the night hours, the camp was still alive with soldiers going about various tasks beneath the light of the torches. Cooking fires burned, and music and laughter floated among the people.

This time, Nadia walked a different path with Jed as they wound their way among several tents on their way to Saladin's private quarters.

"Jed," a man said in a soft voice.

It was the allamah. He hurried toward them, coming from the opposite direction. "Come with me," he whispered when he grew close.

"What is it?" Jed asked, grasping Nadia's hand.

"In here." The allamah motioned toward a canopy. He stopped inside, taking a deep breath, and looking from Jed to Nadia. "Saladin is waiting for you with his soldiers."

Jed nodded. "We are to dine with him. I am introducing him to my wife."

The allamah shook his head and stared intently at Jed. "No, he is waiting for you *with* his soldiers."

Jed stared back. "What do you mean?"

"I cannot say any more," the allamah said. Then with a pitying look, he glanced at Nadia, then started to move past them.

"Wait," Jed said. "Tell me what's going on."

"I can only warn you," the allamah said. "I was never here, and I never spoke to you." The man sidestepped around Jed and hurried away.

Jed leapt toward him and put the allamah's neck in a hammerlock, holding a knife to his throat. "Tell me everything you know, or your blood will stain this very ground."

The allamah struggled against Jed but failed.

"Saladin knows everything," he said, closing his eyes. "He knows your wife's parentage, and he knows she's a Christian."

"She's Islam," Jed said. "You performed the conversion yourself."

"Saladin isn't happy that she's from outside our tribe," the allamah said. "You are promised to one another, but Saladin says he'll not have the bloodline tainted."

Jed went still. He lowered the knife and released the allamah, who bent over and put his hands on his knees to catch his breath.

"What else did he say?" Jed asked in a cold voice.

The allamah didn't look up. "He's ordered your capture."

"What about Nadia?"

"They're coming for both of you," the allamah said. He straightened. His face had paled to alabaster.

Jed looked at Nadia.

The look of defeat and fear in his eyes pierced her very core.

Still looking at her, Jed said to the allamah, "Create a distraction. Anything. I need some time."

The allamah hurried away, leaving only Jed, Nadia, and Kazbech beneath the canopy. The sounds of the camp seemed to echo inside Nadia's head as she imagined every shout, every call, every word as coming from soldiers looking for them.

"Jed?" Nadia whispered.

He stared at her for a moment, and pulled her into a fierce embrace. Then he moved her veil aside, exposing her face, and kissed her long and hard. When he released her, she was breathless. The tears coursed down her cheeks.

"What are we going to do?" she whispered. She hoped he'd tell her he had a plan. That he had a horse ready. That they had someplace to go that was far away from Saladin.

Jed didn't answer her question but removed the leather cord from around his neck. He wrapped it around her wrist three times, then tied it into a knot.

"Jed?" she said, her voice choking on her own tears.

His hands were on her face again, his lips pressed against her forehead. "I regret nothing, my Nadia," he said. "Always remember that I loved you first."

And then before she could say anything more, he released her and turned to Kazbech. "Take her to safety and always watch over her. Guard her with your life."

Kazbech nodded, his eyes black in the night. "I will."

Then with a single glance at Nadia, Jed turned and hurried out from beneath the canopy.

"Jed!" Nadia whispered after him. The sounds of the camp came into sharper focus, loud and clear. Men were calling to each other, shouting, and on everyone's lips was the word, "betrayer."

Nadia shivered at the men's voices rising in the night.

She was barely aware of Kazbech's grasp on her arm as he led her out of the enclosure and away from Jed's tent. She couldn't comprehend where Kazbech was taking her, just that she was no longer with Jed, and that he was possibly fleeing for his life.

And then Kazbech was running, pulling her along, his knife in one hand. She stumbled alongside him as they skirted other tents and finally arrived at one of the corrals. Kazbech helped her onto a horse, then climbed up behind her.

"We can't leave him," Nadia gasped out, trying to push Kazbech away. "We have to go back."

"He'll find a way out," Kazbech said, keeping a firm hold on her. He maneuvered the horse out of the corral, and then they were racing across a valley floor beneath the lonely moonlight.

Nadia turned as much as possible to watch the war camp with its torches and soldiers. What was happening back there? Had Jed escaped? Then she turned forward again, allowing herself to relax into the movements of the galloping horse as Kazbech held her in his strong grip.

Squeezing her eyes shut, the tears burned again. What had gone wrong with Saladin? Jed had seemed so sure that his father would accept her into their family. He had been looking forward to their introduction.

Nadia didn't know how much time passed before Kazbech slowed the horse from a gallop to a trot. The night was still deep when he brought the horse to a halt in a small valley. Nadia looked around, not recognizing their surroundings. She had no idea how far they'd ridden.

As Kazbech helped her off the horse, she shivered against the cold night air. The sting of the wind had kept her numb when riding, but now the cold seeped into her skin, into her bones. Kazbech led the horse to the well by an olive tree. When he returned, he said, "The well water is too bitter for humans. The horse probably won't drink much." He offered his goatskin of water, and she lifted her veil to drink.

"I have no food," he said.

She took a long drink, then handed it back. Even if they had had food, she wouldn't have been able to eat. "Thank you," she murmured. She couldn't help looking toward the direction they'd traveled, as if she could still see the war camp, or perhaps Jed riding toward them through the night.

But the moon's pale glow lit up only empty terrain.

"We should try to sleep for a couple of hours before the sun comes up," Kazbech said in a low voice.

Nadia turned toward him. "I won't sleep until Jed has joined us."

Kazbech nodded and removed his cloak from his shoulders. He draped it over her. The extra layer of warmth felt good, yet she could not enjoy it. She knew she was exhausted, but her nerves were so tight that she couldn't rest. She started to pace the small area, and Kazbech settled onto a nearby rock and watched her.

Finally she turned to him. "Do you think he got away?"

He didn't say anything for a moment. "If anyone could escape Saladin's soldiers, it would be Jed."

Nadia wasn't exactly comforted. "What if he's captured? What will his father do?"

"Find a way to teach him a lesson," Kazbech said in a slow voice. "Perhaps force him to denounce your marriage."

She sucked in a breath. "Is that possible? Would his word make our marriage invalid?"

"If Saladin declared it invalid." Kazbech moved to his feet and walked toward her.

Nadia had to tilt her head back to see his face. His eyes were darker than Jed's, his face more square, but he was a handsome and powerful man.

"There is a saying among my people," Kazbech said. "Do not fear tomorrow when you must live today." He'd spoken it in Arabic, but Nadia had no trouble understanding.

"Is that how warriors sleep at night?" she replied in Arabic.

His brows shot up, and one side of his mouth lifted. In all the times Nadia had spoken with Kazbech, she hadn't seen him even close to smiling. He was reserved in his display of emotion whereas Jed wore every emotion for all to see.

"Have you studied languages all your life?" Kazbech asked.

Nadia had to step back. She wasn't used to interacting so closely with other men. Jed, of course, was different, and besides, he was her husband now. "I wasn't as gifted in the arts and music as my mother had hoped I would be. I spent more time with my brother Humphrey's tutors than he likely did." She smiled at the memory of following her brother around and sitting in on his lessons. As long as she was quiet, the tutors didn't send her away.

"You have a gift," Kazbech said.

She stared at him intently for a moment. She didn't want kindness and compliments. She wanted Jed.

"How long have you known Jed?" she asked.

"My father worked for his father, and Jed and I grew up doing a lot of the same things," he said. "He's like a brother to me."

Nadia nodded. It made sense why Jed trusted him so much.

"Come," Kazbech said. "At least sit down. We might have a long wait."

She pulled the cloak tightly about her, then sat down, leaning her back against the rock where Kazbech crouched. She breathed in the night air, and wished she wasn't so far from Jed. Her mind was leaping to all kinds of conclusions, and none of them made her heart rate slow down.

She closed her eyes, listening to the night sounds of the

desert, to the wind, the insects, and the distant howl of jackals. When she next opened her eyes, she realized she'd fallen asleep, leaning her head against Kazbech's leg.

Dawn had come and gone. The sun had cleared the horizon, the heat of it making her skin moist. She lifted her head and looked up. Kazbech was awake, his arms folded across his chest, his eyes on the horizon. She realized he must have been cold all night without his cloak.

"Have you seen anything?" she asked in a hoarse voice.

Kazbech looked down at her. "Not yet. I'm glad you slept, though."

"Did you sleep?"

"No," he said. "I thought one of us should stay awake in case there was any sign of Jed." He stood from the rock and arched his back. Then he picked up the goatskin from its place on the other side of the rock and handed it over to her.

She took a couple of swallows of stale water, wiped her mouth, then handed it back.

Kazbech took a drink, but she knew it wasn't nearly enough for a grown man. It wasn't enough for her, either. She climbed to her feet and steadied herself against the rock. She felt light-headed and hungry.

"Someone's coming," Kazbech said.

Nadia followed his gaze. "Where?" And then she saw it. A dark form moving through the morning light took shape against the brown of the harvested fields. A man on horseback.

"Jed?" Nadia breathed, starting to walk.

"Wait," Kazbech said, grabbing her arm. "We don't know who it is. Anyone could have followed our tracks." His hand slipped to her hand, and he pulled her around the other side of the rock. "Get down."

"What about the horse?"

Kazbech looked over his shoulder. The horse was several paces away lashed to an olive tree. "We'll be discovered soon enough, but I don't want the rider to know I'm with a woman. The stakes will be much higher if he finds out." Methodically, he removed the long knife from the belt of his tunic.

Motioning again for her to be quiet and put on her veil, he moved to the front of the rock, knife in hand, to await the rider.

Nadia moved slightly to get a view of the rider. Her heart thudded louder than the sound of the approaching hooves.

"Raahil," Kazbech said under his breath. He turned toward Nadia's hiding place. "It's the allamah."

She rose and hurried to join Kazbech as the rider approached. Sure enough, the allamah was coming toward them, gripping the reins of his horse as he slowed the beast.

"What news do you bring?" Kazbech asked immediately.

Allamah Raahil dismounted and wiped the perspiration from his face. He was breathing hard, and his face was flushed with heat. When his gaze met Nadia's, she felt her stomach twist.

"What's happened? Where's Jed?" she burst out. She didn't know why she felt like crying. If Jed was all right, wouldn't he have traveled with the allamah? Unless there was to be another meeting place?

The allamah nodded at Kazbech, then gave a small bow before Nadia. "It is with great regret that I bring terrible news," he started.

"No!" Nadia cried out.

Kazbech grabbed her arm, holding her still. "Tell us."

The allamah wiped his face again. His eyes flitted back and forth from Nadia to Kazbech. "Saladin has ordered Jed's execution."

The strength left Nadia's legs, and she sank to the ground. "How can that be?" She looked up at the men. "We need to return to the war camp to stop Saladin. Jed is his own son . . . how can a father order such a thing?"

"Saladin has declared Jed's marriage to a woman outside the bloodline as an act of treason," the allamah said in a careful voice.

"He refuses to be lenient in this, not even for his son. Jed might have hoped that your conversion to Islam was enough, but he was wrong."

"We need to go back," Nadia said. She grasped Kazbech's hand. "Take us back."

"Your execution has also been ordered," the allamah said in a quiet voice. "To return is to die."

CHAPTER THIRTY-THREE

TEL AVIV, ISRAEL

"Dammit." Omar finished reading the incoming text then pushed back from the balcony railing of his apartment in Tel Aviv. "You were right." He walked into the living room where Mia sat on the couch, her laptop propped on her knees.

She looked up, curls wet around her face from her recent shower.

They'd been back in Tel Aviv less than two hours, and now this. Omar held out his phone so she could read the text from Simon Greif.

She read the message. "The Sayids escaped the police?"

"I don't know if the police actually ever had them in custody," Omar mused, sitting next to Mia on the couch. At least Chad and Aamira were safe, under protection somewhere in Jerusalem, where they were still accessible to Omar and the Israeli Department of Intelligence, but hidden from the Sayid family. The Sayids wouldn't dare cross Israel's borders in search of their daughter.

"What are you thinking?" Mia asked, laptop forgotten, her full attention on him.

"Chad and Aamira will have no life and no future until those guys are in custody and found guilty in a court of law." He met Mia's gaze. "So there's only one thing we can do. We've got to bait them."

"How?" Mia asked, her expression genuinely curious.

Omar hesitated. Mia had followed him on too many bizarre adventures, and he wasn't sure how she'd take this one. "I'm going to draw them out of their hole or cave or wherever they're hiding," he said. "Make them want to seek me out."

Mia lifted a single brow. "How?"

Rising to his feet, he grabbed a book from the kitchen table. It was an art book that depicted the collections at the National Portrait Museum in London. He flipped open to the pages that contained photographs of the Passion paintings. "Here." He pointed to the page. "I'm going to buy the artwork on the black market from the Sayids themselves. They've undoubtedly removed the poetry."

Mia feigned interest. "Really? You just happen to have millions of dollars lying around and a way to get in touch with a black market dealer?"

Omar set the book down on the coffee table and grinned.

"No," Mia said. "Not Naim Bata."

But Omar was already dialing a number into his phone. Naim was in witness protection where he'd been for several months after his father's black market enterprise had been brought to its knees by the Prime Minister of Turkey. But if anyone could pull off this sort of coup, it was Naim. It only proved that one needed to keep enemies close.

The phone rang twice before Naim answered.

"Zagouri," Naim said.

"How did you know?"

Naim chuckled. "When paintings are stolen in London, and then the hometown where the paintings originated makes national news, and one painting is found in a half-burned warehouse, but the rest are still missing . . . Then suddenly I receive a phone call from a restricted number. I put two and two together. You're on a treasure hunt, aren't you?"

"Can you help me?" Omar asked. He looked at Mia, who

shook her head. She'd picked up her laptop, though, and was tapping away at something.

Naim sighed heavily. "What can I possibly do for you from here? I'm on some Greek island, enjoying the beach by the way, but I'm not exactly in the thick of things any longer. My father's arrest ensured that even the legitimate parts of his business have now failed."

"I need names and contact information," Omar said.

"I don't think I can help," Naim said. "I'm trying to keep a clean slate, and when I do get my life back, I've got plans."

Omar couldn't help but smile. "With your girlfriend Leyla?"

"With Leyla." The smile was plain in Naim's voice, even through the phone.

"Well, I don't want to put you at risk," Omar said. "But I need names if at all possible. Once I have the financing arranged, I can make a serious offer under an assumed name. I plan to be at the pickup place myself . . . and I'm banking at least one member of the Sayid family will be there to collect the cash." He lowered his voice. "The Sayid family is bad news, Naim. Take your father's crimes and multiply them a dozen times, and you have Taheer Sayid."

"Really."

"There are at least a dozen honor killings in their family dating back the last forty years or so," Omar continued. "My cousin Chad fell in love with a young Muslim woman at his college in London."

"Let me guess," Naim cut in. "She's a Sayid."

"Yes, and her brother is Ehan Sayid."

Naim whistled. "He was one of my father's buyers."

"So—"

"What's your best email?" Naim asked. "I can have a couple of viable contacts to you within the hour. With my referral, they'll trust you."

"Thank you," Omar said. "I won't forget this, my friend."

"That's exactly what I want you to do," Naim said. His voice was no longer amused. "Forget this conversation, and forget that the connections came from me. I'm serious about becoming legitimate once I get out of this witness protection program. I'm not messing around anymore."

"Agreed," Omar said, but he couldn't stop the grin from spreading across his face. He hung up and turned to face Mia.

She didn't say a word, just rotated her laptop screen to show Omar.

The breath left his chest. A picture of Chad and Aamira had been posted—separate photos arranged side by side—and the headline: "Sayid Heiress Abducted by British Citizen."

"He won't be able to live this down," Mia said in a soft voice.

"No." Omar sank onto the couch next to her, staring at the photo and the headline.

"He'll need a new identity," Mia continued.

"Yes," Omar agreed. He was stunned at the power the Sayid family still had, wherever they were hiding.

His cell phone dinged with an incoming email. It contained three names and phone numbers from Naim.

Mia looked at the phone screen with him. "There's so much that could go wrong with this."

"There is," Omar said, his voice devoid of emotion. "Are you in?"

Mia glanced at the laptop once more then said, "Definitely. Let's reel in the bastards."

Omar pulled her into a fierce hug, and she squeezed him back. Moments later, he was on the phone with Raul Culver. After a convoluted conversation establishing Omar's credentials and his connection to Naim, Omar gave Mia a thumbs-up. Culver had just agreed to float the money, with a significant interest rate, of course.

The next phone call wasn't so simple. Mr. Martin required transparency. Otherwise he would never buy Omar's story, his motivation for wanting to acquire these paintings. If anyone could get the word out about a very wealthy and very interested buyer for the Passion paintings, sans the poetry, then Martin had to be on Omar's side. Martin would, naturally, take a higher-than-normal commission, but he could guarantee to keep Omar's identity secret.

Ten minutes later, Omar sank onto the couch next to Mia. "I've either masterminded the most brilliant plan in history, or I've just committed the stupidest act ever."

Mia grabbed his hand and linked her fingers through his. "I'm coming with you, so I'll make sure this doesn't blow up in our faces."

"Both literally and figuratively?" he clarified. He leaned over for a kiss and gratefully received one. "Remember when I asked you to marry me?" he whispered.

She drew back. "Which time?"

"The most recent time."

Mia looked up at the ceiling. "I do, and I also remember what I told you." She looked at him, her eyes narrowed.

"Are we any closer to a *yes*?" he asked, with a hopeful smile.

"How is this a good time to discuss marriage?" Mia asked. She pushed against his chest as Omar tried to pull her into his arms.

He chuckled. "Is there ever a good time? I mean, if we talked about it last week, I would have been in London, and you were in France. If we talked about it two days ago, we were driving across the desert, trying to get Joseph to a hospital in Amman. If we'd talked about it yester—"

She placed a hand over his mouth. "Hush. I get it."

He raised his brows in question.

She smiled and lowered her hand.

"So?" he prompted.

"So, I guess we might be a little closer to something more permanent," she said, her face flushing a beautiful pink.

“Because I keep proving I’m an amazing guy?” Omar asked.

She tilted her head. “You are quite amazing, actually.” She wrapped her arms around his neck just as his phone rang.

Of course. “Hold all your thoughts right there.” When he saw the number for Mr. Martin, he straightened and answered. “That was quick,” he said.

Mr. Martin was suave. “I have a verified lead. But they want a good faith deposit of one million dollars.”

Omar gave a low whistle. “Do they think I’m stupid?”

“This is how it works,” Mr. Martin said. “They want proof of funds, and it doesn’t hurt to see how stupid you’re willing to get.”

“All right,” Omar said, leaning forward and propping his elbows on his knees. “What’s your advice?”

“Wire in the one million, then wait.”

Too much, even if it was someone else’s money. Omar calculated. He thought again about consulting with Simon, but that would slow things down too much. Besides, he was already running outside most legal channels. And the more people he put in the loop, the greater likelihood of his cover being blown.

When he was ready to make the purchase, he’d call for backup if needed. “Email me the wiring instructions,” he told Martin. Then he hung up and walked into the kitchen before calling Culver.

Culver laughed when Omar told him the deposit amount. “I hope the Israeli government loves you,” he said. “You know this can go one of two ways.”

Omar closed his eyes. He knew. But it appeared Culver wanted to trot him through several cautionary scenarios. “The money could disappear into a black hole, never to be recovered,” Culver said. “Or you could have a deal, and you’ll be at physical risk if you insist on meeting the seller in person.”

“I insist,” Omar said.

“Very well,” Culver said. “The transaction will take about fifteen minutes. Once it clears, I’ll send you a confirmation by text.”

"Good," Omar said. "And thank you."

"Remember my interest rate starts tomorrow and accrues daily," Culver added.

"I remember." Omar hung up and turned to Mia.

She was on her laptop, the screen open to the government's secure portal.

"What are you doing?" he asked.

"We'll need a private jet," Mia said, as she entered her request.

"That could take forty-eight hours to get approved."

"We'll be long gone before any approval is made. I'm only creating a paper trail." Mia looked up at him. "In case things go south, there will be a record that we at least attempted to follow protocol."

"You don't have to come with me," Omar said, rubbing the back of his neck. "Even if this thing ends up smelling like roses, I'll probably still get fired."

Mia stood up. "Well, it's a good thing I like you more than my job."

"Really?" he said.

"Really." She moved closer and wrapped her arms around his neck.

"That's better," he murmured against her lips before he pulled her into a kiss. Mia's body melded against his. They hadn't been alone much over the past several weeks, and he missed her.

Mia kissed him back, teasing him, since they both knew a single text could send them back into the field again.

The next couple of hours passed agonizingly slowly. Omar knew it could take hours for things to come together, or even another day or two.

When his phone finally buzzed, he looked away from his laptop where he was in the Israeli database, browsing descriptions of stolen artifacts. He read the text aloud to Mia. "The transaction has cleared, and now . . ." he started to say. Another buzz. Just like clockwork.

He turned the phone so Mia could see the block of information that had just been transferred. It seemed the Sayid family was anxious to get the stolen property off their hands.

"Cairo?" Mia said. "Why do they want to do the transfer in Cairo?"

"Neutral territory?" Omar suggested.

"I guess you could call it that," she said, but her frown didn't disappear. "Something's wrong."

Omar looked at the screen and reread the instructions. Meeting scheduled for Cairo at 5:00 a.m. in a leather goods shop, old part of the city. "What do you think?"

"It's too neat, too simple," Mia said. "I don't see the Sayid family hiding out in Cairo. I think it's a setup."

Omar turned toward the balcony. He stared at the blue sky over the shimmering Mediterranean Sea. Mia was right. It was too neat. She came to stand beside him and linked her arm through his.

"They already have the deposit money," Omar said. "But they don't trust me yet, so they're being cautious."

"Right," Mia agreed. "What do you want to do?"

"Counteroffer with a different location?" Omar suggested. "Someplace more neutral. Throw them off, make them think I have something to hide as well."

Mia laughed. "Exactly. Then they'll trust you more."

Omar pulled out his phone and typed in his next instructions to Mr. Martin.

"So, where are we going?" Mia asked.

"Alexandria."

Her eyes widened. "You're not going to bring my father into this?"

Omar shook his head. "There's a compound near the airport. Quite a distance from your father's place." Mia's birth father was the now-exiled Coptic Pope, His Holiness, Patriarch Stephanus II.

Mia seemed to relax.

"But I do need your father's help with one thing," Omar said. "I need to hire some bodyguards. You think he can refer me to an organization?"

"You're kidding," Mia said, drawing away and staring at him. "You have the entire Israeli undercover operations department at your service. Highly trained men and women who are some of the best snipers in the world."

"The Sayids will smell us coming a dozen kilometers away." He rested his hands on Mia's shoulders and gazed into her brown eyes. "You'll stay hidden in the vehicle, so you can be backup if things go wrong. They'll see me traveling with local bodyguards, and think nothing's amiss."

"All right. That makes sense. I guess we still need a jet."

Omar grinned in agreement.

CHAPTER THIRTY-FOUR

HORNS OF HATTIN

"We need to go back," Nadia repeated to the allamah, knowing that if she didn't return to the war camp and prostrate herself before Saladin, to beg for Jed's release, then he'd truly be lost to her. Forever.

The sun was burning a fiery hole against the sky, and the allamah wiped his face once again. He'd been riding hard for hours toward the hideout Nadia shared with Kazbech.

"Kazbech," she said, scrambling to her feet. "Take me back to the war camp, or I'll ride there myself."

"You'll end up dead," Allamah Raahil said. He glanced up at the sky. "It is probably too late already."

Nadia stepped toward him. "What do you mean?"

"His execution is scheduled for sundown," the allamah said. "Even if you were to make it before sundown, you would not be allowed to see Saladin."

"But he's my father-in-law," Nadia whispered, dumbfounded that a father could sentence his own son to die. "Please." She grasped Kazbech's arm.

She could see her own pain mirrored in his eyes. Kazbech and Jed were like brothers. "If we don't try—"

"It's more than foolish," the allamah cut in. "Even I cannot return. They'll have figured out that I left to join up with both of you."

“Kazbech,” Nadia said again, ignoring the allamah. “I don’t care what happens to my own life; I must try to stop Jed’s execution.”

He gave a single nod. “We’ll leave right away.”

“You are a fool,” the allamah said. “Don’t say I didn’t warn you. Your blood will not be on my hands.”

“Thank you for delivering the news,” Kazbech said in a calm but firm voice. He walked toward the olive tree and untied the horse. Then he led it over and helped Nadia mount for the ride back.

The allamah watched them but said nothing.

When Kazbech climbed up on the horse, he looked over at the allamah. “Where will you go?”

“I will return to my homeland,” he said. “I’m a marked man now.”

Kazbech reached around Nadia, taking up the reins. “May Allah be with you.”

The allamah nodded and turned away toward his own horse, drinking from the well near the olive tree.

Then instead of mounting, he led the horse away from the two of them.

“Will he be all right?” Nadia asked Kazbech. “Where’s his homeland?”

“His father and his grandfather worked under Saladin, so he must be referring to his roots,” Kazbech said. “Which I believe are in Upper Mesopotamia.” He slapped the reins and the horse jolted forward, starting into a trot. Kazbech slapped the reins again, and the horse increased its speed.

Nadia gripped the saddle, holding herself upright, although she needn’t have worried. Kazbech’s arms were a solid wall keeping her on the horse.

The heat of the sun stifled them, and as they rode, Nadia kept track of the yellow disk as it crawled across the sky. They had to make it back to the war camp before sundown. They just had to.

But the horse grew tired a couple of hours in, and Kazbech was forced to let it canter instead of run.

The afternoon was late when Kazbech drew the horse to a stop. Nadia blinked away the stupor that had overtaken her. "Why are we stopping?"

"The horse is fatigued," Kazbech said. He dismounted, and extended his hand toward Nadia.

She slid off the horse, and took a moment to steady herself by holding onto Kazbech's arm.

"We'll have to travel the rest of the way on foot," he said. The horse dispiritedly stood in a mangrove of tall prickly bushes where Kazbech had led it.

"The horse is finished?" Nadia asked.

"For today," Kazbech said. "It will need a day's rest." He motioned with his hand. "Come, we have a ways to go."

Nadia glanced at the lowering sun. "Will we make it in time?"

"Allah willing," Kazbech said.

To Nadia that meant that something else would have to delay Jed's execution. She trudged through the rocky terrain, keeping up with Kazbech as best as she could. She knew he was moving slowly for her benefit.

She wondered if she should send him ahead, but knew she should be the one to make the request. Pride and honor would prevent Saladin from changing his mind unless a woman entreated him. Her gender would work to her advantage this time.

By the time the sun touched the horizon and continued its descent, they had still not reached camp. Nadia's clothing was soaked with perspiration, and she had never been more thirsty in her life.

The Hattin plateau finally came into sight. Nadia increased her pace with some special reserve of extra stamina. Kazbech looked at her and wondered. When she saw the guard patrol they'd have to bypass, she once again pulled on her veil.

"I can go alone," she told Kazbech. "Maybe they will take more compassion on a single woman traveling to beg for Saladin's mercy."

But he shook his head. "You don't understand Muslim warriors. You will be captured immediately. At least the guards know me and perhaps might make an exception. Let me do the speaking."

The sun's globe was completely behind the western mountain now, although its light still spread orange across the sky.

A guard rode up to them. He reined to a stop and said, "Kazbech? Who travels with you?"

"Jed's wife is with me," Kazbech said, looking up at the man on the horse. The guard's brows were thick and his beard scraggly. "We are here to petition Saladin for Jed's release."

The guard spoke bluntly. "You plan to bury his body?"

Nadia's breath stilled. "He is dead?" she asked, although she wasn't supposed to speak.

The guard moved his horse closer. "You are the Christian woman?"

"She is Muslim, just the same as the rest of the tribe," Kazbech said, moving to stand in front of her.

But Nadia wanted answers. She stepped out from behind Kazbech. "Has Jed been killed?" she said in hoarse voice.

The guard looked her up and down. "Yes, Jed was executed, but Saladin will be very interested in meeting you."

Executed? The word left Nadia staggered. Impossible to believe. How could he be gone? Somehow she was still standing, although her mind and heart were slowly going numb. She couldn't accept this reality. The guard had to be lying.

"Ah, there's the funeral procession now," the guard said, and waved his hand in the direction of the plateau.

"No," she whispered. She watched in horror as a couple dozen soldiers walked behind four other men carrying a litter. Upon it was a body draped with cloth. Her stomach clenched with nausea. "Where are they taking him?" she choked out.

"He will receive a traitor's burial," the guard said. "No tomb, no marker befitting his accomplishments in life. Saladin was generous to let him be buried with his head."

Nadia shuddered, unable to take her eyes away from the procession as it moved to the edge of the plateau. The litter was set on the ground, and the soldiers brought over rocks, placing them on top of the body. This was Jed, a shrouded corpse, this was her husband who had been executed, a man who no longer breathed the air around him.

"They are leaving him there?" Nadia said in a trembling voice.

"He can't be buried on tribal land, you know," the guard said. He climbed off his horse and extended his hand toward Nadia. "I will escort you to the burial site so that you can offer your respect."

A couple of other guards from the perimeter of the plateau had noticed them, and shortly trotted over on horseback.

"What's happened to Raynald's wife and stepson?" Kazbech asked before Nadia could respond to the guard's invitation.

"Saladin has sent them back to Al Karak under guard," the guard said. "But this woman is wanted by Saladin. Come, I'll ride you into the camp and present you. Then you may pay your respects at Jed's grave."

Nadia's need to see Jed, or settle for visiting his grave, intensified. She'd been too late to plead for his life, too late to trade her own for his. The least she could do now was pay her respects and try to explain to her father-in-law that Jed was not a traitor. She was about to step forward and go with this guard. Maybe she could somehow plead for Jed to be given an honorable burial. But Kazbech grasped her arm. "She stays with me. With Jed's death, there is no place for her at the camp."

The guard smirked. "I don't think Saladin shares the same opinion." His gaze narrowed as he looked at Kazbech. "He'll be the one deciding, not us."

"No," Kazbech said. "Turn your horse around and return to your post. The woman leaves with me."

"Ah," the guard said, his voice rough now. "I see how it is."

Simultaneously, the men lunged at each other. Nadia jumped back. Fists flew, then knives came out. She heard the thundering of horses' hooves moving toward them, but she couldn't take her eyes off the dueling men. And then Kazbech had the guard pinned to the ground, a blade buried deep in the man's thigh.

Kazbech straightened up and yelled, "Get on his horse!"

Nadia bolted into action and mounted the guard's horse in an act of sheer and athletic grace, Kazbech right behind her. And then they were galloping full speed away from the plateau, two other horsemen in pursuit.

Kazbech rode hard, and the horse sprinted through the desert. Twilight covered the land, and as it grew darker, they were able to increase the distance. Nadia didn't want to be captured by the guards, but the war camp was the only place she could restore her husband's honor and clear his name. But with Kazbech injuring that guard, they'd be in more trouble now. When darkness fell completely, Kazbech slowed the horse. Nadia looked behind them; there was no sign of the pursuers.

"What happened back there?" Nadia asked. "Why did you attack that guard?"

"He was ready to kill me to get to you. And you would have joined Jed in a grave if you'd gone with him," Kazbech said.

Nadia squeezed her eyes shut. "But what if Saladin will listen to me? What if he'll clear Jed's name?"

When Kazbech said nothing, her tears started. Then Kazbech turned the horse so that they faced the direction of the plateau. In the distance were the tiny bright specks of the cooking fires. All else faded to black. "He's gone," Kazbech said in a low voice. "Whatever mercy Jed thought his father might extend, he was wrong. He's been given a traitor's burial, and Saladin has sent a message to everyone in his army and everyone who passes by the plateau. Disobedience will never be tolerated in Saladin's tribe."

Now Nadia's tears were copious, and sobs rose up within her, until she was gasping for air, trying to breathe.

Kazbech's arms came around her and pulled her against his chest as she turned into him and cried over her husband's fate.

CHAPTER THIRTY-FIVE

ALEXANDRIA

The landing strip was well cared for, at least that's what the pilot had told Omar and Mia. The bumpy landing testified otherwise. But Omar didn't have time to be choosy. In less than an hour, he'd be facing one, perhaps two Sayid men, and he had no idea what to expect.

Mia was already unbuckling her seatbelt and reaching for her jacket when Omar turned away from the small, oval window that didn't show much outside but a few runway lights and darkness beyond. The area was desolate, but that's how Omar wanted it. He didn't want to meet the Sayids in the public market of a large city.

"Ready?" Omar asked Mia, and she nodded. He reached for the leather case beneath his seat. Two million dollars in cash was heavier than he realized. Hefting the case with one hand and grabbing his jacket with the other, Omar followed Mia down the short staircase off the plane.

"Two hours?" the pilot asked. He was framed in the open door, already lighting a cigarette.

"At least," Omar said. "But don't worry, we're paying you by the hour. And there's a bonus once we get back on Israeli soil."

The pilot nodded, then lowered his voice. "It's not the pay," he said, as if making confession. "We're close to the former Jewish Quarter—the one that's always in the news."

Omar knew what he meant. Civil unrest had broken out more

than once in the past couple of weeks near the former Jewish Quarter in Alexandria. And the jet was clearly marked with Hebrew writing.

Omar fished out an ID from his jacket. "If anyone asks you questions, tell them you're working with the Egyptian government." He handed the ID up the staircase to the pilot.

"This is you?" the pilot asked, looking at the picture on the ID, and then back at Omar.

"Yes, it's a few years old, all right?" The man in the photo had a thick mustache and closely-cropped hair. And he sported a deep tan.

"We'll be as quick as possible," Mia said, tugging on Omar's arm.

The sound of an approaching truck echoed in the night.

"Not a truck," Omar muttered as they walked away from the plane. He eyed the small truck and marveled that this was the best the private security company could do.

Two men sat in the back, rifles slung over their shoulders. Two other men sat inside the cab. As Omar and Mia approached the truck, the driver climbed out and greeted Omar.

"This is your best vehicle?" Omar asked in Arabic.

"Our larger SUV is in repairs," the man said, and extended his hand.

Omar shook it. "What's your name?"

"Mosa."

"Tell your man in the cab to climb into the back," Omar said, and then gestured toward Mia. "She'll ride up front with us."

Mosa glanced at Mia.

"If anything happens to her, you'll pay," Omar said. "Let your men know that as well."

"Of course," Mosa said, giving him another look, then sizing up the private jet. "You're from Israel?"

"We're with the government," Omar said. "On a top-secret mission." He figured if anything went wrong, at least the security company would know which embassy to contact, not that the Hebrew lettering on the jet wasn't a strong hint.

"Please tell your pilot to turn off his lights," Mosa said.

Omar turned to the jet, where the pilot was still smoking at the top of the stairs. Omar motioned with a hand-check for him to turn off the lights. The pilot disappeared inside the jet, and a moment later the entire thing went dark.

"Let's go," Omar said, opening the door on the driver's side. Mia climbed in first, so that she sat between Omar and Mosa. Omar settled into the driver's seat and checked his weapon and ammunition. Then he took out his ID that read Mr. Ali Faaris. The man in the picture had a mustache, and since Omar didn't have time to grow one, he had to make do with a costumer's version. He pressed the mustache to his upper lip.

"All set?" Omar asked Mia.

She nodded. Her full veil already covered her face.

Omar turned the truck around. The drive was only fifteen minutes from the landing strip, but Omar took a longer, more indirect route to shake any possible surveillance. He hoped the Sayids expected his plane to fly into the main Alexandria airport and were monitoring arrivals there.

After ten minutes, they pulled off the main road and onto the gravel stretch that led to the compound. Omar slowed the truck. He positioned a small digital camera on the dash and turned on the recording device. Lights were on inside the compound, and Omar hoped for a meeting outside, where the dark would assist his disguise.

The firefight at the warehouse in Al Karak had been brief, but Omar didn't want to take chances.

"Stay in the truck, out of sight," Omar told Mia. "Unless I signal for you. Those lights are going to be like a beacon."

She said nothing, which meant she was agreeing with him, at least for now. He hoped he wouldn't need her as backup. When they drew closer to the compound, she ducked beneath the dashboard.

Two vehicles sat parked in front of the compound, one a sedan, the other a black SUV. It seemed *they* had the right vehicles for this operation. A couple of men were smoking, the orange glow of their cigarettes setting off white trails of smoke.

Three other men looked to be bodyguards. They stood with rifles in their hands, not aiming, but not standing down, either.

Omar stopped the truck twenty meters away, and turned on the miniature camera he had attached to the collar of his jacket. He climbed out of the driver's seat. Mosa followed with his men who had quietly descended from the bed of the truck. Omar gripped his own pistol in his hand and watched the reaction of the two men with cigarettes. They dropped them on the ground, then straightened from their positions leaning against the sedan.

With Mosa at his side, Omar motioned for the other hired guards to wait by the truck, and he and Mosa started toward the two men. Omar recognized Taheer Sayid immediately. Aamira's father. The second man required Omar to spend a few more seconds sorting through his memory. Kahul Sayid, Taheer's brother. Omar glanced around to see if Ehan was among the group. Not in sight. Perhaps he was further inside the lit-up compound.

"I assume you need two vehicles because the paintings are in one of them?" Omar said in Arabic.

Taheer waited a moment before answering. He scrutinized first Omar, then Mosa. "You have the money?"

Omar nodded. "With one of my men." Behind him, a bodyguard had been commissioned to carry the leather case. Omar had no doubt that Taheer would demand a visual check of its contents before handing over the paintings.

Taheer released a low chuckle. "They look like rent-a-cops." He didn't know how close to the mark he really was. "And you're Ali Faaris? How come I've never heard of you before?"

Omar was ready for this question, and he decided to speak as much truth as he could, using his father's background as his own. "I live in Morocco. I think we have a few acquaintances in common."

"Like who?" Taheer asked.

"Mr. Martin, for one, and Mr. Bata," Omar said, naming Naim's father who was imprisoned the year before, crumbling his black market dynasty.

Taheer shook his head. "Mr. Bata didn't deserve his fate."

"He's a smart man, though," Omar said. "And can afford the best lawyers."

Taheer narrowed his eyes, studying Omar much more closely now. "Let's see the money."

Omar nodded to Mosa, who signaled the guard with the leather case. As the guard approached, Taheer and his brother Kahul motioned for their own men to come closer. The guard set the leather case at Omar's feet. "Help yourself," Omar said.

Surprisingly, Kahul was the one who stepped forward and opened the case. The money was new and banded into neat chunks of cash. Kahul counted through the stacks, then lifted his head. "Two million," he said. "It's all here."

"Can I see the paintings now?" There were six of them, but the Sayids had agreed to sell only two. Omar didn't care about the number of paintings or the amount he had to pay; he just wanted the paintings for evidence.

Taheer lit another cigarette. At least somebody at this scene was relaxed.

"Bring the painting," Taheer said to one of his thugs. The man moved to the back of the SUV, and moments later he carried out a narrow crate.

When he opened the crate, it didn't take much examination by Omar to know it was original. He'd studied these paintings enough. And he knew the Sayid family wouldn't have had time to hire an artist to create any counterfeits.

But Omar still had a part to play. "This is not the painting I asked for."

"What do you mean?" Taheer said. "It's the Passion, number 8. That's exactly what Dr. Martin said."

Omar groaned. "I wanted number 9." He waved his hand toward the painting. "This one is worth a fraction of the price you asked for."

Taheer laughed, shaking his head. "The Passion collection has been relocated."

Omar lifted a brow, letting Taheer know that he knew exactly what *relocated* meant. "Do they have Nadia's poems concealed within them still?"

This time Taheer acted surprised. "You know about them?"

"Any serious collector carrying my kind of cash knows these things," Omar countered.

Taheer paused for a moment. "They've been removed and are not for sale. The painting or nothing. But we'll keep your deposit if you back out."

"Of course," Omar said. "Let's see the other painting, then I decide if we have a deal. And my deposit will be returned in full."

Taheer nodded to his man and said to Omar, "You've not done business much on the black market, have you?" He was watching Omar too intently, and Omar began to wonder if he should have worn a fake beard as well.

Just as the guard brought around the second small crate, a man came out of the compound and strode toward them.

Ehan.

Omar felt a chill. Ehan was more likely to recognize him than the father or uncle, especially if Ehan had researched Chad's family at all. Which, no doubt, he had.

It appeared that Ehan had been injured in the gunfight in Al Karak. He walked with a limp, but he wore a tailored suit and a smug look on his face. Looking at the young man in person made Omar feel sick.

When Ehan stopped near his father, Omar busied himself, hiding his face by inspecting the painting. It was time to conclude this transaction and get out of here.

The guard popped open the crate and pulled out the second painting. Omar nodded. "Looks like the original," he said.

"No complaints about this one?" Taheer said. "You seem to suddenly be in a hurry."

"He had complaints?" Ehan walked closer to Omar.

Ehan in close proximity to Omar wasn't going to be a good thing. Aamira had told Omar and Chad about his temper. All of the things her brother had said and done to her. Not only was Ehan a bad seed and the worst brother possible, but he was also an international thief who enjoyed making others miserable.

Omar felt his free hand curl into a fist as Ehan neared. He stopped just a few feet away from Omar. "What are your complaints?"

"I asked for 9, and I don't appreciate a substitute," Omar said. Time was up, he had to get out of here. He had plenty of video footage now.

In a quick motion, Ehan reached out and tugged at Omar's mustache. It came off his face without resistance.

Omar brought up his pistol, pointing it directly in Ehan's face. "That wasn't a smart thing to do."

Ehan smiled. "I thought it was you." He didn't move, not with the pistol aimed between his eyes. But he didn't seem bothered that Omar had sighted him.

"Father, don't you know who this is?" Ehan said.

Taheer stepped forward, his own gun aimed at Omar.

"Omar Zagouri," Ehan said. He glanced at the bodyguards Omar had brought. "Came solo, did you? That surprises me. Must be getting cocky."

Now Kahul also moved in closer so that Omar was surrounded by all three Sayid men, everyone's weapons at the ready.

"Where's my sister?" Ehan asked.

It was Omar's turn to smile. "She's not your sister any longer. Remember, you renounced her membership in the family." He looked at Taheer. "She told us everything, by the way. Her testimony has been filed by the Israeli government and sent to the

Jordanian authorities. This case now goes far beyond your little village. Investigations into the deaths of other women in your tribe have also been opened."

Ehan's eyes widened, but then he replaced his surprise with a smooth smile. "It's easy enough to get a testimony destroyed. You'd be surprised at how many court officials can be bribed."

"I'm sure you know how it's done," Omar said, inching forward, keeping his gun steady.

Taheer's guards were all pointing their weapons, and Omar's hired bodyguards had approached the group. Omar hoped Mia would stay hidden inside the truck. The Sayid men wouldn't show any mercy to a woman. One false move, and both sides would be gunning each other down.

"So, you've come for the paintings?" Taheer said with a laugh.

"I don't want the paintings," Omar said. "I want you." There was no neat and pretty way out of this, and Omar knew it. He took another step forward, but Taheer was holding his ground. Omar knew he had to move fast before this turned into a shooting fest. Another step forward, and he knew he was too close for comfort now, so he lunged for Taheer. Omar reached him before he could scramble out of the way, wrapped his arm around the man's neck, then pointed his gun at the man's head. "Everyone put your guns down," Omar called out. "It would be my pleasure to take out a member of the Sayid family tonight."

Ehan took a step back, lowering his gun.

"Drop it," Omar said, staring at him.

Ehan nodded to the others. "Put down your guns." One by one the guards, and then finally Kahul, put their weapons on the ground.

"That wasn't so hard, was it?" Omar said, wondering exactly that . . . why had they been so compliant? Then he realized Ehan was no longer looking at Omar, but up at the sky.

A low rumbling came from above—the unmistakable sound of a helicopter.

"What the hell?" Omar said, also looking up now. He didn't recognize the markings of the chopper, but he didn't have time to read them because two shooters inside the helicopter started to fire.

Omar hit the ground and rolled, losing his grip on Taheer. He thought he heard Ehan laugh. When Omar looked over at the man, Ehan pointed to the helicopter that was circling back, guns pointed down. "I'd like you to meet the Mika'il Order." Then he moved for cover with the other men, leaving Omar exposed in the open.

Omar rolled away from the chopper's gunfire, then scrambled to his feet and made a run for the compound. He had to draw the gunfire away from the truck and Mia. Behind him, Mosa ran, too, cursing every living thing.

The only good thing about the helicopter's arrival was that it gave Omar a brief opening while the Sayid men took cover. Omar yanked the door open to the building and ran into a foyer. The place was empty, but the room beyond was not. A couple of tables were set up with several rifles laid out on them. It seemed he'd found the weapons stash. Impeccable timing.

He grabbed a rifle and several clips and ran to the window. Opening it, he aimed outside, searching for the helicopter. It sounded like it was directly over the compound.

"I need something bigger caliber," Omar said to Mosa, while keeping his eyes trained upward. "Anything there?"

The chopper cleared the compound, still flying low. Omar needed to keep the chopper away from the truck, but he wouldn't do much good if he got himself killed.

"Ah, here's a rocket launcher," Mosa said, reaching under the table.

"Load it and give it to me. Now!" Omar eyed the chopper. It was close enough that he could see the black clothing of the shooters and the glint of their machine guns against the compound's lights. "We need to kill the lights," Omar shouted over the noise.

"Here," Mosa said, setting the launcher down by Omar. "I'll find the lights."

Omar crouched by the window and checked the equipment on the launcher. He'd used one of these during a training weekend, and about all he could remember was that his ears rang for days.

Just as he aimed the launcher, some of the compound lights shut off.

"Thank you, Mosa," Omar said, as he pressed his finger to the trigger. The rocket thudded out of the barrel of the weapon, and Omar nearly lost his balance from the recoil.

He scrambled back up and watched the rocket neatly clip the nose of the chopper. Somehow the pilot kept it stable, and now Omar knew he was in trouble. The shooters wouldn't show any mercy now.

"Another rocket!" Omar shouted.

Mosa was next to him in a moment, breathing hard, but in his blessed hands, he carried two rockets.

Omar dropped to his knee and reloaded the second rocket, propping the launcher on the windowsill. Now the helicopter shooters found the range for Omar's side of the building. Mosa picked up an AK-47 and started to fire out the window by Omar's side.

"Watch out!" Omar yelled, and sent another rocket on its way.

This one found the tail of the helicopter and thudded home with a blast of light, vaporizing the rear rotor and causing the airborne machine to tilt and spin out of control even as Omar reloaded yet again.

Mosa cheered, but Omar wasn't finished.

While the helicopter careened away from the compound to crash-land in a nearby field, Omar aimed at the Sayids' SUV and pulled the trigger again. The blast that exploded the SUV lifted Omar and Mosa off their feet. Omar landed on his back. He was definitely going to have trouble hearing after this.

He rolled over, groaning, but knew he was the lucky one. He had to get to Mia. He pushed himself to his feet. His back and neck throbbed, but he could still walk, so that was a plus. He grabbed another rifle and clips off the table.

"Are you all right?" he asked Mosa.

Mosa grunted. "I'm alive."

"Let's get out of here," Omar said. "We're sitting ducks in this building."

Mosa moved with Omar to the front door. The Sayids were getting to their feet as well, a burning SUV behind them. In the field beyond, fierce flames consumed the downed helicopter. Unfortunately for Omar, there were three Sayids, plus their guards, between him and the truck.

Omar and Mosa were outnumbered, especially since it looked like their hired bodyguards were still taking shelter, or in shock, or killed or injured. But he and Mosa had fresh firepower.

Ehan Sayid spotted Omar and started to move toward him, his limp more pronounced now. When Ehan raised his gun, Omar knew only one of them would make it out of this alive.

CHAPTER THIRTY-SIX

ANCIENT KARAK

Nadia paced the bedchamber in the Karak castle. It was two months since Jed's death, two months since Kazbech had returned her to the fortress of Karak. Her mother's greeting had been lukewarm at best. Stephanie hadn't fled with Azzo but had faced Saladin and tried to negotiate with him. The light had gone from her eyes with all of her concessions, and now she was more focused on keeping Humphrey out of Saladin's grip than on the fact that she was a widow for the third time—and her daughter was a widow too.

The memories of the night Nadia had arrived with Kazbech still tumbled about in her mind. He'd prostrated himself before Stephanie, and begged for her mercy. She, of course, had granted it. But when she heard the whole of Nadia's tale of marriage and flight and Jed's death, Kazbech had been sent away and Nadia strictly confined to her rooms. Her mother was worried that if Saladin discovered she was harboring Nadia, he would renege on his mercy.

Nadia was all but forgotten.

Meals were delivered twice a day, her chamber pot emptied once a day. Once a week she was allowed a stroll outside with an armed guard. On one of these brief walks she had spotted Kazbech among the laborers rebuilding a castle wall. So he'd been put to work and not banished after all. That fact brought her a strange sort of comfort. Kazbech had said once that he and Jed were like brothers. And Nadia had to be satisfied with this modest earthly connection that remained to Jed.

Her only comfort was the daily visit of her handmaiden, Miriam. The short visits at least gave Nadia a chance to speak with someone each day.

Nadia stopped at the window opening with a view of the courtyards below. Her stomach lurched, although she'd taken only a few bites this morning. For three days, she'd thrown up her morning meal. By evening she was so hungry that her body decided to accept the food. Now she turned and bent over the washbasin, emptying her stomach until there was nothing left. She stumbled to her bed and collapsed upon it. She had no fever.

The lock of her door turned, but Nadia stayed on the bed, unable to lift her head. And that was how Miriam discovered her.

"You're ill again, my lady?" Miriam's voice seemed to screech through Nadia's head even though the handmaiden spoke in her usual gentle tone.

"I threw up again and was too dizzy to stand up," Nadia said.

Miriam pressed a cool hand against Nadia's forehead. "There is no fever." And then her eyes widened.

"What is it?" Nadia demanded, although it sounded like a very weak demand.

"When was your last menses?"

Nadia was quiet as she remembered. Since before the battle between the Muslims and the crusaders.

"Before your marriage?" Miriam asked.

Nadia propped herself up on an elbow. "Yes." Was Miriam thinking . . . Was she . . . "You are with child." Her voice was barely above a whisper, but she might as well have shouted it, because the words seemed to expand and completely immerse Nadia.

"I'm carrying Jed's child," Nadia said. "I'm . . ." She covered her mouth with her hand. Closing her eyes, she felt the tears burn.

She was carrying her husband's baby. A child would be born with no father, no identity, and no name. A part of Jed would live on, but what kind of life would the child have?

Miriam grasped her hand. "We must tell your mother," she said. "Perhaps she will show you more kindness."

"No," Nadia said. She knew exactly how her mother would react. Nadia was already in hiding, and her mother had refused to see her in person these past weeks. Their only communication had come through a handful of notes. "Saladin still controls Karak, and my mother is his puppet. She doesn't want Saladin to know of my existence, and she'll demand that I get rid of the child." Nausea forgotten, Nadia sat up on the bed and smoothed back her tangled hair. "I must leave."

"You are in shock," Miriam said. "You can't possibly travel in your condition."

"I *must* leave," Nadia repeated. She rose from the bed, and with her hand over her belly, she walked to the window. "I am carrying my husband's child, and I must honor his wishes." Realizing she was carrying Jed's child pumped courage through her. She would leave this prison, no matter the risk or the cost.

"How can you know his wishes?" Miriam asked.

The question angered Nadia, and she turned to face the old woman. "My husband was a Muslim and second-in-command of one of the most powerful desert tribes of the land. He was betrayed by his own people and his own father. I will not raise this child of his in captivity. His child will be free and grow to be strong." The words poured out of her, coming from a place of strength and determination she didn't know she had. "I must leave this castle-prison and find my own future."

Miriam stared at her, mouth open.

"When it grows dark tonight," Nadia said, "deliver a message to the slave Kazbech. Tell him to meet me at the canal bridge." She had imagined many times escaping her prison, but not until now was she willing to take the risk.

By nightfall, Nadia felt better, as she did every night. But on this night she prepared to sneak out. She drew on one of Miriam's cloaks, and when Miriam arrived, Nadia embraced her handmaiden for the last time. She exited the chamber wearing Miriam's clothing, hood pulled up. With her she carried a small satchel of belongings.

The guard outside her chamber said nothing, and Nadia hurried on her way, down the stairs, out into the garden. There she followed the same path she used to take when meeting Jed.

This time she was alone, with not even her handmaiden to accompany her. The night air was pleasantly cool, and after so many weeks of being locked in her bedchamber, she welcomed it. She wanted to remove her hood and let the wind fan her neck and scalp. But she did not dare risk being recognized.

She was nearly to the bridge when a terrible thought crossed her mind. What if Kazbech didn't come? What if he couldn't get away from his slave quarters? Her heart thudded as she neared the bridge, and then she saw him. A dark form emerged from beneath the bridge, and Kazbech stood up in the moonlight.

She wanted to run to him. Instead she walked quickly to where he stood and motioned for him to crouch yet again beneath the bridge. And this time she joined him.

The moonlight came in from the side, but they were in near darkness as they sat together.

Nadia wasted no time in speaking. She told Kazbech that Miriam couldn't stay holed up in her bedchamber for long before their deception was discovered. Her mother didn't want anyone to know that Nadia was hiding within the castle walls, but she also wouldn't be pleased if Nadia escaped. Nadia tried not to think about Miriam's punishment. It was the second time the handmaiden had put her life on the line for Nadia. If Nadia's stepfather were alive, Miriam would have been executed for negligence. But Stephanie had very little power, practically living as a guest in her own castle, and an order of execution might have to come down from Saladin himself.

"Kazbech," Nadia said, looking into his dark eyes. His face had thinned, and there were deep shadows beneath his eyes. The life of a slave was never easy. "I am with child."

He said nothing for a moment. Then, "Jed's child?"

A swell of anger started up inside her, but she tamped it back down. "Of course. We were together for only a short time, but it was enough. I've been ill every morning for the past week, and my handmaiden has confirmed it."

"Will your mother be merciful?" Kazbech asked.

It was a reasonable question, but definitely not one that mattered much anymore, given all this effort to rendezvous with Kazbech.

"I don't want my child to become a political pawn," she said. "*If* I'm allowed to carry it to full term. But I will no longer live beneath her roof or under her rule. This child is the beginning of a new dynasty. One that will make Jed proud."

Kazbech was watching her closely. "What is your plan, my lady?"

"I will travel to Armenia and appeal to my sister Isabella," Nadia said. "This child will be raised as a royal, and when the time is right, we will raise an army and take our revenge on Saladin."

Kazbech didn't blink, didn't move. "You think your Christian sister will take in a Muslim woman and her child? A child with a grandfather who just defeated the crusaders and executed Raynald and now controls all of your mother's lands?"

Nadia stared at him. It was perhaps the longest speech she'd ever heard Kazbech make. "I do. My sister will understand once I explain everything." But as she spoke the words, she realized their absurdity. If her mother would force her to get rid of the child or use the child as a pawn, her sister would do the same. Most likely, her sister Isabella would send her back to her mother.

Shaking his head, Kazbech said, "You have been raised inside castle walls which keep you ignorant of the ways of the desert tribes. No Muslim warrior would ever fight for a man raised in a Christian kingdom, especially a man whose father was denounced by Saladin. Do you not understand that Saladin is second only to Allah in the eyes of our people? Saladin has restored the Muslims' land after decades of oppression and thievery and murder by the crusaders."

Nadia looked away, not able to withstand the censure in Kazbech's eyes.

"What then?" she whispered. "Where am I to go?"

"You're certain you are with child?" he asked in a low voice.

She thought of Miriam's question about the timing of her menses. There was no other explanation. "Yes."

His hand grasped hers, startling Nadia into looking up at him. "You will come with me."

"As a slave?"

"We will leave tonight, just as you planned." His gaze flickered to the satchel she'd brought with her. "But instead of traveling to meet your sister, we will go to a village near Damascus. The town of my mother's birth. We will tell everyone that we are married, that the child is mine, and when the boy becomes a man, we will tell him about Jed."

She stared at him for a long moment. "And you will say we are married?"

"Yes," Kazbech said, leaning close and tightening his hold on her hand. "Jed was like a brother to me, and when he asked me to watch over you, my oath was like giving my own blood. I will never break it."

She nodded and looked at their interlocked hands. She knew she could trust Kazbech with her life and with the life of Jed's son. She would not be able to find another man like him. A lonely life stretched out before her if she didn't accept Kazbech's kindness. Perhaps they could make it a happy life someday. Until now, she hadn't realized the length that a mother would go to protect her child. "Then we will marry in truth." She looked up at him to see his reaction.

He hadn't moved, didn't seem to be breathing.

"This child will need a father, one who is loyal and dependable and courageous. You are all of those things, Kazbech."

Still he didn't move.

"Is it so unfathomable?" she asked in a light tone. "Marriages are arranged all of the time."

"This would be a business arrangement?" he finally asked, and Nadia didn't miss the sketch of disappointment fleeting across his face.

She placed her hand over her stomach, thinking of the tiny life growing inside of her. She felt sure this child was a boy, and if so, she'd name him after his father. She'd raise him to be a good man, a fair man, one who would accept love marriages within his tribe and not use death as a weapon of control.

"There is a Bedu camp not far from Karak," Kazbech said, breaking into her thoughts. "We will ask the holy man to marry us."

"Thank you," she said sincerely. "You have saved my life many times, Kazbech, but it is in this that you show your true honor."

He lowered his gaze for a moment, as if he were trying to make a decision. When he looked up, she saw only resolve. "We must leave tonight. We'll travel to the Bedu camp and marry at first light. Then we'll continue to Damascus."

"All right," she said, her voice falling to a whisper. Her life was changing yet again. And this time it was with a new man, and a new place, and the start of a new family.

Kazbech climbed to his feet and extended his hand to her. She grasped it and let him pull her up.

He didn't let go of her hand. "Follow me. We will walk to the camp, and Allah willing, we'll secure horses once we are there." He glanced at the satchel slung across her body. "Do you have anything to trade with?"

"Some jewels," she confirmed. "And a knife." She drew it

out of her satchel and handed it to Kazbech. They would not get off this plateau without a fight.

Kazbech's grasp tightened on her hand, and they walked along the canal bank, close to the water and out of sight of any passersby. Once they found a trail that led off the plateau, Kazbech led her to a grouping of palms. They crouched there, and Kazbech whispered, "You're about to discover Jed's secret of how he came onto the plateau."

Nadia's eyes widened, but she remained silent.

"Come with me now," Kazbech said, rising, but staying hunched over.

Nadia mimicked his motion, and they hurried across the expanse of ground that separated the palms and the edge of the plateau.

As they neared the edge, Kazbech dropped to the ground again, taking Nadia with him.

Lying in the dirt, face down, she questioned whether or not there was another way off the plateau. Kazbech picked up a rock and scooted closer to the edge. Nadia edged next to him and peered over the side. Although the night was heavy, the moon and stars gave off enough light that she could see the guards about thirty paces down, sitting at their posts, overlooking the desert floor below.

Kazbech pointed to the guard that was almost directly below them, and then with perfect aim threw the rock straight at the guard's head. The sound of the rock hitting his skull made a sharp crack, and the man toppled. Nadia gasped, covering her mouth with her hand to stifle her own sound.

And then Kazbech was pulling her arm and they half-ran, half-slipped down the side of the plateau, following no particular path. It was a desperate, reckless action. The closest guard was perhaps a hundred paces away, and Nadia knew he would soon notice his missing companion. Although Nadia's breath was now coming fast, Kazbech didn't slow his pace, but continued down the side of the plateau.

Rocks scraped Nadia's skin, and bushes caught on her clothing. More than once something snagged and ripped.

Finally, at the base of the plateau, she was able to stand on two feet and catch her breath.

"Hurry," Kazbech said. He turned to look at her, scanning her from head to toe. "We can't stop now." He glanced up the ridge, and Nadia followed his gaze.

Although they were too far away to hear anything, it was obvious that another guard had found the injured man. It was only a few short moments before a search started.

Nadia and Kazbech ran. They sprinted across the moonlit ground, and down another rise, then back up. Kazbech turned to the north, continuing at a pace that Nadia found increasingly difficult to match. At last he slowed down, and although his walk was brisk, Nadia was able to keep up.

They walked for what seemed like hours through the darkness, through the gray, shifting colors just before dawn. When the first yellow glow of the sun began to appear on the eastern horizon, Kazbech drew her to a stop.

She looked around and saw only sand and rocks and more hills. Kazbech handed over his goatskin of water, and she took it, drinking greedily. When she finished, she wiped her mouth and said, "I drank more than my share. I hope we're close."

He nodded, his mouth curving into a bare smile. "We are." He pointed toward the east, where the sky had softened from gray to a pale yellow. "One more hill, and we are at the Bedu camp. Are you ready?"

Nadia gazed up at him. This man was taller than Jed, his eyes darker, and his face more square. Her heart didn't flutter when she was around Kazbech like it had with her husband. But Kazbech's loyalty and goodness endeared him to her.

She stepped close to him and lifted her hand to his face. The surprise was immediate in his eyes, but he didn't move away. She ran her fingers along his cheek and then across his soft, short beard. His eyes seemed to darken, and his gaze intensified. She knew this was unexpected, for him as well as for her.

"Kazbech, I want to thank you for your sacrifice," she said.

He started to protest, but she placed two fingers on his lips.

"You are the most loyal man I know," she said. "And I will be honored to marry you."

Kazbech blinked several times, and then he tilted his face so that it rested against her palm. "What should I call you?"

Nadia started at that question. Then she realized she'd never heard him call her by name, only "my lady." It was fitting that she continue with the Muslim name Jed had given her. "Nadia," she said, and a smile lit up her face.

And then an extraordinary thing happened. Kazbech smiled back. It was the first time she'd ever seen him smile. She'd been wrong all along. Kazbech was a handsome man, a beautiful man.

She lifted up on her toes and kissed the edge of his mouth. For a moment, he didn't move, and then his hands settled at her waist. He turned his head before she could withdraw and captured her lips with his. The kiss was brief and warm, and over almost as soon as it began. Nadia could feel the restraint from Kazbech. He was holding back.

Once they were married, Nadia knew he would have no cause to rein in any passion, unless she wished it. As she stood in his arms, with the new dawn blossoming around them, she knew she didn't want her marriage to be one of convenience only. She wanted love and passion and joy. She found that she was smiling again, and Kazbech was smiling back.

She linked her fingers with his and said the only thing she needed to. "Let us go meet the holy man."

CHAPTER THIRTY-SEVEN

ALEXANDRIA

Although most of the compound's lights had been shut off, Omar could see the whites of Ehan Sayid's eyes quite clearly. Maybe it was due to the flames of the burning SUV, or fifty meters away, the larger inferno of the downed helicopter.

Men were shouting, screaming too, but all Omar could hear was the thud of his own pounding heart. His hearing had been severely impaired by launching those three rockets from inside the compound. Mosa was next to him, holding his ground. The man was turning out to be a stand-up guy. When Omar had first jumped in the truck with the hired bodyguard, he hadn't known what to expect.

Mosa hadn't caved. He'd done everything Omar had asked of him, and now they stood together, facing not one but three Sayid men. Taheer and Kahul had just climbed to their feet and were gaining their bearings.

It wouldn't be long now, Omar realized. But it would be worth it. If only he could tell Mia to start the truck and drive the hell away. No reason for both of them to go down. She had plenty of video footage.

"You're a lunatic!" Ehan shouted at Omar.

Frankly, Omar was surprised he could hear Ehan. The human body really was amazing.

"I've heard about stunts you've pulled off," Ehan continued, closer now. In fact, he was ten feet away. "I see the stories weren't all wrong."

"Is that a compliment?" Omar said.

"Take it however you want," Ehan said, keeping his gun level.

Omar's rifle was also level, and he had no doubt Ehan's finger was getting itchy.

"Any last words?" Ehan asked, his gaze moving from Omar to Mosa, although his gun remained stationary.

"You first," Omar said.

Mosa shifted slightly next to him, keeping his rifle aimed as well.

If this continued, all of them would be dead in a simultaneous exchange of fire.

"I think the time has come and gone for talking," Taheer said. His shirt had been ripped at some point, and he strode toward Omar, a death glare in his eyes.

Omar attempted to think of this man as Aamira's father, but it was increasingly difficult to do so. The man who faced him now—dirty, disheveled, and seething with anger—was just another pathetic terrorist. A man who'd lost his soul a long time ago.

And Omar would be more than happy to take him out. "I agree with Taheer," Omar said, and pulled the trigger.

The Sayid men dove to the ground, somehow avoiding Omar's bullets. Omar flattened himself on the ground as well, dodging retribution. Ehan was headed straight toward him, but before Ehan could take aim, his rifle was shot out of his hands.

Ehan dove toward the ground, covering his head. When he realized he hadn't been shot, he scrambled for the fallen rifle. Omar looked up to see Mia walking toward them.

"Get down! All of you!" she yelled at the Sayid men. "Face down!"

She swung the automatic weapon in a short arc and fired a burst above their heads, and.

"Don't move or the next bullets are in your hearts," she called out. Something popped in the crackling flames of the SUV. Mia kept her rifle aimed at the backs of the now prostrate Sayid men.

Behind Mia the other hired bodyguards appeared. One of them proceeded to disarm the Sayid guards, who soon lay on the ground, face down. Mosa's other two men flanked Mia.

Hiring these thugs had been the best move of Omar's life.

"I'll grab the handcuffs," Mosa said, on his way to the truck. Moments later he returned and knelt down. While Omar kept his rifle trained on the Sayids and their guards, Mosa did the honors.

"It's going to be a tight fit," Omar mused, as he yanked the first man to his feet. One by one he helped the men to their feet, then steered them toward the truck with some encouragement from the barrel of his rifle. There he made them sit down in the open bed. "Cover their heads," Omar told Mosa. "I don't want them making eye contact. And cuff their ankles together. All together. I don't want them getting any ideas to jump off my truck."

Mosa smiled and set to work.

"This is going to cost extra, you know," Mosa said with a smirk.

Omar held up the leather briefcase that had survived the mayhem. "I just happen to have some extra cash on hand. It's your lucky day."

Mosa met Omar's look with one of his own. "If I thought you were serious for one minute, you'd be my new best friend."

Omar shrugged. "A couple million or not, I think we're definitely friends." He slung his rifle over his shoulder and stuck out his hand. Mosa shook it, gripping hard. "Oh, and nice rockets."

Mosa laughed. "I only wish I could have been the one firing them."

"Next time, my friend," Omar said, clapping Mosa on the shoulder.

"Omar," Mia interrupted. "How about we get out of here?"

He turned to Mia and pulled her into a hug. She wrapped her arms around him. "I thought you were done for when you ran into that blasted building."

"We were just trying to find a few more weapons," he answered.

Mia placed her hands on her hips. "You knew there were weapons inside?"

He gazed at her for a moment. Her face was moist with perspiration, her eyes huge in the firelight, and her brows lifted in question.

"No, we were just trying to keep the helicopter away from the truck," he said, dropping his voice.

"I can take care of myself," Mia said, but there was a glint in her eye.

"I know you can," Omar said. "But I think that if anything happens to either of us, it's better me than you."

"And why is that?"

"Because you're irreplaceable," Omar said, tightening his hug. "Simon Greif could hire another Omar tomorrow, and the world wouldn't know the difference." Mosa started up the truck's engine. It was time to go. Then Omar said, "What's wrong, Mia?"

She was shaking her head and wiping at her cheeks with a bandanna. "I'm just glad you walked out of that building, or I would have been really mad."

Omar leaned down and kissed her. Too short, but plenty sweet. "Come on," he said, drawing away reluctantly. "We've got to deliver these guys to the authorities."

CHAPTER THIRTY-EIGHT

JERUSALEM

The knock came on Aamira's door sometime in the middle of the night. When she opened her eyes and saw that the clock next to her bed blinked three in the morning, her heart jolted. "Coming," she called out.

Aamira scrambled to her feet and crossed the room. She looked through the peephole and opened the door. "Chad," she said.

She hadn't seen him since their brief reunion after Al Karak. They were both staying in Jerusalem, and had been able to text and call each other, but the government had kept their locations separate in case of a security breach.

There were a couple of police officers with Chad.

"What's happened?" she asked, her heart continuing to race.

Chad reached out and grasped her hand. "Your father and brother have been caught and taken into custody."

Aamira brushed the tears from her face with trembling hands. "What about my mother?" she asked. She knew from her research that her mother would also be a person of interest to the authorities.

"She's been questioned, but no charges have been filed."

Aamira didn't know whether to be relieved or disappointed. Her mother was aware of the crimes, yet had done nothing. On the other hand, Aamira was sickened by the thought of her mother sitting in a prison cell.

Aamira turned from Chad and tried to gain her composure.

Chad said softly. "I know this is a lot to process right now. You can ask any questions you want as time goes by." He placed a gentle hand on her shoulder, and she closed her eyes. "They're going to be locked away for a long time. They had the Mika'il Order trying to protect them, so now that entire organization is under investigation too. Generations of secrets and wrongful deaths will be exposed. Not only has your family been apprehended, but warrants are out for dozens of other individuals." He turned her to face him and with his thumbs removed the tears from her wet cheeks. "But most importantly, you're going to be safe now. You'll have your life back."

"*Our* life back." She leaned against him, and Chad wrapped his arms about her.

"It's over, sweetheart. Finally over."

She nodded against his chest.

The two policemen had moved down the hallway to give them privacy.

"Omar wanted you to have something," Chad said in a quiet voice.

Aamira released Chad, and he picked up a briefcase at their feet near the door. He handed it over, and said, "It's poetry written by your ancestor, Nadia. You can finally know the true story of her life."

She stared at the leather case. "This is . . . priceless."

"Actually, yes," Chad said with a small laugh. "Yes, it is. Omar said the same thing, but he said it's up to you to decide. You can keep the manuscripts or donate them to a museum."

"May I read them first?" she asked.

"Of course."

"Thank you." She barely spoke above a whisper. Her throat was tight with emotion, and even though her life had changed completely over the past few weeks, she'd never felt more blessed and humbled. She brought the briefcase to her chest and held onto it tightly. She'd just been given part of her history, something that had led to tragic killings. And now, the killing curse had finally been stopped.

"Chad?" Aamira started. "How did my father and brother get caught?"

Chad chuckled and ran his hand through his hair.

She narrowed her eyes. "What?"

He shoved his hands into the pockets of his pants and rolled back on his heels. "Well, the information I have so far sounds pretty sketchy. I never know whether or not to take my cousin at his word. But according to Omar, it involved about three million in cash, a pretty crazy shootout in Alexandria, and, of course, a helicopter."

CHAPTER THIRTY-NINE

DOWNTOWN JERUSALEM

Omar tried not to check the time again. Mia was at least twenty minutes late. They'd agreed to meet at the CoffeeShop patio, then catch a taxi back to Tel Aviv together. Omar had already ordered his coffee and Mia's tea, which had arrived five minutes earlier. The beverages were cooling.

Omar had spent most of the day writing up his report for Simon Greif about how he'd brought down the Sayids. Greif, already in communication with the Jordanian government about opening an investigation on the Mika'il Order, was hell-bent on exposing more corrupt individuals who supported honor killings, now dubbed as *the killing curse* in top circles.

Leaning back in his chair, Omar stretched out his legs. What was taking Mia so long? She'd been given a new assignment and had to go through a briefing, but briefings never took more than a couple of hours.

He was just about to text her when a movement in his peripheral vision caught his attention.

She was walking toward him from the main part of the café. She wore a dress—one he hadn't seen before. Had she been shopping? He supposed he should be annoyed that she'd gone on an errand without letting him know she'd be running late. In their line of work, running late could mean something serious had happened. But somehow, he couldn't find the words to criticize anything about her just now.

The dress was an ivory wraparound that hugged her curves, and she wore dangling silver earrings that set off her lovely dark curls. He could have waited hours for this.

She made a face when she saw him ogling her, slid into the chair next to him, then turned her cheek.

Obediently he leaned forward and kissed her soft skin.

"You smell great," he said, giving her a half smile.

She took a sip of the tea, but said nothing.

"And you look great," he continued. "New dress?"

Her dark eyes flashed as they met his. "Thought you'd never notice, you cold man."

Omar moved close again, and she leaned in and kissed him on the mouth, the way it should be done.

"I brought you something," she murmured.

"More than the dress?"

She smiled, and Omar felt his heart pulse.

"Better than the dress."

He took a long look. "I don't think that's possible."

Mia shook her head and removed the purse strap from her shoulder. She opened the clasp and slid out a thumb drive.

Omar's heart rate went up a notch. He wasn't positive he knew what was on the drive, but he could guess. "Did you scan Nadia's poetry?"

She grinned. "I did."

He picked up the thumb drive and turned it over. In his hand he held the stories of a woman from generations ago. Secrets of a woman who had sought vengeance on Saladin, the most powerful Muslim leader to ever live.

Despite the excitement he felt about finally having a chance to read Nadia's words, he slipped the thumb drive into the shirt pocket of his button-down. They were alone on the back patio since Omar had paid the waitress to give them privacy.

"You're not going to pull it up on your phone right away?" Mia asked, looking genuinely surprised.

"I'm not." Omar grasped her hand and linked their fingers. "Because even this can't compete with your dress."

Mia laughed, and he was pleased to see her olive skin tinge a sunset pink.

"In fact," he continued. "I have a confession to make."

Mia maintained her amused expression. Omar knew he couldn't completely put how he felt about her into words, and of course he'd tried and failed time and time again, so now was the moment to show her how serious he was.

"Do you remember this CoffeeHouse?" he asked.

Mia shrugged. "We've come here a few times."

"We met here that first time," Omar said. "After our first heist together."

Her eyes widened. "So we did." The smile on her lips was soft. "I remember."

"I think I knew then that I wanted to marry you." This could go badly, but he was hoping for the best.

Mia looked away, but she wasn't frowning. And she didn't pull her hand away from his. Omar took that as a good sign.

"You couldn't possibly have known that." Her tone was serious.

"If I hadn't experienced it firsthand, then I would have agreed with you." Omar let his thumb gently drift over the back of her fingers. "But I realized that I've been going about it all wrong."

Now she looked at him again, with a more intrigued expression.

So far Omar was doing well. "I neglected a very important tradition."

Mia blinked in confusion.

Omar held up his phone as if to demonstrate his point. "I called your father today and asked for his blessing."

Mia's lips parted as she stared at him. "You called my *father*? He doesn't take phone calls."

"I know," Omar said. "But when I explained to his secretary why I was calling, I was put through."

Mia blinked again. "What . . . I don't believe it."

Omar pressed send on the private contact he'd pulled up. Two rings later, the call was answered on the other end. "This is Omar Zagouri," he said. "I have your daughter here." He held out the phone to Mia. "It's your father."

"What's going on?" she mouthed, then answered the phone.

Omar watched as Mia started to talk with her father. He knew it had been months since they had last spoken. When an assassination attempt had been made on her father's life, security at his Alexandria compound increased. The patriarch had even cut off communication with his daughter.

It was still odd to think of Mia's father as the patriarch of the Coptic Church. But he'd never known of Mia's mother's pregnancy. It wasn't until years later that he found out, after he'd already entered the Coptic priesthood, and had taken a vow of celibacy under the Holy Synod. Naysayers against the church had tried to use the information, that the Coptic pope had a daughter, against him.

Mia gazed at Omar as she spoke with her father. She didn't look angry, in fact, she looked . . . astounded.

Omar hoped that was a good thing.

"You gave him your *blessing*?" Mia asked in a low voice. Her eyes filled with moisture, and Omar's heart sank.

She was upset.

"I don't know," she continued, blinking rapidly. She fell silent for several moments, then she said, "For what it's worth, thank you . . . yes . . . yes, I love you, too."

She hung up and didn't say anything, but stared down at her tea.

Omar's heart was pounding and not in a good way. Was she angry, embarrassed, impressed?

"Mia," he said, pulling out a small alabaster box from his jacket pocket. "I know I've asked you to marry me before, and I know that you've had your reasons to say no."

Now her look was difficult to fathom. A warm wind stirred the curls about her face.

"Even with your father's blessing, I know that this is a risk for both of us." Omar could feel his nerves taking over. He made his signature neurotic move of scrubbing his hand through his hair as he gripped the jewelry box with his other hand. "But that's exactly why I want to marry you. We never know what will happen next, or even what will happen tomorrow. I'll take whatever time is given to us. I just want it to be together."

Mia exhaled. "Omar . . . we've talked about this before. It would be going against every agent code ever written. And my own mother was killed because it was a way to get back at me. If we marry, then we both become greater targets."

"And I've told you that no one has to know about our marriage," Omar said. "Maybe my parents and your father, but that's it. Even Simon Greif doesn't need to know."

Mia shook her head, and Omar could feel he was losing her again.

"At least look at the ring," he said. Opening the alabaster box, he slid it across the table.

She sighed and looked down. Then her eyes widened. "Where did you get this?" She picked up the thick silver band set with a diamond and a row of emeralds.

Omar smiled. "Sometimes when an artifact hasn't been on display for a few years, a museum curator can be talked into trading for it. Especially if he's sorely in need of funds and wants to get the first look at some poetry."

"This looks twelfth century," she mused, examining it.

"Thirteenth. It belonged to Isabella of Angouleme, who married King John."

"A queen, huh?" Mia said. Her gaze connected with his again. "I could never wear this, Omar. It's priceless, and I can't wear any jewelry that singles me out."

"You could wear it between assignments," Omar said. He reached for her hand, drew it toward him, and took the ring and slid it on her finger. He lowered his voice. "You could wear it when it's just the two of us."

Mia kept her gaze on the ring.

What was this woman thinking? Omar felt he was close, yet still so far away. When she looked up at him, he said, "I know that life is never a sure thing, and it never will be. Everything about us is taking a chance. But I still want you to be my wife."

After a heartbeat, she said, "Do you know why I was late?"

This conversation wasn't going exactly as he had hoped. "Why?"

"I got caught up reading Nadia's words," she said. "She gave up her entire life to marry the man she loved. And even when he was killed, she didn't return to her family. She continued forward and married another man in order to give her child a father and to raise the child in honor of his name."

"Marrying *me* doesn't sound so bad then," Omar said. "You don't have to give up your family, or your job."

She didn't laugh, though. "You don't understand," she said in a quiet voice, brushing back a strand of hair that was blowing against her face. "I have to give up myself."

Omar stared at her, seeing that she was perfectly serious. "What do you mean?"

"I mean," she said, with a full pause, "that it will be a full commitment."

He waited for more. He felt the stirring of disappointment, an all too familiar feeling. "Before I met you, and before you drove me absolutely crazy, I felt the same way." He traced his fingers over the hand that still wore the ring. "But things changed, and I want to be fully committed to you."

"I—I just don't want to let you down," Mia said softly, leaning toward him.

"I don't think that's possible," he said.

Her gaze connected with his, and he could see her struggle. But he could also see that she loved him too.

"Keep the ring," he said. "Engaged or not, I bought it for you."

A slight smile curved her lips, and she moved closer still. She brought her hand to rest on his shoulder. "Maybe you're right."

Omar's heart nearly stopped. What exactly was he right about?

"Maybe we shouldn't let time pass us by," she said, her face only a breath away from his.

He didn't dare breathe.

"I mean my father likes you, and," she shrugged, "I *am* in love with you."

"Are you . . . are you accepting my proposal?" Omar managed to say.

She smiled. A brilliant, beautiful smile. "I am."

Omar pulled her into his arms and tugged her onto his lap. She laughed as he started to kiss her, and after a few moments, her laughter merged with his as she kissed him back.

Omar didn't care who in the CoffeeHouse saw them kissing, and it seemed Mia didn't mind either. When they finally broke apart, Omar said, "I knew the hardware would convince you."

"Hardly," Mia said with a smirk. "You know I can't be bought."

"I'm just happy you're wearing it now."

Mia kept her arms looped about his neck and leaned close to whisper. "I have a surprise for you."

Omar wasn't sure his heart could tolerate much more excitement. "What is it?" he whispered back.

"My next assignment doesn't start for eight days," she said, gently fingering his neck with the back of her nails. "So what am I going to do with all that free time?"

Omar chuckled. "I'll take time off too and come up with a few things." He stood, bringing her up with him, and kissed her again.

When she finally pulled away, the look on her face let Omar know he'd lost his heart forever.

"We should get out of here," she said.

Omar tossed a couple of bills onto the table, and said, "I couldn't agree more."

AUTHOR'S NOTES

The historical portion of this novel details the well-documented Horns of Hattin battle during the Second Crusade, which was fought during the twelfth century between the armies of Salah ad-Din Yusuf ibn Ayyub (Saladin), and Raynald of Châtillon (also known as Reginald). Saladin, a Kurdish warrior who was a champion of Islam, became the Sultan of Egypt. He's legendary for evicting the crusaders from Jerusalem.

Raynald broke his truce with Saladin by invading a caravan that contained some of Saladin's family members. This led to the King of Jerusalem, King Guy, asking Raynald to return the stolen property. But Raynald refused, and war was Saladin's answer. On July 4, 1187, Raynald was taken prisoner at the Battle of the Horns of Hattin. After a devastating loss by the crusaders in which the Muslims had every advantage, Raynald was escorted to Saladin's tent. Historians claim that Saladin himself beheaded Raynald.

The contemporary portion of the novel follows a modern character who is in peril by her family. Even in the year 2017, the year of this novel's publication, honor killings still occur in many parts of the globe. Most reports of honor killings never make it to media outlets. When my sixteen-year-old daughter and I were watching the Academy Awards in 2016, and the short documentary film *A Girl In The River: The Price Of Forgiveness* won an Oscar, my daughter asked, "What's an honor killing?" I knew right then that I needed to include this hideous tradition in my next novel in order to bring more awareness about a practice that has only recently been outlawed in some countries. In short:

"*A Girl In The River: The Price Of Forgiveness* is by

Pakistani director Sharmeen Obaid-Chinoy. The 40-minute documentary tackles the tough topic of honor killings in Pakistan, from a rare point of view: a survivor's. Saba, an 18-year-old girl, was shot and thrown in a river by her own family for secretly eloping with her lover — and lived to tell the tale." (http://www.npr.org/sections/goatsandsoda/2016/02/29/468582341/this-oscar-winning-film-could-help-end-honor-killings-in-pakistan)

According to Phyllis Chester, "Wherever an honor killing is committed, it is primarily a crime against young people. Just over half of these victims were daughters and sisters; about a quarter were wives and girlfriends of the perpetrators. The remainder included mothers, aunts, nieces, cousins, uncles, or non-relatives. Honor killings are a family collaboration. Worldwide, two-thirds of the victims were killed by their families of origin." (*The Middle East Quarterly*, http://www.meforum.org/2646/worldwide-trends-in-honor-killings)

What makes an honor killing different from other types of murder? "Premeditated killings of family members, primarily women, who are thought to have brought shame or dishonour to their family by engaging in certain behaviours considered unacceptable (e.g. pre-marital or extra-marital sexual relationships, or relationships with boys not approved by the family), are often referred to in media reports as 'honour killings'." (http://www.justice.gc.ca/eng/rp-pr/cj-jp/fv-vf/hk-ch/p1.html)

Historically, honor killings have been enacted for centuries. In ancient Roman times, the *pater familias*, or patriarch of the family, had the right to kill his adulterous wife or unmarried sexually active daughter. In England, King Henry VIII had his fifth wife, Catherine Howard, beheaded for alleged adultery. The practice of honor killing dates back as well to pre-Islamic times when Arab settlers in Pakistan practiced the tradition of live burials for newborn daughters (female infanticide was outlawed by the Prophet Muhammad). Ancient Babylon perpetrated the view that a woman's virginity belonged to her family. (See: http://www.justice.gc.ca/eng/rp-pr/cj-jp/fv-vf/hk-ch/p3.html)

Sharif Kanaana, professor of anthropology at Birzeit University, observes that, "What the men of the family, clan, or tribe seek control of in a patrilineal society is reproductive power. Women for the tribe were considered a factory for making men. The honor killing is not a means to control sexual power or behavior. What's behind it is the issue of fertility, or reproductive power." (http://www.justice.gc.ca/eng/rp-pr/cj-jp/fv-vf/hk-ch/p3.html)

According to the Honour Based Violence Awareness Network (http://hbv-awareness.com), more than 5,000 honor killings per year are reported. Many more are not reported. Countries that have released honor-killing statistics include Egypt, Jordan, Lebanon, Morocco, Pakistan, the Syrian Arab Republic, Turkey, Yemen, and other Mediterranean and Persian Gulf countries. Reports of honor killings have also come from France, Germany, and the United Kingdom. India is another country with a high number of honor-based crimes, possibly an average of 1,000 per year (http://hbv-awareness.com/today/). The BBC reported that more than 1,100 women were killed in honor-based murders in Pakistan alone in 2015 (http://www.bbc.com/news/world-asia-35943732). North America and South America are not exempt from this tradition.

Change starts with awareness.

ACKNOWLEDGMENTS

I'd like to extend my appreciation to the many people who've helped me on this book. Namely my parents, S. Kent Brown and Gayle Brown, who read the early draft and gave me valuable feedback. Thank you to Susan Alyworth, who has been a diligent beta reader on this series and a good friend. And thanks to my agent Jane Dystel for her guidance and encouragement.

I was privileged to once again work with Charlotte Herscher who has been the editor on this series from the beginning. I also appreciate Dan Born's willingness to once again add his copyediting talents to this series and keep all things consistent. Thanks as well to proofreader Lisa Shepherd who is always willing to work with my deadlines.

Thanks to the support my father-in-law Lester Moore continually gives as he hands out my books to people near and far. I'm grateful for my writer friends who keep me on track, more so than they know, Taffy Lovell, Julie Daines, and Jaime Theler. Additional thanks to my husband, Chris, and my son, Kaelin, and my daughters, Kara, Dana, and Rose, and their continual support of my writing.

ABOUT H.B. MOORE

Heather B. Moore is a *USA Today* bestselling author of more than a dozen historical novels and thrillers, written under pen name H.B. Moore. She writes women's fiction, romance and inspirational non-fiction under Heather B. Moore. This can all be confusing, so her kids just call her Mom. Heather attended Cairo American College in Egypt, the Anglican School of Jerusalem in Israel, and earned a Bachelor of Science degree from Brigham Young University in Utah.

Sign up for Heather's email list: hbmoore.com/contact
Website: HBMoore.com
Facebook: Fans of H. B. Moore
Blog: MyWritersLair.blogspot.com
Instagram: @authorhbmoore
Twitter: @HeatherBMoore

Made in the USA
Las Vegas, NV
18 April 2023

70754880R00204